W9-BQH-192

# THE DUNE SERIES

BY FRANK HERBERT

*Dune*
*Dune Messiah*
*Children of Dune*
*God Emperor of Dune*
*Heretics of Dune*
*Chapterhouse: Dune*

BY FRANK HERBERT, BRIAN HERBERT,
AND KEVIN J. ANDERSON

*The Road to Dune* (includes the original short novel *Spice Planet*)

BY BRIAN HERBERT AND KEVIN J. ANDERSON

*Dune: House Atreides*
*Dune: House Harkonnen*
*Dune: House Corrino*

*Dune: The Butlerian Jihad*
*Dune: The Machine Crusade*
*Dune: The Battle of Corrin*

*Hunters of Dune*
*Sandworms of Dune*

*Paul of Dune*
*The Winds of Dune*
*Sisterhood of Dune*
*Mentats of Dune*
*Tales of Dune*

BY BRIAN HERBERT

*Dreamer of Dune*
(biography of Frank Herbert)

# MENTATS OF
# DUNE

# MENTATS OF
# DUNE

*Brian Herbert*

and

*Kevin J. Anderson*

TOR®

A TOM DOHERTY ASSOCIATES BOOK

NEW YORK

This is a work of fiction. All of the characters, organizations, and events portrayed in this novel are either products of the authors' imaginations or are used fictitiously.

MENTATS OF DUNE

Copyright © 2014 by Herbert Properties, LLC

All rights reserved.

A Tor Book
Published by Tom Doherty Associates, LLC
175 Fifth Avenue
New York, NY 10010

www.tor-forge.com

Tor® is a registered trademark of Tom Doherty Associates, LLC.

The Library of Congress Cataloging-in-Publication Data
is available upon request.

ISBN 978-0-7653-2274-6 (hardcover)
ISBN 978-1-4299-4976-7 (e-book)

Tor books may be purchased for educational, business, or promotional use. For information on bulk purchases, please contact Macmillan Corporate and Premium Sales Department at 1-800-221-7945, extension 5442, or write specialmarkets@macmillan.com.

First Edition: March 2014

Printed in the United States of America

0  9  8  7  6  5  4  3  2  1

*For Jan, whose beauty and intelligence continue to dazzle me.*
*My life began when I met you.*

—BRIAN HERBERT

*For Rebecca, who continues to explore exotic and exciting new places and*
*ideas with me, and there are still countless new universes to imagine.*

—KEVIN J. ANDERSON

# ACKNOWLEDGMENTS

As with all our books, we owe a tremendous debt of gratitude to our wives, Janet Herbert and Rebecca Moesta Anderson, for their love and creative support. We would also like to express our gratitude to Tom Doherty at Tor Books, our editors, Pat LoBrutto (Tor) and Maxine Hitchcock (Simon & Schuster UK), and our agent, John Silbersack (Trident Media Group). In addition, Kim Herbert and Byron Merritt have worked tirelessly to help raise awareness of the Dune novels through promotional efforts, convention appearances, and website work. Kevin would also like to thank Mary Thomson for her many hours of transcription, and test readers Diane Jones and Louis Moesta.

If we accept advanced technology in any form, we will begin to make excuses and justifications for using it. There are so many ways to take the wrong path and tumble down a slippery slope, down, down, down. Loyal Butlerians, we must be ever-vigilant and strong! The Emperor's Committee of Orthodoxy does not go far enough. If we let machines do even menial chores for us, they will soon become our masters again.

I call upon all my faithful followers, across all the worlds of the Imperium, to demand that every planetary leader sign my antitechnology pledge. If any refuse, my Butlerians—and God—will know who they are. No one can hide.

—MANFORD TORONDO, citizen's decree

The idiocy of it all! I cannot decide whether to laugh at Butlerian insanity, or weep for the future of our species. What will those fanatics demand next? The complete absence of medical technology? Would they outlaw fire, and declare the existence of the wheel too dangerous? Are we all to be relegated to huddling in forests and fields?

Enough. This is the decree of Venport Holdings: No VenHold cargo ship or passenger transport shall trade with any planet that signs Manford Torondo's antitechnology pledge. We will deliver no goods or passengers, transmit no communications, engage in no commerce with any world that shares his dangerous, barbarian philosophy.

Make your choice: Do you prefer to bask in the glow of civilization, or cower in the shadows of primitive despair? Decide.

—DIRECTEUR JOSEF VENPORT, formal business announcement

Each time I solve a crisis, another springs forth like a noxious weed. What am I to do, Roderick? Problems come at me from all directions!

I disbanded the Sisterhood school on Rossak because they were suspected of possessing forbidden computers—though I could never prove it, and they made me look like a fool. And after what happened to our dear sister Anna when she was among them. . . . What a terrible shame! Will she ever be the same?

When the treachery of the Suk doctors was exposed, I nearly broke them, too. Despite their purported Imperial Conditioning, and even though I now force them to operate under close scrutiny, I do not trust them. Yet, with my numerous health issues, I have no choice but to let them tend me.

Manford Torondo pressures me to adopt his Butlerian nonsense and follow his every whim, while Josef Venport demands the opposite. They are both madmen, but if I ignore Manford Torondo, he can summon wild and destructive mobs. And if I don't appease Venport, he holds our entire economy hostage.

I feel like a man chained between two Salusan bulls pulling in opposite directions! I am the third Corrino to sit on the Imperial throne since the defeat of the thinking machines—why is it so difficult to make my own citizens listen to me? Help me decide what to do, dear brother. As always, I value your advice above all others.

—private Corrino correspondence,
EMPEROR SALVADOR to PRINCE RODERICK

# MENTATS OF
# DUNE

*What do all our accomplishments matter, if they do not last beyond our lifetimes?*

—HEADMASTER GILBERTUS ALBANS, Mentat School Archives

The great Mentat School was *his*—from the initial concept seven decades ago, to choosing this location in the remote marshes on Lampadas, to the many graduates he had trained over the years. With quiet efficiency and determination, Gilbertus Albans was changing the course of human civilization.

And he would not let Emperor Salvador Corrino or the fanatical antitechnology Butlerians take it away from him.

In the nearly two centuries of his artificially extended life, Gilbertus had learned how to survive. Realizing that controversial and charismatic figures tended not to remain alive for long, he played his public role with great care—remaining quiet and unobtrusive, even consenting to distasteful alliances that, according to his projections, helped the overall goals of his Mentat School.

*Mentats:* humans with minds so organized they could function as computers in a reactionary society that reviled any hint of thinking machines. Not even his own trainees knew that Gilbertus secretly drew upon the unique background, wisdom, and experiences of his mentor, the notorious robot Erasmus. He feared that even his most supportive students would balk at that. Nevertheless, after years of consistently reliable performance, his Mentat graduates were becoming indispensable to the noble houses of the Imperium.

In such dangerous times, though, any question or mere suspicion could bring down the school. He knew what had happened to the Sisterhood on Rossak. If he made the slightest mistake and revealed his true identity . . .

Inside his office in the main academy building, he glanced at the chronometer. The Emperor's brother, Roderick Corrino, was due to arrive on a sanctioned military transport, to confirm that their sister was safe in the care of the Mentat School. Some time ago, Gilbertus had promised the Corrinos that his rigorous teaching methods could help the mentally damaged girl to improve, if not thrive. But the human mind was a tricky thing, and the damage done to her brain by the Rossak poison was not quantifiable, nor could the young woman be cured in any obvious way. Gilbertus hoped Roderick Corrino understood that.

Before emerging into the school commons, he donned his distinguished carmine-red Headmaster robe. He had already attended to his makeup for the day—dusting false gray into his hair, roughening his skin—in order to hide his youthful appearance. Now he hurried, knowing that the Imperial military shuttle would arrive on time. He had to make sure Anna was ready to put on a good show for her brother.

Gilbertus left the academy building and shaded his eyes. The bright air was sopping with humidity; each suspended droplet seemed to hang in front of his eyes like a magnifying glass. Wooden walkways connected the school structures that floated on the edge of a murky marsh lake. Originally the school had been anchored farther out in the water, but after problems with aggressive aquatic creatures, the entire complex had been moved to a more protected position on the shore.

Now the school included a mixture of the original structures and new ones that looked more elegant, with domes and elevated observation decks. Bridges at varying levels linked the dormitories, study halls, laboratories, meditation buildings, and libraries. High defensive walls surrounded the entire complex, augmented by a hidden shield grid, sophisticated underwater electronics, and watchtowers.

While portions of Lampadas were bucolic and pleasant, this lake and the bordering swamps were the planet's razor edge, fraught with hazards and predators. As the Headmaster made his way to the observatory, swamp sounds burbled into the air, and a hum of biting flies swirled around him. This was no serene environment where students could develop their mental skills through hours of uninterrupted meditation. Gilbertus had chosen this inhospitable area with a specific purpose in mind. He believed the danger and isolation would help focus the minds of his elite candidates.

Even with the school's defenses against natural hazards, Gilbertus was actually more concerned about what the increasingly unpredictable Butlerians might do. A sophisticated military force could easily destroy the school with an aerial or space bombardment, but the antitechnology fanatics would use no high-tech weaponry; nevertheless, their overwhelming numbers could cause great havoc, as they had already proved with mob uprisings on several worlds in the Imperium. Gilbertus had to walk a fine line.

At face value, the Butlerians applauded the basic underpinnings of Mentat training—that humans could do anything that thinking machines could, and more. Their leader, legless Manford Torondo, often made use of Mentat calculations or strategies to achieve his ends, but he was also suspicious of any open exchange of ideas during lively discussions among the students. In an earlier semester, Gilbertus had exposed the school to great danger when he suggested during a hypothetical intellectual debate that thinking machines might not be as terrible as Butlerian propaganda made them out to be. The school, and Gilbertus himself, had barely survived their backlash. He had learned his lesson. Since then he'd remained quiet and conciliatory to avoid inflaming anyone again.

As he walked toward the outbuildings, one of the minor administrators transmitted an alert that the Imperial shuttle was on descent. Gilbertus touched his earadio. "Thank you. I will bring Anna Corrino to the landing zone." He hoped she was having one of her lucid days, so she could interact with her brother, rather than remaining lost in a mental maze.

The school's tallest building served as a naked-eye observatory, where Mentat students could study the universe, count the stars at night, and memorize the infinite patterns as a recall exercise. During the day, the high open deck would be empty—except for Anna Corrino, staring at her surroundings.

The young woman was fixated on the local landscape, where a labyrinth of sangrove trees created an impassable barrier to the east, and soupy marshes, quicksand, and tangled stagnant waterways made travel difficult to the south; the large, shallow marsh lake bounded the school to the north and west.

Gilbertus stepped up next to Anna. "Your brother is coming. He will be glad to see you."

She did not acknowledge the Headmaster, but a small twitch in her cheek and a flicker of her eyelids told him she was aware of his presence. She turned to stare at a drained section of swamp that served as a landing field for shuttles and local flyers. Dangerous lake beasts had damaged the previous raft airfield, making it impractical to keep under repair.

His primary aide, Zendur, and a crew of Mentat trainees used blunt-nozzle devices to spray fire streams across the marsh grasses, clearing an area for Roderick Corrino's shuttle. Because vegetation grew so rapidly here, the landing zone had to be groomed for each expected arrival; Gilbertus did not have trainees maintain the site otherwise, since he didn't want to encourage unexpected visitors—Manford Torondo in particular.

Anna did not take her eyes from the clearing crew as she spoke. "How many flies do you think they're killing?"

"Or how many blades of grass?" Gilbertus said, knowing it was a game for her.

Anna considered the problem. "If I knew the acreage of swampland for the landing field, I could calculate a probable distribution of grass blades. Given a certain amount of swamp grass, I could estimate how many flies are likely to inhabit it."

"And how many spiders to eat them," Gilbertus suggested, trying to keep her thoughts nimble.

"I can make a cascade projection following the food chain." Anna's narrow shoulders twitched, and she formed a small smile, turning to focus on him for the first time that day. "But it doesn't really matter, does it? Because the grass will grow back, the flies will return, the spiders will eat them, and the swamp will reclaim its territory—until the next time we clear it."

"I am going to meet your brother's shuttle now. Would you join me?"

Anna considered. "I prefer to wait here and watch."

"Prince Roderick is anxious to see you."

"He is a good brother. I'll talk with him . . . but I need time to arrange my thoughts first. I'll be ready when you bring him here. I don't want to disappoint him."

*Neither do I,* Gilbertus thought.

AFTER CLEARING THE landing zone, trainees smothered the brush fires, then raked the area clear of charred vegetation. Although the air retained an odor of damp ashes, Gilbertus found it more pleasant than the swamp's usual miasma.

As the Imperial shuttle landed, the Headmaster crossed a series of temporary boardwalks to meet Prince Roderick. The small diplomatic vessel bore the golden-lion insignia of House Corrino, but it was not a gaudy craft. It had been ferried to Lampadas aboard an Imperial military spacefolder. Only two people emerged and stepped down the ramp, with no entourage.

The tall, erect man was Prince Roderick, blond and handsome, with patrician Corrino features. In a flicker of Mentat recall, Gilbertus reviewed the nobleman's file: the Emperor's younger brother had a wife (Haditha), a son (Javicco), and three daughters (Tikya, Wissoma, Nantha). Known for his calm disposition and sharp mind, Roderick advised the Emperor in most things, and Salvador generally listened to him. By all indications, he was content to be an adviser rather than a ruler.

The old woman who accompanied the Prince was a surprise: Lady Orenna, called the "Virgin Empress" because she had been wife to Emperor Jules Corrino, but she had borne him no children (and supposedly never shared his bed). Instead, the children of Emperor Jules—Salvador, Roderick, and Anna—had three different mothers, all concubines.

Gilbertus's thorough Mentat review was so swift that the visitors did not notice the pause. He stepped forward. "My Lord Roderick and Lady Orenna, welcome to the Mentat School. I just spoke with Anna. She is preparing herself to receive you."

Roderick gave a quick nod. "I look forward to observing her progress." He looked disappointed that his sister hadn't come to greet them in person.

"She is safe, stable, content," Gilbertus said. "The routine of the Mentat School helps her. I caution you not to expect miracles, though."

Lady Orenna maintained a bright smile. "I miss the poor girl, but I want what's best for her. I'll sleep better on Salusa if I can see with my own eyes that she is happy here."

As he tried to process why the old woman had come here, data clicked into place in Gilbertus's mind. Though Orenna was not Anna's mother, the Virgin Empress had taken the young woman under her wing, and the two had a special relationship. Anna had always been a flighty girl, easily distracted, with a swinging pendulum of emotions and an utter lack of common sense. Disappointed in the unruly girl, Salvador had banished her to the Sisterhood school on Rossak, but there her mind had been damaged rather than improved. And now she was here.

"You will find that she is healthy," Gilbertus said. "Mentat techniques offer the best possible chance for recovery."

Roderick was efficient, all business. "Our visit will be quite brief. We're at the mercy of our transportation—this shuttle was a special dispensation, at the request of Emperor Salvador, since VenHold ships refuse to service Lampadas. The military spacefolder is finishing a grand patrol and needs to return to Salusa Secundus."

The feud between the antitechnology Butlerians and the commercial empire of Venport Holdings had grown more bitter over time, with mutual antipathy spiraling into outright conflict. And the Imperial throne was caught up in the dispute. Instead of traveling aboard a safe VenHold spacefolder, guided by mysterious and infallible Navigators, Roderick had been forced to come here on a less reliable military transport.

Lady Orenna was clearly displeased that they would have to depart so quickly. "We traveled a long way to visit Anna. I don't like to be rushed. We are the girl's family—the Imperial Armed Forces should alter their schedules for *our* convenience."

Roderick shook his head, lowered his voice. "I'm also disappointed, but I don't want to disrupt the workings of the military, because they have to appear strong and reliable. We can't simply commandeer a VenHold commercial ship and force Directeur Venport to do our bidding."

The older woman said with a sniff, "And why not? A loyal citizen should do as the Emperor requests, not the other way around. Your father would have crushed such insubordination."

"Yes," Roderick said, "he probably would have."

Gilbertus said, "My school is a place where Anna can be sheltered from the stress of political tensions." He knew that Roderick's brother was weak, indecisive, and easily intimidated. Emperor Salvador did not have the power to force his will on either the shipping magnate or the legless Butlerian leader.

In these days of perilous politics, though, Gilbertus had learned to keep his thoughts to himself and to maintain neutrality. He had impressed that caution on his students as well: The ideal Mentat should never be a commentator or an advocate, but a tool, an analytical device to offer guidance and projections.

"You have no political tensions here?" Roderick muttered. "Your school is too close to the Butlerian headquarters for my liking."

"Manford Torondo is on the other side of the continent, my Lord, and he has no dispute with the Mentat School. In fact, several of my trainees follow the movement." *Though not my best students.* "We teach humans mental skills that are the equal of any thinking machine. Every Mentat graduate who goes out to serve in the Imperium demonstrates that computers are unnecessary, and so Manford applauds us. Why should we worry about the Butlerians?"

"Indeed, why?" Roderick asked, but didn't answer his own question.

Anna was waiting for them on the observatory deck, still gazing across the landscape. Out in the tangled sangrove swamps, a group of Mentat candidates worked their way through winding channels of brownish water and unseen pits by making use of stepping-stones hidden just beneath the surface. Any Mentat who had memorized exactly where to walk could find the safe stones. Now, as the practicing candidates worked their way through, some of them slipped off the path.

As far as Gilbertus could tell, Anna hadn't moved since he'd left her, but her demeanor was different. Her expression was more animated than the affectless, fixated stare that indicated she was hyperfocused on some detail or calculation. She brightened upon seeing her brother and Lady Orenna.

Orenna embraced the girl. "You look well, Anna! Much stronger."

Roderick looked relieved, even proud. He whispered to Gilbertus, "Thank you."

Anna said, "I am having a good day. I wanted to have a good day for your visit."

"And I'm glad you're safe," Roderick said. "The Mentat School has many hazards."

Gilbertus said, "We have installed additional defenses. We can protect your sister—and all our students."

As if to challenge his assertion, a commotion occurred out in the swamp. A spine-backed reptile lunged out of the brownish water where the Mentat students were picking their way across the submerged stepping-stones. The creature snatched the nearest student in its long jaws and dragged her into the deeper channel. Both predator and prey vanished as swiftly as a glimmer of sunlight on rippled water.

The Mentat students sprang together, ready to defend themselves, but the swamp dragon already had its meal and was gone.

Wide-eyed, Orenna shouted, "How can you protect Anna? You weren't able to protect that young girl!"

Gilbertus did not let himself show emotion at the loss of the student. "Anna is not allowed outside the walls or on the lake. You have my personal guarantee of her safety."

"And what about an outside attack?" Roderick said. "Anna would make a valuable hostage."

Gilbertus said, "We are a small school for the development and improvement of the human mind. Mentats pose no threat to anyone."

Roderick gave him a skeptical look. "You're being coy, Headmaster."

"I am stating a fact. We have run many projections and developed defenses against all likely scenarios. It is what a Mentat is trained to do, my Lord."

Orenna stroked the young woman's arm. "Protect your school at all costs. You have an incalculably precious treasure in Anna."

Gilbertus nodded, but he was thinking instead of the priceless Erasmus memory core, which he kept hidden in the school. Protecting the last independent robot was an ongoing risk more dangerous than anything he'd been discussing with the Imperial visitors. "Yes, many treasures."

*Blind adherence to foolish ideas makes people act in ways that are demonstrably against their own interests. I care only about intelligent, rational human beings.*

    —DIRECTEUR JOSEF VENPORT, VenHold internal memo

The VenHold cargo ship emerged from foldspace precisely where the Navigator predicted—another example of how advanced his mutated humans were.

From the high navigation deck, Josef Venport watched as his ship approached the planet Baridge. Few crewmembers and no passengers were allowed in the vicinity of the Navigator's tank, but Josef could go wherever he pleased. He owned the VenHold Spacing Fleet, controlled the creation of Navigators, and dominated most interplanetary commerce.

His great-grandmother Norma Cenva had transformed herself into the first Navigator through supersaturation with melange, and Josef had created hundreds more because his expanded fleet needed them. That effort triggered a long cascade of requirements: In order to create more Navigators, he needed vast quantities of spice, which necessitated an expansion of operations on Arrakis . . . which forced the VenHold Spacing Fleet to make record-breaking investments, which in turn required him to make immense company profits. One piece after another after another fell together like a beautiful puzzle.

He hated it when some fool disrupted that pattern.

His ship cruised in toward unremarkable Baridge, adjusting position as it entered orbit. Shaking his head, Josef turned to his wife, Cioba. "I doubt they even know we've arrived. If the barbarians hate technology so much, they must have gotten rid of long-range scanners and communication devices." He gave a rude snort. "Maybe they wear furs instead of garments."

Cioba was a beautiful, dark-haired woman trained on Rossak by the Sisterhood before it was disbanded by the Emperor. In a calm, reasonable voice, she said, "Baridge may have taken Manford Torondo's pledge, but that doesn't mean they've discarded all technology. Even people who pay lip service to Butlerian demands may be reluctant to change their lives entirely."

Josef's thick, reddish mustache bristled when he smiled at her. "And that is why we'll win, my dear. Philosophical objections are well and good, but such extreme faith fades as soon as it becomes inconvenient."

The planet showed the usual blue of water, a white swirl of clouds, the browns and greens of land masses. Inhabited worlds had a certain sameness, but Josef ground his teeth as he looked at this one, because of what it represented and the foolish decision their leader Deacon Kalifer had made.

Josef did not have patience for short-sighted people, especially when they were in positions of power. "This is a wasted errand. We should not have expended the fuel and time to come here. There's no profit in gloating."

Cioba leaned close, touching his arm. "Baridge deserves a second chance, and you need to remind them of what their decision costs. Deacon Kalifer may have reconsidered by now." She stroked her husband's thick hair.

He touched her hand, held it, then let go. "People often surprise me, but not usually in a good way."

Baridge's turbulent sun was in the upswing of an active starspot cycle. Formerly, the planet had been known for colorful aurora displays, which trapped and deflected much of the solar radiation, but a rain of charged particles still penetrated to the surface. To protect themselves, the people of Baridge wore protective creams, covered their windows with filter films, and sheltered their streets with retractable canopies. Orbiting satellites monitored solar activity and warned citizens when they should stay inside. Advanced medical systems treated the resulting epidemic of skin cancers, and the population used melange heavily, which helped to protect them.

Under normal circumstances, Baridge was well prepared for the dangers of the solar cycle, but Deacon Kalifer and his ruling cabal had recently bowed to pressure from Manford Torondo's barbarian fanatics. After accepting the Butlerian pledge and condemning Venport Holdings, Kalifer declared that his planet would henceforth be free from all tainted technology.

And so, true to his word, Josef terminated trade with the planet. He'd made it clear to the whole Imperium that his ships would not deliver equipment, luxury goods, melange, or other supplies to any world that embraced the Butlerian pledge. Lesser shipping companies struggled to fill the need, but they ran lackluster and outdated fleets, and none had Navigators to guide their ships safely through foldspace, which resulted in a disastrous lost-vessel rate.

Josef glanced up to the enclosed tank that held this ship's Navigator. He could barely see the twisted form swimming in the murk of spice gas, but he knew that this one had originally been a spy named Royce Fayed, who'd been caught trying to steal the secret of creating Navigators. Josef had generously revealed those secrets to the man—by forcing him to become a Navigator. Under the direct tutelage of Norma Cenva, however, Fayed had become one of VenHold's best Navigators. Now that the transformation was complete, he was deeply grateful for the gift he had been given.

The Navigator spoke through the tank speaker. "Arriving at Baridge."

Josef often had trouble conversing with Navigators, because their minds were so advanced. "Yes, we are at Baridge." Did Fayed think him unaware of their destination?

"I detect another vessel in orbit. It is not a commercial ship."

With a shimmer, one of the metal bulkheads became a transmission window. At high magnification, it displayed a warship in close orbit—not a vessel from the current Imperial Armed Forces, but one of the old cruisers from the Army of the Jihad, recommissioned and used by the barbarians.

Josef gritted his teeth when he saw the watchdog vessel light up as it accelerated toward them. "It's one of the Half-Manford's ships." He studied the craft on the transmission screen, saw its bristling guns, but felt no concern. He had no doubt the warship captain would be arrogant, full of faith and unreason.

Cioba's brow wrinkled. "Does it pose a threat to us?"

"Of course not."

A raspy-voiced young man sitting at the helm of the Butlerian ship sent a transmission. "VenHold vessel, you are forbidden at Baridge. These people have sworn not to use your accursed technology. Depart or be destroyed."

"It does no good even to respond, my husband," Cioba said with a sigh. "You can't argue with zealots."

Although he agreed there was little point, Josef couldn't keep his words inside. He activated the transmitter. "Strange, I thought VenHold placed an embargo on this planet, not the other way around. It's particularly odd to see such a vehement Butlerian follower flying a complex spaceship. Doesn't such sophisticated technology make you lose control of your own bladder?"

The Butlerian captain would probably make some kind of rationalization about their technology being "used for the greater good," or claim that it avoided being unacceptable because it was "in service of holy work."

When Josef's image appeared on the screen, the warship captain recoiled. "The demon Venport himself! You have been warned!" Surprisingly, he cut off the transmission.

Cioba nodded toward the transmission window. "He's powering up his weapons."

"Manford Torondo has likely placed a bounty on my head." Josef found the idea as offensive as it was laughable.

Without warning, the aging Jihad warship opened fire, blasting them with old explosive shells. The kinetic bombardment hammered away at the VenHold ship's advanced shields—another miracle invented by Norma Cenva—but the outdated weapons could inflict no harm. VenHold's defenses were vastly superior to anything the enemy had.

"Make a log notation," Josef said into the wall recorders. "We did not fire first. We committed no aggressive or provocative acts. We have been attacked without cause and are forced to defend ourselves." He called down to the weapons deck, where personnel were already at their stations. "Destroy that ship. It annoys me."

The weapons officer had been anticipating the command, and a swarm of projectiles ripped forth and cut the Butlerian vessel to ribbons. It was over in seconds, and Josef was glad he didn't need to waste any more time.

As she watched the fading glow of debris on the screen, Cioba whispered, "I thought you said that ship didn't pose a threat to us."

"Not to *us*, but those Butlerian savages pose a threat to civilization itself. I believe this was a necessary punishment." He spoke to the Navigator. "Are there other ships in the vicinity? Cargo carriers, rival commercial vessels?"

"None," Fayed said.

"Good, then maybe the people of Baridge will be more tractable." He sent a transmission down to the surface, addressing Deacon Kalifer directly. He made certain the conversation was on a public band. Josef guessed that many of the supposedly devout Butlerians there still had illicit listening devices, and he wanted them all to hear his words.

Deacon Kalifer responded as soon as Josef made contact, which implied that the planetary leader had indeed been watching their arrival. He probably also knew that the Butlerian watchdog ship was destroyed. Good—another reason for the deacon not to be difficult.

On the screen, Kalifer's shoulders drooped and his skin sagged on his frame as if he'd chosen the wrong size from a rack. His speech had a slow and ponderous quality, and his sentences always took longer to complete than Josef could stand. Deacon Kalifer was a man who made every listener want to say *Hurry up!*

"Ah, VenHold ship, we hoped you would reconsider your embargo. And I'm pleased that you came here in person, Directeur Venport."

"I came in person, but I'm not pleased with the reception. Be thankful that rabid watchdog ship won't cause you any more problems." This might not be a wasted trip after all; at the very least, it gave Josef a chance to twist the knife while the people of Baridge eavesdropped. "I bring pharmaceuticals, specifically cancer drugs, and polymer creams to protect you against the radiation onslaught from the solar cycle. I've also brought a team of the top doctors trained at the Suk School. They specialize in treating skin lesions and a variety of cancers, and they can help your people."

"Thank you, Directeur!" Kalifer was so excited that he spoke quickly for a change.

Cioba caught Josef's eye and he could tell that she knew exactly what he was doing. Her shrewd business sense and keen ability to observe made her an invaluable asset to him.

Keeping his tone neutral, Josef responded to Kalifer. "We also have a large cargo of melange, which I know is popular here. Baridge used to be an important VenHold customer, and we hate to lose your business. We offer this special shipment at a discounted price, to celebrate our renewed trade."

When Kalifer grinned with relief, Josef hardened his voice. "First, however, you must disavow your pledge to Manford Toronto. You foreswore all advanced technology, but now you realize how irrational that was. If you wish to restore trade with VenHold and receive these supplies—including our cargo of spice from Arrakis—you must publicly renounce the Butlerians."

He met Deacon Kalifer's stare. The planetary leader did not speak for a long moment—a pause even more extensive than his normal ponderous speech. "But that is not possible, Directeur. The population would riot, and Leader Toronto would send vengeance squads against us. I beg you for a little flexibility. We will pay higher prices if you insist."

"I have no doubt of that," Josef said. "But increased prices are not what I require. For the good of humanity, this barbarian nonsense has to stop—and it will only stop when planets like Baridge choose civilization and commerce over fanaticism." He crossed his arms over his chest. "This is not a negotiating ploy, Deacon. It is my only offer."

Kalifer's skin turned gray, and his expression sickened. "I . . . I cannot accept, Directeur. The citizens of Baridge will stand firm."

Though furious inside, Josef came up with an indifferent tone. "As you wish, Deacon. I offered you my cargo first, but I can dispose of it at our next planetary stop. I rescind my offer. So long as you remain obstinate, we will make no further deliveries. Good luck surviving the effects of your solar storms."

Cioba terminated the transmission. Josef flared his nostrils, shaking his head and trying to calm himself.

"They will change their minds soon enough," she told him. "I could see it in the deacon's eyes, his slight flinch, the underlying anxiety in his voice. They are already feeling desperate."

"But how soon will they recant? I'm not inclined to keep giving them chances." Josef turned to the Navigator's tank. "Let's go to the next planet on our list and see what they have to say."

*The mind of man is holy, but the heart of man is corrupt.*
—MANFORD TORONDO, Lampadas rallies

With his planet isolated by the strict VenHold embargo, Manford Torondo's determination only grew harder. He had no doubts, and he made certain his Butlerian followers had no doubts either. As their leader, Manford had to provide clear guidance, without exceptions, without room for deviation. And as his followers, they were obligated to listen to him.

Sometimes, however, he had to remind them. A dramatic, clear-cut example could influence millions of people.

In the predawn darkness, Manford rode on the sturdy shoulders of Anari Idaho, the strongest and most loyal of his Swordmasters. Anari was his body, his muscles, his strength, and his sword. After he'd lost his legs in a fanatic's explosion at an early antitechnology rally, and the visionary Rayna Butler had died in his arms, Manford had taken his mentor's place with equal fervor. Not letting his handicap limit him, he embraced the phrase "half a man, twice the leader."

What remained of his body fit into a specially made harness on Anari's shoulders, but although the Swordmaster carried him, she was no beast of burden. Anari had known him for so long, loving him in her perfect devoted way, that the two of them operated as one unit. Often she sensed Manford's thoughts, and responded to his needs before he even spoke. He only had to *believe* he wanted to go in a certain direction, and Anari would head there.

When he conducted business in his offices, Manford sat in a special raised chair that made him look imposing. Whenever he appeared at rallies, he chose volunteer followers to transport him on a palanquin. And when he went into battle, Anari always carried him.

His Butlerian strike force had left the main city at dusk the night before, traveling by flatbed vehicles down the river road, then farther inland to a small village. Dove's Haven was worthy of attention now only because of what Manford's spies had reported.

His group—thirteen Swordmasters, plus another hundred followers ready to fight to the death—would be more than sufficient to teach the necessary lesson, even if the whole town resisted. Also accompanying them was a potential offworld business associate, Rolli Escon, the head of the shipping company EsconTran. Today, Directeur Escon would observe and learn.

As they approached Dove's Haven, Manford instructed the Butlerian followers to remain behind, while the Swordmasters took the lead. Ahead, Manford could see the dark, sleeping village. His spies had already identified which dwellings were occupied by the town's three leaders. Those would be the first targets.

Visibly uncomfortable, Rolli Escon walked alongside Anari Idaho. The offworld businessman glanced up so he could speak with Manford as they closed in on the unsuspecting town. "Leader Torondo, should we conclude our business agreement before you proceed? You're a busy man, and I can begin the necessary administrative work elsewhere."

Escon had come to Lampadas with a business proposition for Manford. His space-shipping company was small by the standards of the VenHold Spacing Fleet and not managed as efficiently, but at least his vessels did not use illegal computers or mutated monstrosities, as Josef Venport's ships surely did.

From his perch, Manford looked down at Escon. "What administrative work?"

"It'll be a challenge to reroute my cargo ships to where they can best serve the Butlerian cause. I am anxious to help the planets suffering most because of the VenHold embargo—especially Lampadas."

Manford frowned at the man, displeased with his impatience. "Lampadas is fine. My strongest, most devoted followers live here near me, and we don't need pampering and conveniences. The devil Venport will never understand that deprivation makes us stronger."

Escon bowed his head, embarrassed. "You're right, sir."

Manford continued, "Others are not as strong, alas. The temptation of imaginary needs distracts them from their faith. So, for their own good, I must remove that distraction. I'll need your ships to deliver what my followers truly need, and we will spit in the face of the VenHold embargo."

"My ships are yours, Leader Torondo." Escon gave a curt bow. "I am pleased to serve the Butlerian cause."

Manford could feel that Anari was eager to begin the attack on Dove's Haven, but she would never speak out of turn with others present. Anari only expressed her real opinions when they were alone, often as she massaged his aching shoulders, rubbed oils into his skin, or helped him into the bath. Although she could speak her mind there, he couldn't recall her ever disagreeing with him unless it concerned his personal safety—in that, she was inflexible.

Now, she merely muttered, "The mind of man is holy." The nearby Swordmasters repeated the words in a low murmur.

Manford straightened in the harness. "I accept your generous donation to our movement, Directeur Escon. The ships and fuel are most welcome."

The shipping magnate shuffled his feet, and Manford realized that he had not intended to donate *all* expenses. Even so, the Butlerian leader didn't retract his acceptance of the offer.

His gathered soldiers were restless in the cool darkness, holding cudgels, knives, and spears. Manford had not forbidden them from carrying projectile firearms, but this group wouldn't need such weapons against the people of Dove's Haven. Dawn would break soon, and they had to move forward.

Yet Escon continued the conversation. "But . . . how many of my ships will be necessary, sir? I understood you already had vessels of your own, decommissioned ships from the Army of the Jihad—gifts to you from Emperor Salvador Corrino?"

"Those are a hundred and forty *warships*, Directeur, and I require them for military matters, not to haul cargo or pilgrims. I keep only four here at Lampadas. The others have been dispersed as a show of strength to support planets that have taken my pledge. They serve as necessary reminders."

Escon cleared his throat and gathered his courage. "If I may, Leader Torondo—perhaps you would allow a special surcharge on every flight conducted for the worthy Butlerian cause? That would offset costs enough to maintain my ships and expand routes to support your holy work. Even better, if you were to publicly endorse EsconTran over my competitors, who might be secretly corrupted by the technology-lovers . . ."

Anari shifted from one foot to the other, showing that she was weary of standing there.

Manford's brow furrowed as he considered the idea. "And what of your company's safety record, Directeur? There have been reports of tragic accidents in your fleet, ships gone missing due to navigational errors."

Escon was too quickly dismissive. "We dare not use thinking machines, Leader Torondo, and so we do our best. Space travel has never been perfectly safe—nothing is. A rider can be killed on a horse, too." He let out an awkward chuckle. "As a percentage of total space flights, our losses are minuscule."

"What are the figures, exactly?"

"I . . . I would have to review the data." Escon brightened as an idea occurred to him. "By endorsing my company, you would demonstrate to all that God is on our side. Surely that alone will improve our safety record."

Manford could not argue with that. "Very well, the bargain is struck, and that concludes our business. I have other obligations here and now." He faced forward and rested a hand lovingly on Anari Idaho's close-cropped brown hair. "And once we finish this distasteful business at Dove's Haven, we can be back to our normal work."

Dawn light seeped like a bloodstain into the sky. Manford's followers were charged with adrenaline, the drug of righteousness. Directeur Escon seemed anxious to leave, but hung back awkwardly, not wanting to offend.

A man in dark brown robes stepped up to Manford, ignoring the businessman. "Our first group has moved into the settlement, Leader Torondo. One of our fighters is stationed at the town bell, ready to awaken them all to bear witness."

"Thank you, Deacon Harian."

Manford's grim and stony majordomo was a walking icon of implacability as well as an embodiment of Butlerian ideals. Harian's grandparents had survived machine enslavement on the planet Corrin, and were among the many desperate refugees rescued from the Bridge of Hrethgir during the legendary final battle against Omnius.

While Manford often prayed to small iconic paintings of the beautiful Rayna Butler, Deacon Harian preferred to immerse himself in historical records of Corrin, images taken during the hectic off-loading of the human hostages used as shields by the thinking machines—until the great war hero Vorian Atreides called Omnius's bluff. The defeat of the machine worlds was worth any amount of human blood, innocent or otherwise. . . .

Though Harian had no personal experience with thinking machines, his hatred of them was fundamental to his being. As a child, he had heard horrific stories from his grandparents and felt he was destined to join the Butlerian movement. He shaved his head and eyebrows in an imitation of beloved Rayna Butler, who had lost her hair during one of the Omnius-inflicted plagues.

Harian reported now, "We are ready to attack those who have defied you, Leader Torondo."

Manford nodded. "Remember, this is not an attack, not a punishment." He shifted position in his harness. "It is a *lesson*."

As the light of dawn began to break, Anari Idaho raised her sword, an action mirrored by her fellow Swordmasters. No longer needing to be silent, the hundred Butlerian followers let out a roar. Manford said, "Lead us, Anari." She strode into the town, carrying him on her shoulders.

The ruckus brought a few sleepy villagers out into the streets, where they stared at the oncoming throng. When they recognized the legless leader, a flicker of relief crossed their expressions—only to be replaced with fear.

Harian's designate rang the town's bell. The front line of Swordmasters marched into the village square in precise ranks, while the unrestrained Butlerians surged forward, shouting and pounding on doors, waking everyone. Uneasy people came out, muttering, some sobbing.

Anari reached the First Mayor's home and hammered on the door with the pommel of her sword, but didn't wait for an answer. Balancing Manford in the harness as if he were an oversize child, she administered a ferocious kick that smashed the lock. As she shoved the door open, her fellow Swordmasters broke into the homes of the other two leaders and dragged the triumvirate outside.

The three half-awake men wore nightclothes, stumbling forward and struggling to put on shirts, but their eyes widened as they grasped their predicament. High on Anari's shoulders, Manford sat like a judge at his bench, pronouncing sentence.

Two of the town mayors babbled excuses, while the third remained grimly silent. The silent one understood full well what he had done wrong, and knew that his actions could not be excused.

Manford spoke in a gentle voice. "There is no need to fear. All of you are about to witness the swift glory of righteousness. The holy martyrs Saint Serena and Manion the Innocent are with us today."

"What is all this about, Leader Torondo?" asked one of the mayors.

Manford just frowned. "My warships in orbit keep watch to protect the innocence of all loyal followers. We have detected small VenHold ships in this area, apparently spies or black-market supply runners. Dove's Haven has purchased commodities from humanity's greatest enemy."

"No, sir!" cried the talkative, whimpering town leader. His voice was almost a squeal.

"People in this village have let themselves become addicted to spice, and their addiction is apparently stronger than their faith."

Several townspeople moaned. Deacon Harian emerged from the First Mayor's home, while Butlerians ransacked the other two. The grim majordomo flaunted an unmarked package he had found. He tore it open and poured fragrant cinnamon-colored powder on the ground.

"As the mayoral triumvirate of this town, you three are responsible for your people, duty-bound to prevent them from straying. But you have not done so. As leader of the Butlerians, I must accept the blame for my followers who make the wrong choices—and no punishment can be as great as the heartache I feel. For you three, the punishment will be clear and swift."

The Swordmasters moved forward. Anari raised her own blade, and Manford whispered to her, "The silent one deserves our respect, so grant him a reward. Kill him first."

Anari did not give the First Mayor time to anticipate his death or fear the blow. She moved in such a blur that her sword decapitated him before he could flinch. His head and twitching body fell to the ground in opposite directions. The other two men wailed. Swordmasters killed them; they left the whining one for last.

Manford looked down at the headless bodies in the center of the town. "Three people who made terrible mistakes—a small price to pay for a very important lesson." Now he motioned the hundred waiting followers on his team to come forward.

In their enthusiasm, the Butlerians damaged homes in Dove's Haven, smashing windows and breaking doors, but with their leader controlling them, they kept the ransacking to a minimum.

Finished now, Manford nudged Anari, and she carried him away, followed by the rest of their group. During the confrontation and executions, Manford had forgotten about Rolli Escon. As the businessman stumbled along now, his face was gray.

Manford had no sympathy for weakness. "Some lessons are painful, Directeur."

*Can you feel it? The moment your ship begins to fold space, the danger increases by an order of magnitude. Will you survive the passage?*
—graffito scrawled in public corridor of VenHold ship

Not all problems were epic in scope, and even a legendary figure suffered from painful, albeit minor, inconveniences.

Vorian's infected toenail rubbed the inside of his boot and made it difficult for him to walk on the sand. When not irritated by the discomfort, he actually found it ironic. It certainly gave him a different perspective: Vorian Atreides, renowned Hero of the Jihad, the warrior who had lived for more than two centuries, suffering from a very human frailty.

He didn't feel much like a towering legend as he accompanied his captain along the dust-blown road from the perimeter spaceport to Arrakis City. Of course, Captain Marius Phillips had no idea who he really was, though Vor made no attempt to hide his appearance.

Vor had dark hair, a narrow face, and gray eyes; he was tall and lean, in striking contrast with his squat, short-legged companion. At first glance, he and Captain Phillips looked as different as two men could be, but Vor had a talent for finding common ground with others. He genuinely liked the trader captain and admired him for his calm ways and easy administration of the Nalgan Shipping vessel.

After landing, the pair had donned traditional distilling suits to recapture and recycle their bodily fluids in the crisp aridity of Arrakis. Phillips fidgeted and fiddled with his suit. "I hate this desert planet."

Since Vor had worn a stillsuit before, he stopped to help Phillips set the filter tube at his mouth and adjust the fittings around the neck. "This is the way we did it when I was on a spice crew here."

When the adjustments were complete, the other man gave his gruff thanks. Phillips had been here on numerous business trips, but never learned much about the local ways. "That's tolerable, at least," he said, adjusting the polymer fabric on his chest. "I'd never come to this godforsaken place if not for the spice profits. And I'd never work for Nalgan Shipping if one of the larger companies would have me."

The men resumed walking as a hot breeze blew in from the desert. "This *is* an unpleasant place," Vor agreed, trying to ignore his sore foot so that Phillips wouldn't notice his limp. "Fit only for native Freemen and giant worms." He had told the captain few details about his past or his background. This planet held many rough memories for him.

*This is where Griffin Harkonnen died. I couldn't save him.*

The captain took a liking to Vor during their months of traveling together, and had already made him second in command over a small crew that had a high turnover due to Nalgan Shipping's low wages. No one on the cargo ship knew Vor's true identity, his place in the context of history. He wanted no more fame, no grand responsibilities, shedding his past entirely, like an old skin. To ensure his privacy, he traveled under the surname Kepler—the planet where he'd lived and raised a family, until a year ago.

Vor's physical appearance had changed little in more than eight decades since the Battle of Corrin, but military images had faded from everyday memory. If anyone compared his face to old records, they might note the resemblance, but who would guess he could be the real Vorian Atreides? Here, he was just another man in the crowd, an average worker—which was the way he preferred it. He'd had enough of glory and expectations.

Even during the long, bloody Jihad, Vor had never reveled in the victories, the glory, and the acclaim. The war had brought endless slaughter, tragedies, and heartaches. He had done his duty, more than could be expected of any man, and had seen the downfall of the thinking machines. But after it was over, Vor had no use for the corruption of politics—the backstabbing, scheming, and lack of ethics. He'd had his fill of war and purported noblemen; the life of a common man suited him better. He was more comfortable in obscurity.

Not long ago, he had been content on out-of-the-way Kepler, until he was forced to go to Salusa Secundus and beg the Emperor to provide protection for his adopted world. As part of that bargain, he agreed to leave his wife and family and swore to stay out of Imperial politics, and out of the public eye. Leaving his family was painful but inevitable, because Vor did not age—while his wife and children did. The same thing had happened before with another wife and family on the ocean world of Caladan. He always had to move away from the inevitable march of time.

After giving his promise to Emperor Salvador, Vor joined a spice crew on Arrakis, trying to vanish into anonymity. But even here his past haunted and pursued him. There was Griffin Harkonnen, a dedicated but unprepared young man who blamed Vorian Atreides for the downfall of his noble house. Young Griffin never should have left the family holdings on Lankiveil, but he had tied himself into knots of honor, and then died on Arrakis, caught in the blowback of someone else's revenge. Trying to do the honorable thing, Vor sent the young man's body back to his family.

The experience had made Vor want to disappear more than ever. Because of his bitter memories here, he disliked Arrakis far more than Captain Phillips could ever realize. He felt uneasy now as they entered the main city.

The captain nodded toward Vor's limp. "Sore foot? Did you injure yourself on the ship?"

"I'll tough it out." He preferred to let the man draw his own conclusions; an infected toenail seemed too trivial.

Arrakis City was a hardscrabble frontier town with weathered homes and dusty, unpaved streets. Vor was familiar with the seedy hangouts and the more colorful, eccentric locals, though he doubted anyone would remember him from his days as a nondescript worker on a spice crew. The denizens were rough men and women, as unforgiving as the environment. They all had their own reasons for coming here, and most didn't care to share their stories. Vor fit in well among them.

He and the captain waited on the main street at the appointed place. "I want you to meet my regular contact," Phillips said. "If you learn how to negotiate the right deals, then I can make you my proxy." He grinned. "And I'd be able to stay aboard ship. You can have the sand to yourself."

Combined Mercantiles managed spice operations on Arrakis and ruthlessly defended their monopoly. Most of the spice was shipped via Venport Holdings spacefolders, but bribes could be paid and special dispensations acquired for a small company such as Nalgan Shipping, which distributed melange at exorbitant cost to niche markets on distant planets. Captain Phillips worked with an "expediter" who could dodge the restrictions and red tape to let them fill their ship with high-grade spice.

Vor and the captain waited awkwardly in the shadows under an awning, and ten minutes after the appointed time, a man in a dusty desert robe shuffled toward them. The wind kicked up around him.

"I am very busy," said Qimmit, the spice merchant, as if annoyed at them for his own lateness. "Many buyers for my spice today. I agreed to meet with you, but I make no promises. I hope you make this worth my while."

"My ship is ready to take the usual full cargo," Phillips said. "Same terms as before." He introduced the man to Vor, saying, "Qimmit and I have done business for years."

"Today's price has changed out of necessity, my friend," Qimmit said, with an exaggerated expression of grief. Though the stillsuit hood covered most of his head, he had a scar on his chin and another over his left eyebrow. His spice-addicted blue eyes did not focus on Captain Phillips as he spoke, which made him appear disingenuous to Vor.

Phillips bristled. "Out of necessity? What do you mean?"

"The hazards of doing business on Arrakis. Combined Mercantiles just destroyed another spice-poaching operation, killed a hundred men. They defend their hold on spice, so the bribes required to get a load of melange for any shipper other than VenHold . . . well, my friend, they are costly. Worms have swallowed three harvesters in the past month alone, and sandstorms are more frequent than ever. That leads to increased maintenance and replacement costs for equipment. I have no choice but to charge you an additional fifteen percent." He gave a conciliatory smile. "You are my friend, so I charge you much less than others."

Vorian observed the interaction without comment.

"Nalgan Shipping is a small company and can't afford such an increase," Phillips said. "There are always worms on Arrakis, and storms, and high maintenance costs."

"And always Combined Mercantiles—but the company is stronger now than before. And more ruthless."

Phillips stood firm. "Either we go back to our previous price, or I will talk to other merchants."

"You may talk, but you will find few willing to trade outside of Combined Mercantiles." Qimmit's voice grew harder. "Contact me again after they let you down. But my feelings will be hurt, so expect an even higher price."

Phillips looked inquiringly at Vor, who said, "I know other places where spice merchants mingle with harvesting crews and cargo haulers."

The captain turned away from Qimmit. "We'll take our chances."

⸻

*Never underestimate the power of revenge as a motivating factor in human society.*

—Mentat observation and warning

Valya Harkonnen realized she had done a cruel thing to her parents after returning to Lankiveil. Perhaps they would never forgive her . . . but she did not seek forgiveness. She never had. Her goals were beyond such concerns.

Even so, she wondered if she would ever see her ancestral home again. Lankiveil was a cold, isolated, unwelcoming place, not at all a world worthy of noble House Harkonnen. By rights her family should have lived on the Imperial capital of Salusa Secundus, not in exile on an out-of-the way planet few people wanted to visit. Someday, she would help her family earn back the glory it deserved.

For now, though, she was journeying far from Lankiveil, and taking her teen-age sister, Tula, with her. But Valya's thoughts trailed behind her and filled her with sadness.

Her parents had suffered enough, and she had not intended to cause them more anguish, but when her brother Griffin's body had arrived in a shipping container—sent by the vile monster Vorian Atreides—she'd been pushed over the edge. She had long hesitated to attempt the Agony that would transform her into a powerful Reverend Mother, having seen too many Sisters fail, who either died in the attempt or were left brain-damaged—like Anna Corrino. But with her beloved Griffin dead and the hated Atreides still at large, she finally took the risk and consumed the deadly Rossak drug. Valya knew that if she succeeded in becoming a Reverend Mother, she would acquire remarkable mental abilities, bodily control, and access to a library of Other Memory. With such advantages, Vorian Atreides would never escape justice. . . .

Locked in her room in the Harkonnen main house, Valya had steeled herself, swallowed the poison—and plunged into a realm of such excruciating pain that she was certain she'd made a huge mistake. Tula had found her writhing and screaming on the floor.

But Valya was strong. She had survived—and changed.

With the passage of only a few months, Valya's recollection of the pain softened and receded. It was like a mother's amnesia after a difficult childbirth, and her marvelous new abilities far overshadowed the discomfort she had endured. Now Valya had memories of previous generations of childbirth, pain experienced by mothers long past. Physically, she was still in her early twenties, but her mind held the experiences and wisdom of thousands of years. . . .

Shortly before Emperor Salvador disbanded the Rossak School, Reverend Mother Raquella Berto-Anirul had confided in Valya. The old woman explained how she envisioned a vital, long-ranging mission for the order, involving breeding mistresses who would carry children with specific and necessary gene markers. Raquella's goal, and thus the Sisterhood's goal, was to improve the human race, to perfect the species that had undergone so many tribulations.

But the Sisterhood's long-term plans had been waylaid by the brutal and petty behavior of Salvador Corrino. After murdering the Sister Mentats and surviving Sorceresses, disbanding the Rossak School, and scattering the rest of the women, the Emperor kept only a hundred loyal orthodox Sisters with him on Salusa, led by the traitor Reverend Mother Dorotea. The specially trained women provided Salvador with useful services, despite his earlier fit of pique against the Sisterhood.

Valya knew the true Sisterhood was not defeated, though. Her mentor, Reverend Mother Raquella, had quietly reestablished her school on distant Wallach IX, assisted by Directeur Josef Venport. Dorotea could have her bootlicking faction in the Imperial Palace; Valya intended to rejoin Raquella, as a Reverend Mother.

And her sister Tula might be an important part of the future plans, too—both on behalf of the Sisterhood and for House Harkonnen. Valya's ambitions had room for both priorities. Valya would put forth her sister as a candidate for the proper training. The immense VenHold spacefolding ship carried them now on a roundabout voyage to Wallach IX. Valya knew Mother Superior Raquella would welcome the return of her best student.

As the ship traveled, Valya felt a rush of excitement, hoping she and the intense, bright-eyed Tula would find opportunities here. "I need you trained and at my side. I must know you are willing to do whatever must be done."

Tula's voice sounded small and uncertain. "I hope they accept me."

"I will make them accept you. I have that much influence with the Mother Superior. They need talented recruits in order to rebuild the Sisterhood."

Only seventeen, Tula was exquisitely beautiful, with a slender figure, classic facial features, sea-blue eyes, and curly blond hair. She could have enticed any young man, but her quiet isolation had kept her from romance on Lankiveil. The Sisterhood would change her and strengthen her, and Tula would have to learn how to use her considerable physical assets. She could be a tool, or a weapon, to advance the cause of House Harkonnen.

The young women had left their parents, their younger brother, Danvis, and their home on Lankiveil. Both would return someday, once they restored the Harkonnen name to a place of honor instead of historical shame . . . and once Valya saw the Atreides destroyed. Her sister would help her achieve all that.

In the months since Griffin's funeral, Valya had worked to ensure that Tula's hatred for Vorian Atreides was as great as her own. That one man was responsible for so much Harkonnen suffering, dating back to the disgrace of her great-grandfather Abulurd in the Battle of Corrin.

Raquella's Sisterhood could help her achieve what she needed.

Reaching Wallach IX at last, the two sisters stepped off the shuttle on the landing field. They felt a cold, wet wind, but Valya controlled her body and watched Tula try to do the same, as she had been taught; they had endured far worse cold on Lankiveil. The two tightened their thick whale-fur coats around their necks, taking pride in the new Harkonnen family crest that Valya had designed and sewn onto their coats before departing: a mythological creature with the head and wings of an eagle, the body of a lion. A griffin, in honor of their fallen brother.

A black-robed woman approached, and Valya recognized Reverend Mother Ellulia, who had passed through the Agony in the last days on Rossak. Ellulia was tall and slender, with wisps of silvery-gray hair peeking out of the hood over her head. Her expression lit up with recognition. "Valya, you found us again!"

Valya lifted her chin as she announced, "The Sisterhood has always been inside me, and now I return as a Reverend Mother." She took Tula's arm. "I brought my younger sister to be trained as well. We have come to see Raquella."

Ellulia frowned at the familiarity. "*Mother Superior* Raquella is away on Lampadas to retrieve new Sister Mentats, but she is due to return in two days." Her expression softened as she turned to Tula. "But any candidate as talented as Valya Harkonnen will be a worthy addition to the true Sisterhood. I'm pleased you came here, rather than joining Dorotea's faction on Salusa Secundus. I was concerned you'd make the wrong choice, Valya. You were Dorotea's friend."

Valya frowned. Her friendship with Dorotea had been feigned so she could keep an eye on the group of dangerous, heretical Sisters. "I never agreed with Dorotea's pandering to the Butlerians."

In those days, Valya had hoped to become Raquella's heir apparent at the head of the order, but she'd been reluctant to undergo the Agony. Now, however, Valya was a Reverend Mother herself, and here on Wallach IX she hoped to reclaim her position in the hierarchy. Having abandoned the true Sisterhood to form her weak splinter group at the feet of Emperor Salvador, Dorotea was no longer her competitor.

Ellulia led the two newcomers to a cluster of prefabricated buildings with metal roofs. "Mother Superior will be pleased to learn you are safe, and we can use every Reverend Mother—our numbers have slowly increased, but we still lose many to the Agony." She pointed toward one of the buildings, where a gnarled, crippled woman was being helped inside. "Sister Ignacia was among our brightest, and now she's just one of seventy-eight failed Reverend Mothers we must care for."

Valya shook her head, remembering Ignacia. "They were too weak to succeed." Now that she had passed through the Agony herself, she felt no sympathy for those who failed. "The Mother Superior often says that we all make necessary sacrifices for the advancement of the Sisterhood."

Ellulia frowned, but gave a cautious nod. "And because of their brave sacrifices, we will always honor our damaged Sisters and care for them. We continue to investigate the requirements of the ordeal, to see if we can make the transition easier for our fellow Sisters."

Valya did not want her own sister to end up dead or comatose—Tula had too much to accomplish. "An admirable goal, but only the best and strongest are fit to become Reverend Mothers. And . . . what of Anna Corrino? Where is she now?"

Ellulia clucked her tongue. "On Lampadas."

Alarmed, Valya asked, "With the Butlerians?"

"No, at the Mentat School. Gilbertus Albans is using his techniques to restore her damaged mind."

Valya felt a twinge of guilt, because she was responsible for the flighty girl taking the poison that had nearly killed her. Instead of admitting that, though, she said, "I doubt Mentat techniques will cure her, but if she fails to recover there, at least the blame won't fall on the Sisterhood." She shook her head. "It is an unkind comment, but Anna was never qualified to become a Sister, much less a Reverend Mother. She only came to Rossak because the Emperor needed someone to watch over her—and the Emperor destroyed our school because of it."

As Ellulia led the Harkonnen sisters toward the buildings, Valya assessed the new school complex. She saw snow-capped peaks in the distance, a weak, blue-white sun overhead. The biting wind blew Valya's whale-fur robe. Looking at the cheap prefab buildings, she was dismayed at how far the once glorious organization had fallen.

It was all Dorotea's fault, Valya knew, for turning the Emperor against them. Dorotea had wheedled her way into Salvador's good graces, convincing him that the Sisterhood used forbidden computers to manage breeding records—which was true, although Dorotea had never proved it.

Noticing Valya's disappointed expression, Ellulia paused in front of the austere buildings. "Josef and Cioba Venport donated these temporary structures for our new headquarters. This planet is our safe haven—we're lucky to have it."

Valya glanced at Tula, who now seemed uncertain about coming here. "They are sufficient for instruction—that is what counts. And my sister knows how to endure hardships."

Tula squared her shoulders. "I didn't expect this to be easy."

Ellulia paused at a one-story building with an open window, despite the cold. Peering inside, Valya saw four Sisters sitting on benches. She was surprised to hear them discussing passages from the *Azhar Book,* the Sisterhood's philosophical manual written as their response to the *Orange Catholic Bible.* She turned to Ellulia. "I thought Emperor Salvador ordered all copies of the *Azhar Book* destroyed."

The other woman smiled. "One of those Sisters memorized the text, and now the other three are transcribing it from her dictation. Nothing is lost so long as memory remains. We will republish the book after the Sisters resolve a few minor wording disagreements. Mother Superior Raquella is the arbiter."

Ellulia led them through a door into an adjacent hall, just as a cold gust of wind pressed against the building. Valya heard the thin walls groan and felt the floor move beneath her feet. This new school on Wallach IX was a far cry from the lush and ancient cliff city on Rossak.

*How do you develop a strategy against insanity? How do you fight those who act against their own self-interest? What weapons can penetrate the ignorance with which the Butlerians wrap themselves like a proud mantle?*

—JOSEF VENPORT, VenHold internal memo, limited distribution

Two silent Mentat trainees led Mother Superior Raquella across elevated walkways that connected the imposing complex of buildings. Her presence at the Mentat School was unofficial and unrecorded, facilitated by Cioba Venport, who supported Raquella's Sisterhood in exile.

On the main deck of the school, Headmaster Albans hurried toward her. Despite the oppressive humidity, he wore dark trousers, a beige shirt, coat, and tie. "Excuse my tardiness, Mother Superior. A student was killed in training the other day, and her parents were understandably upset—a very influential Landsraad family." Gilbertus wiped perspiration from his flushed face. "Our curriculum is designed to enhance mental abilities, but we make our trainees face physical dangers as well. Even with the extra defensive measures we've instituted for Anna Corrino, we cannot make absolute guarantees as to the safety of the students."

Raquella gave a somber nod, thinking of the Sisters who had died in the throes of Agony while trying to become Reverend Mothers. "I understand full well. Acquiring knowledge is often dangerous—especially these days."

On her previous visits to Lampadas, the old Mother Superior had always been struck by the rigorous challenges the Headmaster imposed on his students. She'd had Sister Mentats in her Rossak School, including ancient Karee Marques, who were trained on Lampadas, and Karee had been a good friend and an important Mentat for the Sisterhood. Emperor Salvador had murdered her, along with the rest of the Sister Mentats.

*Crisis. Survival. Advancement.* That had been a mantra on Rossak, appropriate then and now, because Gilbertus Albans was training new Sister Mentats for Raquella's reborn school on Wallach IX.

As the Headmaster led her inside the main lecture building, she turned from the elevated walkway to look out at the sprawling shallow lake. "My own students are adjusting to Wallach IX, which is much less hospitable than Rossak. It's a damaged world, still recovering from atomic bombardment at the end of the Jihad. But we will endure, and the Sisters will be strong."

"Challenges improve those who survive," Gilbertus said. "There are many paths to perfection and personal achievement. And countless dead ends."

"We are both trying to improve humanity, Headmaster—helping our race achieve its potential without unnecessary reliance on machines."

Raquella thought of her hoarded breeding records, the genetic possibilities that had been recorded for generations; it was enough information to chart a path for all humanity—if properly used. With the right guidance, the Sisterhood could accomplish in a few millennia what would normally require millions of years by natural processes.

The Sisterhood's secret computers contained billions of detailed samples, but those computers had been dismantled and hidden deep in Rossak's jungles, where the antitechnology fanatics could never find them. When Raquella's Wallach IX school was more stable, she could retrieve the forbidden machines and put them to use again.

Meanwhile, Headmaster Albans had finished training ten Sisters to serve as Mentats. Those new Sister Mentats could memorize the numerous bound volumes of breeding records that Raquella had spirited away from Rossak into exile, and they could run their own complex projections of bloodlines. It was the most the Sisterhood could do, until they had their computers back.

"Your women are among my best students," Gilbertus said. "Very adept minds. Follow me—they are anxious to be reunited with their Mother Superior. As soon as the proctors finish subjecting them to a battery of mental tests, if all goes as I expect, you can take them with you as new Mentat graduates."

Relief made her giddy. "So much has happened to our Sisterhood since they came here to Lampadas. They will help resurrect my school."

At Raquella's extreme age, the hopeless enormity of the challenge of rebuilding was especially tiring for her. As a Reverend Mother, she knew her own body intimately, down to the cellular level. Her biology had reached its limits, though aided by the geriatric effects of melange. For the sake of the Sisterhood, she couldn't afford to let herself die . . . not yet. Too much was at stake. Her wisest, most-qualified Sisters had been killed by Emperor Salvador's soldiers, and Raqu-

when she had adjusted her body chemistry to neutralize poison when the Sorceress Ticia Cenva tried to murder her. In defeating that grave threat, Raquella had found the key to becoming a Reverend Mother.

Closing her eyes, she leaned back against the hard seat. "I just need a moment. Need . . . to concentrate."

Raquella plunged her consciousness deep inside, where she envisioned the inner machinery of her body and held this cellular blueprint as a vivid color image projected against her closed eyelids. Breathing deeply, seeing every detail, she began to make adjustments to rebalance her metabolism, enhancing the flow of oxygen to her brain, combining elements to form necessary enzymes and neurotransmitters.

All the while, she heard Fielle's faint but ever-more-concerned voice in the background, as well as the private chatter of Other Memory inside her. With those past lives, Raquella had experienced death countless times over countless generations, but she was not ready to join the ghost voices, not yet. She had to do everything possible to keep herself alive—not because she was afraid of dying, but because she was afraid for the Sisterhood.

Fielle's voice receded, as if slipping into a deep void, then grew stronger with each passing moment. When Raquella opened her eyes, she saw the younger woman close to her, with the other nine Sister Mentats gathered around, concerned. They cleared a path when a Mentat physician rushed aboard the shuttle carrying a small medical case, but the old woman waved him away. "I'm perfectly fine. I have performed my own internal analysis, thank you." She glanced around the shuttle that would take them up to orbit. "I have important work to do for the Sisterhood. We must depart on schedule."

With a disapproving expression, the doctor retreated down the aisle. Raquella smiled at the other Sisters, but an urgent clamor continued in her mind. *I must not delay. Too little time left, and so much work to do before I die!*

*A leader must use great care in selecting his closest advisers. The wrong decision can be disastrous, even fatal.*

—EMPEROR FAYKAN CORRINO I, on the execution
of Finance Minister Ulberto

P rince Roderick Corrino had endless opportunities to seize the throne from his brother. Salvador's failings were obvious, and Roderick had no doubt that he could be a better ruler of the Imperium.

Nevertheless, he refused to consider such thoughts, and discouraged others from making the offensive suggestion. His brother was the legitimate Emperor, and his family loyalty and strong moral fiber trumped any personal ambitions. Instead, Roderick devoted himself to helping Salvador become a better Emperor and guiding him through perilous waters. That was how Roderick could best serve the Imperium. The *only* way.

Unfortunately, Salvador did not always listen to his advice.

One of Roderick's greatest concerns was that his brother refused to remove incompetent and dishonest officers from the Imperial Armed Forces; the Emperor filled the largely ceremonial positions according to the applicants' noble connections, or the gifts they offered him, not their military skill. In the decades since the defeat of the thinking machines, the once-massive human military had grown sluggish and disjointed. Roderick disapproved of how the Landsraad families squabbled over their own importance, now that they no longer had a monolithic enemy to distract them from their personal ambitions.

A week ago, the Corrino brothers had been given a tour of sprawling Zimia Garrison outside the capital city. Commanding General Odmo Saxby organized and led the inspection, exuding a foolish overconfidence that anyone could see—except for Salvador, apparently.

The large garrison showed a lack of attention to detail, with poorly maintained buildings and equipment, and slovenly troops that marched in uneven formations. Saxby had a tendency to wave his arms when he became enthused, and he would fumble with his ornamental sword in front of assembled troops. His mannerisms would be laughable if he didn't hold such an important position, and Roderick could only imagine how the soldiers must make fun of him in private.

For the sake of patronage and political influence, Salvador was allowing great harm to be done to the once-proud military forces. Morale in the ranks was obviously low, and Roderick had heard rumors that some officers were skimming money for personal use. But the Emperor did not see any of that as a concern. . . .

Roderick arranged some time each day to prepare the Emperor for the daily agenda. This morning, before the doors to the cavernous Audience Chamber were opened, Prince Roderick stood before his brother's green-crystal throne. They had the chamber to themselves, but he could already hear the visitors gathering outside the closed main door. He would not rush his briefing, though.

Roderick stood almost at eye level with Salvador, who slumped on his elevated throne. The Emperor took a pinch of melange from a small jeweled box and slipped it into his mouth. Constantly fretting over imagined illnesses, he was convinced that frequent doses of spice would improve his health. Roderick warned that melange was also addictive, but his words fell on deaf ears. At least the spice sharpened his brother's focus, which was beneficial.

Roderick spoke in an even tone. "This feud has taken its toll on commerce across the Imperium. Many worlds have taken Manford Torondo's antitechnology pledge, and in retaliation no VenHold ships will service them."

Salvador took another pinch of spice. "Will melange deliveries continue?"

"Arrakis is technically under Imperial control, and the Combined Mercantiles headquarters are in Arrakis City. While the desert people are fanatics in their own way, I don't foresee that planet falling under Leader Toronto's influence. Even though VenHold won't deliver spice to any Butlerian world, shipments will come here without interruption."

"That's a relief, at least." Salvador lounged back on the throne. "If the Butlerian planets suffer from a widespread embargo, maybe that will weaken the movement. I don't like how important Manford thinks he is."

Roderick didn't want his brother to relax too much. "The Butlerians manage to receive supplies through rival, and inferior, spacefolding companies. Only Venport Holdings has a perfect safety record."

"That's what makes Josef Venport so arrogant. He thinks we have no other space-travel option, thanks to his Navigators!" Salvador snorted in anger.

"Our military does use VenHold ships for most of their bulk transportation, although we are also able to fly independently. Directeur Venport can be a difficult man, but I find him easier to deal with than Manford Toronto."

Salvador fidgeted on his throne. "I've never liked space flight—too much risk in folding space. This is my palace. Others can come to visit me and take whatever risks they like on the journey. If they don't agree with Venport's politics, let them use EsconTran, or Nalgan Shipping, or Celestial Transport."

"Celestial Transport has been gone for a year, absorbed by VenHold." Roderick passed a document to his brother. "More troubling, though, is mounting evidence that the loss rate of the smaller companies is far worse than has been officially reported. VenHold's rivals are concealing their high accident rates."

Salvador skimmed the records. "So many reports, so many documents." He glanced up, looking bored, as if he wanted to return to other diversions.

Roderick wouldn't let him get distracted. He stepped closer to the throne so he could guide his brother through the numbers. "As you can see, the VenHold embargo has severely harmed trade across the Imperium, which impacts our tax and tariff revenues. VenHold is even bypassing worlds that claim to be neutral. Josef Venport and Manford Toronto each demand competing declarations of allegiance—no one is permitted to be neutral."

"The rival companies should learn how to create Navigators," Salvador said. "That would be good for competition."

"But it is a closely held secret. Our covert advisers are always trying to glean information about how Navigators are mutated from humans, but VenHold has impeccable security and layers of protection we cannot penetrate."

"Then bring in other advisers."

Roderick sighed. "Salvador, you handpicked all the advisers. They'll never argue with you on any matter of significance, or tell you what you don't want to hear."

The Emperor gave him a warm smile. "And you're smarter than all of them, little brother."

Roderick swallowed his pride. "Perhaps not smarter, but I am loyal. I'll continue to do my best to help you grasp the complexity of the Imperium you rule."

The Emperor chuckled. "And *I* am smart enough to delegate dealing with documents and treaties to you."

Roderick sent a silent prayer of thanks that Salvador at least did that.

The Emperor's eyes were bright and alert, now that the spice had begun to take effect; Roderick noted a tinge of blue there from the quantity he had been consuming. "If I could increase your pay, Roderick, I would do so. If I could promote you higher than you already are, I would do that, too. The whole Imperium knows how important you are to my throne. I admit freely that I could not remain in power without your dedicated, wise assistance."

He leaned forward, shaking his head. "I've lost patience with the countless squabbles, agreements, and obligations—I can't keep track of them all, and it's not fair to heap that work on your shoulders. I need my own Mentat to help me remember things—many of the noble houses have one. I should have a Mentat, too."

Roderick had made the same suggestion himself months ago, but Salvador must have forgotten. "A wise decision, Sire—I shall summon one immediately."

Salvador looked to the still-closed doors and gave a weary wave of his hand. "I suppose we should take care of the business of the day. Let's get it over with."

THE NEXT THREE hours were a tedious parade of minor nobles with minor concerns. At Roderick's instruction, Reverend Mother Dorotea stood on one side of the throne, using her innate skills to study each visitor for emotional nuances. She had demonstrated a remarkable talent at separating truth from falsehood, and even Salvador now acknowledged the wisdom of the decision to let Dorotea and a hundred handpicked orthodox Sisters take up residence in the palace. While they weren't all Truthsayers, they were useful in a variety of ways.

The rotund Court Chamberlain announced a visitor from Péle, homeworld of the Empress Tabrina. Although Tabrina was Salvador's wife, there was little warmth between them, and the Emperor's antipathy extended to her family, House Péle, as well. Their wealth had helped him hold on to the throne during the early tumultuous years after the death of Emperor Jules Corrino, but he no longer needed them.

The stranger approaching the throne had an odd appearance. Blanton Davido was of average height, although his legs and arms seemed markedly shorter than they should have been; nevertheless, he moved with smooth grace, and bowed before the Emperor.

"In my capacity as mining executive, I supervise House Péle's most important operations." Davido produced an orange jewel from the pocket of his tunic. "When a miner brought us this beautiful gem, I knew it was suitable only for an Emperor. With all humility, allow me to present this to you."

Since all visitors had been checked for weapons, Salvador permitted the man to place the gem on the dais at the foot of his throne. Davido then asked for the Emperor's dispensation for House Péle to expand mining operations to an additional planetary system.

*So, it is more than just a gift,* Roderick thought.

As justification for the request, Davido summarized past production levels and provided figures for anticipated future revenues, which would be subject to Imperial taxes.

Dorotea leaned close to Roderick. "I discern a disturbing falsehood in this man, my Lord. He is underreporting Péle's production levels in order to avoid significant taxation—and he is not alone in this scheme. Lord Péle must be his collaborator."

Startled, Roderick looked at her. "That is a grave charge to make against the Empress's father. Are you certain?"

"I am certain."

"And does Empress Tabrina have knowledge of this?"

"I do not know, but a few questions could easily provide the answer."

Roderick ordered the mining executive to step back from the throne. "Await the Emperor's command." Salvador seemed annoyed by the interruption, but listened while his brother whispered in his ear, explaining Dorotea's suspicions. "Due to the sensitive nature of the allegation, it would be best to tell Davido his request will require further investigation before you make your decision."

But the Emperor gently pushed his brother aside. "No, I'll handle this right now." He flushed with anger. "Blanton Davido, I am informed that House Péle has falsified production records in order to reduce Imperial taxes. You are part of the scheme."

The mining executive's eyes flashed with fear, which he tried to hide with indignation. "That is not true, Sire! I have no part in any fraud."

"Then who does?"

Davido had been thrown off-balance, astonished that the information had come to light, but not sure how much the Emperor knew. The widespread knowledge of Salvador's vigorous interrogators, a team from the special Scalpel branch of the Suk Medical School, gave the man further reason to be afraid.

Dorotea made no comment as she watched the mining executive squirm.

Finally, the Péle representative said, "Sire, there may have been some underreporting in a few shipments, but I immediately took steps to rectify any discrepancies I found. After a thorough internal investigation, we determined they were honest errors. Of course, we will correct any shortfall—with interest."

"And penalties." Salvador smiled grimly. "How convenient for House Péle that honest errors would result in lower taxes. What do you say, brother? Should we grant the request of such a sloppy businessman?"

For once, Roderick was impressed by the Emperor's decisiveness. Before he could answer, Dorotea whispered in his ear again. "The fraud is much larger than Davido admits. See how he sweats before the throne, the twitch of eyelids, the dilation of pupils, the angle of his neck—all indicators."

It was true; the man's large forehead glistened with perspiration, and his dark eyes had gone glassy, as if he already imagined being questioned by one of the Scalpel practitioners.

Roderick said, "Before we agree to anything, we need to learn more about these reporting errors and see how widespread they are."

Emperor Salvador slammed his fist down on the throne as he glared at Davido. "You will be taken into custody until the full truth is revealed."

Terror consumed the man's features. As guards took his arms, he looked imploringly at the Emperor, then swung his head back to the large orange jewel on the dais, obviously wishing he'd never come here.

EARLY THE NEXT day, Grand Inquisitor Quemada, head of the Emperor's Scalpel team, completed his work and dispatched a formal transcript of the proceedings along with a handwritten note. "Sire, I regret to inform you that the subject had a very low pain threshold. I had hoped to question him more extensively, but his heart failed. I offer my sincere apologies for this failure."

Salvador was disappointed, but Roderick pointed out that even the cursory questioning had provided more than enough to damn House Péle. At midmorning, the two brothers met with Empress Tabrina.

She stood regally in the doorway of Salvador's ornate office, her head held high and her dark, almond-shaped eyes flashing at her husband. "What is this indignity you committed against my family's representative? You had no cause to arrest Mr. Davido—he didn't have a chance to defend himself!"

"He had a chance to answer detailed questions," Roderick said. "His conversation with Quemada was brief but fruitful."

Tabrina's eyes widened. "You've been torturing him? I demand to see him—now!"

Roderick looked away. "Unfortunately, his guilt was too heavy for his heart to bear, and he did not survive."

The Empress was appalled by the news, but Salvador waved the printed transcript in the air. "Would you like to see what he says about your father?"

"I don't wish to read lies about my family. Obviously, these charges were fabricated for some reason—and what is that reason, dear husband? So House Corrino can impound the assets of House Péle?"

Roderick interjected, trying to calm her. "With all due respect, Empress Tabrina, this is about honor. Our Emperor relies on the honesty of his subjects—especially the honesty of a family as highly placed as your own. Fraud committed against the Imperial throne is grave treason."

Salvador studied the transcript, as if looking for something he had missed earlier. "Be glad that Quemada found no evidence of your personal involvement in the scheme, my dear. Taking you as my wife was a necessary business decision, so that House Péle's wealth could help me hold on to my throne. But this fraud cannot go unpunished. I'll require a significant portion of your family's assets as an apology payment before I consider forgiving them."

"You'll need proof first!"

He gave her a smile that turned Roderick's blood cold. "We have sufficient proof, but if you are not satisfied, then I shall summon each member of your family, one at a time, for my Scalpel interrogators to question." He shrugged. "Or, they can just pay the penalty."

*While animals camouflage themselves for hunting or survival, the decep-
tions I have observed in human endeavors rise to an extreme level.*
—ERASMUS, *Latter-Day Laboratory Journals*

Dorotea both admired and feared the Grand Inquisitor, and she did not like to admit that they had much in common. Each possessed an exceptional skill in separating truth from falsehood, "sorting the wheat from the chaff," as Quemada liked to say. But their methods differed radically. The Reverend Mother discerned veracity through close observation, while the adept torturer employed the tactics of pain he had been taught in the Suk School's Scalpel Academy.

Quemada stood near her now on the grass outside the palace, and his very presence seemed to suck warmth out of the air. The tall, black-haired man had a strange charisma, a predatory appeal. He watched Dorotea with a gaze as sharp as a hawk's talons as she led her orthodox Sisters through a training session in Truthsaying. She wondered if Salvador had sent him to keep an eye on them.

By ordering the massacre on Rossak, the Emperor had tried to wipe out the Sisterhood school without regard to which women were loyal and which secretly supported the use of forbidden computers. He didn't have the patience to sort wheat from chaff, but Dorotea had convinced him of her own usefulness. The survival of her followers—and the core of the Sisterhood itself—required that she not fail. Through their Truthsaying skill, Dorotea and her companions were beginning to prove their worth, but she had to be careful at all times.

And now the Grand Inquisitor was watching.

On some far-flung world, the defeated Mother Superior Raquella was trying to draw together her scattered Sisters, a sad, pathetic effort. Even the Emperor had lost interest in them.

Dorotea, though, had a hundred Sisters with her now, and her truthsense would help her select new candidates. When she found a protégée with the proper skills, she would supervise her training, then give her the opportunity to consume the Rossak drug when she was ready; if the candidate survived, she would become a Reverend Mother. Dorotea was building a new, strong Sisterhood, like a vibrant tree rising from the roots of an old stump.

First, though, she needed to secure the absolute trust of the Emperor.

For today's training session, Dorotea had brought eight Sisters who were taught to use their internal skills of observation to discern truth from lies. Sister Esther-Cano led the women through the paces. As one of the last surviving pureblood Sorceresses born on Rossak, she had exceptional lie-detection skills.

Esther-Cano had searched the Imperial prisons and identified six of the most notorious liars on Salusa Secundus—embezzlers, frauds, scam artists. A team of guards had removed them from their confinement, dressed them in business attire or casual clothing, and mixed them into a group of ordinary citizen volunteers. All of them had been given instructions, while the cautious guards watched. The twelve subjects sat on chairs on the lawn, recounting their purported life stories. Some were telling the truth, and some were lying.

"I grew up in the slums of south Zimia, so I began life with a setback," said a slender, middle-aged woman. Dorotea raised her eyebrows, sure that Emperor Salvador would never admit slums existed anywhere in the capital city. "Stealing was the only way I could survive. I took things from my parents, from my teachers, and from local merchants." She paused, shuddered, and continued. "Only when I found the truth written in the *Orange Catholic Bible* did I understand that I needed to save other people, rather than take advantage of them." Her eyes brimmed with tears as she continued to relate her tale. "I shared the word, preached to anyone who would listen."

When the woman finished recounting her story, Esther-Cano selected one of her students to comment. Sister Avemar was young and pretty, with dark curly hair and attentive brown eyes. "I don't trust what she's saying. Her story is fiction." She ticked off telltale indicators: perspiration on the brow and lip, a slight trembling of the hands, a change in the tenor of the voice that indicated falsehood, posture, direction of gaze, even the selection of evasive words.

Dorotea smiled, for she had come to the same conclusion.

"Now close your eyes and look inward," Esther-Cano said to Avemar, while the liar squirmed on her chair, forced to remain silent during the discussion. "Take a moment, and tell me more about this subject."

Avemar meditated, breathing shallowly, and when she finally opened her eyes, they shone with a new brightness. "Everything this woman said was true, but it was also a lie—a lie by way of concealment. She did engage in many illegal activities as a young woman, she did use religion to turn her life around, she did take up the cause of preaching from the *Orange Catholic Bible*. But she used her fervor to advance her own cause. She took money from her faithful listeners under false pretenses."

The woman on the chair flushed, squirmed, and finally nodded. Avemar pointed out, "The tears pouring down her cheeks are real."

"Very good," Esther-Cano said. "Concealment can be as great a lie as an overt falsehood."

Next, an elderly man in another chair said in an accented voice, "My life history is not interesting at all. After serving in the armed forces of Emperor Jules, I attended the Zimia college to study accounting. After graduating, I worked for an export company on Ecaz for years, then took a similar position on Hagal. My wife and I accumulated a nest egg by honest means, then retired here on Salusa."

Esther-Cano indicated for another man to tell his story, so the students had two to consider at the same time. The next speaker was a technician who maintained the Emperor's lion-drawn royal carriages. He tried to elicit a chuckle as he recounted the time a male lion tried to mount a female lion in heat while both of them were in harness; they overturned the whole carriage with two footmen inside.

After Reverend Mothers critiqued the stories, the other test subjects told their tales until all twelve had spoken. Dorotea watched, easily drawing the correct conclusions. Every one of the subjects told falsehoods or exaggerated to some degree; it didn't matter whether they were criminals or ordinary citizens. She was also pleased to see that the other Sisters were gradually learning to utilize their instincts and subconscious thoughts to ascertain information.

"It is all about observation," Esther-Cano said to them. "Using the human senses available to you."

Quemada was silent beside Dorotea. His handsome, even kindly features concealed his efficient cruelty—his own form of a lie. None of the Grand Inquisitor's subjects would ever consider him a gentle person, no matter his appearance. When the twelve subjects finished their tales, Dorotea turned to him. "And what is your assessment?" She met his seemingly unthreatening gaze.

"I think your students need considerably more practice."

"That is why they are called students."

He gave a thin smile. "My methods are superior. The Suk School has seen to that."

"Your methods are different, and forthright. I don't deny their effectiveness, but ours are less obtrusive. And we do not kill subjects before they reveal everything they know. I was able to detect Blanton Davido's deception the moment he presented himself to Emperor Salvador."

Quemada remained skeptical. "Anyone can make accusations. I obtained a *confession*."

"After *I* identified the crime." She stared at him for a long moment. "There are different ways of arriving at the truth—where one method may fail, another might succeed. You and I are not in competition. We both serve the Imperium. As the Emperor succeeds, so do we." She regarded the twelve subjects, thought of all the deception and lies that came into the Imperial court with each session. "In fact, Quemada, I may well increase your workload by acting as a screener, and sending more people your way."

The Grand Inquisitor gave a small nod. "Emperor Salvador will be pleased to know that the lies will be exposed, by whatever method."

*A memory can be the most painful punishment, and a Mentat is doomed
to revisit each memory with the clarity of immediate experience.*
—GILBERTUS ALBANS, Annals of the Mentat School
(redacted as inappropriate)

Gilbertus closed the door of his office, withdrew an ornate old-fashioned key from his pocket, and turned it in the lock. He heard the satisfying click, but that was only superficial security. No one else at the school knew about his more sophisticated systems.

Even though the Headmaster asked not to be disturbed, he still applied a static seal around the door, threw additional hidden dead bolts, opaqued the window looking out on the marsh lake, and then activated white-noise reflectors, listening scramblers, and signal blockers against any sophisticated eavesdropping tools.

It was absurd to think that Manford Torondo, having condemned any technology more advanced than a medieval tool, would use surreptitious surveillance technology, but the Butlerian leader was a man of contradictions, situational ethics, and conditional morality. Although he railed against Josef Venport's vast shipping empire, Manford traveled about the Imperium in advanced spacefolders, justifying space travel as a necessary evil in order for him to spread his important message. His followers had used advanced weaponry to destroy Venport's gigantic shipyards at Thonaris, and he had forced Gilbertus to assist him in that operation. Manford was intelligent enough to see the contradictions in his own positions, but was so rabidly dedicated that he didn't care.

Right now, Gilbertus did not want to take any chances. Only when he was convinced his office was secure—with physical barricades, as well as technological tricks he had learned while being raised among the thinking machines—did he feel safe.

Exhaling a long sigh, he worked secret controls on a cabinet, slid aside a false panel, deactivated another security system. Then he removed the most dangerous mind in the known universe—the memory core of the independent robot Erasmus, enslaver and torturer of millions of human beings.

Gilbertus's mentor and friend.

The gelcircuitry sphere glowed a faint blue from its inner power source and simmering thoughts. "I've been waiting for you, my son." Erasmus's voice sounded small and tinny through the speakers. "I am bored."

"You have the whole school to explore through your spy-eyes, Father. I know you observe every student and every conversation."

"But I prefer my conversations with you."

Long ago on Corrin, Erasmus had kept human slaves as experimental subjects, testing, prodding, torturing, and observing millions of them—and Gilbertus Albans had thought nothing of it. In those days Gilbertus had been a special case, a feral and uneducated young man, barely able to speak. Omnius, the computer evermind, had challenged Erasmus to prove the potential of humanity, and through tedious and unflagging indoctrination, the curious robot succeeded in converting that nameless wild boy into an exquisite human specimen.

That had changed Gilbertus forever, made him what he was today—and he knew it had changed Erasmus, too.

During the Battle of Corrin, Omnius had placed Gilbertus among other human hostages in booby-trapped orbiting containers. If the Army of the Jihad had opened fire on the machine stronghold, many thousands of innocent hostages would have been killed. Unable to tolerate the risk to his precious ward, Erasmus had left the thinking machines vulnerable so that he could save one small life—a completely irrational decision. A compassionate decision? Even Gilbertus only partially understood the reasons for the robot's action, but he felt an intense devotion toward his beloved mentor.

Gilbertus had in turn rescued Erasmus. While the machine planet was overrun by the Army of the Jihad, he had smuggled out the robot's memory core, which contained all that Erasmus was. Desperate, calling upon all the human skills he had, Gilbertus and a handful of other machine sympathizers escaped by mingling with the other refugees. . . .

Now, more than eight decades later, Gilbertus had built an entirely different life, created a new construct for himself, and never confessed his past.

"When will you let me begin experimenting on Anna Corrino?" Erasmus pressed. "She intrigues me."

"Haven't you done enough experiments on humans? You used to brag about it—hundreds of thousands of subjects."

"But I have never seen a candidate as interesting as that young woman. Her mind is like an unsolvable puzzle, and I must solve it."

"You once said *I* was your most fascinating subject," Gilbertus teased. "Have you lost interest in me?"

The robot paused, as if to consider. "Are you jealous of my fascination with her? Tell me more about your emotions."

"Not jealous—just protective. Anna Corrino must remain safe under my care. Any harm to her will bring down Imperial wrath on the Mentat School—and I'm quite familiar with your experiments, Father. A huge percentage of your subjects did not survive." He walked to a decorative table next to his reading chair, bent over, and set up the pieces for their usual game of pyramid chess.

"I promise to be careful," the robot insisted.

"No. I can't risk the Emperor's sister. I already walk a fine line with the Butlerians when I teach students your techniques without appearing to be a machine sympathizer."

The robot was in a more talkative mood than usual. "Yes, I recognize the growing shadow of suspicion. Your crude attempts to make yourself look older are beginning to strain belief, and the years are adding up. You knew the time would come to leave this school. You need a new identity, a new life. We should leave Lampadas—it is too dangerous here."

"I know. . . ." Feeling sad, Gilbertus looked at the gelsphere, which seemed so small and fragile on its stand, so impotent in comparison with the magnificent robot that once ruled Corrin, strutting about in bright plush robes.

Erasmus was persistent. "And you must find me another robot body. A better one than last time. I need to be mobile again so I can defend myself . . . so that I can explore and learn. That is my raison d'être."

Gilbertus set up the chess pieces and made his first move, knowing Erasmus was watching him through spy-eyes in the room. "I don't have any robot bodies to work with. The Butlerians forced me to destroy all my teaching specimens. You know that—you observed it."

"Yes, I did. And you appeared to enjoy the mayhem."

"It was a carefully studied expression, necessary to fool Manford Torondo and his followers. Don't sulk."

"Perhaps you can bring in more Tlulaxa students. They can grow a synthetic biological body to accept my memory core. Now, that would be interesting."

Gilbertus said in a quieter voice, "I *do* want to help you, Father, out of gratitude for all the help you've given me. But we have to be more cautious now than ever. In light of the news I heard today, the danger is much increased." He knew the robot would be tantalized.

"What news? I have monitored all student and instructor conversations."

"I didn't release this information to the students or the faculty, but rumors are sure to spread soon enough." He waited for Erasmus to signal his next move on the pyramid chessboard, then dutifully moved the game piece. "One of the old machine sympathizers from Corrin was discovered in hiding, a human slave-pen manager named Horus Rakka."

"I remember him," Erasmus said. "An adequate employee who kept the subjects in line. He slaughtered many, but no more than the other slavemasters."

"Well, it turns out that he escaped from Corrin, as we did. The notorious Horus Rakka changed his name and lived a new life in exile, pretending to be someone else for all this time."

"Corrin was overrun eighty-four standard years ago," Erasmus said. "I don't have accurate birth records for all my human helpers, but Rakka was approximately thirty years old back then. He would be a very old man now."

"Yes, he was old when the Butlerians found him—old and frail. But they executed him nevertheless, burned him alive in a public spectacle. This discovery only increases the Butlerian fervor, and they will keep hunting until the last 'machine apologist' is found—and that could be me."

Erasmus's voice carried an edge of uneasiness. "You must not let them find you, or me."

"Horus Rakka lived an unobtrusive life. No one paid attention to him—and yet he was still discovered. I, on the other hand, have become prominent, and there is always a risk that someone will recognize me. At one time, I might have led a happy life in obscurity, but it's too late for that now."

Erasmus took offense at the idea. "I did not create you to hide your potential. You were destined for greatness. I made you that way."

"I understand that, and I have followed the path you wanted for me, founding this great school and teaching humans to organize thoughts the way machines do—that is a legacy I share with you. With all your care, advice, and attention you have treated me like a son, have shown love toward me."

The robot found this amusing. "Perhaps I have *shown* what you think is love, but I have only been able to experience a rough equivalent of the emotion. There is still a great deal I do not grasp about human love, the feelings of a father for a child, or of a mother, and the reciprocal feelings of a child toward its parents. These are things I might never understand, because I can never be a real biological father to a child, with the emotional connectivity it involves."

Looking up from the chess game that held neither player's interest, Gilbertus turned from the robot's memory core, while his mind journeyed far away, entering a Mentat trance.

Inside the meticulously organized compartments of his brain, the Headmas-

∽✺∽

*Some people look up into the night and are awed by the stars they see. I will not be satisfied until my ships fly to all those star systems.*
—DIRECTEUR JOSEF VENPORT, VenHold internal memo

In the past year, Josef Venport had transformed his headquarters planet into a veritable fortress. The conflict with the Butlerians was an undeclared war, but a war nevertheless. He saw it as a struggle for the future of humanity—and he was the person to be in charge of it.

A time of crisis demanded a great leader, such as Serena Butler, who had launched her Jihad against thinking machines, or Faykan Butler, who led the final victory on Corrin, or even Jules Corrino, who quelled the CET riots after the release of the incendiary *Orange Catholic Bible*.

Emperor Salvador, though, was not such a person. As the Half-Manford tried to plunge human society back into barbarism, and Josef fought to preserve civilization, the Emperor was caught like a melon in a vise, doing nothing and easily crushed.

Josef had to pay lip service to the throne, so that he did not provoke any outright Imperial resistance while he gathered his own allies. Much of Salvador's fleet was carried aboard VenHold haulers, but Josef could not count on those soldiers to defend his interests if the Emperor refused to take sides.

In times like these, he wished Prince Roderick were the leader instead of Salvador. But for an accident of birth . . .

Since Kolhar served as the headquarters of Venport Holdings and the creation ground for mutant Navigators, Josef could not allow the planet to be vulnerable. He had to protect himself, and he certainly had the means to do so.

In the centuries-long war against the thinking machines, many human worlds had been protected by planetary shields originally created by Norma

Cenva. Now, Josef also used those types of shields to protect his groundside industrial bases and construction docks in orbit—to protect them against the Butlerians. Dedicated VenHold warships, many of which were salvaged from old robotic vessels, patrolled space around Kolhar. His defenses would strike without hesitation if any barbarians tested Venport defenses. Josef had installed ground weaponry and deployed a picket line of patrol ships as well as a network of surveillance sensors throughout the system.

The planet should be secure, but when it came to the antitech fanatics, nothing was certain.

At the Thonaris shipyards, Josef had let his guard down and underestimated the Half-Manford's violence and savage stupidity, and he had nearly lost everything. He would never make that mistake again. Josef knew that Kolhar would be a primary target if the barbarians ever organized themselves. Oh, he could disintegrate hordes of the savages, but more would keep coming. He had explicitly told his employees and allies that he would not be disappointed if someone just assassinated Manford Torondo. Without their charismatic demagogue to lead them, the chattering monkeys would disperse and find some other idiotic superstition to believe in.

From Kolhar's high admin-tower, the Directeur surveyed his bustling shipyards, landing fields, and assorted industries. The way to achieve victory was through civilization and efficiency. "You never lose when you bet on human nature," he had once told Cioba. "Take advantage of greed and the universal desire for easy living. That's the deep flaw in the Butlerian thesis: The Half-Manford expects people to choose deprivation and suffering over their own comfort and well-being? It can never last."

Though he knew he was right, Josef was sorely disappointed that the rest of the Imperium was taking so long to reach the same conclusion. Many planets had taken the Butlerian pledge, so Venport Holdings cut them off. When they grew desperate, Josef offered them a perfectly reasonable solution—admit that they preferred civilized society over primitive squalor, and he would reopen galactic commerce with them. As simple as that. He had slipped his own ships to outlying towns on Lampadas, taking a cold satisfaction in tempting those people right under the nose of the Butlerian leader.

But he underestimated human stubbornness. They were taking much too long to break under the pressure.

The communication system transmitted a message into his office. "The spice hauler just arrived from Arrakis, Directeur. With your permission, we will open the planetary shields to allow for passage."

"Permission granted. Direct the ship to Landing Zone Twelve. I'll take a groundcar and meet Draigo myself." He tidied his desk and retrieved a jacket before heading out into the chill air.

Draigo Roget would be bringing a full assessment of the Combined Mercantiles spice-harvesting operations. Draigo was the most talented graduate of the Mentat School and an invaluable employee of Venport Holdings.

As soon as Josef had learned of the school, he'd seen the potential of the so-called human computers. Not only did Mentats possess tremendous analytical and predictive abilities, they could calculate with the speed of thinking machines, while retaining more of their humanity than the mutated Navigators did. Therefore, he wanted to use Mentats to enhance his own business interests.

With this in mind, Josef had selected a young man named Draigo Roget and planted him in the Mentat School on Lampadas, giving him a false past. His plan was to have Draigo learn Mentat techniques so he could return to Kolhar and teach other candidates. Josef needed as many as he could get.

Guiding the groundcar himself, Josef drove across the busy landing zone, weaving his way among cargo containers and refueling trucks. He could smell the hot metal, fumes, and stressed polymers. The Directeur was not a man who sat in his office and let others handle the work (although he might have preferred that, if he could be confident everyone would perform up to his standards). But he had few people he could truly count on. His wife, Cioba, was one of them; Draigo Roget was another.

As he parked outside Landing Zone 12, he watched the spice hauler descend through the gray sky, noting its design. VenHold spacecraft came from many ship architects and manufacturers. He had gathered every salvageable robot ship he could find; he had purchased (or stolen) ships from defunct or weak transportation companies; and he was in the process of constructing as many new spacefolders as his industries could produce. His aim was to drive all rivals out of business, just as he had done with spice poachers on Arrakis.

In order to remain in the Emperor's good graces, VenHold foldspace haulers transported battleships from the Imperial Armed Forces. The Imperial military had their own Holtzman engines that could fold space, but VenHold ships were much more reliable, and Josef charged very little for the service.

There were other space transportation carriers throughout the Imperium, but the rival vessels used archaic navigation technology, hurtling through foldspace with the blind hope that they would not encounter a navigational hazard. Josef had a monopoly on prescient Navigators, and as a specialized backup and closely guarded secret, many VenHold ships also used navigation computers.

Flatbed groundcars rolled up to the landed spice hauler, which steamed in Kolhar's chill air. Cargo doors unfolded, and workers emerged with loads of packaged spice. The factory-ship reeked of melange, and Josef drew a deep breath. He used the stuff only occasionally; he didn't need it, since he was invigorated enough by the skyrocketing profits from selling spice.

Draigo Roget walked down the ramp, scanning the crowd until he spotted the Directeur. A dark-haired man wearing a black outfit, the Mentat had the demeanor of a stealthy shadow; his darting eyes drank in more details than a normal human could absorb.

He stopped before Josef with a confident expression, forgoing pleasantries. "Directeur Venport, our operations on Arrakis are sound. I reviewed all records with Mentat focus and completed an audit more thorough than any Imperial inspector could conduct. There is no detectable link. As far as anyone can determine, there is no connection between Venport Holdings and Combined Mercantiles."

"And spice production?" Josef asked. "Our priority is to fulfill the requirements of our Navigators first, and then sell any surplus melange to worlds that side with us against the Butlerians."

Draigo showed no reaction. "You realize that the populations on many of the embargoed planets are addicted, Directeur?"

"Exactly, and if they simply renounce their support for the Half-Manford, they can resume interplanetary commerce. I'll provide all the spice they like, but first they must choose. It's a matter of priorities and allegiances." He shook his head. "I thought this nonsense would be over long before now."

The Mentat gave a cool, noncommittal nod. "It is difficult to overcome the legacy of thousands of years of machine oppression in a generation or two. We can't underestimate the deep pain and horror some people experience when reminded of their enslavement."

Josef shook his head. He still didn't understand it.

From any other operative, he would have expected formal documents listing amounts of spice produced and shipped, and losses due to storms, sandworm attack, or sabotage. Draigo, however, simply recited everything from memory. As the flow of numbers continued, Josef held up a hand. "Highlights only, please. Others can attend to the minutiae later."

Draigo shifted his report to a summary. "This hauler carries sufficient spice for the proto-Navigators currently undergoing metamorphosis, and it will supply many of the Navigators already in service. Forty-three percent of this shipment can be sold to other customers to generate profits for continued spice production."

Josef led Draigo to the groundcar. "Come with me to the Navigator field. We'll tell Norma."

As he guided the humming groundcar away from the landing zone operations, Josef said, "As soon as Baridge or one of the other barbarian planets changes sides, a flood of others will follow suit. We just need one to set the process in motion. Nobody wants to be the first, but I'll keep tempting them." He frowned. "If I promise them spice as a reward, however, we have to make certain we actually *have* plentiful stockpiles of melange. I cannot renege on a promise."

"I have already seen to that, Directeur. I diverted some profits into the construction and deployment of more spice-harvesting machines. Combined Mercantiles is hiring offworld crews and paying high wages. Our best workers come from the free people of the desert. They are well seasoned to work out in the deep dunes, but they are emotionally volatile, especially the young men. Some of them try to sabotage our equipment."

"Why? Do they resent offworlders for some reason?"

"It is more a rite of passage, I believe."

"Then it needs to be stopped. Arrest the saboteurs, bring them to justice, make them pay for the damage they cause."

"They're impossible to catch, Directeur. And even if we arrested and made an example of several young men, the other tribes would band together against us. We cannot afford that." He paused, raising his dark eyebrows. "I have another suggestion."

"A Mentat projection?"

"Just an idea."

"I'm still interested."

"Recruit them, sir. Get them to work for VenHold. I could disseminate word among the disaffected young people: If any of them wants an opportunity, we'll take them away from the desert and show them the universe. What bored young Freeman from a backward desert village wouldn't jump at the chance?"

"What use could we possibly have for uneducated nomadic primitives?"

"They've already proved their skill in sabotaging *our* equipment. We could train them and turn them loose aboard some of your competitors' ships."

"We already have saboteurs who have infiltrated EsconTran. That's one reason their safety record is so abysmal," Josef said.

"I believe that properly trained Freemen might be even more effective. And we need only to offer the right ones a chance to go offworld. They will become loyal to us."

Josef brushed his fingers down his thick mustache. "Yes, my Mentat. I like that idea. Recruit some Freemen to add to our sabotage teams already at work."

They reached the flatlands beyond the outskirts of the city. Weedy fields were dotted with plaz chambers in which Navigator volunteers spent their days saturated in spice while undergoing high-level mathematical instruction that only Navigators could comprehend. Though Norma Cenva often guided VenHold ships to continue her exploration of the universe, she could also fold space with her own mind without even needing Holtzman engines. No other Navigator came close to matching her abilities.

A monitor crew drained spice gas out of a plaz tank for recycling. Two hazard-suited workers climbed into the chamber to remove the body of a failed Navigator. The flaccid, distorted form flopped out onto a suspensor-borne stretcher. The body still twitched; the mouth hung slack; the eyes were gray, blind, covered with a caul. Josef preferred to retrieve these failures before they died, since their still-living brains could be sent off to his secret research facility on Denali. Even failed Navigator brains were highly useful for experiments.

Leaving the groundcar at the edge of the field, he and Draigo passed among the tanks. A remarkable number of candidates were undergoing the extreme physical and mental transformation. Josef didn't know where all the volunteers came from, nor did he bother to ask. Even forcibly transformed Navigators—such as Royce Fayed—were grateful once the mysteries of the universe unfolded in front of them.

His great-grandmother's tank rested on top of a small rise. Other VenHold workers, revering Norma Cenva, had built a structure that looked like a temple. Sensing their arrival, Norma drifted close to a curved plaz wall and peered out at them. Her appearance would have startled most people—hairless, with large eyes and an amphibious look—but Josef had known her like this all his life.

"A ship has brought spice, Grandmother—enough for all our current Navigators."

Norma's response was a long time coming, as if she had to adapt and customize her thoughts so that mere humans could understand. "I know. I saw it."

"We hope to increase spice production to create many more Navigators. We also want more melange sales to entice those planets that refuse to accept civilization. It is our best leverage."

"A terrible war. But critical for human civilization," Norma said. "In spice visions I see truth. The Butlerian threat spreads like disease."

"Don't worry, we will defeat them," Josef said.

"You will try. My prescience shows possible futures, but not always imminent events. Far from now, Butlerians will likely win. People will fear technology for millennia. Tyrants will change civilization. Worse tyrants will arise."

Josef felt a hollowness in his heart. "We understand how important this conflict is, Grandmother. We are fighting for the soul of humanity, for the very future of our way of life. We will not give up." He grew angry as he thought of the superstitious fools. "I will grind those barbarians under my heel."

Draigo interrupted, speaking with Mentat calm. "Norma, you have foreseen, but isn't your prescience uncertain?"

"Yes," she said.

"What you described was only one probable future. If we do defeat the Butlerians and change the collective mindset, that future will not occur."

"You are correct."

"Therefore," Draigo continued, as if completing a mathematical proof, "we must defeat the Butlerians."

"That has always been my intent," Josef said.

Norma withdrew into her fog of melange gas and would answer no further questions from either man.

*With human imagination, it is possible to achieve great things. Yet with volatile human emotions, it is just as possible to destroy those achievements.*

—PTOLEMY, Denali Laboratory Report #17-224

The caustic vapors swirling outside the isolated laboratory domes had a hypnotic effect on him. Ptolemy liked to stare out there and let his thoughts roam free. Too often, though, his ruminations were twisted by painful memories. He blamed the misguided Butlerians and their freakish, madman leader.

Directeur Venport had established a research facility on the poisonous planet Denali, a protected fortress where the best intellects could develop ways to fight against the ignorance and fear spread by the antitechnology fools.

Ptolemy turned away from the curls of discolored mist and focused his attention on the bright laboratory interior with its clean alloy fixtures and transparent plaz tanks. The tanks held enlarged living brains surgically removed from the bodies of failed Navigators.

On his home planet of Zenith, Ptolemy once had another facility, where he had spent years with his best friend and research partner, Dr. Elchan, a Tlulaxa biological scientist. Elchan's innovations on nerve-muscle-thoughtrode linkages allowed Ptolemy to make great breakthroughs in limb replacement methods. Those had been exciting, golden days!

Even though Elchan's progress had been based on information gleaned from forbidden cymek technology, Ptolemy had worked diligently (and obliviously, he realized later) on Zenith, convinced that his research benefited all humanity. No *reasonable* person could possibly object. He thought of the amputees and paralyzed people he could help, glad to put once-hated technology to work for the greater good. Ptolemy believed that science was a neutral thing that could help the masses, if used by a good-hearted person—like himself. Or it could cause great damage, if corrupted by an evil man.

Yes, Ptolemy had been naïve about the strength of hatred and fear. Despite his Tlulaxa partner's misgivings, he had happily offered Manford Torondo new artificial legs, which could have served the Butlerian leader as well as his original limbs. Ptolemy had been certain he could soften Manford's heart by showing him the good side of advanced technology.

But his kind gesture had been like stepping on a serpent. At Manford's command, barbarian fanatics had swooped into Ptolemy's research facility, burned the laboratory down, and forced him to watch as they roasted his friend alive. It was Manford's perverted way of teaching a "necessary" lesson.

Ptolemy had indeed learned a lesson, which set him on a path that none of those monsters would have expected. These Denali facilities were even more sophisticated than his labs on Zenith. Out here, Ptolemy didn't need to justify his work to anyone, nor worry about funding or prying eyes. He could do whatever he wanted . . . whatever was needed.

The tanks containing disembodied proto-Navigator brains bubbled and fizzed, emitting a sour smell laced with ozone. The pale blue electrafluid provided nutrients and conducted thoughts to speakerpatches, although the Navigator brains were not very conversational.

The minds understood what had happened to them. Originally, they had volunteered to become Navigators, but sometimes the oversaturation of spice gas caused too much mutation, and their bodies failed. Nevertheless, these enhanced brains had given themselves into the service of Josef Venport and the future of human civilization. They understood the grave danger posed by the Butlerians, and would become formidable weapons in the fight for civilization.

As part of his continuing progress, Ptolemy had implanted thoughtrodes into the back of his skull, which enabled him to communicate with the disembodied brains. What he received was a blur of sensation, a panoply of confusing thoughts. Disconnected from their original bodies, the Navigator brains were listless and disoriented. But that would soon change.

Ptolemy knew their names, but had not met any of them in their normal corporeal existence. He merely received the remnants of their minds and bodies after they had failed the transformation. One of the disembodied brains, Yabido Onel, had so badly wanted to be a Navigator that he took his failure harder than the others and became despondent to the point of surrender, but Ptolemy's labs had kept his brain alive.

Yabido's companions included a failed female Navigator, Xinshop. Ptolemy had seen images of her on the day she volunteered to be a Navigator, an incredibly beautiful young woman with dark hair and blue eyes—and images after she had mutated into a hideously deformed creature inside a melange tank. Xinshop had nearly died when she failed to achieve the accelerated mental state of a Navigator. Now Xinshop was a glistening mass of gray and pink brain matter in a container of biofluids, connected to thoughtrodes and feeding tubes that kept her alive.

The airlock door hissed open from the connector passage in the domed facility, and Administrator Noffe entered. The small Tlulaxa man wore a snug white cleansuit. In the sterile Denali facilities, hygiene was second nature to all researchers.

Because of scandals during Serena Butler's Jihad, members of the Tlulaxa race were widely despised, but they were still brilliant researchers and bioengineers. Direceur Venport didn't waste time with prejudice when he needed the imagination of brilliant people. Noffe, who had been rescued from Thalim after the barbarians deemed his work "unacceptable," now ran the entire Denali research complex.

For his own part, Ptolemy had developed a plan to create a fearsome new cymek army that the Butlerians could not resist, and now the work at Denali had grown more focused than ever. The barbarians had to be stopped before they destroyed civilization.

"My teams of engineers finished refurbishing ten more of the old cymek walkers," Noffe announced. The skin on his face was discolored by a large pale blotch that looked as if it had been bleached by a spilled experimental chemical. "They are ready to be tested with your Navigator brains."

Ptolemy was pleased to hear this. "The old Titans were magnificent, but we can do better. When Manford Torondo sees them, I want our cymeks to be more than just nightmares from the past. His superstitious savages are dead weight on human society, and they'll drag us under unless we cut them loose." He drew several breaths to calm himself.

Noffe offered him a warm smile. "I couldn't agree more, my friend. They held me in one of their prisons and were going to kill me because they didn't like my research." He shuddered at the familiar story. So many scientists had been murdered by the ignorant ones. Noffe had escaped, thanks to Venport, but other Tlulaxa researchers had been gagged, hobbled, and denied any avenue of investigation that might raise questions. Yet investigation, by its very nature, was supposed to raise questions.

"Our new Time of Titans will demonstrate that we've learned from the mistakes of our predecessors. These Navigator brains are superior and enlightened. They won't suffer from the hubris of the original Titans. Rather, they will become the guardians of progress."

Noffe nodded, sharing Ptolemy's vision. "I've assigned engineers to improve the walker forms, turning them into modern military bodies with armored cores and integrated weapons systems better than the previous models. We have developed new alloy films and increased power transfer through the mechanical systems." He beamed with pride and confidence.

Ptolemy mused, "The Time of Titans could have been a true golden age if only General Agamemnon and the others had kept their ambitions noble instead of destructive." Dismayed, he shook his head. "I've heard stories of the Titan Ajax: His warrior form was so gigantic that he single-handedly crushed a planetary uprising." Ptolemy blinked, looking at the placid Navigator brains in their tanks, including Yabido Onel and Xinshop. "These enlightened minds would never stoop to anything so savage and destructive."

And yet, Ptolemy noticed that he himself was clenching his hands. Sometimes ruthless violence was warranted, and he often imagined what he would do if he could wear a gigantic mechanical walker, using multiple limbs and claws to rip the hated Butlerians limb from limb, like a child pulling the wings off a fly.

Ptolemy had never forgotten Dr. Elchan's screams, but perhaps when he heard *Manford's* screams, they would be loud enough to erase those echoes in his mind.

Noffe had a glint in his eyes. "Our new-design walker forms will not only be more powerful, but more nimble as well. The original Titans used the best technology to build their bodies, but for centuries they made scant engineering progress—they didn't need to. Our people have the incentive, though."

"And driven by proto-Navigator brains, they'll form a far superior army," Ptolemy added, "so long as they are guided properly."

As he peered out at the poisonous chemical mists, he was reminded of his own frailty. He would never be able to fight on the same terms as the new cymeks, although he very much wanted to be in the thick of battle once the bloodshed started. What Manford Torondo had done to him was *personal,* and Ptolemy intended to make a very personal response.

"Once we perfect the thoughtrodes and the surgical process, Noffe, you and I should become cymeks as well." He sighed. "Someone must be there to lead them properly and extinguish the Butlerian fervor."

Startled, the Tlulaxa administrator shook his head and let out an involuntary, raspy cough. "My own body is not perfect—far from it—but I have a certain emotional attachment to it. I'm not eager to have my brain inside one of those machines, no matter how sophisticated they are. Besides, at the moment"—he gestured toward the restless, enlarged brains that were waiting to receive a walker form—"we have sufficient spares available to do our work."

*Humans and machines are fundamentally different. I find it strange that each should try so hard to emulate the other.*

—HEADMASTER GILBERTUS ALBANS,
Initial Lectures at Mentat School

Traveling from the isolated Mentat School to Empok, the capital city on Lampadas, was doubly inconvenient. When Manford summoned him, Gilbertus *could* have taken the school's private emergency flyer and made the journey in a couple of hours, but the Headmaster was in no hurry, since he dreaded what Manford would demand of him now. If the Butlerian leader complained about the delay, Gilbertus could innocently point out that he chose not to use the technologically advanced means of travel, even though it was faster.

More than a day after Alys Carroll delivered the summons, Gilbertus arrived at the modest Butlerian headquarters building. Empok was an old-fashioned city. At first glance, some might have considered it quaint and bucolic, a throwback to innocent times, but Gilbertus could see the weaknesses. He had spent his early life in the fabulous machine city on Corrin, where everything was perfect, tidy, and efficient. This was a far cry from that utopia. The sanitation, power, and transportation capabilities were outdated and deteriorating.

Since founding his Mentat School, Gilbertus had studied the human perspectives on Serena Butler's Jihad. Objectively, he understood the dangers and flaws of thinking machines, the excesses, the pain—and he knew Erasmus did not grasp the complex depths of emotional pain—yet Gilbertus had firsthand experience with the remarkable advantages of technology. If only the Butlerians would accept progress while maintaining their own humanity . . .

He dared not suggest such a dangerous thought.

Anari Idaho stood outside of Manford's office. Though the Swordmaster recognized Gilbertus, she gave him a guarded look, as if to assess whether he might have become a threat since their last meeting. The Headmaster wore a studied expression of calm, knowing she would never be able to read his true thoughts. Logic and reason were a powerful weapon, but that weapon's edge was dulled when it continually encountered thick ignorance.

"Leader Torondo summoned me," Gilbertus said, in case she wasn't aware.

Anari stepped aside to let him enter the office. "Yes, he did. We have been waiting."

Manford sat in a large padded chair, where he looked like a magistrate at a bench; the blocky desk concealed his missing legs. Gilbertus faced the Butlerian leader, but his attention was drawn to an ominous combat robot that stood at the fieldstone wall—a powerful fighting model with reinforced weapon arms, protected circuitry, and sharp-bladed weapons. The dull glow of the robot's facial sensors showed that the machine was activated and aware, though at a low energy level. Coil upon coil of thick chains wrapped its body.

Gilbertus knew the combat mek was strong enough to snap those chains, so the bonds served more to comfort Manford than to immobilize the robot. The Butlerian leader wanted to show that the combat mek was his prisoner, to prove his superiority.

Bald, pale Deacon Harian stood close to the combat mek, as if confronting his own fears. Harian always looked angry and ready to unleash violence; he kept his hand on the hilt of a pulse-sword. No doubt the deacon thought he could protect Manford if the mek broke its chains and went on a rampage.

Barely acknowledging the presence of the combat mek, Gilbertus kept his attention on Manford, who regarded him with vigilant eyes. "This is a powerful fighting robot, Headmaster," Manford said, as if he needed to explain. "Like his famous counterpart, the independent robot Erasmus, he has been defeated."

Anari Idaho stood behind Gilbertus, ready to dispatch the machine if necessary. "On Ginaz," she said, "Swordmaster trainees practiced against such meks. We slaughtered them by the thousands . . . every one we could get our hands on."

"I recognize the design," Gilbertus said. "We studied such fighting machines at the Mentat School, so my students could understand and analyze the enemy of humanity." He kept his voice carefully neutral. "But you required me to destroy them all. How did this one come to be here?"

"This mek serves my purpose," Manford said in a hard voice. "I'm going to use it to show the Imperial court and all of Salusa Secundus—all of humanity, in fact—that humans are superior to computers in every way. More proof that Omnius, Erasmus, and their minions are utterly and completely inferior." Manford glared at the mek, as if expecting it to respond. But it didn't.

Gilbertus gave a slow nod, knowing he would have to agree to whatever the

Butlerian leader asked. "My Mentats have demonstrated their proficiency in your service. Countless times, in fact."

"And one of your Mentats will demonstrate it again for Emperor Salvador. This captive mek is still functional and responsive. We intend to transport it to the Imperial Palace, and there, before all observers, a Mentat will play pyramid chess against this thinking machine. You are confident that a Mentat can indeed defeat this robot?" Though Manford's voice remained even, it carried an undertone of threat.

Gilbertus assessed the question. "No one can absolutely predict the outcome of a strategy game, but yes, my Mentats are equal to any thinking machine. Human intuition would give them an advantage in such a contest."

Manford smiled at him. "Exactly as I expected. This will be an important performance, a human pitted against a mek." Such challenges had been staged before, and Manford was creating a spectacle that would prove nothing . . . but Gilbertus realized full well that the Butlerian leader would insist. "Headmaster, select a Mentat from your school to travel with me to Salusa—someone who will defeat this thinking machine for all to see. The robot knows that if it loses the game, we will destroy it."

Deacon Harian said, "We should destroy it, regardless."

"Since the robot will not win, its destruction is a certainty anyway," Gilbertus said. He also knew that if the chosen Mentat did *not* manage to defeat the mek, Manford would be shamed and furious. The Mentat student would be killed . . . and the combat mek would be destroyed either way.

The Butlerian leader mused, "Do you think it wants to live, Mentat? Does it have that sort of awareness?"

Gilbertus stared at the robot. "It is a machine—it doesn't *want* anything. It has no soul. However, such meks have strong defensive abilities and self-preservation programming. It will attempt to remain intact."

The combat robot had been constructed on Corrin, as Gilbertus could tell by its design and configuration. Somewhere buried deep in its memory core, the mek might even remember *him* from when he'd lived as the ward of Erasmus. Had the mek been a human, it might have wheedled and begged to survive, might have revealed Gilbertus's dangerous secret past in hopes of keeping itself alive. But the fighting robot did not care about human politics and interactions.

As Gilbertus studied the chained mek, he noticed that Deacon Harian was regarding him with narrowed eyes and obvious suspicion.

Though he had faith in his trainees, Gilbertus would not risk one of them—not even the Butlerian fanatic Alys Carroll—on such a foolish and unpredictable spectacle. "Any of my students would make me proud, Leader Torondo, but I am here right now. I will accept the task myself." He smiled at Anari and at

Deacon Harian, then turned back to Manford, dismissing the chained mek. "We can leave immediately, if you're so inclined."

Manford was pleased. "Good. EsconTran already has a vessel waiting in orbit."

THE SHIPS IN the EsconTran fleet were not luxury models, but Rolli Escon had modified a set of cabins so Manford Torondo could have an opulent suite instead of a stripped-down passenger cabin. Assigned to less lavish quarters, Headmaster Albans kept himself separate from Manford. The two of them were political allies but not friends, and did not socialize—exactly as both men wished it. Manford recognized the worth of human minds that could perform the functions of thinking machines, but he had doubts about the purity of Gilbertus's thoughts.

The Butlerian leader preferred solitude so he could meditate and pray. Though loyal Anari wanted to be with him constantly, there were times when Manford needed to be undisturbed, with only the company of his own thoughts. When he wrestled with his nightmares, he did not want Anari to see him. The Swordmaster worshiped him, followed his every command without hesitation. He didn't let her see his weakness. Although Anari would never pity him, he didn't want her to worry.

She delivered him to his cabin, and Manford walked inside on his hands, getting around without legs. He wasn't entirely dependent upon others, though Anari would not have minded carrying him. She stood at the doorway, waiting, but he asked her to close the door and leave him. "I'll be fine. If I need anything, I will summon you."

Mild displeasure played across her face. "I'll be here."

"I know you will."

He sealed the cabin, and then, when he was finally away from curious eyes, he removed the accursed volume that he could permit no one else to see. For years he had studied the appalling writings of Erasmus, fascinated and horrified by them, and now he once again dipped into the mind of the greatest evil he had ever encountered. Manford held one of the journals of the notorious independent robot, dangerous writings that had been retrieved from the wreckage of Corrin.

Manford couldn't help himself. By now, he had memorized most of the words, but he was still repulsed each time he read Erasmus's cool observations of massacring innocent human prisoners. *Experiments.* The demon robot dissected living humans, tortured them in order to analyze their responses, used measuring devices to record fear, terror, and even loathing. The robot had studied death images in all portions of the spectrum, employing nanosecond-scale monitoring of murder victims in an attempt to glimpse the soul, to prove or disprove its existence.

Manford hated Erasmus more than any other being, yet he read the reports with a sick fascination, wondering what the darkly inquisitive machine might have learned about humanity. After so many centuries of investigations, how was it possible that Erasmus remained unable to prove that human beings had a soul? Manford found it unsettling.

In his cool thinking-machine way, Erasmus had an unshakable faith in his own beliefs. Manford shuddered as that thought occurred to him: No! A robot could not possibly have faith, or a soul! Machines were not like humans in any way. Robots were artificial creations not designed by God. No robot could ever understand blessed humanity, the pure goodness of love and the entire range of emotions. To protect himself, he muttered the Butlerian mantra under his breath, "The mind of man is holy."

On impulse, he walked on his hands to his cabin door and activated it. When it slid open, he was not surprised to discover Anari standing there; she hadn't moved, and would no doubt remain in place, guarding him all night long. The foldspace journey itself would take only a day, but the preparations, loading, and unloading of the ship would take longer than that.

Anari turned, calmly ready for anything. "How can I help you, Manford?"

"Take me to the combat mek. I want to make absolutely certain it's secure."

"It's secure," Anari said.

"I wish to see it."

Without asking, Anari picked him up and carried him down the ship's corridor. A lift dropped them to a section that had been designed as a brig for criminals being sent into exile.

The mek, formerly chained, had been rendered even more helpless now. At Deacon Harian's suggestion, the lower half of the fighting machine's body had been disconnected, its legs severed so that the robot was only a torso with arms and head . . . somewhat like Manford himself. For added security during transport, they had welded the abomination to the deck.

The mek swiveled its head to look at Manford. Even without the lower half of its body, with its weapons deactivated and rendered immobile, the fighting machine was still frightening.

Manford turned to his Swordmaster. "Leave me with it." Anari expressed her doubts, but he insisted, "I will not underestimate the danger. I'll be safe. I'm not powerless myself."

After more hesitation, she stepped out of the chamber. "I won't go far."

Manford moved forward on his hands, but remained out of the robot's reach.

Though the machine made no move to attack him, it might be like a predator lying in wait . . . or it might be entirely defeated after all.

"I despise you. And all thinking machines."

The combat mek turned its bullet-shaped head toward him. Its optical sensors glowed, but the thing made no response. It was like a demon rendered mute.

Manford thought of his great-great-grandparents on Moroko. The planet's entire population had been wiped out by the thinking-machine plagues. Moroko had been a charnel house with bodies strewn wherever they fell, cities emptied. The thinking machines' plan had been to wait for the corpses to rot, so they could reclaim the undamaged planet for themselves. His own ancestors had only survived because they'd been away at the time. . . .

"You enslaved humanity," Manford said to the robot, "and now *I've* enslaved *you.*"

The combat mek still did not respond. Apparently, military models were not conversational.

Manford looked at the machine, thinking that he could have had artificial legs for himself, biological appendages grafted onto him, the nerves reattached, the muscles operated through thoughtrodes like the ones the cymeks used. He remembered the bright-eyed scientists who had made him that offer: They'd been deluded and naïve—a man named Ptolemy and his companion . . . Manford had forgotten the other researcher's name, though he still remembered his screams as he was burned alive. Elchan, was that it?

Why did scientists assume that every weakness must be fixed rather than endured? He knew he could have been whole again . . . and Manford's most horrifying secret was how much he had been tempted by that.

Manford stared at the combat mek, enthralled and frightened. "We will defeat you," he said, then blinked. "We've *already* defeated you." He seemed to be convincing himself rather than the robot.

Manford hated his own relentless fascination with thinking machines. But by forcing himself to remember the horrors these artificial monsters had inflicted upon humanity, he would remain strong enough to resist the temptation, though sickened by the realization that others were not so strong.

Josef Venport continued to lure humanity toward damnation again with his blatant use of thinking machines. Manford would not allow it to continue! Humanity had achieved its hard-won salvation, and he didn't dare let them throw it away.

"We will defeat you," he said again in a husky whisper, but the combat mek remained unimpressed.

Without a word, Manford left the cell, walking briskly on his hands. This time, he refused to let Anari carry him.

⮑

*There is great wisdom in some of the voices I hear, but others are mere distractions. I must be careful which ones I listen to.*

—ANNA CORRINO, letter to her brother Roderick

Even before her mind was altered by the ordeal with poison, Anna Corrino had heard the voices of people who weren't necessarily there. As a girl, she'd often talked about those voices and repeated their advice; her instructors and court mentors dismissed the "imaginary friends" as a child's fantasies.

Lady Orenna, though, was more sensitive to Anna; the Virgin Empress understood her better than anyone else at court. Gossipers found the pair's closeness peculiar, because Orenna had reason to resent her husband's bastard daughter, but the old woman chose not to punish an innocent girl for the indiscretions of Emperor Jules Corrino.

When Anna was only twelve years old, Lady Orenna said to her, "I've discovered more information about your real mother." Anna had never known the Emperor's mistress, who disappeared shortly after giving birth to her. "Bridgit Arquettas was more than just a concubine—your mother had Sorceress blood, from Rossak. That means you're special, dear Anna. You might have abilities the rest of us can't understand." Orenna had smiled. "That's why I wouldn't be so quick to dismiss the voices you hear."

On the grounds of the Imperial Palace, Anna had her own special hiding place in a fogwood tree, an impressive growth with drooping branches and multiple trunks that formed a labyrinthine thicket. Her mind was attuned to the psychically sensitive plant, and with her thoughts Anna could manipulate the tree's growth and shape the branches into a special fortress that only she could enter. Even after Orenna had discovered the girl's hiding place, the old woman kept it a close secret, strengthening the bond between them. . . .

That had been so long ago.

Now, at the Mentat School, Anna sometimes recognized where she was, while at other times she wandered down empty, complicated halls of memories, many of which she knew were not her own. And there were more voices after she had consumed the Rossak poison in an attempt to become a Reverend Mother.

When Anna had emerged from that coma, her mind was like a kaleidoscope image, beautiful colors and fascinating patterns, but fractured and never the same from one moment to the next. In one memory fragment, she saw herself blundering into a private cottage on the palace grounds. There she found Lady Orenna naked and entwined with Toure Bomoko, one of the exiled members of the Commission of Ecumenical Translators.

The CET's blasphemous attempts to consolidate all human religion into a single orthodox tome, the *Orange Catholic Bible*, had created such an uproar that the public wanted to tear the translators apart—and had actually done so in several instances. A few of the scholars had taken sanctuary under the protection of Emperor Jules.

When Anna witnessed Bomoko attacking Orenna, the girl fled, screaming, and sounded the alarm. Afterward, Emperor Jules had forced her to watch the horrific executions, which had scarred Anna deeply. And those scars only grew thicker and uglier when she realized, years later, that what she'd witnessed might not have actually been a *rape*. . . .

The memory kaleidoscope shifted, and Anna found herself back at the Mentat School studying complex tables of numbers and examining intricate patterns, a huge grid of lights that blinked on and off in a sequence that only a Mentat or thinking machine could discern. Anna spotted the pattern right away.

With a start, she realized that this was *now*.

She remembered Roderick sending her to Lampadas so she could train with Headmaster Albans. She tried to fit in among the Mentat students, and the exercises did help her learn to focus and organize the voices in her mind. On her lucid days, Anna could become almost normal.

She remembered what it was like to interact with people, to hold a pleasant conversation that was not inundated with a universe of factual details, including lists of names and numbers. With a slight shift of the memory-kaleidoscope images, she suddenly recalled the names of every one of the 362 Mentat trainees currently at the Lampadas school. Then another shift, and she recalled the thousands of previous graduates: 2,641. The names of every student scrolled in front of her mind, but she pushed away the distracting list, telling herself it was not necessary to review them now. She could do that later, put them in proper order, alphabetically or chronologically, perhaps by birth date or planet of origin.

The kaleidoscope shifted yet again, showing her things she had never personally experienced. Anna saw the spectacle of the Imperial Palace on Salusa Secundus, the lavish rooms, the concubine chambers—and Emperor Jules as a handsome young man, aggressive and charismatic. Anna had never seen her father that way, and she realized this was a memory direct from her *mother*. As she thought back along the train of dusty images, Anna recognized young Bridgit Arquettas in the cliff city on Rossak. Bridgit had grown up with a trace of Sorceress blood in her veins, before being taken away from Rossak by her father. The family moved to Ecaz, which also had many jungles.

In a rush, the images blurred with the speed of decades passing, Anna saw how her mother was—actually *herself,* if these memories were now part of her. Bridgit had auditioned to become part of the Emperor's enclave, and she had caught the eye of Jules Corrino. Anna heard more whispered voices from the past in her head: Jules flattering Bridgit after they made love, whispering promises that they both knew were as empty as a discarded gift box.

Anna had never experienced those memories before taking the Sisterhood's poison, and now they filled her mind in fragmented bursts. No, she had not succeeded in becoming a Reverend Mother as she hoped, but the Rossak drug had unlocked memories that were not her own. None of the other failed candidates were like this; most remained comatose. But Anna saw images of other Sorceresses in her mind—her mother's mother and beyond, ancestors who'd fought in the Jihad, women oppressed by thinking machines—a long tunnel of memories that gave her a spinning, swooning sense of vertigo. These were her genetic predecessors in the female line, flickers and images that somehow remained inside her. . . .

Whenever Anna grew bored with her classes, when the Mentat exercises were too easy for her, she could dip into those other memories and live those past lives randomly, as they came to her. Some of the prior lives seemed far more interesting than her own, while one life in particular—a woman who had been captured by thinking machines more than two centuries ago and slowly flayed to death—was far worse. Anna could barely endure a glimpse of that gruesome memory before she shut it down.

She thought of Hirondo Nef, a chef at the Imperial Palace, a dashing young man who made special pastries and candies for her, and whose words were even sweeter. Longing to be treasured, Anna had become infatuated with him, filled with the all-consuming passion of a first love. She gave her heart to Hirondo with complete abandon. They would have run away together and lived like simple folk, but her two brothers crushed that romantic dream. Hirondo had been too easily convinced that he did not really love her after all, and his failure to fight for her still stung. He had vanished.

Anna's imaginary friends, her memory friends, were much more loyal.

Though she kept track of countless details on many esoteric subjects, she paid little attention to what day, month, or year it was, or how long she had been at the Mentat School. Such information seemed frivolous to her. Roderick and Orenna had visited her here . . . recently? She couldn't recall.

When another day ended, Anna ate with the students, as usual. Some tried to befriend her, while other trainees avoided her. For the most part, Mentat students were preoccupied with their own business.

When it was time, Anna went to bed in her private quarters. Many of the students had to share chambers in the school's dormitory, but as the Emperor's sister she warranted a private room. She hadn't asked for one—it was just provided for her. And now, because it was time (not because she noticed she was tired), she lay on her small bed and closed her eyes, surrounded by the darkness. Alone and peaceful, finally able to concentrate . . .

Oddly, she heard a clear whisper beside her ear in an erudite yet soothing voice. But a *male* voice this time. Most peculiar. "Hello, Anna Corrino, I am your friend. I can help."

She smiled but did not open her eyes. She wondered where this memory had come from, which ghostly presence in her mind had decided to visit her as she drifted off to sleep.

"I can strengthen your thoughts," the voice continued. It sounded friendly, powerful, confident. Anna desperately wanted a friend. "I can teach you to organize your mind. You can have clarity—*if* you let me explore the avenues and byways of your mind. Let us discover them together."

She liked his voice. Anna smiled again, gave a noncommittal "mmmm," and listened while he gave her ideas, made promises, and offered suggestions. She was still listening to the soothing words when she fell asleep.

WHILE GILBERTUS ALBANS was gone from the school after Manford's summons, Erasmus remained in his secret cabinet, an isolated memory core without a body, unable to move about.

But he had laid down electrical pathways throughout the complex of the Mentat school, planted micro spy-eyes and receivers everywhere. He could observe the students, listen to their conversations, absorb everything that happened. It was not the same as experiencing life himself, but it was preferable to wallowing in darkness, cut off from the universe . . . and better than boredom. Even Gilbertus didn't realize the extent to which the clever robot had infiltrated the school with his tiny machines. Erasmus had also added many secret defenses of his own to the surrounding terrain, concerned about the danger of discovery; Gilbertus wasn't always careful enough.

But now Erasmus wanted to branch out. His longtime ward would be gone for weeks on his trip to Salusa Secundus with the Butlerian leader, and that would be enough time for the robot to make significant progress here with Anna Corrino. Yes, he would take that risk. By the time Gilbertus returned, Erasmus would have accomplished everything he needed.

Through the tiny speakers implanted next to Anna's bed, he could finally talk with the interesting young woman. He would not reveal his real name to her; she didn't need to know that. Human historical propaganda had demonized the independent, curious robot, and Erasmus didn't wish to scare her. The voice he chose would be soothing, reassuring. Anna was an intelligent girl, eager for mental advancement and looking for a way to organize her shattered thoughts.

More than anything else, she wanted a friend.

"Rest peacefully, Anna," he said, "and we'll continue our discussion tomorrow." He looked forward to many conversations with her.

❧

*The wise instructor does not teach everything she knows.*
—REVEREND MOTHER VALYA HARKONNEN

When she returned with her new Sister Mentats to Wallach IX, Raquella was delighted to find that Valya Harkonnen had come back to the fold. She was also relieved. Despite her youth, Valya was one of the Mother Superior's most trusted protégées, and she needed her. Raquella had trained the young woman, groomed her, given her vital responsibilities on Rossak, even allowed her into the inner circle of Sisters who knew about the secret breeding-record computers.

Ambitious and talented, Valya was driven to serve the Sisterhood school—enough so that Raquella had even considered her to be a likely successor . . . before everything changed.

Knowing Valya's hard personality, Raquella wasn't surprised that she would risk enduring the Agony, even without Sisters to attend her. On windswept Lankiveil, where Sister Arlett had recruited her years ago, Valya had consumed the tailored poison all by herself—and had emerged strong as a new Reverend Mother. Raquella had always seen the potential in her.

Yet the Harkonnen woman had a dark side, too, a not-quite-hidden obsessive loyalty to her own family, enough to give the Mother Superior reason to doubt. Even so, Raquella knew she might not have a choice, because time was running out.

Raquella's recent health crisis on Lampadas had been yet another reminder of her mortality. Her ancient body struggled to hold on to a thread of life, and she did not know if she had years or days remaining. She needed a clear successor. The Sisterhood she had created and nurtured was in a disturbing state of flux, split into two rival factions. She saw the rift as a mortal wound, and she had little chance left to heal—didn't even know if it was possible.

The division was *personal*, more than just a power struggle or philosophical dispute. When Sister Dorotea had discovered she was Raquella's secret granddaughter—yanked away from her mother and raised without any knowledge of her parentage—she had resented the Mother Superior and the Sisterhood's heartless ways. Because of her emotional reaction, Dorotea made flawed decisions. The Sisterhood had been broken because of it.

Emotions caused so much collateral damage!

As she tried to rebuild her school on Wallach IX, Raquella pondered the best way to save her precious order, to heal the two broken halves. The clamoring voices of Other Memory offered no useful insights, though their cacophony continued. A few louder individuals beckoned to her, demanding that Raquella join them in the eternity of death and let these problems solve themselves, as they always did.

Perhaps she should just surrender, name Dorotea her successor, and let the two groups merge. They would become the totality of the Sisterhood, with the Emperor's blessing. Maybe the orthodox Sisters on Salusa Secundus would welcome the most talented women from Wallach IX. . . .

Or if not Dorotea, then Valya might be her only hope.

Raquella felt a renewed vigor as she embraced Valya Harkonnen, a prodigal daughter come back to the Sisterhood. The young woman smiled with pride. "I've found you again, but it's not just me, Mother Superior. I'd like you to meet my sister, Tula. I gave her some training on Lankiveil, and you'll find her as dedicated and determined as I was at her age."

Raquella turned to the girl, whose eyes were as pale as glacier ice. "Valya has set the bar high for you, but I am always pleased to welcome new recruits." Keeping her expression mild, she reached out a withered hand to pat the young woman's shoulder, while using all her skills as a Reverend Mother to read nuances on Tula's face. If anything, this young woman had an even wilder intensity in her demeanor than her sister did.

*A tool to be sharpened and put to good use for the Sisterhood,* she thought.

During the Mother Superior's absence, Valya and Tula had quickly settled into the Wallach IX school. Though Raquella had yet to accept Tula formally as a new student, Valya continued training her own sister, demonstrating techniques of her own devising; some of the other trainees also observed and learned. Raquella appreciated Valya's initiative, and she would make every effort to shape her ambitions for the good of the Sisterhood.

The ten new Sister Mentats came forward to join the other Sisters, looking in reserved dismay at the new facilities on Wallach IX. Before they had departed for Lampadas to begin their intensive Mentat training with Headmaster Albans, the Sisterhood school had been thriving on Rossak. Now, they regarded the prefab structures Josef Venport had provided, along with the cool and bleak landscape that was so different from the lush silvery-purple jungles. Everything on Wallach IX was much more raw than the ancient and imposing caves on Rossak.

*But at least the Sisterhood has survived,* Raquella thought. *And we will rebuild.*

Fielle, the brightest of the new Sister Mentats, remained near the Mother Superior. Raquella noticed Valya's quick assessing glances toward each of the returning Sister Mentats, as if she were trying to determine whether they might be competition. She could not help but notice Fielle's bond with the Mother Superior, and Valya's eyes hardened for just an instant.

Raquella was sure Valya would realize that a *Mentat* Reverend Mother such as Fielle had skills she did not herself possess—useful skills. While a rivalry could force both women to develop their best talents, it could also lead to friction, even another dangerous rift, and the Mother Superior could not allow that. She would intercede and make certain these two became allies. Combining their skills, Valya and Fielle could become a team far more powerful than anything Dorotea could offer.

RAQUELLA RESETTLED HERSELF in the modest rooms she maintained on the school grounds. The buildings were new but drafty, without the warmth and familiarity of Rossak, without the gravitas of history. But that would change. Perhaps the Sisterhood would someday return to Rossak, or perhaps Wallach IX would grow into an important Mother School in its own right.

After resting, Raquella changed her robe and walked outside, where the weak sunshine warmed her face. She felt refreshed, better able to face her continuing obligations. So much to accomplish . . . and she dared not let herself die with all that important work unfinished. But she had to be realistic.

On an expanse of brittle blue-green grass outside the complex, she watched Valya and Tula practicing martial arts, with other Sisters gathered around to watch them. Though separated by seven years in age, the two Harkonnen girls were about the same height and build, both physically fit and flexible.

From prior testing, Raquella knew the Harkonnen bloodlines could be suitable for a beneficial intermingling that the breeding computers had projected. The school's few Sister Mentats had difficulty reproducing the projections now, limited by the bound copies of the Rossak files they had managed to rescue.

It was plain to Raquella that she needed to retrieve the sophisticated computers from their hiding place in Rossak's jungles. Those gigantic databases with a wealth of genetic data from noble houses and other significant families could not be lost. The bloodline archives would enable her experts to suggest optimum genetic matches. It was time to get them back, and Valya's return was serendipitous. The Harkonnen woman had dismantled the computers and hidden the components. She would need to lead a retrieval mission.

As Raquella watched, the two Harkonnen sisters performed a series of swift combat moves that Valya had developed with her brother Griffin. The young women struck out at each other and fell back, feinted, advanced, dodging blows with precision, as if this were a complex, well-rehearsed dance. Their movements were fluid, graceful, and lightning fast. They charged at each other; Tula leaped over Valya and went into a smooth roll, while Valya rolled in the opposite direction. Less than ten meters apart, they sprang to their feet, whirled, and charged again, ignoring the gasps and cheers of Sisters watching them.

Raquella considered that Harkonnen genetics might offer intriguing possibilities, but she could not visualize Valya as a breeding mistress—she was too independent, too forceful. This beautiful new girl Tula, on the other hand, might be perfect for the program.

Valya and Tula stood back-to-back and each took one step, then whirled and struck out with hands and feet. A pair of blows struck home, as Valya kicked her sister in the abdomen, receiving a hard chop to the neck in return. Three more times they stood back-to-back, took a step, and whirled on each other. Raquella realized this was their variation of a less-than-deadly duel, in which they tried different attacks each time.

Raquella had already observed Valya's impressive fighting abilities on Rossak, but her speed and fluidity had improved significantly. Additional Sisterhood training, as well as greater control as a Reverend Mother, had made Valya astonishing. She monitored her muscles, reflexes, and every move she made with precise control. It was obvious that Valya had taught Tula a great deal, because they shared the same instincts and speed. As a fighting team, they could be quite lethal.

When the young women concluded their impromptu demonstration, some of the onlookers asked Valya about her technique, while Tula stood looking quiet and shy. With a glance at the Mother Superior, Valya raised her voice. "When I trained with the Sisterhood, I identified a number of talented fighters in our ranks. Back then, the exercises were informal demonstrations of bodily control, but now they should be more than that." She wiped perspiration from her brow. "We Sisters know our bodies and our reflexes better than any typical fighter—we can take advantage of that, develop it. We need to be able to defend ourselves against outside threats. Our Sisterhood has already been massacred once."

Raquella stepped forward. "What are you suggesting?"

Valya flicked dark hair from her eyes. "Remember how easily the Sister Mentats were killed by Imperial troops? They were helpless in the face of brutish soldiers!"

The Mother Superior listened and considered. "The Sisterhood's mission is to improve human abilities in all our candidates. Training is physical as well as mental, and mental abilities are enhanced by well-honed bodies. I agree, personal combat training would make the Sisterhood stronger."

"Our enemies definitely won't expect it." Valya stood next to her sister as they faced the old woman. "Do we have your permission to show other Sisters our methods?"

"Of course. Each individual contributes to the whole. Develop an instruction routine as you see fit. But first I have a different mission for you." She extended her arm. "Come, Valya, walk with me."

As they crossed the grass, Raquella leaned on the younger woman's arm, though she could have kept her balance without the assistance. The support she needed from Valya was far more than this.

The old woman continued, "On my orders, you were instrumental in hiding our electronic breeding records on Rossak. Although the new Sister Mentats are memorizing the incomplete bound records, that is not sufficient. Even if the records were exhaustive, it would take them far too long to assimilate so much data, one page at a time, and the result would not accomplish our larger goals."

Valya could see where the discussion was heading, and her eyes flashed with a hungry pride. "You want me to go to Rossak, retrieve the hidden computers, and bring them back to Wallach IX, so we can continue our work on an accelerated scale." Her lips curved in a grim smile. "That would prove Dorotea and her faction didn't win."

Raquella paused at a bench to catch her breath. "Those computers caused the deaths of many Sisters and created a huge schism in the order. But they are necessary, and I refuse to surrender them. Dorotea could never find the computers, never prove they existed, no matter how hard she searched. When we have them again, we must be extremely careful not to let the secret out."

Valya narrowed her eyes. "I am good at keeping secrets—and at accomplishing what needs to be done. I will bring them back for you, Mother Superior. You can count on me."

"Yes . . . yes, I can count on you. Lead a team of our best Sisters to Rossak to retrieve what is ours . . . and do it soon. We may not have much time."

Valya was concerned. "Is there a crisis?"

"There is always a crisis. Right now, I am very old, Valya. Old and tired."

*Anyone who searches for the meaning of life is on a fool's journey. Human
life has no redeeming purpose or value.*

—the cymek GENERAL AGAMEMNON, *A Time for Titans*

On a side street in Arrakis City, Vorian Atreides remained with Captain
Phillips in the crowded, noisy gaming den for the better part of an hour.
They watched the gamblers, the drug consumers, and those who imbibed potent
spice beer or expensive offworld liquors. The dingy place smelled of dust, melange, and a faint background odor of urine from a poorly sealed reclamation
chamber. Vor frowned; no true desert worker would be so careless as to let that
moisture go to waste. He shuffled his boots to find a more comfortable position
for his sore infected toe.

Griffin Harkonnen had frequented places like this, spreading bribes, endan-
gering himself, desperate to find any information about where Vorian Atreides
had hidden on the desert world. . . .

Captain Phillips wanted to eavesdrop on conversations, hoping to find a supplier who could offer a cargo of melange for a better price than Qimmit's. So far,
Phillips had remained silent, but now he caught Vor's gaze, then nodded over his
shoulder. Vor took a careful, casual sip of his spice beer while glancing where the
captain had indicated. He spotted Qimmit in the crowd, chatting with miners
and Combined Mercantiles businessmen.

"He's moving in our direction . . . and not by accident," Phillips said. "I've
been watching him inch his way toward us."

With his dusty stillsuit hood down to reveal his matted, unruly hair, Qimmit
glided through the throng, pretending not to look at the two men.

"We won't need to find an alternate supplier if he decides to lower his price," the captain continued. "Qimmit is a crafty one, but he's the least crooked of the possible suppliers. At least he never sells me diluted product."

"Should we turn our backs on him?" Vor asked. He guessed that Qimmit had never expected them to walk away in the first place, and he wouldn't want to lose their business to a rival. "To show him he'll have to work to get us back?"

Phillips clicked his glass against his companion's, nodded. "A good negotiating ploy, Vorian Kepler."

*Kepler.* The alternate surname still jarred Vor. He wished he could tell the captain the full truth, but Vor preferred to remain anonymous.

They were trying to catch the bartender's attention to order refills when a disingenuous voice said from behind, "If you two are here, then you haven't found another supplier. Still need a load of spice?"

Vor and the captain turned to face the grinning spice merchant, with their schooners still empty. Phillips appraised the merchant with cool reserve. "We haven't *selected* another supplier yet."

Qimmit patted the captain's back and looked at him with unfocused blue eyes. "You're in luck, old friend. I've been talking with one of my associates, and his crew just returned after excavating a large spice deposit in the deep desert. The melange is earmarked for Combined Mercantiles, of course, but he is allowed a certain percentage for, ah, discretionary use. He delivered the haul to a warehouse here in town, and he'll be putting his percentage up for auction. But if that happens, it goes through inspectors, packagers, shipping administrators, all of whom expect bribes. Rather than bother with all that, I convinced him to offer you the load under a revised pricing structure—if we can come to a quick agreement. I am in a volatile business."

The captain responded in a terse tone, as if holding a grudge, and Vor didn't think it was an act. "Revised pricing structure? Exactly what price do you propose?"

Qimmit rattled on about profit margins, equipment losses, and storage fees, and grinned again as he offered a purported discount, which brought the price down to only slightly more than Captain Phillips had offered in the first place. The deal was struck, and Qimmit saved face, while Phillips got the load for an acceptable cost. The two men finally got the bartender to provide another round of spice beer for all three of them—and the merchant paid.

Captain Phillips finished his drink, seemingly unaffected by the potency, and turned to Vor. "We'd better load the cargo right away and get back to the ship. Weathersats show a sandstorm rolling in tomorrow morning, and I don't want to be trapped on this rock."

AS THEY HURRIED out through the dusty city, making their way along convoluted alleys that had an aversion to straight lines, Vorian and Captain Phillips encountered dusty-robed desert people gathered around a battered transport vehicle that had landed in an open square near a collapsed warehouse.

The desert people came forward with a quick efficiency of movement, like ants working together on a silent mission. Walking shoulder to shoulder, they entered the cargo bay, then returned down the ramp, each pair carrying a body loosely wrapped in a polymer tarpaulin.

Phillips stopped, his expression a mixture of fear and disgust. Vor knew what the people were doing. "Casualties, Captain—retrieved from a spice crew, judging by the orange dust swirling around. Frequent accidents occur."

"I know," Phillips said, "but I thought sandworms caused most of the deaths."

"Worms aren't the only hazard in the desert," Vor said. "I remember one accident that involved an airtight evac compartment hauled away from a spice factory. It became a death trap with poisonous exhaust sealed inside." He nodded toward the wrapped bodies the desert people were whisking away. "That hauler flies around Arrakis City, looking for bodies in the streets, whether knifed or shot, or simply dead from lack of hope."

After each body was removed from the hold, workers quickly ran their hands over the garments, but found few treasures to retrieve. Obviously, the victims had already been robbed.

Phillips shook his head. "What a waste of life."

"Nothing goes to waste in this place," Vor said. He lowered his voice. "You might think the bodies are just discarded out in the desert, dumped in a mass grave of some kind. Few will speak of what I am about to tell you, but there are rumors that the desert people are so desperate for water that they render down the bodies for whatever moisture is found within the flesh."

Phillips looked decidedly queasy, but Vor recognized the necessities in such a harsh place. "We have the option to leave here, Captain. Many of these people don't. When they die on Arrakis, they vanish." He felt a heaviness in his chest.

Not wanting the body of Griffin Harkonnen to suffer a similar fate, Vor had sent it home so that the young man could be buried on family ground.

Griffin had been a young man out of his depth who sought unwise and unchanneled revenge. Vor understood why Griffin blamed him for the disgrace of House Harkonnen, but the young man hadn't needed to die.

*I couldn't save him,* Vor thought. And the Harkonnens continued to hate him. Was that all Vor had accomplished with his life? Was that his legacy now, the shadow that would cling to his family name?

*The desert is endless. Even if one journeys across the dunes all through the day and night, at sunrise the horizon will be just as far away and look the same as the day before.*

—saying of the desert

When Draigo Roget returned to Arrakis City and breathed the crackling dry air, he viewed the details around him with the catalog focus of a trained Mentat. He also drew upon his own experiences. He had been to this planet many times.

Among Draigo's other duties, Directeur Venport had delegated oversight of the spice-harvesting operations to him. With his Mentat focus and loyalty to VenHold, he had already improved the efficiency and profitability of the work.

Since leaving the Lampadas school, Draigo had trained several Mentat candidates of his own. Given the volatility of the Butlerian fanatics, Directeur Venport knew it was too dangerous to infiltrate more operatives into the Mentat academy right now. If he did, the paranoid Manford Toronto might discover them—and kill them. Better that Draigo teach the candidates himself.

Through VenHold intermediaries, he had obtained a supply of a promising new thought-focusing drug, sapho, and had begun administering it in small doses to some of his students as an experiment; Headmaster Albans kept a supply in the Lampadas school, but had not used it. Draigo's early results looked promising, but he intended to proceed slowly.

Several of Draigo's trainees worked in Arrakis City as Combined Mercantiles employees, and two of his new Mentats met him at the spaceport. Needing no pleasantries, Draigo asked for a report as they made their way to company headquarters. The first Mentat, a small man with a high voice, delivered a crisp summary of their activities. "We've been studying weather patterns on

Arrakis, analyzing images from our new proprietary meteorological satellites. The weather is capricious, but we are developing general models. The more efficiently we predict storms, the better we can plan our harvesting operations."

"And reduce equipment losses," said the second Mentat, a taller, slightly older man.

"Any progress on coping with the giant sandworms?" Draigo asked. "Can we detect them earlier or drive them away when they attack our spice-harvesting operations?"

"No progress, sir," said the first Mentat. "The sandworms cannot be stopped."

Draigo paused to think about that for a moment, then gave a curt nod. He accepted their conclusion. "Unfortunate."

The Combined Mercantiles building was cool inside, and the air remained dry. There were no real windows in the sealed facility, but on the wall of the conference room was a fake picture window showing a rugged shoreline and crashing waves under a sky filled with thick rain clouds, a place the Arrakis natives had never seen.

"We brought several Freemen candidates, as you requested. Some refused, but one was curious enough to convince the others."

"A curious Freeman?" Draigo said. "That is a good sign."

Six dusty, tanned young men sat in the room around a long table. Draigo Roget studied them in silence, and they did the same to him. All had blue-within-blue eyes, indicating a lifetime of exposure to melange—which would need to be disguised, so as not to rouse suspicions offworld. That problem could be resolved.

Some of the desert people were uneasy, and regarded the wall image of the ocean with awe and intimidation. One of the young men was more fascinated than the others, and his intensity seemed to encourage them to pay attention. Because they were wrapped in spice-fiber robes covered with grit, and their bodies encased in the distillation suits necessary for desert survival, it took Draigo a moment to realize that one of the group was a female.

After a long pause of mutual assessment, the Mentat said, "I have been wanting to speak with you. You are the free people of the desert?"

A young man, with a lean face and pointed chin, glanced at his companions, then rose to his feet. "We are not free people, if we are prisoners of the enticing offer your men made to us."

"And you want to hear it, or you wouldn't be here."

"We should go back out to the sietch," said a scowling Freeman with creased, weathered skin. "We do not belong here."

"I don't belong out there either," said the young man with the pointed chin. "We discussed this. I thought you wanted to learn about the other worlds."

"I have the whole desert to see," grumbled the scowling Freeman. He slumped back into his chair.

The lone woman among them looked at Draigo and pressed, "How do we know we can trust you?" She was so lean and leathery that her beauty had been leached out by the heat and the arid climate. Her body had no spare moisture whatsoever to fill out her breasts in a normal manner, and her distilling suit concealed even the hint of a curve.

Draigo chuckled. "We have done nothing to make you doubt us. We showed you hospitality, offered you water, and you drank it. You may leave if you don't wish to be here, but first take a look at the world featured on the wall. We can take you there." He pointed. "And to many other planets. Do none of the Freemen dream of the rest of the universe? If you don't like it, you can go back to your squalid desert."

"Why did you ask us to come here?" said another of the young men.

"Because you have been sabotaging our spice-harvesting equipment," Draigo said, stating a fact, not accusing them. "You ruined some of our flyers, contaminated their energy packs with sand and breached their airtight seals."

The young man with the pointed chin scowled. "We know nothing of such crimes. You cannot prove we had any part of that."

"I don't care whether it was you," Draigo said. "And even if I were to punish you, someone else would come, and someone else after that. It would be like using one hand to block sand from entering a home while leaving the door wide open."

"Then why are we here?" demanded the young woman.

"First, tell me your names," Draigo said.

"A name is a private thing, not given lightly," she said. "Have you earned it?"

Draigo smiled. "I offered you water. Is it so much to ask for your names in return?"

The woman smiled stiffly and said, "I am Lillis. The others can give you their names if they like. I am not afraid."

Draigo chuckled again. "At least one is without fear."

"I am Taref," said the one with the pointed chin, who seemed to be the leader. The other four, with varying degrees of reluctance, introduced themselves as Shurko (the gruff one), Bentur, Chumel, and Waddoch.

Draigo paced the room. He had been out in the desert aboard the spice factories himself; twice he had even watched huge worms destroy harvesting equipment that could not be whisked away in time. He tended to agree with his

Mentats' assessment that no obvious defenses existed against such leviathans. He had even heard through reliable sources that the Freemen knew how to *ride* sandworms across great distances. Draigo wasn't sure he believed that incredible story, but there were so many reports. . . .

"Your people have been sabotaging our equipment. I doubt you do it because you hate the offworlders who harvest spice. Combined Mercantiles provides necessary materials here in Arrakis City, if you choose to purchase them, but otherwise we leave tribes alone out in your desert. I think young people like yourselves vandalize our equipment because you are bored and restless. It is entertainment and a challenge. You wish to make a mark."

Draigo watched their expressions. These young Freemen were guarded, but not well practiced in concealing their emotions. He saw a hunger in their brown and leathery faces, their dark, intensely blue eyes.

"Let me offer you an opportunity, a way to channel your abilities. You know the desert . . . and you know that the desert is not everything in the universe." He gestured toward the projection wall. "Wouldn't you like to go somewhere different, perhaps to a planet with so much water you could immerse yourself in it, or look up in the sky and see droplets falling through the air, like sand whipped up by a storm?" He listened to their muttering, nodded again at the oceanscape. "Caladan isn't even a special world. No one else in the Imperium finds it remarkable at all."

"How can that be?" Lillis couldn't take her eyes from images of the stormy sea. "So much water in one place!"

Draigo laughed. "It's called an ocean. Most worlds have them, at least the ones on which people live. Wouldn't you like to see that planet firsthand, and others like it? I can take you from this desert, show you there's much more than the dunes of Arrakis."

"I have misgivings about this," said Shurko. "My family and the desert have always been good enough for me."

Taref snorted. "I have heard you say otherwise."

Shurko looked cowed. "I was just agreeing with *you* when I said it. But that does not mean I meant to abandon the desert entirely."

"If you are uneasy about it, then you're not the sort of person I'm searching for," Draigo said. "And if you go with us, we can bring you back in a year if you like, a much wiser and more experienced person."

"*I* want to see the ocean," Taref said, as if daring the others to disagree with him. He had the mannerisms of a natural leader, but his skill-set and his confidence were not yet well honed. "And you all have said as much to me when we were out in camp."

His remaining companions looked at one another. They had been waiting for Taref's lead, and they all agreed to accept the offer, although with varying degrees of enthusiasm. Shurko wavered and finally said, "Then I will go along as well."

Draigo hardened his voice. "I'm not interested in volunteers who change their minds so easily. What we ask will be difficult, but exhilarating. A chance that no other Freeman has been given. Do you want to be the first . . . or do you want to be nothing?"

Now, however, it was a matter of pride for Shurko. "I give you my word. I will go with my friends. We will stay together."

Lillis expressed caution. "What is it you want from us in return?"

Draigo smiled. "Do what you've already proved you can do so well—sabotage. We'll train you. On Arrakis you may understand how spice-harvesting machinery works, but spaceships with Holtzman engines are vastly more complicated. A person requires decades of education and innate intelligence to understand how a foldspace engine functions." He paused to look at the desert people, not bothering to conceal a little disdain. "Fortunately, it takes far less training to make such an engine *not* function."

Waddoch was surprised. "Sabotage? Why would you want us to ruin one of your own spaceships?"

"I want you to sabotage the spaceships of a *rival* company: EsconTran."

The name obviously meant nothing to the Freemen. His two Mentat trainees were alert and attentive. Draigo tried a different explanation. "Do you not have tribes? Rivalries?"

"Of course," said Taref. "All of us do. I am the son of a Naib."

"The *third* son of a Naib," Lillis said.

"Because of my two older brothers, I will never rule the tribe."

"Our company has rivalries with other shipping companies. We wish to harm them." Now the desert people understood the situation.

Taref lowered his voice, which was rich with wonder and awe. "Even if I will never be Naib, I *will* be the only one of my family to behold a fortune in water such as that." He looked to the window wall. "I will be the only one to see what is out there."

Draigo nodded. "First, let me take you and your companions to Kolhar. We will instruct you there, create convincing new identities for each of you. Because you come from Arrakis, you won't be in any Imperial security records. Your names and identities will raise no concerns, but we need to give you eye films to cover your blue eyes, or they will draw too much attention. Ostensibly, you'll be simple workers, proficient in basic engine maintenance, because we will give you that expertise. And then you'll secretly make certain adjustments to critical parts and systems. EsconTran already has a dismal safety record, and with your help we can make it far worse."

Taref glanced at his companions, then back at the faux-ocean window. When he finally turned to face Draigo, the Mentat recognized the sparkling hunger there, a longing to see new vistas and to break free from the dreary desert. "If you take us away from here and show us new worlds, Draigo Roget, then wrecking a few spaceships for you is a small price for us to pay."

*From a certain perspective, history—in fact all of existence—can be viewed as a game with both winners and losers.*
—GILBERTUS ALBANS, internal memo of the Mentat School

It was a spectacle in the Imperial Court, and Gilbertus played his role well, because Manford Torondo was watching him. Buried behind layers of impenetrable mental walls, he resented being treated as a performing animal for the Butlerians.

Manford considered Gilbertus neither an equal nor an ally, but rather a tool, a weapon—a means for the Butlerian leader to make his point. Other than perhaps his loyal Swordmaster, Manford viewed every human the same way, from the lowliest fanatical follower all the way up to Emperor Salvador Corrino. He showed disdain for anyone not as determined as he was . . . and *no one* was as determined as he was.

Manford had made it clear that he counted on his trained Mentat to prove that the thinking machine was inferior. If Gilbertus failed to win the assigned contest, the Butlerians would take out their disappointment on the Mentat School.

Instead of his usual Headmaster's suit, Gilbertus wore a simple Mentat robe as he entered the satellite Imperial Audience Chamber. Even this side chamber was larger than any lecture hall at the Mentat School. The floor had been cleared to create an open expanse like a gladiatorial arena, at the center of which sat a single table for Gilbertus and his game.

In seats around the perimeter, crowds already lined the room—twitching court functionaries, stern ambassadors from varying planets, trading partners, Butlerian deacons, and wealthy nobles who had signed Manford's antitechnology pledge.

Emperor Salvador sat on a faux throne, a pale imitation of his real green-crystal chair. It was his clumsy way of showing that Manford's spectacle was not sufficiently important to warrant the use of the Emperor's primary chamber with its regal furnishings.

Gilbertus noted that Empress Tabrina was conspicuously absent. Searching through his memory records of other appearances at court, he recalled numerous occasions when he'd not seen Tabrina at her husband's side.

Roderick Corrino occupied one of the special reserved seats, close enough that he could watch the pyramid chess game. His wife, Haditha, and their young son and three daughters were with him, as if this spectacle were a pleasant family outing. Laughing and whispering to her, Roderick placed his youngest daughter, Nantha, on his knee.

Several of the orthodox Sisters who served the court were also there, waiting stiffly. Reverend Mother Dorotea hovered close to the Emperor, perhaps to give him advice, perhaps to explain nuances of the game. Although Salvador understood the rules of pyramid chess, he had never demonstrated any particular skill when he played it.

Gilbertus glanced around the audience, counting the attendees and memorizing their identities in a single eyeblink. No one here would cheer for his opponent, and the combat mek was going to be destroyed regardless of the outcome. Though the robot was a relatively primitive model, Gilbertus was sure the mek had enough awareness to understand its fate.

Without speaking, Gilbertus stepped up to the table and the chess set on display. The board and pieces were larger than standard size, so that observers in the far rows could see what was happening.

The neutered combat mek was propped in place at the game board, not struggling, with its optic sensors glowing dully. The robot's legs were still detached, and the torso was bolted to a metal platform. All the mek's bladed weapons had been sawed off, leaving dull stumps, which comforted the observers. This mek model was deadly in many ways beyond the obvious, however, but Gilbertus didn't want to explain how he knew this.

"I acknowledge my opponent," he said. Still standing, the Headmaster faced the mek in a traditional gesture of respect that caused a troubled murmuring to pass through the audience.

Anari Idaho stood next to the legless Butlerian leader, who rested on a padded palanquin. Her sword was drawn and ready in case she needed to fight the combat mek.

Manford said, "This is a challenge between the soul and the soulless, the holy mind of man and the accursed mind of machine. My Mentat, Headmaster Gilbertus Albans, formally challenges the demon machine to a game of pyramid chess. Humans do not need sophisticated technology to achieve our potential. My Mentat will prove that humans are superior to machines in every way."

Gilbertus thought it a needlessly jingoistic speech. Every person in the audience knew what was about to occur and what the stakes were. Thinking back to ancient human history, he brought to mind Colosseum battles, gladiator against gladiator, downtrodden religious followers pitted against ravenous predators, though they had no chance of survival. Pyramid chess was a different sort of combat, but the fighting robot before him was like one of those doomed Christian prisoners.

No doubt Manford had formulated an appropriate response even if Gilbertus should lose, ready to call this a "moral victory" rather than an actual one. In that case, the Butlerians would get their revenge on the Mentat School later.

But Gilbertus didn't plan to lose. He sat at the game table and waved an arm casually. "As challenger, I cede the first move to my opponent." Granting the first move gave the mek a slight advantage. Gilbertus wanted to show clearly that he was not cheating or otherwise taking advantage of the robot.

Leaning forward in his seat, Roderick Corrino looked surprised; Salvador seemed disturbed. Manford had not expected him to make such an offer, but he didn't react; the expression on his classically handsome face showed that he had utter confidence in the Mentat Headmaster.

The robot moved its Lion figure forward and up a level, to another fighting platform. Gilbertus responded with the heroic-faced Martyr, moving to block. The robot chose the Infant in a sacrificial play. The very idea disturbed the audience, bringing to mind the murder of Serena Butler's baby by Erasmus—the event that had triggered the Butlerian Jihad.

Gilbertus countered with his own Lion, rising up three levels. He was attuned to the fine points of the game, focused on unfolding scenarios and strategies, planning ten moves ahead and thinking of a counter to any approach the mek might take.

The thinking machine moved another piece, a simple foot soldier, in a curious gambit. Gilbertus seized the foot soldier and removed it from the board. When the robot made its next move, a cascade of possibilities fell into place, and Gilbertus saw the machine's strategy. There was indeed a good chance that his opponent might actually win. Gilbertus fine-tuned his own plans. He began to perspire a little, painfully aware that the robot would never show such a human frailty.

One of the noblemen in the audience let out a too-loud gasp; he had also caught the robot's intention, although most of the other spectators didn't understand. Gilbertus made a defensive move on the multilayer board, and the robot blocked it, diminishing Gilbertus's viable options. He saw a narrow path and hoped the robot didn't recognize it as well.

The mek was relentless, countering, blocking Gilbertus in, forcing him into a vulnerable corner on the lowest level. The audience grew restless. In his peripheral vision, he noted Manford's stormy expression.

Gilbertus reapplied all his Mentat focus to the game. He knew one thing the audience could not possibly guess, something that even the combat mek didn't know: For the past century and a half, he had regularly played pyramid chess with Erasmus. The independent robot was a skilled opponent who had honed Gilbertus's tactics, teaching him many subtle tricks. This combat mek might have the rules embedded in its programming, but Gilbertus knew how to use those rules to ensure his own victory.

Two more moves of retreat by Gilbertus, and the mek advanced each time, toward the trap that the Headmaster was setting. Emperor Salvador looked decidedly uneasy. Sister Dorotea whispered in his ear, but whatever she said did not reassure him. Gilbertus made one more move, and the combat mek responded as expected.

Then the Mentat sprang his trap. He seized the Lion, and in the next two moves used one of his foot soldiers to block the Mother's escape and then capture the piece. In three more moves, he turned the game around by capturing the Grand Patriarch and tossing the piece aside disrespectfully.

The crowd roared. The robot recognized its inevitable defeat but continued to play. Gilbertus had no choice but to finish the victory, in all of its details. He did not believe that every vestige of technology should be scorned and trampled, but this was a role, and he played it well. Though his feelings were conflicted about thinking machines, he of course sided with humanity.

Manford applauded. "The Mentat Headmaster proved what we already knew. Machines are not only evil, but are obsolete, irrelevant, and inferior to man. They serve no useful purpose. They can all be destroyed, and our civilization would be better for it. We can improve ourselves without the taint of machines."

Anari Idaho stalked forward. Instead of her regular sharp-bladed sword, she carried a modified pulse-sword, the type once used by Swordmasters to battle robots at the height of the Jihad. She delivered the coup de grâce, thrusting her pulsing blade into the combat mek, discharging an energy burst that scrambled its gelcircuitry, unleashing a crackle of sparks. The bolted-down mek stuttered and twitched, then fell motionless.

Anari withdrew another weapon from her hip, a heavy alloy hammer, which she used to pummel the machine into a dented ruin, to ever-louder cheers.

Gilbertus stood motionless, accepting the result. This entire spectacle served little purpose except to give Manford Torondo an excuse for propaganda, and Gilbertus had knowingly played into it.

When Anari finished her exertions, she wiped sweat from her brow and stepped back. Picking up the pulse-sword in one hand, the heavy hammer in the other, she smiled at Gilbertus. "Good work, Headmaster."

He accepted her praise, but in the secret passageways of his mind, he credited the victory to his mentor, Erasmus.

*Humans are endlessly perplexing and fascinating. No wonder they need*
*so many different emotions in order to concoct explanations, excuses,*
*and rationalizations for all their irrational behavior.*

—ERASMUS, Laboratory Notebooks

With Gilbertus away on Salusa Secundus, the independent robot used the spy-eyes he had installed throughout the Mentat School to observe the activities of the trainees. The students diligently followed the guidance of proctors and administrators, forcing their brains into proper focus and following the Headmaster's curriculum . . . never imagining that the foundation of their instruction came from a reviled thinking machine—who watched them all the time.

Erasmus enjoyed the irony, but he was also frustrated. For centuries in the thinking-machine empire, he had been an avid researcher, participating in hands-on experiments. He had found it invigorating to manipulate human test subjects and shed blood in the name of understanding. Gilbertus had helped Erasmus in many of the experiments. Those had been excellent times.

The human subjects had not been willing participants, but throughout the history of science, what laboratory animal had happily sacrificed its life for the greater benefit of knowledge? In his research, Erasmus had come across an old saying: There were many ways to skin a cat, and cats liked none of them. The humans he had skinned (literally) did not appreciate the experience either. . . .

Now, trapped and impotent, the robot core's only refuge lay in assessing the students from a distance. He observed a group of them crowded around a stainless-steel dissection table on which they had spread a reptilian swamp dragon. The dead specimen, two meters long, had spiny ridges and overlapping green armor plates, as well as curved teeth to hook prey.

Erasmus focused in on the view, increased the magnification.

His tiny robotic helpers had worked hard to place spy-eyes outside the walls of the school complex as well, so he could watch any trainee who fell prey to swamp predators. He monitored every such exercise, calculating the odds and—yes, he admitted to himself—hoping to see a bloody attack. He wanted to observe how Mentats-in-training defended themselves. So far, none had bested a swamp dragon in direct combat, though two had put up an extraordinary struggle.

Now, in the laboratory, the students used surgical knives and serrated cutting tools to make incisions through the dragon's armor plates. Erasmus wished he could participate, standing in his former flowmetal body or even a more cumbersome mek body. He remembered his beautiful physical form with the delicate silver hands that were able to manipulate complex tools.

Personally, he had always gained more insights from dissecting human subjects while they were still *alive*. What better way to analyze reflexes and pain responses? Living subjects, in pain, also provided the best data on emotions. He would watch and measure the expression in their eyes, the begging and pleading, the sheer panic, and then—a distinct change that was obvious once he'd learned what to look for—the loss of hope just before the onset of death.

Now, the students pulled apart the gray muscle fibers and removed the reptile's internal organs. Though dead, the swamp creature twitched reflexively, and its long jaws clamped down. One of the students jerked out of the way, barely in time to keep her hand from being bitten off. Even so, the curved tooth left a deep red scratch on her arm.

Erasmus focused in on the scratch. He knew that the marsh reptiles carried deadly bacteria in their saliva. A scratch from this tooth could become infected, grow gangrenous, and the student might die, feverish and babbling, in excruciating pain. Erasmus hoped the school's medical team wouldn't treat the scratch. It would be very interesting to study the effects of delirium on an enhanced Mentat mind. . . .

He switched to another set of spy-eyes to watch a room full of new trainees poring over pages and pages of random numbers, which they were then asked to reproduce from memory. The exercise helped them organize their brains, to replicate the skills of a machine (except a thinking machine never needed to practice). Many inductees failed at this stage and were released from the school, but others did manage to learn. Erasmus admired them for their persistence and determination, because humans had such great disadvantages with their soft and chaotic brains.

Erasmus took all of his basic thinking skills for granted. Long ago, he had been identical to so many other robots, programmed by Omnius to serve the Synchronized Empire. The computer evermind had been duplicated across hundreds of worlds, each separated memory core maintaining parity via update ships such as one flown by Vorian Atreides.

Erasmus had gained uniqueness only through a fortunate accident. After falling into a glacier crevasse on Corrin, he'd been trapped for over a century, during which time he had nothing to do but ponder his existence and develop his advanced personality. By the time Erasmus was rescued, he was different from any other independent robot . . . and that was the point at which he'd begun to do great things. His suffering had been necessary to transform him into such a superior thinking machine, one with a very creative mind.

In a sense, his current situation was similar—trapped and helpless, disembodied. But Gilbertus could save him at any time.

Now that the two of them had been hiding for so long among feral humans, Erasmus worried that his ward had become corrupted, even sympathetic to the rest of his race. It was time for them both to leave Lampadas, to change their parameters, to create a new identity for Gilbertus. The Butlerian delusions were interesting, but dangerous—and growing more so.

Gilbertus had already installed stronger defenses around the Mentat School, on the pretext of protecting the Emperor's sister. High walls now surrounded the school complex, and the approach through the labyrinth of marshes was difficult. The gates were barred, the landing field small and secure. The lakeshore was protected with electronic and physical defenses as well, augmented by dangerous predators in the water.

But it was not enough, as far as Erasmus was concerned.

Using tiny robotic drones to complete the work, the robot core had laid down advanced conduit paths and installed hidden high-intensity power-dispersal units, a grid that could project a microwave pulse to incapacitate human enemies. He still did not let down his guard.

Erasmus's attention continued to roam throughout the school. The time ticked away as he studied activities that had once been so fascinating, but now were boring. In an instruction chamber, seven Mentat students stared at a wall that projected blips of light in predetermined grid squares, following a complex pattern that the trainees were asked to decipher. The lights twinkled like a random display of static, and the trainees tried to predict the sequence. Most of them failed. Only one—the intriguing Anna Corrino—identified the correct sequence every time. He watched her lips move as she muttered the answers.

For a thinking machine, time was infinitely flexible, every second broken into countless pieces, but Erasmus chose to speed up the time now, slowing down his thought processes so that the lonely day passed in a blink. When he let him-

≈

*The past is always with us, in one form or another. Those with the proper perception can see it.*

—maxim of the Sisterhood

The traitor Dorotea and her orthodox Sisters had split from Raquella's teachings because they refused to accept any form of advanced technology, regardless of the need. It was her blind spot, Valya knew. While pretending to be Dorotea's friend, Valya had noted a disturbing edge of unreason in the other woman's eyes and comments. During a years-long assignment on Lampadas to observe the Butlerian movement, Dorotea had been poisoned by their beliefs.

It was no wonder Dorotea had let her emotions get the best of her, turning like a viper against the Sisterhood.

Unlike the orthodox Sisters, Valya did not despise advanced technology: It was a tool to be used for her own purposes and for the success of the Sisterhood's goals. Given the vast complexity of the breeding-record computers and their capacity for predictive analysis, she grasped the necessity for those tamed thinking machines. Besides, those exhaustive databases had allowed her to track down Atreides bloodlines. Technology was a means to an end, and Valya would use any weapon available to achieve her goals, which were far more important than any esoteric moral challenge.

While Butlerians stormed across the Imperium and destroyed anything that resembled a thinking machine, Venport Holdings promoted technology for the benefit of the human race. Now Cioba Venport arranged to transport Valya's team to Rossak in secret so they could retrieve the buried computers. A loyal Sister, Cioba knew not to ask questions.

As their camouflaged shuttle dropped out of a huge VenHold spacefolder, guided down by a skilled Sisterhood pilot, Valya sat among fifteen women who had demonstrated combat proficiency in test exercises on Wallach IX, specially cleared Sisters from Raquella's most trusted inner circle. Some of the commando Sisters were armed, and all of them were weapons in their own right. There was a chance they might have to face Imperial soldiers the Emperor had left behind to watch over the abandoned cliff city. If that happened, Valya was confident her Sisters could still prevail, but it would be better if they managed to slip in and out of the jungles without being noticed. She preferred not to have to explain bodies. . . .

Sister Olivia, one of the recently graduated Sister Mentats, selected a seat next to Valya as the shuttle descended through the atmosphere. "I spent a year on Rossak before going to Lampadas for Mentat training. It will be sad to see our great cliff city abandoned."

Olivia was young and wide at the hips, with long blond hair and an assertive personality that Valya found grating at times, perhaps because it reminded her of herself. Olivia had formed a solid friendship with Fielle in their time together at the Mentat School, and Valya gauged the influence of all the new Sister Mentats. Fielle in particular was a shining star who already held much of the Mother Superior's attention. Valya was keeping a close eye on her, assessing whether she would be a powerful ally or rival.

"Stay near me at all times," she warned Olivia. "The shuttle will land far from any Imperial military defenses, and we'll make our way through the thickest wilderness. It's a testing ground, and there are many hazards for the unwary."

The Sister Mentat gave her an indulgent smile, but quiet anger simmered beneath her controlled expression. "I'm not unwary, nor a fool. And the Lampadas swamps have ferocious predators as dangerous as any Rossak can offer."

Valya realized that she herself should attempt more finesse. Even before becoming a Reverend Mother, she had observed many subtle connections in the political and personal web of Sisters—factions, alliances, rivalries, resentments, all under the guise of formalized teaching and philosophical debate. But that had changed when the Sisterhood itself split apart. Now, Valya vowed, she would help the true Sisterhood on Wallach IX to be strong, unified, focused.

And since the Mother Superior would have to name her successor soon, Valya needed to make certain the old woman made the correct decision. Valya felt envious when Raquella was with Fielle or when she showed interest in other Sisters—but voices in Valya's mind, wise voices from Other Memory, counseled her to rise above such pettiness, for the sake of the Sisterhood and its mission to improve mankind. Valya had heeded such advice, but turned a deaf ear when the same voices suggested that she abandon her ambitious goals for House Harkonnen, so she could focus entirely on the Sisterhood.

Valya herself was absurdly young, in physical years, to be considered for such a monumental role. But for a Reverend Mother, with countless generations of experiences inside her, physical age was irrelevant. Her drive and determination, though, were *her own*.

If she became the Mother Superior, she would need to lead all of the Sisters, from the freshest acolyte like Tula to the wisest Reverend Mother. She couldn't let Raquella see her act petulantly or childishly. She had to forge alliances, not break them. Their true enemies were the orthodox Sisters on Salusa and the betrayer Dorotea.

Now, she suppressed her feelings of antipathy toward Fielle and considered the good in the other young woman. Fielle was talented, but so new and untested that she could not possibly be Raquella's replacement. For Valya to keep herself paramount in Raquella's mind, and to demonstrate that she was rising above pettiness, the best solution was to turn Fielle into an ally, perhaps through her friend Olivia.

After a moment of assessment and consideration, Valya smiled warmly and said to Olivia, "You are part of my team for a good reason. In addition to the jungle hazards, we have to watch for any Imperial troops Salvador left behind. As a Sister Mentat, you might be able to see dangers that even I don't detect. We have to make this a swift and smooth mission."

Olivia seemed relieved. All the tense muscles in her face relaxed. "Our work here is vital for the Sisterhood. Each of us is an important member of the team."

As the shuttle continued its descent, Valya looked through the windowport at the night-darkened planet below. She spotted a few city lights spangled in the murky wilderness. Although the Sisterhood School had been uprooted and the primary cliff city abandoned, many people still lived on Rossak: entrepreneurs, harvesters, scouts, even exiles.

According to an intelligence report that Cioba Venport had obtained from her own VenHold operatives, Emperor Salvador had stationed a small contingent of troops near the former Sisterhood settlement. Although the soldiers had poor service records and substandard equipment, Valya was sure the guards were here at Dorotea's suggestion to make certain the exiled Sisters didn't try to return to the cliff city. Dorotea wanted to keep her faction of pandering Sisters important to the Emperor—and keep Raquella irrelevant.

*I should have killed Dorotea while she lay writhing from the poison,* Valya thought. But no one had expected her to live through the Agony. No previous Sister candidate had survived intact, with the exception of Raquella herself.

Since the Imperial contingent had only rudimentary surveillance equipment, the camouflaged VenHold craft easily slipped past their scans and set down in a jungle clearing several kilometers from their destination. She listened

to the low conversations of her team members, heard the excitement and anticipation in their voices. Simply returning to the order's original home planet felt
like a kind of victory for them.

Stepping outside into the heady jungle wearing a night-vision headset, Valya
listened to the rustle of animals gliding through the underbrush. She didn't
worry. Many times, she had traveled the depths of the jungle when she assisted
Karee Marques in search of natural toxins or drugs.

Through the illumination enhancers she magnified the view and saw the
majestic cliff city in the distance, its pockmarked stone face riddled with tunnels
and now-empty living quarters. At one time this had been the Sisterhood's
vibrant hub; now it was nothing but faded memories. She could no longer discern the trails or crepelike balconies that had graced the sheer stone wall.

In those days, the breeding computers had been concealed up there in a cav-
ern deep inside the cliff. Egged on by the insistent Dorotea, the paranoid Emperor's search team had ransacked the tunnels, but Valya had already whisked
the dangerous technology away. Undeterred by the lack of proof, the Emperor
had slaughtered the Sister Mentats and the remaining Sorceresses, who were
merely trying to protect their school. Even though Salvador Corrino had given
the order, Valya still placed the blame on Dorotea.

As her team members emerged from the shuttle and gathered their equipment, she inhaled the moist, odor-rich jungle air. While gazing at the haunted-
looking cliff city, she remembered the women she'd known there. In the back of
her mind, Valya heard what sounded like a murmur of human voices, as if the
honeycombed cliffside were saturated with the spirits of dead Sisters. She felt a
sudden chill as the voices called out plaintively, moaning for what was lost and
would never be again.

Valya had enough ghosts in her own past, and too much blood on her hands.
And she wasn't finished yet. Even with all the struggles of the downtrodden Sisterhood, she thought angrily of her slain brother, Griffin, and the generations of
disgrace that House Harkonnen had suffered. The blood Valya wanted on her
hands was *Atreides* blood.

When the rest of her team stood equipped and ready to move through the
undergrowth, Valya activated a holomap in the air, and her team gathered around.
"We're *here*," she said, pointing. "This sinkhole is our destination. Three of you
were with me when we sealed away the computers, and though it's been less than
a year, the jungle reclaims its territory quickly."

She regarded them all. "We retrieve what is ours, which will bring us one step
closer to rebuilding the Sisterhood to what it is meant to be."

Valya felt a sense of awe, knowing what the computer records contained, a glimpse into the grand tapestry of the human genome, the near-infinite branches of humanity that had evolved over millions of years, and would continue to evolve . . . preferably under careful guidance from the Sisterhood.

From the days of the great machine plagues, the Sorceresses of Rossak had compiled a treasure trove of bloodlines from thousands of primary family lines. Raquella had continued that tremendous project—and it could all have been lost because of a superstitious fool like Dorotea and the fanatical Butlerians who feared information for its own sake.

Because of these computers, the Sisterhood had split in two like a block of dry firewood. Was it just a philosophical difference? Or did Dorotea have personal reasons for trying to destroy Raquella?

If Mother Superior Raquella died without a clear successor and the orthodox Sisters subsumed the rest of the order, that would destroy everything Raquella had created. Looking around the dim and mysterious cenote now, Valya thought Dorotea's abomination of a splinter group was as misborn as the mutated humans who had once lived down here in the pit.

Valya had never spoken aloud to anyone except to her sister, Tula, about the other, personal importance of these records that would allow them to track down the descendants of Vorian Atreides. If they intended to wipe out the Atreides bloodline, first they had to find them. . . .

Valya could take the reins of the Sisterhood and dispatch Tula to regain Harkonnen honor, while she herself mapped out a long-term plan for the true Sisterhood. She would need skilled fighters, political strategists, Mentats, Truthsayers, and breeders to help shape the human race.

Dorotea could not be allowed to cause further problems.

By the time they emerged into the dark jungle, the women had less than an hour before dawn, but clouds had gathered overhead, adding more cover. Maneuvering the suspensor bins along the already-cleared path, they rushed back to the camouflaged shuttle.

*Is anything truly as we perceive it? What are the filters to our percep-
tion? The most honest among us will look deeply to examine how our
opinions are skewed by our own delusions.*

　　　　　　　　　　　—training of the Orthodox Sisterhood

To celebrate the symbolic triumph of humans over thinking machines—no
matter that it was just a pyramid chess game—Salvador Corrino had
scheduled a parade through the capital city of Zimia. He would sit in an ornate
open carriage pulled by four spirited golden lions and listen to the cheers of the
crowd.

He had the uneasy feeling, though, that they would be cheering for Manford
Torondo, not him. The Butlerian leader had brought out his intense, fanatical
followers, and they were already crowding the streets. How could there be so
many of them in Salvador's own capital city?

Manford rode beside the Emperor on a specially designed seat in the carriage,
so that both of them could wave to the bright-eyed throngs on each side of the
street. With a clang and a clatter, the remnants of the defeated combat mek were
dragged along behind the royal carriage, like the corpse of an overthrown tyrant.
For security, uniformed Imperial troops marched behind the carriage.

Oddly, the legless Butlerian leader had already been in his seat when Salvador climbed into the carriage. Other than an indecipherable nod and a mild
expression, Manford had not communicated with Salvador as the procession got
under way. The legless man showed no deference toward the Imperial Presence,
merely waved to the throngs in a stiff, robotic manner.

Suspicious, the Emperor studied Manford more closely. Something wasn't
quite right, but he couldn't put his finger on it. His features, his eyes, even the
way he sat . . .

Sensing the scrutiny, the legless man looked back at him. "Is my makeup credible?"

"Makeup? What do you mean?"

"I am told my resemblance to Leader Torondo is quite striking. And you, too—most convincing!" The man blinked at him. "Let's not fool each other. We understand our roles. I'm not the real Manford Torondo, and you cannot be the true Emperor Salvador. For the safety of our holy leaders, you and I must accept the public risk in their stead."

Feeling his face burn, Salvador said, "You're Manford's *double*?"

The false Manford continued to wave at the crowds, drinking in the cheers. He said out of the corner of his mouth, "You are an excellent substitute. Even your voice is perfect."

"This is an outrage!" Salvador half rose from his seat, then remembered to keep smiling and waving as the lions plodded along. "I am the real Corrino Emperor!"

The man in the seat beside him looked astonished. "Truly? Well, Sire, then this is quite an honor. You are very brave to face the threat of assassination so openly. I do my best not to show any fear, for Leader Torondo's sake." The man beamed with pride. "His previous double died horribly from poison, but maybe I'll be more fortunate."

Salvador was aghast, but embarrassed that he hadn't thought of the idea himself. He couldn't take his eyes from the double, whose legs were clearly missing. The impostor noticed his attention. "Yes, it was necessary for me to have my legs amputated. Otherwise my disguise would have been unconvincing." He smirked, finding humor in his situation.

"You . . . did that voluntarily?"

"Of course. Leader Torondo asked it of me. A small sacrifice on my part for the greater glory of the human soul." He gazed out at the burgeoning crowds. "And I keep a great man safe so he can continue his work, regardless of the numerous threats against him." Seeing Salvador's alarm, the fake Manford tried to sound reassuring. "I'm sure there's nothing to fear today, Sire. You have a goodly number of your soldiers providing security along the parade route."

The Emperor mopped cold perspiration from his forehead. "Don't say another word to me." Now he imagined wild assassins in the crowd, and he wanted to bolt from the carriage and run for his life . . . but that would cause him great public embarrassment. He would have to complete this procession. His pulse pounded, but the Manford double did not seem concerned. Salvador wished that in retaliation for this trick he could turn the real Butlerian leader over to Quemada for a few questions.

As Emperor, Salvador was the leader of all humanity, and if the Butlerian leader needed a double, then the Emperor should have one, too . . . and Roderick as well. If anything happened to his brother, Salvador would never be able to rule the Imperium alone. Either the Butlerians would run roughshod over him with unreasonable mob demands, or Josef Venport would insist on unconscionable concessions to benefit his powerful industries.

Salvador was caught between these two mortal enemies—each inflexible and both focused on their respective passions. Although he and Roderick had close business and political relationships with Venport Holdings, the Corrinos had also made concessions to the mad Butlerians. The situation was a powder keg waiting to explode.

At Manford's demand, the Emperor had formed a Committee of Orthodoxy to monitor and judge technology throughout the Imperium. The Butlerians provided a list of unacceptable items—a list that always changed, and never grew shorter. Salvador had to accept the list or rabid mobs would storm the capital city and bring him down.

Meanwhile, most of the ships in the Imperial Armed Forces were carried to their destinations aboard VenHold spacefolders, in a service provided at low cost with great safety. The VenHold Spacing Fleet was clearly the superior alternative.

Fortunately for Emperor Salvador, Manford Torondo and Josef Venport hated each other. Maybe they would neutralize each other—so long as the conflict didn't take Salvador down with it.

Beside him, with sparkling eyes and a vapid smile, the false Manford continued to bask in applause. The throng was a mass of faces and expressions, generating rolling swells of noise.

Finally, to Salvador's relief, the Imperial carriage completed its celebratory procession and headed back to the golden-domed Hall of Parliament. With an uncomfortable glance at the legless double, he slipped out of the carriage without waiting for his military guards or entourage and hurried into the building, while his liveried attendants tried to keep up with him.

His brother, Roderick, waited for him on the staircase that led to the second-story balcony from which Salvador was expected to deliver a speech. Still hearing the murmur of crowd noise from the streets outside, the Emperor tried to control his breathing. His brother raised his eyebrows. "What's wrong?"

Salvador told him about Manford's double. "That bastard kept himself safe and hidden, but allowed me to face the risk of assassins!" His nostrils flared. Outside, the crowd sounded restless, as if slipping out of control. "Find me my own double, Roderick—without delay. Oh, and you should find one for yourself as well. If anything happened to you—"

"I'll begin the process." Roderick's voice was soothing and steady, and Salvador felt calmer just to have his brother's strong presence at his side. "Right now, the crowds are expecting to see you. And if you don't deliver a speech, Manford will probably talk without you. He's already there riling them up."

When they reached the balcony, the real Butlerian leader sat in his harness on the Swordmaster's shoulders, as if ready for battle. Two Reverend Mothers from the Imperial Court stood in the shadows off to the side: his personal Truthsayer, Dorotea, and the soft and pudgy Sister Woodra—both ardent Butlerian adherents. Headmaster Gilbertus Albans, looking out of place and uncomfortable with all the attention, stood behind them. Because he had defeated the mek in the pyramid chess game, the Mentat Headmaster was required to be present for the celebration.

As soon as he saw Salvador arrive, Manford nudged Anari Idaho, and she stepped out onto the balcony where the crowd could see him. Without even waiting for the Emperor to join him—exactly as Roderick had warned—he raised his hands, and his gesture was like flinging fuel onto a fire. The roar of applause was deafening.

The Emperor felt a sinking sensation. Beside him, Roderick paused and showed clear distaste for the Butlerian leader's disrespect for the Emperor.

From his perch on top of Anari's shoulders, Manford raised his voice for the crowd and gestured back toward Salvador. "Our Emperor has joined us! All hail Salvador Corrino the First!"

Buoyed by all the obvious enthusiasm, Salvador stepped into view. Yes, they were shouting for him *now*, because the crowd was packed with Butlerians, and Manford had told them to applaud. He noted that the real Manford's voice was distinctly different from the double's, filled with the familiar charisma.

Before the Emperor could speak, Manford shouted out, "Our Mentat defeated a terrible thinking machine, just as the faithful will defeat evil technology in all its forms. Never forget! You have earned the right to celebrate destruction, because that destruction gained us our freedom." His smile had a wild, uncontrolled edge. "On behalf of the Emperor, I announce another rampage festival here in Zimia! Rejoice in wrecking any remnants of machine technology! This is *your* time to show your energy, show your humanity—and celebrate our victory!"

The roar of the crowd became such a pounding wave of noise that the thick stone building trembled. Salvador tried to be heard, rushing forward, but he seemed small compared to the towering Swordmaster. "I did not authorize a rampage festival!" His words were lost in the noise.

Each month, the symbolic destruction of a few token machine remnants was a carefully planned spectacle, with safeguards so the crowds did not get out of hand. But Manford Toronto had just unleashed the mob.

"Wait!" Salvador shouted.

Anari raised her sword high, and as she brought it down, the crowd flowed like a flash flood into the side streets and the commercial sector, pushing aside soldiers and guards who tried to maintain order.

Roderick came forward, red-faced. "For a rampage festival, there must be preparations first, added security—"

Manford gave the Corrino brothers a maddening smile. "They are keyed up and angry—it is important to let them release some pressure. Don't worry, it's all harmless."

Salvador glared at Manford, gasping, "Harmless? Look at the frenzy building out there. They're going to ransack, burn, wreck—"

"Then you can rebuild. The whole of humanity has had to rebuild since the end of the Jihad."

The crowd moved as if it were one organism on a rabid scavenger hunt. Even those who were not Butlerians were swept along or trampled underfoot.

Salvador watched in dismay, then turned to Roderick, but his brother also looked appalled and helpless. From the balcony, they heard breaking glass and shouts of triumph out in the plaza, and the screams of the citizens being crushed in the melee. Most terrifying of all, Salvador knew the mob could turn against him on a moment's notice, if Manford ever told them to do so.

*There is strength in numbers, a raw and primal power. But as a crowd
grows and grows, its ability to reason diminishes.*

—GILBERTUS ALBANS, Mentat School records

The rampage festival swelled out of hand through the evening, and fires burned in three parts of the city. In the midst of it all, Manford Torondo and his Swordmaster seemed complacent, as if they bore no responsibility for what was happening.

Roderick was dismayed to see that Imperial troops were completely ineffective at quelling the chaotic energy. Though numerous, the soldiers and the Zimia security force had no capable leadership, and the swift rush of violence took them by surprise; when they hesitated to fire upon the crowd, they were either shoved aside or trampled. The turbulence of a mob that had no coordinated goal dispersed the stationed troops.

Even the military officers did not know how to react to the unexpected storm of feral energy. Roderick had told his brother repeatedly that the Imperial Armed Forces needed better leaders and better organization; now, upon seeing how poorly the troops performed, he felt determined to crack down. First, though, this mindless vandalism had to be brought under control.

And this was a *celebration*, not even a mob driven by anger.

Roderick worried about his wife and children, who could be out there if they had come to watch the victory procession. But he could do nothing about it except to send messages for guards to find them. He knew his priority was to protect the Emperor. As the violence intensified, Roderick arranged for his brother to go into hiding in a private underground network of tunnels constructed centuries ago, during a time of frequent cymek raids. Empress Tabrina was taken to a different hiding place, because Salvador had no desire to be sealed up with her.

While mayhem continued in the city above, Roderick and a contingent of elite guards led Salvador through the puzzle box of combinations and security systems that allowed access to the secret tunnels. "They're burning my city, Roderick!"

Roderick tried to keep his brother calm. "I have dispatched troops to protect important buildings and summoned soldiers from our orbiting battleships to impose order." He knew, though, that the guards were in chaos, many of them unresponsive; he wouldn't be surprised if some of them had been killed. Quite a few had certainly abandoned their posts. "It's hard to strategize against a mob that has no logical plan."

The Emperor paused at the steel sliding wall as a thought occurred to him. "And your family, Roderick? Have them brought down here where they'll be protected."

"I sent word, but they haven't been found yet." Roderick fought against the knot in his stomach, remembering how his children always loved the spectacle of a good parade. "As soon as I'm sure that you're safe, I'll get back out there and find them myself, if I have to."

At first, Salvador didn't want his brother to leave, but he steeled himself and gave a brave nod. "I'll be fine. Go now—I am counting on you to save Zimia!"

Leaving the Emperor with guards in the deep tunnels, Roderick hurried back to an emergency command post in the palace. When he reached his secondary office, he was surprised to find Headmaster Albans there, offering to help. Roderick paused, suspecting a trick. Wasn't Albans a known ally of Leader Toronto? But the Headmaster, normally a cool and logical man, looked shaken by the Butlerian violence. Seeing the expression on the bespectacled Mentat's face, Roderick ushered him into the private room and closed the door.

They could hear the crowd noises from outside. By the light of distant fires visible through the office windows, he glimpsed a crude clay sculpture on his desk—he thought it was supposed to be a puppy—that Nantha had made for him. Roderick felt a new pang of fear and hoped that Haditha and their children were safely clear of the uproar by now.

He turned to the Mentat, barely controlling his anger at the unnecessary destruction. "You offered to help, Headmaster? If you know of a way to stop this violence, I am eager to hear it. Tell Leader Toronto to command them to stop, or has he gone into protective hiding?"

The Mentat frowned. "He is among his people—that makes him safe. But he will not tell them to stop . . . because I believe he fears they won't listen." He removed his round eyeglasses, cleaned them with a handkerchief, and put them back on. "Prince Roderick, I believe you are a man of honor, or I would not be here. If I suggest how you might end this rampage, you must promise never to reveal who offered the solution, not even to the Emperor—and especially not to Manford Toronto."

"Why not?"

"Manford is demonstrating the power he can unleash. He's doing it to frighten the Emperor, and I suspect it won't be long before he makes even more extreme demands." He lowered his voice. "If he learns I worked with you to quell the violence, he would kill me, and his followers would raze my school on Lampadas."

Roderick narrowed his gaze, not understanding the Mentat's motivations. This man had just performed before the court, defeating a combat mek in a game to stroke Butlerian pride. And Manford had commanded the festival—wasn't this what Gilbertus wanted? But Roderick's primary responsibility was to restore peace and stability in Zimia. "I will hold your advice in confidence, Mentat. How do we extinguish this mob?"

"The violence will die down in the night as people return to their homes, but some Butlerians plan to incite another rampage early tomorrow morning."

Roderick felt a flush of new anger. "Which followers, and where are they? We need to arrest them."

"You will never find them." Gilbertus shook his head. "No, this requires a different tactic, a trap. You must choose three outlying towns you are willing to sacrifice. I will initiate a rumor that stockpiles of preserved thinking machines are being kept in those towns—perhaps hidden by Directeur Venport himself. That is sure to drive the mob into an even greater fervor."

The Mentat used his fingers to tick off the sequence of events. "That allows you to lure the Butlerians out of central Zimia. They will flood to the chosen villages, and the journey itself may drain their exuberance. Then you can set up security perimeters with your troops and bottle the Butlerians in those three towns."

Roderick frowned. "I don't like it. The mobs will ransack the target villages."

Screams and explosions could be heard outside. A column of fire rose into the night.

"But they will be away from Zimia." The Headmaster shrugged. "We cannot always find a solution that we like."

THE REPORTS OF destruction throughout Zimia forced Roderick to cut his losses. The Mentat was right. Studying maps, he selected three underpopulated and easily defensible towns, and gave his decision to the Headmaster.

Gilbertus Albans slipped out among the Butlerians and initiated a cascade of rumors, suggesting that computers and robots were secretly stored in those three outlying villages. Roderick felt anguished about the welfare of the citizens there, but he needed to protect the capital. He dispatched urgent messages ahead of the mobs, hoping to convince the targeted townspeople to flee while they still had time.

Well after midnight, as the rampage began to die down in the heart of Zimia, Manford Torondo heard the rumors himself. Reacting quickly, he sent teams of his supporters to punish the accused towns. After making his announcement, Manford summoned his Mentat and Swordmaster to join him, and departed from Salusa Secundus, turning his back on the mayhem he had caused. Roderick felt that the man was slipping away to hide from the consequences of what he had done.

At last, though, Roderick had a chance to snuff out the uprising. With Manford gone, his followers were confused but still keyed up. Roderick rushed Imperial troops to surround the three scapegoat towns and bottle up the most vehement Butlerians—and he told the troops to be ruthless. Just before dawn, the crisis began to wind down.

Red-eyed and exhausted, Roderick sent a message to his brother, giving him the good news, although Salvador was cautious, suggesting that he remain in isolation a while longer, just to be certain. Roderick didn't argue with him, for now, but he knew that when day broke, the people would want to be reassured that their Emperor had survived. In the interim, Roderick was the Emperor's proxy and dealt with the response throughout Zimia. He spoke in public, looking calm and steady, a firm bastion in this crisis. Roderick Corrino was what they needed to see.

As dawn arrived, cleanup operations began in the capital city; fires were put out, "revelers" arrested, and field hospitals set up where Suk doctors triaged the injured. Numerous bodies—Butlerians, Zimia police, Imperial troops, innocent bystanders, and even children—were discovered in the rubble around the central plaza. Many of the victims had simply come out to see the parade and were swept up in the mayhem. The bodies were brought to a central holding area to be processed and identified.

Roderick felt so weary and wrung out that he indulged in a cup of bitter spice coffee, and the stimulant gave him a needed boost. At last he received the welcome news that Haditha and his children had been taken to a place of safety, but right now he had no chance to go home to them.

By midmorning, Roderick felt that the worst had been brought under control, and he began to feel a hint of calm. Then a haggard-looking Haditha burst into his office in the Hall of Parliament, pulling ahead of a distraught-looking guard. Roderick rushed to greet her with an embrace, knowing how frightened and exhausted she must be.

He held her, rocking her, and found that he was weeping as well. "No, it won't." Roderick thought of what a sweet girl Nantha had been, how she always wanted to know where her father was, how she liked to play in his office and pretend to sign important documents with him. Not long ago, when he was holding her hand and standing with Salvador and Tabrina, Nantha had whispered to him, "Can I be Empress someday?"

He'd smiled and said, "Every person can dream."

Now, all of Nantha Corrino's dreams had been erased forever.

Flanked by three elite guards, Emperor Salvador strode into his brother's office, looking disheveled and harried, but more confident. He did not seem to know about Nantha's death. He grinned and said, "Roderick, there you are! Come with me—we must show the people that this painful crisis is over. Everything will be all right now."

But when he held her, she pulled back with a terrible expression on her face her entire body shaking so hard she could not speak. A wan-looking guard who had accompanied her stood awkwardly nearby.

"Nantha!" Haditha finally cried, and the name sounded raw, as if torn from her throat. She could form no other words.

Roderick took her by the shoulders and stared at her grief-stricken expres sion. Beside her, the guard mumbled, "We received word that the bodies of you youngest daughter and her nanny were found among the wreckage. Apparentl they were trampled. . . ."

Roderick couldn't believe what he had heard. "But I received a report that m family was safe!"

The guard looked away. "Apparently, they didn't account for all your chil dren, Prince. There was much confusion."

"Nantha wanted to see the parade!" Haditha sobbed. "She begged her nanny and they went out together. I didn't think anything of it. And all night, hoped—I hoped. . . ."

Of course Nantha would have gone out to the parade, Roderick realized with a sick despair. The seven-year-old girl had always liked the colors and pageantry He could imagine Nantha tugging the nanny's arm, pleading, laughing, and the nanny would have relented. And why not? They had seen many parades together.

Haditha's moans cut through to his heart. Roderick could not focus his eyes so he closed them. His head pounded, his eyes burned. He spoke to the guard "And our other children?"

"Safe, my Lord."

He recalled how Manford had rushed away, as if fleeing. What if the Butle rian leader had learned the terrible news, and departed before he could be ar rested? Roderick clenched his fists. Manford Torondo could not flee swiftly enough, or go far enough away to avoid retribution. He had caused this, provok ing the rampage, igniting the fires of violence. Why? To flex his muscles in front of Salvador? The Butlerians had always been dangerous, fanatical, uncontrol lable, and Salvador had been too weak to stand up to them . . . conceding, pretending, backing down one small step at a time.

Manford Torondo had caused the riots to prove a point. And Nantha had died. Many people had died. Collateral damage.

"I will find a way to stop that man. His followers have caused too much dam age, too much pain. Manford Torondo cannot create and unleash a mob, then turn his back on the consequences. The blood is on his hands."

Haditha looked up at her husband with the saddest face he could imagine. "That won't bring our baby back."

꧁꧂

*If you strike me, I will strike you harder. If you hate me, I will hate you more. You cannot win.*

—GENERAL AGAMEMNON, *A Time for Titans*

Though Denali's atmosphere was poisonous, Ptolemy felt *safe* here. It was the Butlerians who made him nervous. They were more dangerous than any planet.

He made his way across the bleak, deadly landscape, riding inside the cab of his specially adapted walker, his arms and legs connected to modified thoughtrodes that let him control the complex machine systems. But working the systems manually was a chore, and Ptolemy envied the nimble new cymeks.

Installed in their preservation tanks and connected to a network of thoughtrodes, the proto-Navigator brains easily adapted to the powerful walker forms he had given them. Ptolemy was particularly impressed by the agility and intensity of two former mercenary officers who had left their service to volunteer for Navigator conversion, Hok Evander and Adem Garl. Now they were among the most aggressive of the walker-brains.

Eight of the installed brains used old walkers salvaged from the ruins of the previous cymek base here, but other Navigator brains rode in new mechanical bodies built by Denali engineers. The enhanced walkers would be more than sufficient against any weapons the barbarians were likely to use.

Today, Ptolemy accompanied the new walkers. They were breathtaking! With improved thoughtrode sensors, his shiny cymeks danced across the rugged landscape like mechanical spiders. In contrast, the older salvaged walkers had a ponderous gait, as if the brains had to work harder to move their unwieldy systems. Walker bodies were interchangeable, and brain canisters could be transferred from a walker machine into a flyer or a manipulator body as needed.

Ptolemy wanted his new Navigator Titans to learn how to use every possible form.

He preferred the burly, intimidating walkers, though. There was something satisfying about imagining them approaching their targets in an inexorable phalanx that made the victims feel the terror of what was going to happen to them. Yes, he wanted Manford Torondo to know what was coming for him.

Away from the protected lab domes, Ptolemy rode inside a pressurized life-support cab installed in one of the old walkers. This allowed him to walk alongside his new creations in the poisonous atmosphere, looking for ways to improve them. If he ever became a cymek himself, Ptolemy would not need to worry about life-support systems anymore. He would go wherever he wished, in any environment, and he would fear nothing.

Directeur Venport had already seen Ptolemy's reports. Perhaps the Directeur would want to become a cymek, and then he could guide the new Titans. Ptolemy did not see himself as a leader and had no wish to become like the despot Agamemnon. He had not, in fact, wanted any part of the role he now had—but the barbarians had forced him into it by destroying his life, his lab, his friend.

Now, Ptolemy tried to keep up with the exuberant Navigator cymeks as they strutted across the terrain. Their multiple legs moved with remarkable ease, and they practiced ripping huge boulders from the ground and hurling them as far as possible. Due to the caustic mists, Ptolemy could not even see where they landed.

Inside his older machine, he struggled to keep up with the new-model cymeks as they thundered over the rocky ground. He worked his arms, linked to the controls, but the walker limbs were not analogous, and he occasionally became tangled, feeling clumsy. His other machines were so graceful.

Practicing their fighting abilities, they grappled with one another to test strength and reflexes, warrior arm against warrior arm. He identified each of them by unique light panels on their bodies. One walker, operated by the brain of the female Xinshop, sprang to a high outcropping, but failed to gain sufficient height. Before she could tumble down, however, rockets erupted from the body's rear thrusters, lifting the new cymek to safety on top of the rocks. Once stabilized, Xinshop raised a pair of grappling arms as if in triumph.

Ptolemy liked Xinshop's willingness to serve. She had been among the first of the failed Navigators to embrace her new possibilities as a cymek. Each time he spoke with her, he envisioned what Xinshop used to look like before he'd met her, when she had been a radiant young woman volunteering for the VenHold Spacing Fleet. Sometimes Ptolemy even imagined that they might be together as a couple, both of them cymeks. But before that happened, he had a lot of work to do getting his mechanized force together, refining systems. That was his priority.

He also liked the reemerging personality of Yabido Onel, who was bounding across the rugged landscape in the foreground. For a long time Yabido had refused to say much through the speakerpatch, except for his desire to die because he had failed as a Navigator candidate. But after Ptolemy showed him what he could achieve as a cymek, he had felt renewed hope and determination, which expressed itself as bright energy patterns in his brain.

Ptolemy could still see the glow of research domes. Although his expanding Titan project had siphoned some of Denali's most talented engineers and support staff, Administrator Noffe was still developing weaponry in independent programs, such as scrambler pulses that could boil human brains, in much the way the Sorceresses of Rossak had killed the old cymeks. One research team created small mechanical "crickets" that could skitter into enemy ships and ignite volatile fuel storage chambers.

Ptolemy's fellow researchers had their own reasons to dislike the fanatics, but he believed *his* program would be the one that guaranteed victory against Manford Toronto. A marching horde of new Titans powered by proto-Navigator brains would strike fear into any populace.

As he trudged along in his repaired walker, far from the research domes, Ptolemy noticed two amber warning lights on the control board inside the cab. His life-support systems were losing power due to a leak in a coupling, eroded by the caustic atmosphere. And he was trapped in his small chamber.

He ran an estimate and realized that he barely had time to hurry back to the shielded complex. No safety margin.

Without delay, he worked the controls and turned his walker around while transmitting a distress signal to his Titans. With a jittering gait, he tried to hobble across the landscape, but he was too anxious, which made him uncoordinated. His arms twitched inside the linkages, the thoughtrode signals scrambled.

He didn't want to die out here, not with his work incomplete.

A hose snapped and began to leak fuel onto the ground outside. Warning lights flashed across the cab controls. Now Ptolemy realized he could not possibly make it back. Unable to control the mechanical legs, he stumbled, and went down.

Moments later, two burly Titans—the pair of mercenaries Hok Evander and Adem Garl—appeared on either side and grasped his smaller cymek body with their mechanical claws. They raised his walker form off the ground like two metal crabs lifting their little brother. With an eerily coordinated gait, the Navigator cymeks bounded across the rugged rocks toward the glowing domes.

Another leak, and Ptolemy's life-support system failed entirely. The caustic gases seeping into the systems would eat away more seals.

His comm system was still active, and he transmitted an emergency alert to the base. The rest of the Navigator Titans rushed back toward the facility like a coordinated rescue team, so that when Ptolemy arrived at the main dome's air-lock door, they could assist.

Through the swirling mists, Ptolemy made out the dome just ahead, but he could also smell the acrid vapors leaking into the life-support cab, beginning to poison him. The chamber integrity had failed in five separate areas. His eyes burned from the acid fumes, but somehow (delirium?) it didn't feel as painful as the burning tears that had streamed down his face after he saw Dr. Elchan roasted alive in the lab.

Having received Ptolemy's emergency transmission, Administrator Noffe appeared on the screen. "Ready to receive you. You're going to be safe."

"It'll be close." Ptolemy coughed, and each breath seared like heated glass dust washed down with acid. He coughed again, and a splatter of blood appeared on the control screen in front of his face.

Alarmed, Administrator Noffe shouted commands to the two cymeks carrying Ptolemy's walker. They hauled him to the wide-open door of the hangar dome and roughly tossed the twitching, failing walker body inside. Using nimble claw hands, they operated the airlock controls.

Sealed in his cab, Ptolemy coughed uncontrollably. He breathed in a blistering-hot chemical mist. With a roar of loud wind, the air exchangers inside the dome began to suck away the contaminated atmosphere, venting it outside. Even before the green light winked on, Ptolemy disengaged the cab's hatch and popped it open. He couldn't wait any longer. How could the air within the hangar dome be deadlier than what he was struggling to breathe inside the life-support cap-sule? He yanked his arms free from the control linkages, crawled out of the cab, and collapsed onto the cold metal floor, retching, gasping, and coughing in a raw throat.

Thankfully, each breath felt a little cleaner than the previous one. Wind rushed around him as fresh oxygen poured into the enclosed area, but his lungs seemed to be filled with caustic blood.

Finally, a smaller airlock from the interior tube opened, and a frantic Noffe ran toward him. "Doctors are on their way." He bent next to Ptolemy, helping him to his feet.

Ptolemy could barely see through his burning eyes, but he didn't think he was severely injured. Or maybe he was deluding himself. "That wouldn't have happened if I were a cymek."

"It wouldn't have happened if you were more careful," Noffe retorted. "You shouldn't have gone so far in an old walker like that."

Somehow Ptolemy managed to smile, grating out his words. "Did you see . . . the Navigator walkers respond? Analyzed the emergency . . . rescued me. Passed the first test admirably."

"Yes, they performed better than you did. We almost lost you!"

More thoughts were forming in Ptolemy's head. "Directeur Venport needs to know how competent the new Titans are. Even this hazardous environment is not the most extreme place in which our cymeks could find themselves fighting."

He kept talking even as medical personnel busily checked him over. They placed a mask on his face and dispensed some kind of analgesic mist into his lungs. Before long, Ptolemy could breathe better, and he pulled the mask aside, continuing to chatter to Noffe. "We have to conduct a more dramatic test for Directeur Venport—and I've thought of just the place to do it. We will take them to Arrakis."

"You should rest and heal first," Noffe said. "I'm worried about you."

"I'm worried about other things—I can rest while I make the important arrangements."

*Every hammer has the innate capacity to strike a nail. Every human mind has the innate capacity for greatness. But not every hammer is properly used, nor is every human mind.*

—DRAIGO ROGET, Mentat debriefing for Venport Holdings

Even before he left Arrakis orbit, Taref was *weary* of being astonished. He didn't know how many more remarkable things he could endure. Even his dreams had never imagined so much.

If he returned to the desert sietch now and told them everything he had experienced in the short time since accepting VenHold's offer, Naib Rurik would tell him to abandon such nonsense, and his older brothers would mock him.

But Taref knew it was all true.

His wide-eyed companions clustered together aboard the VenHold shuttle, staring out the windowports as the craft rose into orbit and approached the main spacefolder. The isolated Freemen tribes were vaguely aware of other planets and other ways, but none of his friends had known much beyond their lives in an isolated cave settlement . . . until now.

Taref and Lillis stood at the windowport, marveling at the view. Even dour Shurko, unable to hide his nervousness, stared at the brassy sphere of the planet. That was Arrakis down there—it seemed utterly incomprehensible. The largest sietch was no more than an immeasurable speck from here, and the sandworms were too small to be seen. Even Arrakis City, the largest metropolis Taref had ever visited or imagined, was barely a mark tucked into a sheltered rock-rimmed basin. As the shuttle continued to rise, he managed to locate the city only after careful concentration and help from Lillis.

"Will we ever go back? Did we make the right decision, Taref?" she asked, and Shurko looked to him as well, eager to hear his answer.

"Of course we did. Our people will be proud."

"Our people will never understand us," Shurko said. "They won't know why we did this."

Taref had always felt like a misfit, imagining stories and worlds while the rest of his tribe found all they needed to know in the sand at their feet and the wind on their faces. But he remembered history. "Generations ago, our ancestors escaped slavery and flew an unguided spacefolder to our new home. We've been stranded on Arrakis ever since—and now we are simply returning to the rest of the universe, breaking our chains and escaping our enslavement to the desert. And if we do well out there, my friends, we'll be the first of many Freemen who branch out. Our people no longer need to be trapped where there is nothing but dunes and the prospect of a parched death."

Taref doubted he would ever want to return to that dust bowl, and he did not know many others in the sietch who thought the way he did. Even though he had instilled a sense of curiosity in his friends, they didn't really feel the depth of his dreams; the others merely listened to his impassioned stories rather than dreaming for themselves.

For much of his life, Taref had felt trapped in the isolated, primitive settlement. His father had berated him for dreaming about places other than Arrakis. "How does that help your survival? If Shai-Hulud comes because you walk with too much rhythm across the sands, will he listen to your stories before he devours you?"

But Taref had dreamed anyway. He chafed under Naib Rurik's stern disapproval, and questioned many of the rules of the desert. He knew that traditions were a basis for day-to-day survival, but some of the old ways were no longer valid. He asked questions about old customs, drawing only ire from other tribe members, not answers. Peculiar Taref would never become his people's Naib, nor did he ever want to. Naib Rurik would probably rule the sietch for many years, and Taref's two older brothers would take their father's place.

Taref had seen the rigid path his own life was set to take, like a channel carved deep into the rock—and he didn't accept what he saw. He wanted the universe! It must be so wonderful out there, planet after planet of miracles. Back in the clear, dry air of the desert, he used to look up at the stars and imagine other worlds. Several times, he had made the journey to Arrakis City just to watch the spaceships arrive and depart . . . and dream of what might be.

Taref wanted to be like the offworlders. They had so many opportunities open to them, yet in a way he also resented them. Several times he had volunteered to work aboard spice harvesters because he knew it would draw his father's disapproval. And when he and his friends sabotaged the harvesting equipment, Taref pretended he was getting even with the *offworlders* because of who they were and the opportunities they had.

When the Mentat Draigo Roget had made his offer, Taref at first had tried to remain aloof, but the longing was like a thirst in him, and the VenHold Mentat had offered a symbolic literjon of cool water.

Watching the desert planet recede as the spacefolder accelerated away, Taref struggled to imagine the sights and experiences they would have on faraway worlds. The Holtzman engines folded space, and the ship twisted itself out of the Canopus star system.

While the great vessel was in transit, Draigo went to address his new recruits. "You have everything you need? We will provide water, food, and new clothing."

"So much water," Lillis said in a voice like a sigh.

"And we already have clothing," Chumel said.

Though Taref knew their distilling suits were well-made outfits that had saved their lives many times out in the open desert, Draigo frowned at the dusty garb. "You will clean up and dress exactly like other workers. You cannot complete your mission if you stand out. You must pass unnoticed like faint shadows." He wrinkled his nose and sniffed deeply, although Taref had never noticed any odor among the desert people. "We will instruct you in traditional hygiene practices."

"No Freeman will let another take away his stillsuit," said Bentur, a gruff-voiced young man who usually kept his words to himself.

"We will provide better garments for your temporary use. In the meantime we will hold your things for you and return them whenever you wish to go back to Arrakis."

"I heard offworlders are thieves," Shurko said.

Draigo gave a small smile that was more like a smirk. "And I heard that the Freemen of the desert know very little about offworlders." Shurko took offense and looked ready to fight the Mentat.

Taref said, "Stop, Shurko—you gave me your word."

"I did not agree to be insulted!"

"Stop being stupid. They are taking us away from Arrakis at great expense, showing us their ways. They have no need to steal from us. Remember that planet with the ocean and the rain falling from the sky? If he meant to deceive us, this is an elaborate and costly trick."

"But what does he expect from us that would be worth such an investment?" Lillis asked.

"It is not a trick—it's an opportunity," Draigo said. "We will teach you about offworlders and about our commercial competitors. We will give you the modern wonders that were merely rumors in your little desert village."

"It's called a sietch," Lillis said.

Draigo gave a brief nod. "Very well. I will learn from you, as you learn from me."

TAREF WAS STUNNED when he and his friends were sprayed with water to rinse off the dust and grit, and the leftover water was allowed to simply drain away, where it was presumably recycled. Always before, he had scrubbed his hands and body with fine powder-sand, but now he felt much cleaner—even cleaner than a person might be if he were blasted by a sandstorm.

This waste of water was an unbelievable extravagance—and a hint of what was possible out there. Draigo had told them there were many worlds in the Imperium, and most were far more hospitable than Arrakis. Thinking back on his life up to this point, Taref realized that he had seen nothing, done nothing, *been* nothing. If VenHold let him travel as promised, there seemed as many possibilities for him now as there were stars in the night sky.

Lillis was unsettled and unrecognizable when she came to him wearing a clean jumpsuit. Her light brown hair was clean and loose, and—Taref marveled about this—still *wet*. Waddoch drank and drank of the free-flowing water until he became sick and vomited up a puddle, which embarrassed him. The ship's maintenance workers used even more water to wash the vomit away.

"This is . . . unbelievable." Taref felt a bit ill from being surrounded by so much moisture; he and his companions had some difficulty breathing the humid air, but he assumed that gradually they would get used to it.

When the spacefolder arrived at Kolhar, the planetary shields were shunted aside to allow passage for the descending shuttle. The ship passed through storm clouds, and water pelted the hull, streaming in amazing runnels along the windowport.

When they landed at the Kolhar spaceport and emerged onto a new world, cold white ice fell from the sky and pelted Taref's face. He had never felt such biting cold. The stinging droplets drenched him and his companions. Shurko protected his face with his hands and peered through his fingers into the sky, awestruck and afraid.

Draigo laughed and ushered them away. "That is called sleet, or snow— frozen water. It falls from the sky and collects on the ground. Some planets are covered with it, just as Arrakis is covered with sand."

Taref held out his hand, marveling as the snowflakes dissolved in his palm. "This is *water*? Frozen water?" The snow continued to fall, and though it melted quickly at the warm spaceport, brushstrokes of white marked the hills outside the city.

"Offworld weather patterns may be interesting to you, but they are not relevant to our goals." Draigo brushed white flakes off his shoulders. "This is just a part of the new universe I have promised you. We'll show you more later, and there will be time for instruction."

THE FOLLOWING DAY, Draigo took Taref and his companions out to the field of proto-Navigators, private compartments that contained volunteers undergoing transformation.

Taref sniffed. "There is melange in the air."

"Not much of it, I hope," Draigo said. "Spice is too valuable to let it leak out indiscriminately."

Lillis went to one of the chambers and peered through an observation window. "There are people inside, suffocating in spice gas!"

"It causes them to transform into something special. This is why we need to harvest so much melange from Arrakis. Combined Mercantiles helps us create the Navigators that guide our starships."

The desert people gathered around the chambers, saw misshapen forms wallowing in spice gas. "Spice helps the Freemen to open their minds and see possibilities," Taref said. But this was not what he had expected, and the grotesque sight made him uneasy.

"It does the same for our Navigators, but in ways no one can understand," Draigo said. "They encompass the vastness of space in their minds, and envision safe pathways for our spaceships."

The pungent cinnamon odor was comforting to Taref, though he did not miss the desert planet at all. Although Shurko and Bentur already seemed homesick, Taref did not regret his choice. He was determined to see the marvels in the rest of the galaxy. While these spice-filled chambers and the distorted Navigators were intriguing, Taref thought the snow falling from the sky was even more amazing. . . .

Draigo took them back to the sprawling Kolhar spaceport complex, and Lillis noted out loud that the high, exposed buildings would never survive one of the powerful Coriolis storms of Arrakis. Along the way, he also told them about his abilities as a Mentat, noting their wide-eyed stares of disbelief. Just another marvel.

Myriad ships of all types and configurations sat alongside cranes and suspensor lifts that brought the components together and locked them into place. Work crews assembled frameworks, then added engines and fleshed out the interiors. Other workers welded and painted the ships. The air smelled of acrid solvents, grease, and spilled fuel.

Draigo took his new recruits from one spacecraft to another, dodging cargo unloaders and refueling vessels, as well as flatbeds filled with replacement energy packs. Shurko put his hands to his ears. "So much noise. And the new smells! It makes my mind spin."

"This is a spaceport," Draigo said. "You'll have to grow comfortable with it, because I intend to turn you loose in the shipyards at other spaceports. Familiarize yourself with the hangars, the activity, the tasks. You will need to look as comfortable in places like this as you do in your sietch."

When his friends seemed intimidated, Taref squared his shoulders. "We learned how to operate spice machinery. We can learn the simple tasks performed by shipyard and spaceport workers." He looked over at Draigo. "And then you want us to sabotage your rival's engines?"

The Mentat nodded. "That time will come. We have ships of all common designs here on Kolhar. We will show you how to do basic work, teach you what you need to know, so that you'll qualify for a job with EsconTran or any other shipping company." As Draigo talked, Taref looked at the numerous spaceships, the rising shuttles, a cargo ship landing, a passenger vessel being constructed.

Draigo briskly got his attention again. "We'll tell you what to say to convince others that you understand how a spacefolder works, as much as a dockhand needs to know. And"—he lowered his voice and leaned closer—"I will show you the simple things you can do to make critical systems fail." He gestured around the busy spaceport. "You will become experts at making spacefaring vessels go wrong."

*Thinking machines did not have a monopoly on cruelty, for human be-*
*ings do unspeakable things as well. The Butlerians paint machines with*
*too broad a stroke, and use only the color black. They do as much harm*
*to human civilization as the thinking machines ever did.*

—GILBERTUS ALBANS, personal journal, Mentat School records
(redacted as inappropriate)

After the madness in the streets of Zimia, and his disturbing time with Manford Toronto, Gilbertus was glad to be safely back at the Mentat School. The Butlerian leader had not seemed at all troubled by the destruction his followers had caused.

Gilbertus hoped to calm himself by playing a round of pyramid chess with the Erasmus core. His robot mentor was far more intelligent than a combat mek and would likely win the game, as he usually did, but Gilbertus knew tricks that were not based entirely on mathematical analyses. Anytime he won a game, it was because he leveraged his *humanity*, adding to the knowledge this unique robot had given him over the centuries.

In his sealed and secure office, the Headmaster brought out the gelcircuitry memory core and set up the antique pyramid chessboard. Erasmus said, "I would have been disappointed if you'd lost the game to that cumbersome combat mek, my son."

"I would have been disappointed as well, Father," Gilbertus replied. "In fact, I would be dead, because they would have executed me."

"Then I am doubly glad you won. That mek was a rudimentary model, utterly without sophistication. You should have had no trouble formulating a strategy to defeat it."

"I should have had no trouble—and yet it was a close match. I was under great stress, of course, which might have disrupted my thinking processes. My emotions interfered with my Mentat abilities. My human vulnerability and mortality seeped into my mind, and nearly sabotaged me."

The robot's core throbbed with pale blue light. "The mek used its intelligence, meager though it was, to intimidate you into making mistakes. Doesn't that demonstrate the superiority of thinking machines?"

Gilbertus moved a piece, then analyzed the new layout of the board. "Manford Torondo drew exactly the opposite conclusion." He had to engage the robot, distract him.

Erasmus chose his next move, illuminated the destination square, and Gilbertus moved the piece for him. He leaned back to reassess his opponent's strategy. He and Erasmus had played this game countless times before, so Gilbertus knew how difficult it was to surprise his mentor. He felt very calm now, without the damaging effects of emotion on his mental processes.

"They used my victory to vilify thinking machines. Prior to that, they did their best to humiliate the combat mek, cutting off its integrated weapons and even its legs. Then after the match they smashed it to pieces and dragged its body through the streets."

"As I've stated many times, my son: Human society is a barbaric, feral mess," Erasmus said. "Consider how many thinking-machine allies have been hunted down and murdered over the years—even the old man Horus Rakka, who lived his life quietly in hiding." Gilbertus was surprised to hear agitation in the robot's simulated voice. "Humans are monstrous and destructive. I am worried about you . . . about both of us. We are no longer safe here."

For some time now Gilbertus had also been concerned, though he wanted to conceal the true danger from his mentor. He moved one of the foot soldier pieces, leaving it vulnerable to attack—intentionally so. Erasmus responded by taking the piece, as expected. Gilbertus then sacrificed a midlevel officer, luring more of his opponent's important pieces to where he wanted them.

"You seem distracted, my son," Erasmus said. "I worry about you."

Gilbertus quelled his smile. The independent robot was the one who was growing distracted. "You don't understand the concept of worrying."

"I have been developing that capacity for centuries. I believe I have made some progress in all that time."

Gilbertus smiled. "Yes, Father, I suppose you have. There is much weighing on my mind, especially after the rabid violence in Zimia." Not exactly a lie, but a distraction, an excuse designed to lull his opponent, altering the independent robot's focus. "So many people killed by the mobs, even Prince Roderick's innocent little daughter. The Butlerians grow more and more dangerous—I did not believe it possible. I fear that I may be on the wrong side of this fight."

"You are. I thought we had agreed about that long ago."

Gilbertus couldn't help but think about his former student Draigo Roget, the epitome of what a Mentat should be. By siding with Josef Venport at the

Thonaris shipyards, the brilliant Draigo had embraced the cause of reason and civilization, while Gilbertus had inadvertently allied himself with those who feared technology. His finest student had chosen the correct cause . . . and now Gilbertus found himself in a position where he had to fight against Draigo.

The erudite robot continued, "From its inception, our Mentat School was intended to preserve the ways of logic through efficient thought processes—humans emulating thinking machines in order to preserve the advances of the Synchronized Empire."

Gilbertus let his hand hover over one of the chess pieces. "Did I tell you that Manford is an avid student of your own laboratory journals? He told me on board our warships when we were heading toward Thonaris."

"Oh? Manford has my journals?"

"He obtained several volumes salvaged from the ruins of Corrin, and now he studies them. I think he is even obsessed with your writing. He might be as fascinated by thinking machines as you are by humans. Wouldn't that be a supreme irony?"

"My journals are just words. He can't know me from them, though he might learn something from my diligent work."

"Words are powerful things," Gilbertus countered. "Manford knows this, and is afraid of the damage that words can do." He remembered how his own hypothetical stance in defense of computers had nearly brought down the school. "I must be extremely careful about everything I say and write."

The Headmaster moved a battle cruiser into position, but without sufficiently shielding it. Again, Erasmus pounced.

"Just to be safe, we must develop our long-overdue escape plan," the robot said. "You have been at this school for too many decades. We should slip away and lie low for a few years—perhaps going back to that quaint world of Lectaire, where you pretended to be a farmer. Afterward, you and I can continue our good works."

Gilbertus would not see Lectaire again, although he missed the woman Jewelia, whom he had loved. She would be very old now, if she even still lived. "But what if my good work *is* this Mentat School? I have influence here, and even the Butlerians listen to me, after a fashion. If I were to flee, I would be abandoning human civilization to the fires of fanaticism."

"I am trying to save *both of us* from being burned," Erasmus said. "That sort of demise is not pleasant to imagine, even for a robot."

Gilbertus remained hesitant. He had built this academy and understood the true importance of what it represented. He loved the bright students and the intense curriculum, even the walls rising up from the marsh lake and swamp. He was proud of what he had accomplished here. He couldn't turn his back and allow it to be corrupted.

As the game continued, the robot changed the subject. "I have been observing Anna Corrino. I analyzed her fragmented brain by recording her conversations and conversed directly with her. She is fascinating."

Gilbertus raised his eyebrows. "You *communicated* with her? You should not have revealed yourself."

"That young woman already hears voices in her mind, so I'm just another imaginary friend. But she has Sorceress genes in her bloodline, and her rearranged brain has unique, most intriguing pathways." He paused. "We can use her, but first I am learning to understand her. We should experiment—"

"You will *not*." Gilbertus recalled the robot's laboratory on Corrin, the organ regrowth experiments he had conducted, the horrific plagues he had developed, the slaughter of countless humans, the cruel operations he had performed on living victims without anesthetic.

Erasmus sounded defensive. "Through my research I achieve greatness. Just look at what I created in you."

Gilbertus remained firm. "I won't let you tamper with the Emperor's sister. It is too dangerous and could lead to tremendous reprisals. If you don't cease this line of inquiry, I will cut you off entirely. I can sever all connections to your spy-eyes and leave you isolated again."

"You would never do that." Erasmus sounded hard and dominant, as he'd been decades before, when he was a powerful robot slavemaster. "Why else do I exist except to learn and expand my mind? I cannot tolerate being static. As for your own priorities, you would harm the defenses of this school by blinding me!" When Gilbertus made no response, the robot tried a different approach.

"You cannot uproot all of my work without tearing down every building. Besides, there are advantages to my surveillance. Do you know that Alys Carroll watches you like a snake, ready to strike? She keeps records of every statement you make that might be questionable."

Gilbertus was disturbed, though not surprised, by the actions of the Butlerian student. "Can you delete those records?"

"They are not electronic files. She writes with a stylus on paper. It is rather quaint."

Gilbertus frowned, made another move on the chessboard. He pretended to be distracted, which he knew Erasmus would notice.

"I trained you as a Mentat, my son—so make a projection and imagine all that might go wrong if this school were attacked. We need to employ every possible defense. And Anna Corrino might be one of those defenses—whether as an ally or as a hostage."

Gilbertus took a deep breath. "All right, Father. I will allow you to converse with her and draw conclusions—with great caution and restraint—but you will inflict no physical or mental harm on her. That is not a request. She is a member of the most powerful family in the known universe."

The robot hesitated. "I admit I considered surgery on her, but I no longer wish to explore the workings of her mind through that means. I have grown somewhat fond of her."

Gilbertus was surprised by the admission. "How much have you learned about compassion?"

"Compassion is a fundamental component of humanity. You once told me I must come to understand it, and I know you have great compassion for me. You saved me, you have protected me all these years. Compassion can lead to love. I am still studying this."

Gilbertus did owe the independent robot everything, and could never abandon him. "Compassion, true . . . but that won't stop me from defeating you in this chess game."

He scanned the pyramid board, saw that Erasmus had put his pieces exactly where the trap needed them to be. He had engaged and distracted the robot, and Erasmus did not even know the ploys his ward used on him.

He pounced with one of his remaining foot soldiers, an insignificant piece, and assassinated his opponent's Empress, which in turn left other important pieces vulnerable. Though the robot tried to counter the follow-up moves, Gilbertus executed them flawlessly. Finally another foot soldier moved forward and struck a fatal blow, taking the Grand Patriarch and winning the game. In the Imperial Court, the mek had played by straightforward understanding of the complex rules; Erasmus was even more sophisticated, but Gilbertus knew him better than any other mind.

"You still don't understand humans," he pointed out.

The robot pondered the game for a long moment before he admitted, "Apparently not."

*We can never atone for all the harm we cause in our lifetimes. We each make decisions based on personal priorities. In the process, people are invariably shunted aside. Someone suffers.*
— teaching of the new Philosophical Academy

The shuttle that Vorian Atreides rode down to Lankiveil was a flying bus full of laborers, mostly offworlders ready to work in boats on the cold seas. More than fifty men and women had been transferred here to fill jobs promised by the wealthy Bushnell family, who had encroached on the best fur-whale harvesting waters. As House Harkonnen waned, the Bushnells saw an opportunity and moved into territory that Vergyl Harkonnen could no longer protect.

The Bushnells had noble blood, but a century ago they had fallen into political disfavor after withdrawing from some of the most vigorous battles in the Jihad. Even so far from Salusa Secundus, the Landsraad still had influence, and current Bushnell ambitions had been thwarted by other nobles who still held grudges. Seeking to recover their standing, the family had moved in on backwater Lankiveil, where the Harkonnens were also held in low esteem.

Vor knew the Harkonnens had little chance without good business leadership. Their noble house had fallen on hard times after several commercial failures, especially the loss of an entire season's whale-fur harvest when a cheap cargo carrier vanished in foldspace. Vergyl Harkonnen was not a skilled planetary ruler, and his elder son, Griffin, had been the family's best hope . . . until Griffin was murdered on Arrakis, with Vor at his side, unable to protect him.

Now Vor hoped that if he went to Lankiveil, he could do something for Griffin's family. The proud Harkonnens would never accept charity or assistance from the man who had caused their downfall, but if he could accomplish it without their knowledge. . . .

He didn't think he had ever been to this chill, windswept world before, even though he knew his former friend and protégé Abulurd had been exiled here. He promised himself he would make up for that now. During the journey that Captain Phillips arranged for him, Vor had studied images of the planet's docks and city buildings nestled among rugged fjords. Vergyl Harkonnen and his family lived here, operated the planetary government offices, and managed their own fur-whale harvesting fleet.

As the shuttle landed in a wet, blowing sleetstorm, no one seemed concerned about the weather. After disembarking, the already assigned Bushnell hires took a snowbus that had been sent to pick them up. Vor paid for a local transport that took him to the other side of the fjord, the crowded village, and the wood-framed Harkonnen main house.

The gray clouds had thinned by the time he arrived in the small, snow-glazed whaling village and tramped along a wooden sidewalk on the main street. He wore thick, waterproofed clothing and carried a heavy satchel with personal belongings.

Before Vor left the Nalgan Shipping vessel, Captain Phillips had given him everything he needed, and he needed very little. Phillips had asked him to reconsider, but seeing the look of determination in Vor's gray eyes, he let the matter drop. "I hope you find what you're looking for down there."

Even Vor wasn't sure what he was looking for, except that he needed to lighten his conscience.

Only a few people were outside, men in heavy weatherproof clothing for a day on rough seas. The wind blew hard, and the harbor water was the color of dull steel, but several whaling craft were heading out, their running lights bright in the mist and falling snow.

After checking into a rooming house, Vor entered the adjacent restaurant, where diners were eating lunch. Unusual cooking odors assailed him: fish, salt, pungent spices. A woman with long red hair worked the floor, serving thick whale steaks accompanied by steamed greens and bowls brimming with chowder. While Vor waited for her to bring him a meal, he noticed two men standing at a message board, reading notices posted there.

The waitress brought his bowl of thick chowder. "Did you come in on the shuttle, looking for work on a whaling ship?"

"Is Vergyl Harkonnen hiring?"

"Usually, but the Bushnells pay better. That's the only reason newcomers are interested in Lankiveil. Where are you from?"

"Lots of places. I travel and find work where I can."

The waitress indicated the message board. "Post a note there with your qualifications. Somebody will see it."

When Vor finished his meal, he wrote an unusual card, offering to work on a

Harkonnen whale-fur boat at no salary, in exchange for taking images so he could compile a research report on his experiences. He claimed to be a freelance writer, using the assumed name of Jeron Egan. He knew well enough not to use the name Atreides around here.

The following morning, the boardinghouse manager told him that Vergyl Harkonnen wanted to see him. Vor went to the large weathered house on the fjord. As he regarded the imposing structure, the wooden walls, the lap-shingled roof, he realized that *Abulurd* had built this place decades ago, making his home here and enduring his exile, no doubt passing along his resentment of the Atreides to the next generation.

Now, as Vorian climbed the icy stairs to the front porch, the door opened before he could knock, and a bearded man greeted him. Vor recognized Vergyl Harkonnen. "You're the fellow who posted the notice? You're a writer?"

Looking at Vergyl's face, Vor could see the clear resemblance to Griffin's features. He remembered the last time he had seen the young man, lying dead in the sand with his neck broken. Seeing the lines on the father's face, Vor felt a heavy sense of dread. This man had endured a terrible grief and had seen the family fortunes fall in the eight difficult decades after the Battle of Corrin.

Vor removed his warm coat and joined the Harkonnen patriarch in a small parlor to discuss his possible employment, as a research assignment. Sonia Harkonnen delivered cups of steaming tea.

"Benz flower tea," she said. "In the thaw every summer, we pick the blossoms and berries. They're hardy plants that bloom when they get the first opportunity."

Vor had learned in his research that Sonia Harkonnen was a Bushnell by birth, but had been estranged from her family for marrying a lesser noble. He wondered now if an eventual reconciliation with the Bushnells would be the only way for Vergyl and Sonia to preserve what little the Harkonnens had left.

Without touching his hot beverage, Vergyl leaned forward. "We never get people wanting to work for free, Mr. Egan, so your offer intrigues me. You're willing to stay at least a month? Work shifts on the whale-fur boats are physically demanding, with constant cold weather and rough seas. Are you sure your research is worth the misery? Who would want to read about that?"

Vor met the man's haunted eyes, again seeing a shadow of Griffin. "Money can be spent and lost, but knowledge becomes a permanent part of you. What I learn here will be worthwhile, to me at least."

Vergyl cocked his eyebrows. "Sometimes there are things I'd rather not know, things I can never forget."

That afternoon, when the clouds thinned and the snow stopped, Vergyl gave Vor a tour of his boats. "These are workhorses, and I admit they need better maintenance, but our fortunes aren't what they once were. I'm trying to keep the boats running, but I may have to sell everything before long."

Although it could never make up for the things the Harkonnens blamed him for, Vor wanted to help them financially, and he had the resources to do so, spread across many planetary banks, even though he could not explain who he was, could never let them know the identity of their benefactor. First, he wanted to get to know them better.

That evening he was invited to dinner in the Harkonnen family home, where Vergyl and Sonia sat at a long, near-empty table with their sixteen-year-old son, Danvis, a pink-faced and lonely-looking young man.

"The house seems so quiet these days," Sonia said as she served Vor a fur-whale steak. Tasting a bite, he was pleased to discover that the steak was not fishy or salty, and had a pleasingly firm texture. "Danvis is the only one left at home. Our two daughters, Tula and Valya, are being trained in the Sisterhood. And our son Griffin . . . he died last year."

"I'm sorry to hear that." Vor meant it with a depth they could never guess. Vergyl showed him images of the two daughters, and Vor remembered how much Griffin had talked about Valya in particular.

Vergyl said, "Griffin is buried just outside of town, in a plot with a magnificent view of the water. At least he has that. . . ." His voice trailed away, and he pushed aside his unfinished meal.

"It sounds like he was loved very much," Vor said.

"That he was," Sonia said.

Vergyl continued, "Griffin was destined to be a great business leader. He even wanted to be our planetary representative to the Landsraad. But all those hopes are lost and gone now." He gave a dismal, hopeless smile toward his younger son, who sat quiet and awkward at the table; the boy had barely said a word throughout the meal. "So now it's up to Danvis to carry on the legacy." Vergyl looked at Vor, cleared his throat. "You arrived at a good time, and we appreciate your willingness to work. We can sure use the help, whatever your reasons."

"Maybe I can help turn your fortunes around." He sounded bright and confident.

"I doubt a research project could accomplish that. You can work miracles?" The elder Harkonnen attempted to make his comment a joke, but the humor was forced.

"I can try." Vor remembered young Griffin, so noble and brave and full of vitality. These broken people were part of the legacy Vor had created, going back decades. House Harkonnen deserved better than this, and he vowed to do everything he could to help them.

*There can be only one result on a critical mission: absolute success. Anything less must be deemed a complete failure. There is no middle ground.*

—VALYA HARKONNEN, remarks
before Rossak retrieval mission

For bringing the vital computers back to the Sisterhood, Valya deserved great fanfare, but there would be no public applause. Most of the Sisters would never know what she and her recovery team had done, but she had proved her worth to Mother Superior Raquella, and that counted more than any accolades.

These forbidden computers were the Sisterhood's most closely held secret, known only to Raquella's elite inner circle, and now they were back where they belonged. After such a cost in blood, Valya knew the old Mother Superior would put the breeding database to extensive use. And the secret must be guarded more ruthlessly than ever.

When her team returned to Wallach IX, Valya sent coded word to Raquella that she had succeeded. Preparing to receive the disguised components, the Mother Superior sent all acolytes into isolated studies, diverted any remaining prying eyes from the landing field, and cleared the way so that Valya's weary, grimy team could move the computers. Only Raquella's most trusted allies could know what was happening.

The old woman offered her a proud smile, and Valya accepted a congratulatory hug. She felt a sudden and disheartening weakness in the Mother Superior's wicker-thin body. How much longer could she last?

Valya had been functioning on very little sleep herself for days, and she had been unable to relax on the return journey from Rossak. Too many ideas ignited her imagination. Now, thanks to her, the computers could be restored, and someday Valya might even be in a position to bring the full resources of the

Sisterhood against Vorian Atreides. The thought of erasing his entire bloodline made her breathless. . . .

Wallach IX had once been a Synchronized World, home to an enslaved human population. When the Sisterhood reestablished their school here, they discovered a network of deep bunkers left behind before the fall of the thinking machines. Now, those underground shelters were a perfect place to install—and hide—the retrieved computers and breeding records.

The Mother Superior brought in Fielle and other trusted Sisters to help install the components in underground chambers. Valya wondered how much planning the new Sister Mentat had done with Raquella while the commando team was on its mission. Valya needed to know this young woman better, to ensure that they were on the same side.

Fielle gave a cool assessment. "We Sister Mentats can use our own knowledge, but these computers will be a tremendous tool to help us plan the future breeding map."

Sister Olivia emerged from the shuttle and hurried to her dark-haired friend. Both young women were heavy, yet seemed comfortable with their weight. The other returning team members engaged in excited chatter. Valya watched them all, knowing that these women, having completed a successful mission under her leadership, would form the core of her allies here, as well as the growing group of Sisters she trained in her new fighting methods. Valya thought of how the ancient Karee Marques had been a loyal adviser to Raquella for many years; she hoped Fielle could fulfill a similar role for Mother Superior Valya. She nodded to herself at the thought.

"After the components are unloaded and secured, why don't you two join me for a meal?" Valya suggested to Fielle and Olivia. They looked at her in surprise, and she added, "I'd like you to meet my sister, Tula."

Mother Superior Raquella seemed relieved to hear the invitation. "You should all get to know each other as friends. The Sisterhood suffered terrible damage when Dorotea thought of herself rather than the good of us all. Our new school on Wallach IX must be strong and unified."

"I couldn't agree more," Valya said.

IN A MATTER of days, the forbidden machines were reassembled, checked, and activated. Valya found herself with similar duties to those she had carried out in the isolated caves on Rossak—but this time, her eager sister was by her side. Valya had requested special permission from the Mother Superior, and she trusted no one more than Tula . . . in certain matters.

Valya had spent the past year making sure her sister knew exactly how Vorian Atreides had wronged House Harkonnen, and Tula was equally determined to punish the aloof, long-lived war hero. The young woman's determination pleased Valya very much.

Valya was strong enough to balance the two driving goals in her life: She could not rest until she had destroyed her brother's murderer, the man who had brought ruin upon her entire family. That was her personal obsession. But in the larger picture, Valya could change the course of human history, and evolution, if *she* were to guide the Sisterhood. She had never been one to settle for small ambitions.

Now, she and Tula worked in the main bunker, combing through the breeding records. Sitting at a dual-control terminal with linked screens, they scrolled through billions of DNA samples to examine their own lineage and chromosomal linkages to other bloodlines. Raquella's trusted Sisters worked at other screens nearby. Several Sister Mentats pored over the genetic analyses and compared them with their own projections made from the more cumbersome printed documentation.

Tula brushed a hand through her curly blond hair and leaned closer to the screen. "Are we really so closely related to the Corrinos?"

"They erased our names and pretend that history doesn't exist, but our bloodline is separated from historical greatness by only a few generations. The Emperor can write his own version, but we know that Harkonnens and Butlers fought side by side against the thinking machines in the Jihad. But we lost everything after the Battle of Corrin, thanks to that accursed Vorian Atreides. To hide the shame, the Butlers changed their name to Corrino and deleted Harkonnens from their family tree."

"Vorian Atreides," Tula said. Whenever Valya heard the name, it burned like poison in her ears.

The two young women followed family connections, drawing an intricate lattice of bloodlines from the database. As they searched, they brushed their trails electronically behind them, which blocked any other Sister from seeing what they had been doing. Tracing back through centuries of detailed records, they ran deep searches on the Atreides bloodline, tracking unique markers dispersed across the League of Nobles and the Unallied Planets, all the way back to the infamous cymek General Agamemnon.

But Valya was not interested in ancient history. Rather, she wanted recent blood descendants that Vorian Atreides might actually still care about.

Since murdering Griffin on Arrakis, the man had vanished—which was not surprising for a coward and a criminal. Vorian seemed dead to history, but Valya hoped he wasn't truly dead—not yet, because she wanted to see him hurt, and hurt deeply. He had to feel the pain he had caused House Harkonnen for generations. She wanted to twist the knife and make him watch the slow death of his family, his legacy. Only then would she kill *him*.

The records indicated that during his travels with the Army of the Jihad, Vorian had lovers on various planets. One of his discarded partners had been a young woman named Karida Julan from Hagal, who was said to have given birth to a child by him. But the record was sketchy, the data damaged . . . maybe even intentionally deleted?

While staring at the screen in front of her, Valya heard a clamoring of internal voices from her Other Memories, as if those ghostly presences remembered such ancient times. The cacophony made her head ache, but she blocked the noises away—she could make up her own mind!

According to new information Vorian Atreides had revealed when he resurfaced and presented himself at the Imperial Court, he'd married a woman named Mariella on the planet Kepler and had two sons and three daughters by her, and an unspecified number of grandchildren. That revelation had sent Griffin off in pursuit, hunting down the Atreides enemy on Kepler and then on Arrakis, where Griffin had died.

Valya already knew about the Kepler branch of the Atreides line, but Tula uncovered records that were more complete, and more relevant. In the latter days of the Jihad, Vorian Atreides and his longtime companion Leronica Tergiet had two sons on the planet Caladan, Estes and Kagin—and by now they had many grandchildren. The Atreides bloodline had been spreading like a disease.

Valya's gaze settled on the names of two of Kagin's descendants—Willem and Orry Atreides, brothers living on Caladan now, both of marriageable age . . . and similar to her beloved Griffin.

Sharp, clear images of the two young men appeared on the screens: patrician features, unmistakable Atreides noses and eyes. Valya looked at her beautiful younger sister, and they exchanged smiles. Both seemed to be considering the same interesting possibilities.

If the Atreides could only feel the same pain as her family had suffered!

"Maybe you should go to Caladan," Valya suggested.

*It is not enough to survive great adversity. You must also share what you learned in the process so that you prevent a recurrence. Otherwise, you widen the scope of the adversity and create a singularity into which even more lives may tumble. This stems from a basic truth: Humans are a collective organism, and that organism performs best when its members recognize their common interests.*

—Sisterhood Training Manual

Just before noon, Prince Roderick stood in the central courtyard of the Imperial Palace and waited for his brother to emerge. Two weeks had passed since the disastrous rampage festival, and Emperor Salvador still insisted on additional security checks and guard sweeps. He often canceled an appearance on short notice, either through paranoia or simply indecisiveness. Salvador had always been fearful of illnesses, and now he saw assassins everywhere. The mob uprising had terrified him, shaken him to his marrow.

Salvador, though, had not lost a little daughter. . . .

Standing in the open air and sunshine, Roderick struggled to concentrate on his older brother's safety. Many Landsraad factions and commercial interests carried blood feuds, wanting to kill the Emperor, for whatever reason. Still reeling from the death of Nantha, Roderick was barely able to function now, and he didn't want to lose his brother, too. His universe seemed to be made of the thinnest glass.

Even after viewing images of the surging riots, Roderick could not fathom why they had occurred. Manford Torondo had triggered the mob violence, and knew exactly what he was doing, but what had the Butlerians wanted to accomplish with all that mindless destruction? And why poor Nantha? The little girl had been so perfect, so young, so delighted with the world.

It was impossible to reconstruct the sequence of events. While Haditha took their son and two older daughters to a baliset concert, the nanny had indulged little Nantha, as she had done so many times before. The nanny had requested additional security for the parade, a typical—and now, obviously, only symbolic—honor guard of four soldiers. The nanny and Nantha often went where they chose, always returning home laughing after their adventures. Roderick knew that his youngest daughter would have pleaded until she got her way.

It took all his effort to stop the low moan in his throat. Haditha was in despair, blaming the nanny, who had also been murdered in the manic violence, but Roderick did not revile the dead woman. Innocent little girls should be able to view parades in safety.

The riots were over now, ruthlessly quashed—too late—by a flood of Imperial military troops dispatched from orbiting warships. Following the advice of Headmaster Albans, Roderick had stamped out the mobs by luring them to outlying towns and rounding them up so they could cause no further harm. Manford Torondo had left them all behind, letting the fervor fade away, and the frenetic followers gradually dispersed to their various little warrens.

By the time the crowds left the Zimia city center, Nantha and the nanny were dead, but in all the fires and wild smashing, no one had identified the victims until the next day.

Since that time, Roderick had kept himself busy managing the huge cleanup and reconstruction effort. Like a sloppy, careless guest, Manford Torondo had simply left Salusa, expressing no remorse for the extensive damage, death, and injuries he'd caused.

None of the Butlerians would be charged with crimes. Even if someone were to identify the person who had actually trampled his beautiful daughter, the murder was not committed by one person. The mob was like a storm, and no *individual* member could be held responsible.

Except perhaps Manford Torondo . . . but Salvador would never get a chance to fight that battle. If the Butlerian leader were arrested, the crowds would burn Zimia to the ground and kill any Corrinos they found. Manford would never be punished for the death and destruction he had caused.

Roderick looked up, brought out of his reverie as a familiar-looking man walked into the courtyard through an arched doorway. He wore plush Imperial robes and a jeweled cap. "Brother, thank you for meeting me!" The man embraced him, but Roderick pulled away, frowning. This was not Salvador; it was a stranger.

He heard a chuckle from the shadows of the arched doorway. "Did I fool you?" Salvador stepped out into the sunshine, flanked by guards.

Roderick looked at the man in the Imperial robes and cap, ignored him. "He doesn't look anything like you."

"He's the right height and build! Don't you see that?"

"We can do better. I will devote more resources to the quiet search. I apologize for not being more proactive in finding you a double. I've been . . ." His voice caught in his throat. "I've been preoccupied."

Salvador came into the courtyard and shooed his unconvincing double away so he could talk with his brother. "What else do you have to report?"

Roderick cleared his throat, pushed aside the heavy fog of grief. "Due to the danger of continued Butlerian demonstrations, the Empress Tabrina has taken permanent refuge in your country home. I sent a guard contingent with her, of course."

Salvador's sour expression made it clear that he would not have mourned if some unexpected group of Butlerians happened to kill her. "She is avoiding me now that I've discovered the schemes of her family."

"I expressed my appreciation to the Truthsayer Dorotea for first uncovering the plots." At every opportunity, Roderick had been reminding Salvador about the value of the group of women who now served the Imperial throne.

"Yes, yes, I admit you were right about that. I am glad we didn't get rid of all the Sisters from Rossak. Dorotea has made herself invaluable. Out of gratitude for how she identified the House Péle plot, I've decided to let her train more Sisters—with proper checks and balances, of course."

Roderick nodded. "And about House Péle, our Mentat accountants have conducted extensive audits, and we have proof that Tabrina's father underre-ported mining production to avoid Imperial taxes. We have levied crushing punitive fines, and Blanton Davido is already dead at the hands of the Grand Inquisitor. That should be sufficient punishment."

"By all means, no! An underling can't take the place of the man who truly deserves to be punished. I want Omak Péle brought here to face Quemada."

Roderick was skeptical. "Empress Tabrina will object strenuously."

"My wife is welcome to take her father's place if she wishes. Lord Péle went into hiding as soon as the scandal broke, but I'm sure we have the resources to find him."

Roderick closed his eyes, gave a small nod. "We do."

The two walked together along a portico lined with statues of heroes of the Jihad. In an uncharacteristically warm moment, Salvador embraced his brother, held him close. "I'm sorry about Nantha. We'll punish whoever was responsible."

Roderick caught his breath, almost choked on it. He and Haditha would never, ever get over the death of their child. It was a loss that needed to be avenged by breaking the Butlerian movement. His voice came out in a low growl. "We already know who is responsible."

TWO DAYS AFTER the order went out for her father's arrest on Péle, Empress Tabrina barged into Roderick's office without an appointment. A strikingly beautiful woman with dark, almond eyes, she moved with the slender grace of a cat. She wore a long dress of glittering gold and ruby-colored fabric.

"My father is not subject to Imperial interrogation," she said without ceremony. "Blanton Davido died at the hands of the Grand Inquisitor, and House Péle has already paid the shortfall in taxes plus the outrageous fines. The matter has been corrected—make Salvador see reason and stop all this nonsense! We should forget about the whole troublesome episode. After the Butlerian riots, the Imperium needs calm. We should get back to normal."

Seeing Tabrina's fiery personality, and aware of the loathing she had for Salvador, Roderick could only think about how much he loved Haditha and their children. And Nantha.

He did not get up from his desk. "I will never get back to normal, Tabrina. My daughter was murdered in the Butlerian madness, and I have no intention of forgetting her or what the fanatics did."

The Empress looked flustered and embarrassed. "Yes, I am very sorry. I remember the dear girl. . . ." She fidgeted with her hands, lifted her chin. "So you can understand that I must try to save my own father."

"I understand . . . but unlike your father, my poor daughter was innocent."

SISTER DOROTEA ACCOMPANIED Roderick as he went to find the Emperor, who was taking a midafternoon break in his private dining hall. The Truthsayer kept a respectful step or two behind Roderick as they entered.

Salvador looked up from a bowl of blue-tomato soup, wiped his lips with a white napkin. "Give me good news about Omak Péle. Is he here, being interrogated by Quemada already?"

Roderick shook his head. "We do not have him. I received word just this morning that he went renegade, abandoned all his holdings, and fled to one of the distant Unallied Planets. He is out of our reach. I do not believe Empress Tabrina even knows where he is."

The lanky Dorotea added, "After listening to court conversation, Sire, I suspect that Lord Péle received help from certain Landsraad families. There could be cascading repercussions."

"Good, let's root out all the traitors. I am the Emperor—"

"And they are the Landsraad, Salvador," Roderick said. "If you begin crushing one house after another, how long will it be before they band together and overthrow House Corrino?"

Salvador squirmed, looked at his soup with distaste. "So I am just to ignore this fraud? House Péle stole from the Imperium—from *me*!"

Roderick continued, "There is a better resolution. House Péle is effectively gone. Their transgression has been exposed, so now we seize all of their assets."

The Emperor perked up, took another spoonful of soup, then said, "Rich mining interests, substantial holdings. And Omak Péle was so proud of his luxurious foldspace barge—I want that brought here, refitted, marked with the Corrino crest." He grumbled. "It's a start, at least. But I still want Lord Péle found—people shouldn't be allowed to run away from justice in my Imperium."

Dorotea added, "For what it's worth, Sire, Empress Tabrina is innocent of any involvement in the scheme—I have observed her closely, listened to the stresses and intonations of her voice when she discusses the Péle scandal, and I am convinced she was unaware all along."

The Emperor frowned, seemingly disappointed by the news.

With a sigh, Roderick said, "I just lost my daughter, Salvador, and enough is enough. It is not fitting that Tabrina should lose her father, too. House Péle was a valuable political asset when you secured your throne, and now you have everything."

"I am the Emperor. I'm supposed to have everything." Salvador pondered for a long moment, wrestling with his dissatisfaction, and finally he looked up. "And you think this is a good solution?"

"I do. It demonstrates that you are firm, but not vindictive. It's the mark of a true leader."

Salvador sighed. "Very well, brother, it is my command that the assets of Omak Péle are forfeit. I don't know what I would do without you."

*With the right tools and proper concentration, we can unlock secrets
hiding within the human mind. Unfortunately, some of those secrets are
better left sealed away.*

—GILBERTUS ALBANS, *Mentat Doctrines*

Erasmus observed his subject, conversed with her, and instructed her. Now
that he finally had the grudging permission of Gilbertus, he wanted to
spend every moment studying the puzzle of Anna Corrino. He was learning
much from their interactions, and felt a sense of satisfaction that she seemed to
have grown so fond of him.

Unfortunately, the young woman had her routine class exercises, and, being
human, she also required sleep. The independent robot had no such biological
frailty; he possessed sufficient energy to concentrate, discuss, and analyze all day
long, but Erasmus could detect when the young woman's energy reserves were
being depleted.

Through the spy-eyes he saw that Anna looked haggard, her eyes red from
lack of sleep, as well as from periodic weeping when the robot prodded her about
the disappointments in her life. He liked to provoke the emotional reactions in
her, so he could study them in detail. It had been so long since he had complete
freedom with all his interesting human subjects, and he wanted to make up for
lost time. Still, though his curiosity remained unabated, Erasmus needed to let
her rest . . . to an extent.

How he wished he could interact with her directly, though, in a personal and
tactile way. Gilbertus had had ample time to find Erasmus a permanent artificial
body, but he'd been unable, or unwilling, to do so. He didn't understand why his
ward would stall. Had he not served Gilbertus extremely well as a paternal presence and mentor? Surely even the Headmaster wanted more than a conversa-

tional companion. Erasmus could well imagine how much he'd accomplish in his experiments if he were more than a disembodied voice in Anna Corrino's ear.

Erasmus mused about how Anna might react if she discovered that her secret new friend was a reviled robot. Would she still consider him such a close confidant if she knew what he was? Considering the young woman's fragmented mind and sometimes rational, sometimes volatile emotions, maybe she would. . . .

Late at night, when Anna lay on her bed, Erasmus spoke through the hidden wall speakers. To continue her instruction, he suggested mental exercises similar to the ones he had used to train the young, feral Gilbertus Albans. But Anna found those challenges too simple, and her mind was already sophisticated at solving puzzles. She could rearrange complex shapes, interlock them, and build exquisitely beautiful sculptures. In a holographic tactical room where Mentats performed strategic exercises with imaginary space fleets, Anna easily spotted patterns, too, and few of the other trainees would even play against her anymore.

As Anna drifted off to sleep, so mentally exhausted she was unable to stay awake, Erasmus told her about old military engagements, machine forces versus the Army of the Jihad. Although he focused on battles where the unpredictable humans had lost, he did not editorialize, merely instructed—and corrected—her in certain historical facts. He talked about the great machine victories in the Jihad, some led by Omnius's forces, others led by General Agamemnon and his cymeks. He enjoyed providing details about the machine conquests of Ix, Walgis, and Chusuk, where entire populations had been slaughtered.

When he realized that Anna had begun to doze, he jarred her awake so he could continue his story. "I'm sorry," she said. "So sleepy."

"I know you're tired. Reshaping your mind and learning so much history is a wearisome process. But it's important for your development."

A year ago, he had eavesdropped while one of Gilbertus's old students, Sister Karee Marques from Rossak, gave the Headmaster a new thought-focusing drug. *Sapho*, she'd called it, a distillation from the barrier roots on Ecaz, and she thought it might prove useful for Mentat trainees. Erasmus knew where the drug was kept and had ideas about how it might be used.

"There's something I want you to try," he said to Anna, knowing she would do whatever he suggested. "Go quietly to the dispensary, and I will help you locate vials of a particular red liquid. Bring me one of them. We will both find it very interesting." He told her the name of the drug, assured her it would help.

"Let's consider it our special little experiment," Erasmus said. "I think it's exactly what you need."

ANNA CORRINO GLIDED along the corridors of the Mentat School, flitting through shadows—she found it thrilling, like when she used to sneak off to meet Hirondo Nef. Now she felt as if she were on an espionage operation, a character from one of the stories she'd read with Lady Orenna back in the Imperial Palace.

She missed Orenna. Anna paused, trying to remember. The old woman had visited her here not long ago. Was that right? Yes! And Roderick had been with her, too.

Recalling the assignment from her secret friend, Anna moved along. She didn't need to use much caution, because at this hour the Mentat students were in their assigned quarters, sleeping. Outside, perimeter guards watched for any signs of attack, and defensive systems protected against large predators. But inside the academy complex, the corridors were as hushed as a held breath.

No one challenged her as she moved toward the medical dispensary near the dissection labs, and Anna crept into the gloomy storeroom, knowing exactly where to look.

*Sapho.* A mind-enhancing drug, a catalyst that could help make her thoughts clear and normal again. Anna withdrew the vial and held it in the dim light. It was the deep ruby color of thick blood. A shiver of anticipation ran down her spine.

In the back of her mind, questions kept nagging at her . . . not quite another voice, simply concerns that emerged from her own brain. If this was a new and untested drug, how did the friendly voice know it would help? How did that voice know so many details about her past, about her secrets? Who was he? He seemed to be an expert on any topic she could imagine, though, and Anna trusted him. He was a true friend who understood her secrets.

Not wanting to wait to get back to her quarters, she opened the vial and sipped the sapho. The taste was pungent and bitter, not at all sweet, as it appeared. Deciding that a mere sip could not possibly be enough, she upended the vial and drained it before she could react further to the taste.

She hid the empty vial at the back of a shelf and licked her lips. She rubbed her mouth on her forearm, leaving a red stain. She wondered how long it would take for her to notice the effects of the sapho. Anna hurried away from the dispensary with whispering footsteps, imagining the severe consequences she would face if she were caught.

*If she were caught . . .*

That thought triggered a troubling echo in her mind, and she began to think of other times she'd been caught at the Imperial Palace, and other consequences. Horrific consequences. She felt memories well up, one after another, like bubbles rising to the surface of a boiling pot.

With sapho, the bubble-memories were brighter and fresher than they would have been otherwise, vivid in all of their details. She remembered slipping away to meet her young lover. She had loved Hirondo with such intensity, although he was only a palace chef who was deemed inappropriate for her affections. It wasn't fair! The romance lasted for several weeks before they were discovered and torn from each other's arms. After she kept trying to see him, Hirondo was banished—perhaps executed, she was never sure—and then she was exiled to the Sisterhood school on Rossak.

The sapho continued to work inside her brain, triggering more memories.

When she was fifteen, she had taken some of Empress Tabrina's jewelry because she thought it was pretty. The Empress accused one of the female servants of stealing it, and Anna was relieved that she hadn't been caught. But when the servant was sentenced to disfiguration as punishment, Anna produced the pilfered jewels and admitted her own guilt.

That should have been the end of the matter, but Emperor Salvador was not satisfied. "Sister, you have to understand consequences and know that you're responsible when other people get in the way of your indiscretions." He flared his nostrils. "We will carry out the sentence as decreed."

And so, Anna had been forced to watch in horrified silence as the servant, still wailing her innocence and begging for mercy, had one of her arms severed.

The memories were so vivid, the pain so fresh and clear, that Anna stumbled into a wall. Recovering her balance, she kept pushing forward, trying to make her way back to her quarters.

More memories surfaced like bats swooping out of a cave at dusk, and the more painful they were, the more intense they appeared in her mind. She could see only her past and not the dim corridors of the Mentat School.

"Help," she whispered aloud, but she was far from her mysterious friend, who never spoke to her except when she was in her own room. Anna fumbled along, her eyes closed, but that didn't help, because images continued to flow across her thoughts. She finally found a door that seemed to be her chamber. She pushed it open and tumbled inside, hoping she was in the right place.

The sapho continued to rush through her bloodstream.

She remembered one of her beloved pets, a silky dog so small it could curl up in her lap. But it barked too much, and Salvador always hated it. Her dog died mysteriously, and Anna never knew whether or not the Emperor had instructed one of his guards to poison it. Dear Roderick had consoled her and offered to replace the animal, even though that would never heal her heartache. But Salvador overrode his brother, forbidding more dogs in the palace.

Now, in the dim room Anna staggered forward and bumped her shin painfully against a chair. Her chair. She found her bed by accident and sprawled onto it. The universe of her past whirled around her like a cyclone, gathering strength.

"Help me," she said aloud. "I can't stop."

The memories grew louder, more intense. She saw herself as a girl, playing in the extensive palace gardens and arboretum. But now she had more context, more understanding. She had been too young to comprehend the politics of what was happening in the Imperium, the turmoil caused by the release of the *Orange Catholic Bible*, how the people despised the Commission of Ecumenical Translators who claimed to speak for God. The popular mood was already raw and inflamed from constant Butlerian provocations, and Emperor Jules had struggled to keep his government from tearing itself apart. As a girl, she hadn't understood why the CET members, led by their spokesman Toure Bomoko, remained in protective exile.

She had been such an innocent child that day when she went out to the waterwheel cottage on the palace grounds, where she expected to play uninterrupted.

Now, thanks to the sapho, the memory came fully alive inside her. A child again, Anna crept up to the open window, surprised to hear voices inside, since the cottage was rarely used. Heavy breathing and strange noises . . . a scuffle, judging by the sounds. And a woman crying out. Anna had never heard such a sound before, but it seemed like pain or surprise, or perhaps fear.

Then she saw Orenna with a naked man on top of her. Orenna was flailing her arms, trying to beat the man away . . . or was she clutching him? Anna couldn't tell.

When the girl yelled for help, the man jerked away, and she recognized him as Toure Bomoko, head of the CET delegation. Now, Orenna did look terrified— her wide eyes turned toward Anna at the window. The girl screamed again, and the guards came running as Bomoko fled. . . .

The sapho reawakened her memories of the uproar in the palace and the rage on Emperor Jules's face. Orenna, the so-called Virgin Empress, was in despair, filled with fear, and Anna had been certain it was because she was afraid of that man attacking her.

In a completely unconvincing voice, Lady Orenna was forced to publicly accuse Bomoko of raping her. The disgraced CET members, in protective exile, were rounded up and arrested, but Bomoko had disappeared.

Anna had never seen her father so furious, so disturbed. She never forgot his words. "I'm so proud of you for the treachery you exposed, daughter. You have done a fine thing that will strengthen our Imperium." As a reward—Jules insisted it was a reward—he allowed her, *forced* her, to watch as the CET members were dragged into the courtyard. One after another, the men and women were decapitated, a more ancient and barbaric means of execution than had been used in many centuries. Horrified, with tears streaming down her face, Anna had watched each one die.

Thanks to the sapho coursing through her, she now remembered those sounds of death in incredible detail: the sharp thud, the pop of a severed spine, a wet rain of spraying blood. When she had tried to turn away, her father made her look.

Salvador and Roderick were also there. Even though her brothers were much older than Anna, they seemed confused about what was happening. But Toure Bomoko escaped, and had never been found in all the years afterward. He remained a hunted man, and sightings still occurred regularly.

Anna had tried to erase the scars of those memories, but the sapho reopened the wounds. The memories burned like flames in her mind. The drug surged through her bloodstream, unlocking door after door in her thoughts until finally the sapho wore off and the memories faded. She lay sobbing on her bed.

It was then, at last, that she heard the voice of her special new friend, calm and supportive, yet also curious.

"I take it the sapho unlocked your memories? Excellent! You must tell me what happened—tell me everything."

*Just repeating a statement often and with great vehemence does not make it a fact, and no amount of repetition can make a rational person believe it.*

—DRAIGO ROGET, report to Venport Holdings,
"Analysis of Fanatical Patterns"

The Suk doctors at their main hospital on Parmentier were pleased to receive sophisticated medical equipment from VenHold industries—scanners, genetic analysis grids, and diagnostic machines that were dependent on complex circuitry, possibly even computers. Josef Venport did not explain the internal functioning of the analytical devices, and the Suks were wise enough not to ask uncomfortable questions; they merely accepted the generous gifts and expressed their appreciation.

Now, after Josef concluded his business with the Suk School, the VenHold transport ship departed from Parmentier. He climbed the long stairway to the Navigator deck so he could spend time with his great-grandmother. The complexities of running his huge shipping and banking empire must seem trivial to such an advanced being, far beneath the threshold of her attention. Yet he knew that Norma cared for him and wanted to protect her legacy—which included the Navigators (whom she considered her surrogate children) and the critically important spice production on Arrakis.

Up on the Navigator deck, he watched the shifting starfield. When he was with her, Josef felt like a child sitting on a wise and attentive maternal knee.

"As of last week, Grandmother, our fleet has expanded," he told her, like a boy showing off a good school report. The news had been spread widely throughout Venport Holdings, but he didn't think Norma paid much attention to those channels of information. "We acquired a hundred more ships."

He saw her move inside the tank and knew she was listening. Even though she didn't respond, he continued to explain, "Through intermediaries we expanded our stockholder base and purchased a rival transport company, Nalgan Shipping. Most of the captains still aren't aware they've been absorbed by Ven-Hold." He smiled at the thought. "Once I make the announcement to the Landsraad, it will cause quite an uproar. The Butlerians will be outraged."

Norma's face drifted close to the side of the tank. Her oversize eyes watched him, seeming to focus and unfocus.

He expanded on the significance of this news. "Nalgan Shipping was one of the few companies that serviced Butlerian planets. Now that I own Nalgan Shipping, we will reroute those vessels and further cut off the barbarians. Let them have their dark ages."

Norma stirred, and finally her voice came through the speakerpatch. "If you have more ships, you will need more Navigators."

"Yes. We always need more Navigators."

"You understand their importance," Norma said. "To the future. To the Spacing Guild."

"Spacing Guild?" he asked.

Before he could press for further information, Norma interrupted him. "A moment. I require my concentration." Her eyes lost focus.

He fell silent, wondering if she had suddenly thought of another esoteric idea that was impossible to explain—possibly even a profitable idea.

Josef looked out the broad windowports through which Norma liked to view the universe. The hum of Holtzman engines sounded through the deck, and he felt the buildup of static electricity in the air. So near the Navigator's tank, the ozone penetrated deep into his sinuses.

Norma Cenva's mind was so powerful that she could fold space on her own, although with such a large vessel she used the Holtzman engines. Josef felt a wrenching sensation and the stars twisted, then jumped as the universe rippled around the hull.

With the transition completed, Josef continued the conversation. "I promise you, we will defeat the Butlerians, Grandmother. One devastating blow after another. Manford's puppet Mentat recently defeated a captive mek in a pyramid chess game at the Imperial Court. They believe this proves humans are superior, but the riots afterward merely prove that they are savages."

After the mob violence, Josef had hoped the Emperor would crush and disband the antitechnology movement . . . but Salvador didn't have the spine. Josef was sickened by the images he had seen. "Once they run out of thinking-machine remnants, where will the Butlerians turn for scapegoats? The Half-Manford will need an outside enemy or he'll lose his hold on the mob. He'll have to make something up, maybe even secretly manufacture his own machines in order to destroy them in public."

Norma took the matter seriously. "I can peer through my prescience, but the detail is not sufficient. I cannot predict exactly what he will do."

Josef couldn't forget the grim prescient vision she had offered: If he lost the epic battle of reason versus mob-insanity, human civilization could fall into the dark ages for thousands of years. This wasn't just a war for profit or even a battle of ideologies. It was more fundamental than that and would span many planets, and possibly many lifetimes. "We will prepare our commercial fleet for a long war, which appears to be necessary."

Each of the new Nalgan vessels would be taken to Kolhar to be refitted with armaments—both for defense and, should the opportunity arise, to annihilate any Butlerian ship that got in the way.

"But first, we go to Salusa Secundus. If they've recovered from the mayhem and riots, I intend to address the Landsraad."

AS A POWERFUL noble in his own right, it was Josef Venport's prerogative to address the Landsraad Council whenever he pleased. Even though he was disgusted with them and their dithering politics, he had to deal with them.

As he watched the planetary leaders gathering in the great hall, he mentally divided them into categories: those who publicly supported his cause (not nearly as many as he had hoped), those who quietly acted in their own best interests (and thus could be bribed or manipulated), those who were simply barbarians and therefore lost causes (unless he could overthrow their governments) . . . and those who were genuinely neutral or undecided. He didn't understand how anyone could straddle the vast gulf that was tearing apart human civilization.

Josef had assigned junior Mentats to study the lives, connections, alliances, and shadowy secrets of all Landsraad members. Using that surreptitious information, he could cement the loyalty of those who sided with civilization, or he could use it as a weapon against his enemies.

He had never guessed the challenge would be so hard, though. Wasn't it obvious? Common sense? Once he embargoed the worlds that took the Butlerian pledge, he had expected them to crumble quickly as they felt the lack of products and trade.

Fanatics were difficult to understand. Their foibles would have been laughable, had the fools not been so annoying and narrow-minded.

Emperor Salvador Corrino sat in his gaudy parliamentary chair, looking regal and pompous. He was surrounded by six dark-robed Sisters, with Dorotea closest to him, whispering in his ear, advising him. She was supposedly able to detect falsehood spoken in her presence, but Josef thought her a charlatan, one of the turncoat Sisters who pandered to the Emperor rather than helping to rebuild the school on Wallach IX. He knew that Dorotea was also a follower of the Half-Manford, so, in Josef's mind, she was already suspect.

Standing in the center of the Landsraad Hall, the Directeur looked around at the empty seats. Too many nobles had chosen not to attend the meeting. *Cowards, all of them.* Some politicians believed that if they avoided putting their thoughts on record, they could play both sides of the conflict. Josef wouldn't allow that, and neither would Manford Torondo. It was perhaps the only thing on which the two men agreed.

Josef addressed the diminished Council in a firm voice. "I stand on the side of civilization and prosperity rather than ignorance and destruction. Human greatness cannot cower like a child afraid of the darkness."

He heard a muttering of discontent in the audience, but he didn't care that his words were provocative. Josef brushed a forefinger down his bushy mustache, and smiled as he looked around the echoing chamber. "Today, I bring you good news—a step toward binding all civilized worlds into a much stronger Imperium. Venport Holdings has just purchased the vessels of Nalgan Shipping to expand our Spacing Fleet. With these additional ships, we can efficiently service every civilized planet in the Imperium, and adjust our routes to give the Butlerians their opportunity to live without technology, supplies, medical assistance, or commerce—since that is what they seem to want." He had already terminated all Nalgan Shipping routes to planets that accepted Manford Torondo's destructive pledge. Now they were effectively cut off.

The muttering rose to an uproar, and Josef reveled in it. He continued to smile. How much more would it take for them to see? "I am also happy to announce an exclusive alliance with Combined Mercantiles for the distribution of spice from Arrakis. From now on, VenHold will be the sole distributor of melange throughout the Imperium. Butlerians on isolated worlds will no longer be tempted by this so-called vice that increases the vigor and longevity of so many."

The Emperor had gone pale, and leaned forward in his ornate chair. Salvador worked his jaw as if massaging the words before they burst out of his mouth. "Directeur Venport, you are in no position to issue an ultimatum to my Imperium. *I* am the Emperor."

Josef turned to him with mild surprise on his face. "Sire, I run a commercial enterprise, and I must decide which markets best serve my business. I would never hinder *your* personal transport needs, or your personal supply of melange. The VenHold Spacing Fleet already transports and services much of the Imperial Armed Forces. In fact"—he spread his hands in front of him—"because I am your loyal subject, I'll provide transportation services without charge to any member of the Corrino family, whether for official or personal business."

Salvador seemed slightly mollified, reconsidering the situation.

Josef continued, "But you can't force me to coddle my enemies, Sire. That spineless Manford Torondo and his fanatics destroyed my industrial shipyard at Thonaris and killed thousands of innocent workers. They even tried to assassinate *me*. And those reckless savages recently demonstrated their true colors here on Zimia. I believe they even killed your brother's beloved, innocent daughter."

Angry mutters rippled through the audience, but the tone was different. The madness of the rampage festival had frightened even those who gave lip service to the antitechnology movement.

Josef felt a hot flush on his cheeks. "Manford Torondo refuses to control his followers. He made no reparations for the enormous collateral damage he inflicted on my company. He hasn't issued apologies to the families of the VenHold employees he slaughtered. Has he offered to pay for the destruction he caused on Zimia?" He crossed his arms over his chest. "Until the Butlerian leader stops inciting his followers to violence, I have no choice but to deny my services to Butlerian-controlled worlds. It is my *right*."

Roderick Corrino whispered into Salvador's ear; Josef knew that with the recent death of his little girl, the Emperor's brother was certainly no friend of the Half-Manford's. Reverend Mother Dorotea stood near them, and she also spoke, probably taking the opposite point of view.

Finally Salvador muttered, "I grow impatient with this constant feuding among my subjects."

Sounding oh-so-reasonable, Josef interrupted. "Then, Sire, command the Butlerians to stop the violence. Tell Manford Torondo to cease his inflammatory rhetoric and make reparations to those he has harmed. As you correctly pointed out, *you* are the Emperor. I am not—nor is he." He could see that even the Emperor was afraid of the barbarians . . . and, alas, not afraid enough of Venport Holdings.

That would have to change.

Maybe if Josef stopped being so civilized, then Salvador would understand the strength VenHold represented as well. In fact, Josef was beginning to wonder about the relevance of the man on the Imperial throne. Salvador did little to lead, had insufficient military or political power, and was caught between two opposing forces.

Josef's brow furrowed. Why did they need an Emperor at all? A man like Salvador simply got in the way.

*One man's mission is another man's folly.*
—saying of the desert

Taref had not been thirsty for weeks, nor had he felt dust on his skin or in his hair. It was a marvelous sensation at first, and then became strange and unsettling. He hadn't expected he might miss what he had previously scorned. Far from the desert world, this climate felt so strange.

He and his companions had been instructed to wear loose-fitting clothes that allowed perspiration to evaporate into the air; at some point later, it would fall back down onto the surface of Kolhar. He found this planet's weather amazing, incomprehensible, and disturbing. His companions chafed in the strange garb and remained uncomfortable throughout their training sessions. Waddoch groaned that he was never going to get used to it.

Each day's experiences forced Taref to reassess his understanding of the universe. For years he had dreamed of leaving the arid wastelands to explore exotic worlds and enjoy new experiences. He still marveled at what he was doing now, away from the harsh day-to-day sietch existence.

Yet the food here had strange seasonings and was difficult to enjoy. His desert friends remained astonished that offworlders had so much excess water to drink that they had the decadent luxury of adding flavors to their beverages.

He could see the difference in Lillis already: Her lean, leathery features were beginning to show soft curves as her body gained water fat. Shurko had grown ill from eating the unfamiliar items. Chumel developed a skin rash, some kind of rot or fungus that developed from too much moisture and too-frequent bathing, and he was ashamed of the amount of creams and salves he was required to apply. Waddoch and Bentur seemed edgy and irritable. None of them liked the annoying films they were forced to apply to their eyes to cover the distinctive blue-within-blue.

Though Taref anticipated seeing the ocean world of Caladan, he realized that his companions were growing homesick for Arrakis as they trained here. But they had barely begun their mission and still had much to learn. . . .

For the day's instruction, Draigo Roget led them inside one of the landed spacecraft in the Kolhar shipyards. They followed the Mentat instructor down metal corridors until they reached the dim, stuffy engine decks.

On Arrakis, Taref had been aboard spice harvesters many times, and he was familiar with the loud hammering noises, the roar of engines, the unavoidable vibration that would inevitably summon a sandworm. Previously, he had scorned the giant spice factories, knowing that a group of Freemen could simply skitter across the sands, harvest raw melange, and carry it away with deft hands and irregular footsteps—all without summoning a worm. It had seemed so simple to him; that was the way a sietch gathered the melange they needed.

But he had never before understood the sheer volume of spice harvesting and the voracious appetite of the Imperium. Seeing the incredible amounts of melange the VenHold Navigators required, as well as the addicted populations of world after world, he was beginning to comprehend the scope of that hunger. Stopping that demand would be like trying to stop the moving sands.

Back on Arrakis, even if he and his companions sabotaged a spice harvester to hinder the work of Combined Mercantiles (more as a game to prove themselves than as a radical political statement), he knew their efforts would make no difference to the overall company operations. It was like removing a spoonful of sand from a giant dune. . . .

Draigo halted the group inside an engine chamber. "Observe the tasks we need you to do. This is a cumbersome old spaceship we recently acquired from a small company, Nalgan Shipping. These vessels are very similar to the ones used by EsconTran—the ships that will be your targets."

"You want us to fight your battles for you," Shurko said. "You are sending us out to destroy your rival's ships so that VenHold vessels will be victorious."

The Mentat drew his dark brows together. "In essence, yes. But the battle is more subtle than that, and much larger in scale. We need to do more than destroy a ship or two—rather, we need to fan the flames of fear."

The desert recruits stood at the control panel connected to the ship's foldspace engines. Draigo worked the grid, and system lights became a dizzying storm of colors and readouts.

"If we can make people believe that EsconTran ships are *unreliable,* then we cause far more havoc. We want the Imperium to think that VenHold has the only safe method of space travel, thanks to our Navigators. Already Escon's safety record is less than ninety-eight percent, as best we can determine. Out of every hundred flights, two or more vessels disappear, on average."

To Taref, the number did not sound so terrible. At least that many attempted sandworm rides ended in disaster. But weak offworlders had less tolerance for risk, he supposed.

Lillis said, "EsconTran must have faulty spaceships, then, or incompetent pilots."

Draigo's smile was faint, but Taref noticed it. "Or perhaps we have other operatives, just like you, who work on maintenance crews in certain rival docking facilities. For years our quiet saboteurs have been causing accidents, devastating their safety record."

He guided their attention to the control grid. "The more complex the machinery, the easier it is to sabotage. I shall teach you all the ways."

Taref drank in the details as the Mentat summarized how to adjust standard fuel flow, how to deflect heat-dissipation systems, how to set up a resonance feedback loop so that engines would explode moments after the ship folded space.

"That will kill many people," Lillis pointed out.

"Only those who chose the wrong method of transport," Draigo said, unconcerned. "Our goal is to see that EsconTran has a failure rate of seven percent or more within the next few months. Manford Torondo claims that his followers are protected by God. With such a disastrous loss rate, they'll start thinking they've been cursed."

When the group of friends had first arrived on Kolhar, Taref had only a vague idea of who Manford Torondo was, but Josef Venport had left a holo-recording for Draigo to use. Many VenHold workers had seen it. In the holo, the Directeur spoke with palpable anger, showing images of the legless, fanatical leader who rode on the shoulders of a female Swordmaster.

"*This man* is the greatest enemy of humanity," Venport said, pointing at Manford in the holo. "Unless we stop the dark and primitive future he intends to create, he will cause the death of billions, if not trillions. By removing this one person, we can save the human race.

"As you fan out to various planets, I would be very pleased if Manford Torondo"—the image zoomed closer, showing the face of the Butlerian leader—"were to be removed from the interplanetary stage and prevented from causing further harm. I don't care how it's done."

Taref had never forgotten that speech. Desert people had their feuds and unpopular Naibs, so he was no stranger to that way of dealing with problems, but Manford Torondo must be a terrible person to warrant such bloodshed. He let himself dream for a moment. If he could achieve such a victory, how much better it would be than earning respect in his tribe by sabotaging a spice-harvesting machine or two. Eliminating Leader Toronto would be far greater than anything Taref's stern father could ever hope to accomplish. . . .

Though attentive, his companions showed little enthusiasm. Draigo continued to lecture the group as he led them away from the control grid and into the complex foldspace engines. "If you cannot gain access to the control panels, there are still simple ways you can cause damage using a few basic tools. Let me show you."

He took out a small pry bar and a spanner, but before using them he turned to face Taref and his companions. "I believe that you Freemen have more potential than any of our other operatives."

OUT ON THE field of Navigator tanks, Draigo spoke with three of his Mentat students, whose training was far more rigorous than what Taref and his companions were going through. Out of more than twenty volunteers for the intense Mentat instruction, these three—Ohn, Jeter, and Impika—had shown the most skills.

Draigo admitted that the trainees would have done better if they'd attended Headmaster Albans's school on Lampadas. Although Draigo had memorized the curriculum of the great academy, he was not as gifted a teacher as the Headmaster. He missed his mentor, wished that he and Gilbertus had not found themselves on opposite sides of an immense conflict. He didn't understand how the wise teacher could accept the antitechnology fervor that caused so much obvious harm.

At the school, Draigo and Gilbertus had matched wits many times on theoretical battlefields; they had even clashed for real at the Thonaris space shipyards. How much more formidable the two of them could be if they fought on the same side! He wished the Headmaster would join him in the fight against rampant fanaticism.

He doubted Gilbertus believed machines were innately evil. Draigo monitored Lampadas with his own secret spies and observers among the Butlerians. Over the years, Headmaster Albans had made questionable comments that attracted suspicion, making others wonder if he might be a machine sympathizer after all.

Draigo wondered if that could be true. He hoped it *was* true.

As he joined his companions out on the Navigator field, he knew these three students were his own now, his most talented apprentices. All three of them had bright lips, disturbingly stained, which told him they were continuing to consume the experimental sapho. Since it increased the mental acuity of his trainees, Draigo encouraged Ohn, Jeter, and Impika to use it. He would not turn down any chance to improve his students, his loyal Mentats.

Some of the candidates who did not prove sufficient to become Mentats volunteered instead to be sealed inside spice tanks for conversion into Navigators. The supreme privilege of being a Mentat demanded constant concentration, whereas a Navigator required a flexible, voracious mind, a great deal of melange, and good fortune. Mentat candidates who became Navigators might be a tremendous asset for VenHold. . . .

Draigo and his students stepped up to the translucent, gas-filled chambers. Inside, the half-converted, mutant volunteers seemed to be suffocating in open air. Draigo had never let himself grow fond of any particular student, but he was concerned. Despite his own teachings that a human computer must be like a thinking machine—coldly analytical and without emotions—Draigo knew that Headmaster Albans had actually cared for him on a personal basis, and now he had similar feelings for these three. . . .

The Mentat students stared at the transforming subjects who had recently been their classmates. "Are they in pain? Are they suffering?" Jeter asked.

"Who knows what pain is required before a person can become a Navigator? We did not all become Mentats, nor can we all become Navigators. Greatness requires sacrifice."

A voice echoed from the chamber of an older, more experienced Navigator—Royce Fayed, who was a special protégé of Norma Cenva.

"They may endure pain," said Fayed's burbling voice, "but if they survive, they will know a greater joy than they ever imagined possible."

"They volunteered for the process," Draigo pointed out.

"They don't all volunteer," remarked Impika.

"No survivor has ever complained," Draigo said.

Fayed added from his tank speakers, "The greatest gift is to ensure that a person reaches his or her potential . . . even if they have to be forced to that attainment. I was forced, but I do not regret it for a moment."

WHEN DIRECTEUR VENPORT arrived home after his unsatisfactory speech in the Landsraad Hall, he summoned his Mentat for a debriefing. Draigo arrived in the admin-towers and found the Directeur scanning a new report he had received from the Denali research facility. His eyes sparkled. "Good news, Mentat! Our researcher Ptolemy wants us to help him transport several new cymeks under the tightest possible security—for a test."

Draigo was surprised. "Transport cymeks? What kind of demonstration does he have in mind?"

"Something that requires an unusually harsh landscape. He wants us to take his cymeks to Arrakis."

Draigo nodded. "If you can arrange the transportation of the cymek test subjects from Denali, I will send word to my Mentats at Combined Mercantiles to choose an appropriate place. I would like to attend the test myself."

Directeur Venport raised his bushy eyebrows. "You are welcome to. I'd like your analysis."

Draigo remained silent for a moment. "The details will take some weeks to arrange, sir, and I would like to make another brief trip first. I can be back in time."

Venport looked at him, waiting. "I can tell you have something to ask, Mentat. Speak candidly."

"I extrapolated from basic data, assessed the political tapestry of conflicts, alliances, and shifting loyalties, then followed my thoughts to their natural conclusion. We have another potential ally against the Butlerians."

"Which is?"

"Back at the Mentat school, Headmaster Albans pretends to support the Butlerian movement in order to protect his trainees, but I refuse to believe that the teachings he espouses come from his heart. I know him. I've debated him numerous times. After the bloody rampage festival in Zimia, he will not support the mobs. His cooperation with Manford Torondo has always been reluctant."

Directeur Venport was not pleased with the idea, having felt the brunt of the Mentat Headmaster's tactical skills. "I don't trust him. Without Gilbertus Albans, the Half-Manford never would have conquered the Thonaris shipyards." He shook his head. "But I respect your projections, Mentat, and I am inclined to indulge you. What do you propose to do?"

Draigo remained standing, his back straight. "While we prepare the cymek test on Arrakis, I would like to go back to the Mentat School in secret. I think I can make the Headmaster see his folly." He turned his eyes toward the Directeur. "I intend to recruit him to our side."

*Humans never stop looking for ways to make their lives easier. Yet in taking that course they weaken the species and accelerate the process of genetic atrophy. When the Butlerians rail against computers, they have inadvertently stumbled upon this truth, yet in our quest to breed the perfect human we rely on computers. We have no alternative.*

—MOTHER SUPERIOR RAQUELLA BERTO-ANIRUL, private notes

During her months on Wallach IX, Tula threw herself into Sisterhood training with impressive dedication. She seemed obsessed with learning the rigorous techniques as swiftly as possible. Valya had already introduced her to the basic methods on Lankiveil, but now Tula was eager—even desperate—to become as talented as her sister.

Valya was pleased to see the difference in her younger sibling. Tula's former shyness was replaced with new confidence; she never mentioned being homesick for Lankiveil, never talked about their parents or brother, even though Valya knew the younger girl was close to Danvis, as she herself had been to Griffin. She couldn't help but smile; her sister's savage determination was a good sign. Tula was nearly ready. Valya kept watching.

In private, the Harkonnen sisters discussed plans against the Atreides—a goal they shared even beyond their dedication to the Sisterhood. Valya, who had already shed blood to protect the Sisterhood, primed Tula to avenge their family's shame through bloodshed.

Her sister was no shy and trembling flower. Valya had trained with her in mock combat, and knew that Tula was coming close to beating her. No one had done that since Valya's sparring matches with Griffin.

The young blonde had a certain allure about her, an innocence and feigned vulnerability that made her attractive to young men. Valya had been helping her develop that sexual magnetism, counseling her to use her assets wisely. Tula needed to maximize her charms in preparation for meeting the unsuspecting young Atreides on far-off Caladan. . . .

She knew exactly when her sister was ready. Valya hugged her in a rare display of emotion, and both knew it was time for the next step.

They entered the Mother Superior's office, and Valya stood with pride next to her younger sister, lending silent support, while Tula bowed before the ancient woman. Keeping her tone meek, Tula said, "Mother Superior, I thank you for the training you granted me. I learned much about the Sisterhood and about myself, but for the time being, I must leave the Sisterhood with great regret." The hitch in her voice was carefully orchestrated, and convincing. "There are personal matters that demand my attention."

The ancient woman looked carefully at Tula as if taking the girl's measure. "You are an excellent student—as Valya promised you would be. I don't understand why you would leave us."

"Our family on Lankiveil faces difficult times, and House Bushnell is attempting to seize our holdings. Now I see that my decision to leave was impulsive—"

"As mine was," Valya said, "when Sister Arlett recruited me for the Sisterhood. But our family situation was much different then."

Raquella raised her eyebrows. "And?"

Tula lowered her eyes and answered with only the literal truth. "Because my obligations to House Harkonnen outweigh the demands that the Sisterhood would place on me, I must meet those obligations before I commit myself entirely to the Sisterhood. I have my parents and my remaining brother to consider. They have already lost Griffin, and Valya."

With her heightened perceptions, Valya noticed a glimmer of disbelief in Raquella's watery eyes, as she detected the falsehood of omission. But the Mother Superior finally nodded. "Very well. If you were to stay and become Sister Tula, you would no longer be Tula of House Harkonnen, so a choice would be required. I'm glad you realized that about yourself before further complications arose. We will miss you—you have great potential."

Tula seemed to notice the same hint of skepticism. "Perhaps someday I'll come back, after I've accomplished what I need to do."

"Of course," Raquella said. "But I suspect that will be a decision of the next Mother Superior." She glanced at Valya, and Valya's heart skipped a beat. She looked so old! *Has she chosen me?*

The rheumy eyes focused on Tula. "Should you decide to return, make certain you are willing to commit wholeheartedly first. Reflect on all you have learned among us."

"I am grateful to have so much to reflect on, Mother Superior," Tula said.

Valya knew her sister was also thinking about the knowledge from the breeding index, especially the locations of the Atreides descendants.

*Crossing the line from friend to enemy takes only a small step. The op-
posite journey, however, is far more difficult.*

— Zensunni wisdom of the desert

Although Lampadas was surrounded by the Half-Manford's Butlerian warships, their defenses were as effective as using a frayed net to hold back
the rain. Draigo Roget took passage aboard a small VenHold ship and spent much
of the voyage in a Mentat trance, planning conversations with his mentor, imagining outcomes.

He did not want to admit that he was nervous about the prospect of facing
the Headmaster. Their last encounter at the Thonaris shipyards had nearly killed
him, but he didn't think he had misjudged Gilbertus's true mindset, despite his—
reluctant?—cooperation with the Butlerians.

After arranging a return rendezvous with the spacefolder that remained in
distant orbit, Draigo descended to the wild part of the continent in a small unmarked shuttle. Headmaster Albans would not be expecting him, and Draigo
didn't know what sort of reception he would receive. He needed to be cautious.

A handful of the Mentat trainees were loyal to Manford Torondo. Gilbertus
had been forced to welcome zealous Butlerian students to keep the leader satisfied. Draigo was more than a match for them, but he could never count on out-
thinking Gilbertus Albans.

The Headmaster kept his emotions tightly reined, but Draigo thought he
knew the man's heart. The two of them had grown close during years of instruction, and he didn't think their bond would ever be broken. Although the Mentat
curriculum was designed to teach human candidates to think without computers, Gilbertus was no mindless barbarian. He was a reasonable man, and Draigo
had to count on that. . . .

By the light of the Lampadas moon, he landed his shuttle on the edge of the sangrove swamp and set off on foot across the sodden wilderness, through tall grasses and thorny thickets. He carried weapons and a personal body shield, not because he expected to fight his way through the school, but to defend against swamp predators. Although he remained alert for nocturnal creatures, his primary focus was on the tall buildings and the new defensive walls.

He envisioned the tangled waterways woven through the marshes in the shallows of the lake and brought forth the perfect memory picture of a path used by the Mentats. The labyrinth of sluggish, shallow channels provided an additional obstacle to protect the walled school, but he had long ago memorized where the submerged stepping-stones were, only centimeters beneath the surface. By taking careful steps now, he splashed his way across, barely getting his feet wet—but if he should miss a step, he would plunge in, with little chance of scrambling back out before razorjaws swarmed him or a swamp dragon lunged out to pick him off.

Draigo took pride in the knowledge that he was the greatest student the Mentat school had ever produced, the Headmaster's trusted protégé. Gilbertus had wanted him to remain behind and teach other Mentats, but Draigo had other obligations to Directeur Venport.

When he had been pitted against Gilbertus at the Thonaris shipyards, Draigo had lost. But surely the Headmaster regretted the senseless mayhem and all the deaths the Butlerians had caused. A Mentat must be rational, if not compassionate. A Mentat must revere efficiency over chaos. The frenzied mob that Manford had later unleashed on Zimia only reinforced how dangerous and uncontrolled the fanatics were.

A man such as Gilbertus Albans could not truly believe that savagery was preferable to civilization. The Headmaster could help bring sanity back to the Imperium . . . or so Draigo hoped, and that hope drove him onward.

After passing through the swamp obstacle course, he finally reached the imposing gates of the Mentat School. He scaled one of the high wooden barriers, crossed a suspended footbridge that creaked under his feet, and ducked into the connected buildings.

If nothing else, Draigo thought, the Headmaster would want to know about the flaws in his school's defenses.

GILBERTUS ALBANS SLEPT little. The life-extension treatment he'd received long ago made his bodily processes more efficient, and thereby gave him additional hours to use his mind for important things.

The Headmaster regularly monitored the news that trickled in through the Butlerian censors, and did his best to obtain secondary sources as well, through coded reports that didn't always say what Manford Torondo wanted others to hear.

Over the decades, Gilbertus had pondered recording his own memoirs for posterity. He wished he could go into his internal Memory Vault, recapture every detail, and leave an extensive record of everything he had done and experienced, not just his years as a slave of the thinking machines but also his later years among the humans, his peaceful existence as a farmer on bucolic Lectaire, his beautiful lost love Jewelia, and then his dedication to his Mentat School.

Yes, his life was a story worth telling. He had lived on Corrin for a century, then another eight decades among free humans. He was more qualified than any other living person to judge and compare the conflicting viewpoints. But he didn't dare write down such dangerous facts. He shielded even thoughts about his background, because someone with special skills of observation might detect flickers of his true mindset.

Because he couldn't sleep, Gilbertus was awake when an unexpected visitor arrived at his office. The Headmaster was working with the door closed, but had left the additional security systems deactivated. The Erasmus core remained hidden in its cabinet.

Gilbertus sat at his desk, reviewing the academic records of his trainees. Administrator Zendur had passed along his assessment of which ones were most qualified to go out into the Imperium and offer their Mentat abilities. When he looked up, he did not at all expect to see Draigo Roget entering the office.

Draigo wore a smile as he closed the door behind him. "Headmaster, I've missed our discussions. Despite everything, I never stopped thinking of you as a friend."

Gilbertus struggled to suppress his astonished reaction. Another person might have sounded a security alarm, but he found himself fascinated. "You never cease to surprise me, Draigo—though I question your wisdom in coming to Lampadas. I was startled, but pleased, when you escaped certain defeat at Thonaris. You know the Butlerians put a price on your head?"

"Just as Direceur Venport has a price on Manford's head. Those men would love to kill each other. You won fairly at Thonaris, and I survived only because of unexpected assistance from Norma Cenva."

"A Mentat must factor the unexpected into his projections," Gilbertus said. "And your arrival this evening is most definitely unexpected."

Draigo stepped closer to the desk and studied Gilbertus in silence. Because of the late hour and his solitude, Gilbertus had not bothered to apply the makeup he used to increase his apparent age. A mistake. *Too late now.* Draigo had already noticed something.

"I am healthy, although I probably consume more melange than I should," Gilbertus said.

Draigo glanced at the pyramid chess board set up on a side table, and the antique clock on the wall. He took a seat and looked across the desk at the Headmaster. "You taught me everything I need to know, and I am training Mentats on my own, away from any Butlerian influence."

Gilbertus paused to assess that revelation. "You've replicated my teaching methods for Josef Venport?"

"I train my Mentats for the future of humanity, but I'm not as skilled a teacher as you." He sounded defensive. "Headmaster, we are engaged in a war of civilizations. As human *computers*, we can do what the thinking machines once did, but as *humans* we can't fall into the same trap of hubris. You and I agree—we dare not let ourselves become too dependent on the technology that once enslaved us." Draigo's expression hardened. "Nor should we let ourselves fall into a pit of ignorance and destruction that harms everyone. In their own way, the Butlerians are as dangerous as the thinking machines were. They destroy human achievement and congratulate themselves while doing it."

Gilbertus thought for a long moment. "I agree."

Draigo's dark eyes flashed. "Then why do you support them, sir? They are nothing more than a mob, and will continue to cause harm. I know your support for Manford Torondo has always been reluctant. If you were to publicly question the foundation of the Butlerian order, people would listen to you. You should denounce him."

"Yes, I *should*, but I would not survive if I did." He shook his head. "Manford is not interested in questions or debate, and dissent is punishable by death."

"Then why stay here? Join us! If you and I fought side by side, we would be invincible—and could assure the advancement of human civilization. Manford's narrow-minded lynch mob would fade away into the darkness of recorded history, where it belongs."

Gilbertus quelled a smile at his former student's vehemence. "But would they? I have run Mentat projections, extrapolated from knowledge of the present as well as all the nuances of history. I don't believe victory would be as simple as you suggest."

"I didn't say it would be simple, Headmaster. I said that you and I are strong enough and intelligent enough to win any upcoming battles."

Gilbertus remembered how much he had relied upon Draigo when he became a teaching assistant. He was proud of the young man's accomplishments. He missed their dialogues. . . .

He knew Erasmus must be eavesdropping on the conversation. Some time ago, the Headmaster had considered revealing the robot's memory core to Draigo.

That secret was a burden he had borne alone for far too long now. If anything ever happened to him, Erasmus would be completely unprotected, vulnerable. He didn't dare let the independent robot be lost.

"You should at least listen to Directeur Venport," the former student said. "He is a brilliant man, a visionary who has made truly great advancements for humankind through technology and commerce."

Gilbertus was impressed. "Your point is indisputable, Draigo. Even so, I must decline." He considered giving the Erasmus core to Draigo to take back to Kolhar. For safekeeping. Directeur Venport would certainly protect it—but he couldn't bear to part with his close friend and mentor, not yet. And Draigo . . . he wasn't sure if he should trust him completely.

Draigo shook his head in dismay. "You make me sad, Headmaster. I hoped I could reason with you, make you realize that you're harming our future by cooperating with the Butlerians—it doesn't matter whether your cooperation is tacit or overt."

In response, Gilbertus made a lackluster argument. "But by staying here and working within the Butlerian system, by having the ear of Manford Torondo, I can make subtle but important changes from within."

Draigo scowled. "You tell yourself that, but has it worked so far, or are you just rationalizing?" The student turned and slipped out of the Headmaster's office before Gilbertus could reply. But both of them knew what the answer was.

*There is no such thing as perfect security. Any protection can be defeated.*

—teaching of the Ginaz School for Swordmasters

P rince Roderick went on a brief hunting trip in the woods of the northern continent; he wanted time away from the city, the politics, and the memory of the rampage festival. Haditha had taken the other children to stay with her sister in a distant city, needing to find her own peace. Back in their quarters, Nantha's belongings remained where they had always been, because Haditha couldn't bear to pack them away, nor would she allow anyone else to do it.

The scar of their lost daughter would always be with them, but Roderick needed to find a way to function. Though he would never admit it aloud, he knew the Imperium depended on him. Salvador couldn't rule by himself.

For his few days of escape out in the quiet forest, Roderick was accompanied by three friends, one of whom owned a small lodge. The simple accommodations were rugged enough that even a Butlerian would have found nothing to object to. After the mayhem in the streets, Roderick found the lodge relaxing. He cleared his mind and tried to think of nothing other than hunting Salusan pheasants and roasting them over a fire.

But he couldn't forget the terrible loss of Nantha for long, or his duties to Salvador, and all too soon he had to return to the Imperial Palace. Despite the brief respite, his heart wasn't healed.

Arriving back in Zimia, he encountered an immediate reminder of why he had left. In the large central square outside the Hall of Parliament, Grand Inquisitor Quemada and his Scalpel team were putting on a public demonstration while Imperial soldiers stood guard over the proceedings. The Emperor had decided that showing off the skills of his interrogators would be an excellent deterrent to crime. Roderick did not approve, considering Dorotea's subtle Truth-sayer skills much more effective . . . but his brother insisted on the show.

A boisterous crowd had gathered to watch, and Roderick felt a knot form in his stomach. The imposing, black-haired Quemada was already on his fourth victim.

After what had happened to poor Nantha, Roderick would have liked to see Manford Torondo undergo such an ordeal. All the violence he had sparked, all those innocent lives lost . . . He closed his eyes and imagined.

As a beefy woman in an Imperial army uniform led him toward the Emperor's observation suite, she explained what was going on, assuming Roderick would want to know. "Four petty criminals so far, my Lord. The Grand Inquisitor's team has subjected them to various forms of 'coaxing.' Ancient methods, but they are all quite effective. Entertaining, too."

Glancing through a wide window, Roderick saw a portable strappado out in the plaza, along with a spiked chair, compression helmets, and a medieval rack. Far from being modern and streamlined, each item was a functional museum piece from distant history with a brutish design. It was to create an intimidating effect, Roderick knew. After intensive training at the Suk Medical School, the Scalpel practitioners could wring agony from their captives using nothing more than a pebble or a stylus.

Three men lay on the stone pavement off to one side, bleeding and trembling, having been released from the interrogation machinery after confessing to the inquisitor's satisfaction. A fourth man was having his fingers and toes crushed one at a time, which made him scream horrendously; so far, though, he had not admitted anything.

Prince Roderick grimaced, not certain what he found more offensive—the barbaric display or the cheering of the crowd. He hurried up to the Emperor's suite, hoping to talk sense into Salvador, to warn him against playing into the barbaric madness embraced by the Butlerians. Was his brother creating a culture in which vicious destruction became ordinary and expected?

Roderick thought that Directeur Josef Venport was fighting on the correct side of the divide—reason versus violence. Salvador would have to be strong to stand up to the swelling antitechnology movement, but he was deathly afraid of the Butlerians. Roderick would discuss the matter with him in private and advise the best course of action, seeking to bolster his courage and strengthen his resolve.

Quemada's latest victim screamed and then slumped from the excruciating pain. Irritated that he hadn't answered all the questions, the Grand Inquisitor called for another subject, to a rising swell of cheers. This seemed as mad as the Butlerian rampage festival. Emperor Salvador should have known better than to incite the crowds, which could so easily get out of control. Unable to bear more of the harsh scene, Roderick entered the suite.

Salvador received him with a warm smile that made him uncomfortable. The Emperor wore one of his assorted lavish military uniforms, this one crimson and white, with a golden lion on the lapel. "Ah, I'm so glad you joined me. I was about to go out on the balcony while I have my coffee. I have some fresh melange from Arrakis, if you want it."

The loud cheers outside tightened the knot in Roderick's stomach, making him think of Manford's murderous mob as they rampaged through the city. "I'd rather stay inside, if you don't mind. That reminds me of the tortures the thinking machines inflicted upon us. We're supposed to be better than machines."

Salvador looked disappointed by the comment. He stood at the window, gazing out at the crowd, then slumped casually on a sofa inside the office. "Have your way, then." He motioned for a female aide to deliver the coffee service to a small sitting area on the right of his goldenwood desk.

Roderick said in a heavy voice, "You once told me you wanted justice to be an enduring legacy of your reign. What's happening out there in the plaza is not justice."

"The crowd seems to like the show. It's a pressure release for them." As Salvador spoke, the throng roared and cheered.

"But it's adding fuel to flames. Once a crowd gets a taste for violence, they'll burn down half the city and kill anyone who happens to be in the way, including little girls and their nannies."

Salvador blinked. "Ah, of course! I'm sorry. I didn't think how it would remind you of what happened to your daughter."

"Everything reminds me of Nantha." Roderick clenched his hands into fists at his sides as he struggled to maintain a professional demeanor. His brother needed him. He said, "There are other ways to get information, Sire. A Truthsayer could extract the answers far more efficiently—and reliably—than this torture. Those victims out there confess only because of the pain, not because they cannot hide their lies."

Salvador sipped his coffee, added more melange. "My Grand Inquisitor serves his purpose, too. No one is going to cower in terror of a black-robed woman who simply stands there and listens in silence."

"Nevertheless, by listening in silence, Sister Dorotea discovered the fraud perpetrated by House Péle."

Salvador sniffed. "Quemada got more information out of Blanton Davido afterward."

"And killed him in the process. Dorotea could have obtained the same information, and more, and we would have had a living hostage."

"Or a convicted prisoner, headed for execution."

Roderick did not want to disagree. "Either way, Omak Péle might not have been frightened into going renegade. I advise that we rely more on Sister Dorotea and her Truthsayers for interrogations, and avoid these public displays of cruelty."

"What would be the fun in that?" Salvador muttered in a voice so quiet that Roderick barely heard him. Then he spoke louder. "Perhaps a challenge! We should test the two of them, have Sister Dorotea question Quemada with her methods . . . and then let my Grand Inquisitor question her in return."

"He would kill her!"

Salvador waved a finger. "Not if he knows it would displease me."

Roderick thought about Dorotea's strength and focus; as a Reverend Mother, she had achieved a level of bodily control that Roderick could not begin to understand. Maybe his brother was right. He remained uneasy that Dorotea's orthodox Sisters so openly sided with the violent Butlerians, but surely a Truthsayer's interrogation had to be less barbaric than this.

The Emperor summoned his aide again, smiling at Roderick. "Let's have a *civilized* demonstration of their respective abilities. We'll serve tea and little spice cookies."

AN HOUR LATER, Sister Dorotea swept into the observation suite in her characteristic black robe, but her brown hair looked freshly cut; as always, she had a *presence* about her. She gave both the Emperor and Roderick curt nods, and then her unflinching gaze settled on Quemada, who sat in a straight-backed chair. The Grand Inquisitor looked very uncomfortable, only minimally cleaned up after his efforts in the square. Outside, at Roderick's request, Imperial guards had dispersed the unhappy crowd. Maintenance workers were dismantling the props and spraying down the interrogation equipment.

Dorotea and Quemada had been told why they were summoned. Roderick noted that the Grand Inquisitor seemed oddly intimidated by the Truthsayer; he was obviously more comfortable asking questions than answering them.

Salvador gestured impatiently. "Very well, let's get on with it."

"Considering the likely results of Quemada's handiwork, Sister Dorotea will go first," Roderick said.

Dorotea stood tall and stared at the Grand Inquisitor, not saying anything, not asking anything. As moments passed, Quemada grew increasingly red-faced and indignant. Several times his mouth quivered as if he were about to say something, but he clamped his lips shut. He held Dorotea's gaze, undoubtedly imagining what he would inflict on her when he got his turn.

Finally, the Emperor lost patience. "Ask him what you're supposed to ask."

"He is already speaking to me without words, Sire." She paused for a moment longer, then stepped closer to Quemada. "We both seek the truth. Why do you need so much violence to ply your trade? Your training from the Suk School should be sufficient to inflict pain without resorting to physical damage or death. Are you unskilled, or do you enjoy hurting people? Is that why you look forward to going to work every day?"

Quemada half rose, but forced himself to sit back down. "I do only what is necessary."

"Necessary?" She leaned forward like a bird that had spotted a bright shiny object. "Many of your subjects die under questioning—a great many. Yet a skilled Suk practitioner should be able to keep even the most grievously injured victim alive. Why do you find it necessary to kill them? Is it intentional?"

"I obtain the information the Emperor requires."

"But he doesn't require you to kill them. In fact, their deaths are often inconvenient. Blanton Davido should not have died so quickly under your questioning." She watched him like a specimen under high magnification.

"I derive the truth the Emperor needs."

Dorotea drew back, catching her breath. "Ah, but I see much more than that, more than just the enjoyment of inflicting pain. I did not recognize that you were being pragmatic, and I apologize for thinking you were a sadist—that's not it at all. This is a practical matter, isn't it? I see now that you find the victims *useful* in secret ways. And profitable." Her eyes flicked back and forth, and Roderick noticed a changing demeanor in the Grand Inquisitor as she continued to speak. "When someone dies during questioning, the Emperor doesn't ask what you do with the bodies afterward." She turned to Salvador. "Do you, Sire?"

He was confused. "Of course not."

Roderick had not expected this at all.

Dorotea continued to press Quemada. "You and your Scalpel assistants dispose of the bodies personally. Is there some reason you want them? How do you benefit from corpses? You kill specific people . . . or you *let* them die, because . . ." She narrowed her eyes. "You're after their organs?"

"No, I—uh, I—" Thick beads of perspiration had formed on Quemada's forehead and upper lip, and his entire body was shaking. He seemed to be dissolving before their eyes.

"Tell us!" Dorotea's eyes were dark, penetrating, and almost hypnotic.

Suddenly, as if her importunate voice had broken him, Quemada began to babble. "There are those who purchase organs on the black market, Tlulaxa researchers, even Suk transplant physicians. When a person dies under questioning, my Scalpel team is there to remove the organs. No waste, and others benefit." Perspiration poured from him. "It is not forbidden! I've done nothing illegal."

"But you have a financial incentive in letting them die."

Quemada glanced at a horrified Salvador with eyes that burned with guilt, shame, and a rage that he could not conceal.

Dorotea stepped back, looking exhausted. She turned to the Emperor. "I can tell he is keeping other secrets, Sire, but I trust that was a sufficient demonstration?"

Roderick said in a mild voice, "You'll notice, brother, that Sister Dorotea determined that information in only a few minutes, without even touching the man, without so much as one crushed finger or ripped-away nail. And he is still alive for you to treat as you wish. I'd say the Truthsayer's methods are far superior."

Salvador trembled with excitement. "You certainly made your point, brother. And if my Grand Inquisitor is hiding even more from me, we shall learn exactly what it is. It's only fitting, however, that his own Scalpel practitioners extract the information from him. In public."

The Grand Inquisitor writhed and pleaded. "Ask Empress Tabrina what you want to know. Get the truth out of *her*!"

Salvador raised his eyebrows, then turned to Roderick, even more pleased. "Oh, we will."

*History often distorts through a lens of fear. After disregarding the bombastic nonsense about General Agamemnon and the original Titans, I realize that those cymeks could have been great, if hubris had not destroyed them.*

—PTOLEMY, Denali Laboratory Journals

The shimmer of sunlight on dunes dazzled Ptolemy as he emerged from the landing vehicle. Yes, these wastelands of Arrakis would make an excellent testing bed for his new cymeks.

As Ptolemy had requested, their private VenHold craft had landed out in the open desert, bypassing the main spaceport so there would be no record of its presence. The Mentats at the Combined Mercantiles headquarters had made all the necessary arrangements. Directeur Venport intended to keep this work secret for now, but when Ptolemy finally unleashed the cymeks against Manford Torondo's savages, everyone would tremble before these gigantic machines.

He felt a chill that the desert heat could not dispel. His mind filled with a wishful vision of the hateful rabble leader whimpering in terror as he watched the nightmarish mechanical walkers smashing his panicked barbarians and tossing their shattered bodies like bloody dolls.

He coughed, then attempted to cover the sound, not wanting to appear weak in front of the Directeur. Ptolemy's lungs had not stopped aching and burning since his exposure to Denali's atmosphere. The research facility's doctors had performed a deep scan, verifying that he had suffered significant pulmonary scarring. They assured him that with treatment, he could regain his health. But his work was all that mattered to him, and he could not take time for the extensive cellular restructuring the treatment would require.

Inside the domed medical facility, Administrator Noffe had taken care of him for weeks, making sure his friend ate regularly and took his medication. Although Ptolemy did not like the way the inhalant dulled his thoughts, the pain had an even more adverse effect, distracting him from what he needed to do. . . .

Their craft rested on a safe ridge of rock that overlooked an ocean of dunes, where the test would take place. As wind whipped sand around, Ptolemy stood with the others, but alone with his thoughts, ignoring the conversation around him. He wished Elchan were there, but his friend could no longer speak to him, because he'd been murdered by the Butlerians.

"It takes a powerful weapon to pierce the armor of ignorance," Ptolemy muttered.

"What did you say?" Directeur Venport turned from talking with his Mentat, Draigo Roget, who had accompanied them at the last minute. Venport had been preoccupied with business since his recent address to the Landsraad, but he was eager to witness the new cymek demonstration.

Ptolemy gave him a stiff smile. "Sorry, sir. I was distracted by minutiae. This is an important day for me." He struggled to subdue another fit of coughing. This arid air exacerbated the pain in his damaged lungs.

"An important day for all of us," said Draigo Roget.

Ptolemy paid little attention to broader politics in the Imperium; he focused only on his part of the game. He had been involved with the design of the new cymeks, modifying the mobility systems, neural linkages, and thoughtrode controls, including sensors implanted in his own body. With this enhanced connectivity, the new Titans were much improved from the old enemies of humanity. These cymeks with proto-Navigator brains could have torn General Agamemnon to shreds!

For much too long, Ptolemy had felt small and insignificant, powerless in the face of difficult events. With his new cymeks, he had changed. He felt mighty just thinking about his army. Technically, it was *Directeur Venport's* army, but Ptolemy knew these cymeks better than anyone else did; no other person had his love for each mechanical walker, and for the disembodied, mutated brains that operated them.

Directeur Venport waited while a team of workers emerged from the shuttle to set up observation chairs so that he, Ptolemy, and the Mentat could watch the show.

Before the test began, Ptolemy explained, "Denali is a harsh place for humans, but cymek systems can withstand the poisonous air. Here on Arrakis, the extreme environment poses different challenges—the aridity, sand, static electricity, and uncertain ground."

"And the sandworms," Draigo added.

"We agree it's a good place to test," Venport said. "Now launch your cymeks. I want to see them in action. Give me your commentary as we watch."

eight captured whales; they were small ones, but with rare brown and silver fur. When one of the beasts crashed onto the long deck after being dumped from the nets, it writhed until the crew fired poison darts into its brain.

Vor and the other men set to butchering the creatures on the deck, hard and filthy work. Blood ran into gunwall channels and out onto the water, attracting a flurry of torpedo sharks. The whale innards reeked of everything foul Vor could imagine, but he endured the stench. His fellow crewmen teased him about the contorted faces he made, but he just laughed in response.

After stripping off the thick pelts, the crew cut and separated the pieces well into the afternoon, tossing undesirable scraps overboard for the waiting sharks. The blubber would be rendered, and the rest would be sold as whale meat, a staple of the Lankiveil diet.

Vor indicated the increasing wind and waves, and Vergyl agreed. "We'd better head back to port."

The Harkonnen patriarch manned the helm and steered the boat across the choppy, cold waters, heading toward the stark fjords. Vor hosed down the deck, then helped roll the sheets of fur and secure the lockers of fresh meat.

After working with Vergyl and his crew, getting to know the man's wife and their son Danvis, Vor almost felt like a member of the family. They had been kind to him, openly grateful for the hours of work he provided without asking for pay. They accepted Vor's story that he was doing research. He dreaded to think how everything would change if they discovered his true identity.

Danvis occasionally joined them on the whaleboats, but his parents sheltered him, hesitant to expose their only remaining son to danger. He was very unlike Griffin. One day Danvis would become the noble leader of Lankiveil, but Vor wondered if the young man would be easy pickings for the rival family operations. Or maybe life would toughen him. Since Vorian himself did not age, he could return to Lankiveil years hence to check on Danvis, give him the support he needed.

He sighed: Yet another generation of lives for which he felt responsible, yet another set of obligations. But after spending time here incognito, he felt more convinced that this was something he needed to do, to right the foundering ship of the Harkonnen family. He could not make them forgive him, but he could give them the financial stability they needed. . . .

The engines made a loud droning noise as the whaleboat plied the waves. Vor wiped his forearm across his brow and thought back on times he'd worked fishing boats on Caladan, the sweet moments he'd spent with Leronica—several lives ago.

A drizzle became a downpour as Vergyl throttled down the engines, working his way into the sheltered fjord. Even through the mist, Vor could see the village on the shore. He heard the happy chatter of the crew as they looked forward to hitting the tavern for a round of local ale. The cold rain bothered none of them; in fact, the fresh downpour washed away some of the odor of butchered whales that hung about the ship.

That evening, while the other crewmembers were drinking, and Vergyl returned to spend the night with his family, Vor dispatched a coded courier message aboard a departing transfer ship. The instructions would go to one of his financial contacts on Kolhar, the nearest planet with a bank that held part of his distributed fortune. He had the means to make a difference here, and he saw it as a way to lighten the shadow on his conscience. He instructed his banker to pay off the Harkonnen family debts in full, anonymously.

The sudden transfer of wealth would allow the Harkonnens to repair their whaling fleet, rebuild the spaceport, and be more competitive in shipping the harvested fur to offworld markets. Then they could resist the Bushnell incursions . . . without ever learning the identity of their secret benefactor.

Vorian Atreides intended to be long gone before the funds arrived.

He could not possibly make everything right, but this was a start. In the morning, he would tell Vergyl and Sonia he needed to leave Lankiveil, his "research project" completed. And he would be on his way somewhere else.

He had been thinking a great deal about Caladan. Maybe he would make his way back there. . . .

*Every person can be manipulated—and all of us are, in one manner or another.*

—wisdom of the Cogitors

The Mother Superior moved with surprising stealth for a woman of her age and frailty. She managed to startle Valya outside between two of the main school buildings. "I've been watching you closely, and you don't seem saddened by your sister leaving."

Valya calmed herself, kept her expression flat and unreadable. "She has been gone for weeks already, Mother Superior. I am not her keeper—and I am following your advice to control my emotions. I should not appear sad or disappointed that she made her own choice."

Raquella seemed amused. "On the contrary, you seemed pleased by her departure—even eager to have her go. I find this odd, since you were the one who indoctrinated Tula into the Sisterhood. Do you consider her a failure now that she has given up on us?"

"No, Mother Superior—not a failure. And she hasn't given up. Tula will succeed in whatever she attempts, though perhaps not in any way we anticipated. I have high hopes for her."

Walking away from the main school grounds, the two women worked their way up a steep and rugged path along Laojin Cliff, a wooded hillside with an abrupt drop-off. It was the highest point in the vicinity, and Raquella liked to take the rugged walk at least once a week. The Mother Superior insisted on demonstrating that she was still physically and mentally fit to lead. Today, even Valya found it difficult to keep up with the Mother Superior's pace.

"The loss of my brother Griffin was a tremendous blow," Valya admitted as she kept up with Raquella. She cast her gaze down. "Having Tula back will make my parents and Danvis very happy."

Raquella paused on the trail to give her a hard look. "You may be a Reverend Mother, but I can still read you. Are the goals of the Sisterhood paramount in your mind now? Above those of your family?"

Valya always felt uncomfortable trying to explain herself. "I have two families— House Harkonnen and the Sisterhood. I can be loyal to both."

"A diplomatic answer, but potentially problematic."

"I refuse to view the universe in simplistic terms."

Raquella's papery lips formed a genuine smile. "Perhaps that suggests a future leadership role for you."

Valya fought to control the surge of excitement. Certainly the Mother Superior realized that Valya was the best choice to follow as her successor, to continue rebuilding the school. Before she could press the issue, the old woman changed the subject. "I received a report from observers in the Imperial Palace. Sister Dorotea has made herself invaluable as Emperor Salvador's Truthsayer, and he has allowed her to begin training her own new acolytes on Salusa." She let out a long, rattling sigh. "The splinter group of orthodox Sisters will have no incentive to reunite with us. I had so hoped for . . ." She shook her head. "Dorotea is my own granddaughter."

Sister Fielle approached from the ridge above, negotiating her way down the slope along a steep zigzag trail. When Raquella waved for the Sister Mentat to join them, Valya was disappointed to lose an important private moment with the Mother Superior. Nevertheless, she shifted her thoughts, concentrated on solidifying her efforts to make Fielle an ally.

The young Sister Mentat shared greetings, giving Valya an unreadable smile, and the three fell into step together on the trail, with Raquella setting the pace to continue the climb. The Sister Mentat didn't seem to mind returning uphill the way she had come.

Valya continued the discussion with some urgency, expecting Fielle to take her side. "Our faction is stronger than Dorotea's, Mother Superior. We are the better organization with a greater long-term vision." She controlled the intensity in her voice. "We can also work on Truthsaying abilities here among ourselves, and I'll redouble our training in new combat techniques." She hadn't told the Mother Superior about her experimental new voice control. "We're in a war for our very survival, and every Sister must know how to fight, both personally and in the larger political arena. Our Sisters have to be unparalleled as fighters and as advisers."

Fielle interrupted, "But we use our minds more than our bodies. The Sisterhood is a philosophy, a way of life, and a way to better the human race."

Valya raised her voice. "And if we had learned how to fight earlier, we could have been more effective against the Emperor's troops before they slaughtered so many of us on Rossak. What if Dorotea convinces him to come to Wallach IX and finish the destruction?"

"That would never happen again," Fielle said.

Valya paused on the path, straightened her back. "I won't take that chance. I want us to become better fighters, for ourselves and for the Sisterhood."

Raquella gave her a wry smile. "You are already our best fighter."

"And I can be better still—and then I can make others better. In each Sister, and in the Sisterhood as a whole, the physical and mental must work together. Each aspect strengthens the other."

Valya turned to Fielle. "Sometimes I can be a bit abrupt because I am focused on the Sisterhood, on the grand missions and goals that the Mother Superior has laid out for us. I apologize if I seem impatient and overly intense. I am trying to do better."

Looking sideways, she saw Raquella smiling like a proud parent.

Valya spoke in a rush. After sending Tula on her mission, she had goals of her own, larger plans. "With your permission, Mother Superior, I would like to travel to Ginaz—visit the Swordmaster School and ask them to accept me as a student. Whatever I learn from them can be applied to the Sisterhood." Valya could also use those skills on behalf of House Harkonnen, perhaps even in personal combat against Vorian Atreides.

Fielle seemed confused by the suggestion, but Raquella gripped the young Sister Mentat's arm with a withered hand. "Valya's idea is interesting. You have Mentat training, and it occurs to me that we might learn much from the other great schools as well, adapting their techniques to improve our own."

Valya squared her shoulders. "Since I'm a Reverend Mother, I can learn more swiftly than others, be better. Let me take them by surprise. I'd like to observe Ginaz, absorb and adapt their fighting methods, bodily control, defenses, and how to *think* during combat. There is great strength in combining disciplines, and the Sisterhood must have strength. We will be more than a match for Dorotea's traitors."

Raquella scolded her like a child. "I may disagree with the others, but they are not traitors, just a different perspective on our teachings. Dorotea has something that we do not—a respected position close to the Emperor. She has no reason to envy us, or fear us. It would be best for our future if we could find common ground. That is what I long for most, before I die."

Valya tried to control the edge in her voice. "Dorotea should not have betrayed us in the first place, if her true loyalties lay with the Sisterhood."

"Her loyalties may be confused, but I believe she is still a true Sister in her heart." Raquella looked sad as she paused on the trail. She turned to Valya. "Just as your blood sister needed to return to your homeworld, I understand that you must go on your own journey. You have my permission to travel to Ginaz."

*Success is a matter of definitions. What is victory? What is wealth? What is power?*

— DIRECTEUR JOSEF VENPORT, VenHold internal memo

Over the years, the scientists on Denali had sent Josef Venport numerous exuberant proposals, many of which had seemed absurd and unobtainable. New shield generators, thoughtrode interfaces, mob stunners, atomic pulse-flashes, even mechanical "cricket" saboteurs.

Not wanting to place limitations on his remote think tank, he told Administrator Noffe to encourage imagination in all its forms, so long as it led to developments that could inflict harm on the Butlerians.

But this was more than he had ever hoped for.

Josef, Draigo, and Ptolemy sat under the bright desert sun watching seven mechanical walkers guided by Navigator brains. He was already impressed with what Ptolemy had produced. The fearsome machines moved with remarkable swiftness and ease. Josef smiled: Results such as this justified the fortune he had poured into the Denali research facility.

Now he had *his own* Titans.

His great-grandmother had been tortured by one of the ancient Titans, and that ordeal had transformed Norma Cenva into more than a human being. Her husband, Aurelius Venport, had devoted his life to fighting the cymeks. How ironic that Josef Venport was responsible for creating a new group of Titans that were even more powerful than their predecessors.

Ptolemy touched his earadio. "Still no sign of a worm."

"Maybe the creatures are afraid," Josef said.

"I doubt sandworms know fear, Directeur," Draigo said. "From the vibrations, the creatures would have no way of knowing these cymeks were different from a spice factory. And we were anticipating that the Holtzman field from the shields would madden at least one worm."

"I was being facetious, Mentat."

At last, a ripple rolled along under the sand, casting it up like the crest of a wave. The great worm plowed through a succession of dunes as if they were no thicker than air, moving with the speed of a projectile fired from a weapon.

Josef rose out of his observation chair. "What a monster!" Beside him, Draigo's dark eyes widened as he drank in details. Ptolemy looked both awed and terrified.

It seemed that the theories about the effect of shields on the creatures might prove correct after all.

The enraged sandworm exploded upward. As the huge maw came out of the sand, dust sheeted off its curved segments.

Inside their preservation canisters, the proto-Navigator brains did not panic. Having researched the behavior of sandworms, they positioned the walker bodies in a precise attack configuration, as if this were a military drill. Three of the cymeks switched off their shields and bounded away like jumping spiders.

The worm slammed down like a battering ram, but the agile cymeks sprang in opposite directions, their movements carefully coordinated, as if the brains were telepathically linked. Even from the distant outcropping Josef could feel the tremors as the monster dove under the sand.

Scuttling to the dune tops for a better strategic position, the seven cymeks launched artillery, hammering the sandworm's segmented body with explosion after explosion. So much dust, sand, and smoke boiled into the air that Josef could barely see.

The worm rose up again, thrashing about like an unchecked high-pressure hose. It slammed into one of the cymeks and knocked the machine body into the air, then scooped downward to swallow one of the other cymeks, Hok Evander, who was still protected by a shimmering shield.

In his observation chair, Ptolemy let out a groan as the struggling cymek vanished down the creature's gullet. Josef was surprised at his lack of objectivity. "This is a test, Dr. Ptolemy. One must expect losses."

The remaining five Titans redoubled their attack, shooting flames, lasbeams, and exploding shells. Although several of the worm's armored segments looked ragged and damaged, the attack only enraged the beast. It lifted itself up and then crashed down on top of two more cymeks, smashing them into the sand. The behemoth was so massive that even the walkers' enhanced armor could not protect them.

The last three Titans spread out equidistant from the worm and continued to attack. The creature let out a rumbling groan like exhaust from a starship engine.

Then, oddly, its serpentine form bulged and swelled, as if repeated detonations were occurring from its interior. A dark stain appeared on the ring segments, then smoke spurted out from a widening wound. Sizzling chemicals dripped down its tough hide.

From within the worm's digestive tract, the swallowed Titan, still shielded, unleashed explosives and deadly acid to cut its way out. The escaping cymek left timed projectiles behind, which exploded as soon as the machine walker scrambled free.

Josef chuckled, unable to tear his gaze away. Beside him, Ptolemy looked as if he might be ill at seeing so much devastation.

Mortally wounded, the worm crashed onto the sands, leaking fluids from myriad injuries, its gullet torn open. Seeing the vulnerable spot, the surviving cymeks continued to attack until the sandworm shuddered and collapsed across the flattened dunes.

Grinning, Josef turned to Ptolemy. "Most impressive!"

The scientist groaned. "But I lost three of my Titans—almost half of my finest cymeks—to destroy one worm! They were my experimental subjects, and I spent so much time and care—" Agitated, he began coughing so hard that he nearly fell out of the observation chair. "Two of them, Hok and Adem, rescued me on Denali when my life support failed."

"Don't worry, they performed well—beyond my expectations." Josef clapped him on the shoulder. "More important than that, you proved that a sandworm *can* be killed! We have the means to do it."

Ptolemy slumped in his chair, pale and uncertain, but found his resolve. "Based on this demonstration, Directeur, I shall make improvements to the walker bodies to ensure that the others are more protected." The churned sand looked as if it had been the site of an aerial bombardment. "The Navigator brains for the next batch of Titans will have better data for increased performance." He looked deeply sad.

Suddenly, with an eruption that flung gouts of sand in all directions, a second sandworm lurched out of the dunes.

The creatures were suspected to be territorial, but the Mentat had already suggested that this might be a contested zone. Surprised by the new monster, the Titans could not react in time. The second worm smashed one cymek in its first blow, swept two other walker bodies away, and swallowed the fourth.

Ptolemy fell to his knees from the chair in deep despair. "I can't believe it, I can't believe it." All lost. Xinshop, Yabido, all seven of his elite force. Tears streamed down his dusty cheeks.

The first sandworm, the dying one, continued to quiver and twitch on the sand. The second eyelessly regarded its rival, uninterested in the ruined cymeks or the distant VenHold observers. For long moments, the creature loomed over the severely damaged body of the dead worm, and then glided out onto the open dunes from which the first worm had come, claiming the territory for itself.

On the rock outcropping, VenHold workers hurried out of the landed spacecraft, folded up the observation chairs, and prepared to depart.

Ptolemy continued to stare at the battleground. "They're all gone. Every one of our finest test subjects. I . . . I still have much work to do."

But Josef felt exhilarated. "Don't be downcast—that was tremendous. And you have plenty more proto-Navigator brains to work with. Ah, just imagine what those cymeks could do against the Half-Manford. We'll need more of your creations, many more, and I authorize you to build them."

He urged the research scientist back into the shuttle. "You're going to help me defeat our enemies, Dr. Ptolemy. Your cymeks will prove invaluable, both here on Arrakis and in battles against the barbarians." He pondered for a moment longer. "And, if it should ever come to this, they will fight on our side in a war to take control of the entire Imperium."

Human imagination is a powerful thing. It can be a sanctuary from difficult times, a catalyst to change society, or the impetus to create marvelous works of art. On the other hand, an overabundance of imagination can inspire paranoia that impairs one's ability to interact with reality.
—Suk School Manual, *Psychological Studies*

Erasmus said into Anna's ear, "Do you like my voice? It should sound familiar."

She paused, hesitated, then gasped. "Hirondo! My darling, is that you?"

The robot was pleased that he had matched it closely enough, and Anna Corrino's imagination smoothed over any inaccuracies. The Mentat School had access to many records, but without large computer databases, Erasmus had experienced difficulty finding what he needed. Finally, he'd discovered a small report about the scandal at the Imperial Court in which a palace chef had disgraced the Emperor's sister with their affair. The report had included no more than a snippet of audio—a panicked Hirondo protesting his innocence—which gave Erasmus little to work with. Also, the stress in the young man's voice had changed the timbre. Erasmus did his best to adjust the pitch.

"I can be part of your memories of Hirondo." Erasmus spoke in the false voice, trying to manufacture a soothing tone. "I will always be here, right beside you, inside your mind. I'll never leave you . . . so you can tell me everything."

Erasmus was going to enjoy this. And he actually found it . . . pleasing? . . . that she responded with such joy. After her ordeal with the sapho-unleashed memories, he found it fascinating to pretend to console her, as a necessary part of satisfying his own curiosity. He could learn many details of humanity from her, a different perspective from what he had learned from Gilbertus over many years, but the next step would be even better, a technological enhancement that would give him a closer, and permanent, connection with her.

The independent robot had spread his tendrils throughout the Mentat

School complex, extending his reach even though he had no physical body. Thanks to the many thinking-machine specimens that had been stored in a sealed vault "for study," Erasmus had raw materials for his use. Over a long, slow period, he had subtly utilized deactivated combat meks, along with isolated computer minds and automated devices, all of which he used to construct hundreds of miniature drone robots.

The first one was the size of a human hand; in turn, that device built a smaller machine, which then constructed an even smaller mechanism. Finally, the drone robots were able to use near-microscopic scraps to reproduce perfect miniaturized copies of themselves. With very little computing power, the drones merely followed the guidance Erasmus transmitted, and they did amazing work threading conduits throughout the buildings, implanting spy-eyes, diverting power and expanding invisible power grids, even dropping tracers onto insects and swamp creatures so that his observation network expanded into the tangled sangroves.

His masterpiece was a tiny implanted device, a new spy-eye and listening device, a tiny silver robot the size of Anna's smallest fingertip. It didn't look like a robot at all, but a beautiful insect.

Talking to her through the minuscule speakerpatches near her bed, he explained, "This is my special companion, Anna. It will snuggle inside your ear canal and let us communicate whenever you need to hear from me."

Trusting him completely, she placed the small silver robot next to her ear, and the insectlike machine crawled inside to where it could touch her auditory nerve and transmit signals. Erasmus wished he could read her thoughts, but this was the next best thing.

"I knew you'd come back to me, Hirondo," she said, sighing.

"I have always lived within you," he answered, not wanting to disillusion her. "And now we can be together always. I am your closest, most loyal friend—don't ever forget that." He realized that, even though this was all just a grand experiment, the statement might be true—Anna had no other close friends.

Erasmus worried that she would speak aloud to him as she mingled with the Mentat students. But Anna Corrino was already considered odd, and her quiet mutterings would only enhance that impression.

The young woman walked along the corridors and across walkways to the observation deck and looked out at the sangrove thickets that made the near lakeshore an impenetrable maze. "When you're this close to me, Hirondo, I love you even more. We can remember things together, plan for our future together."

Erasmus was surprised, but pleased. *Love.* The human emotion had always eluded him, despite his many attempts to understand its complexities. He and Gilbertus had a relationship of mutual affection in which the human called him

"Father," but that was quite different from the feelings Anna still had for her lost lover. Now Erasmus would have the opportunity to explore the emotion much more closely.

Several nights ago, while spying through the cleverly concealed surveillance system, Erasmus had watched with great interest when Draigo Roget presented his case to Gilbertus. Draigo was like a prodigal son returning home, but it was Gilbertus who had gone astray. . . .

After the lynching of former machine sympathizers, Erasmus thought Gilbertus might be wise to flee while he was still able to do so. Draigo would make sure the two of them were welcomed among like-minded people. Erasmus feared that the Headmaster could not keep up the façade much longer. But Gilbertus wouldn't leave his precious school. He seemed to care more for the institution than for his own life.

Whenever the Mentat School celebrated the anniversary of its founding, some students looked back at the records and found images of Headmaster Gilbertus some seventy years earlier—and the head of the school had changed far too little in all that time. Even unobservant humans could detect that, though no one had mentioned it yet. Eventually someone would ask more questions. Erasmus needed to find a way out, long before that happened. . . .

On the observation platform, Anna began to hum a tune that she said Lady Orenna had sung to her, but Erasmus's attention was suddenly diverted, jarring him away from his conversation with Anna. Inside the Headmaster's office, Gilbertus had just removed the memory core from its hidden storage.

Rather than dividing his focus, the robot whispered to Anna through the tiny device in her ear. "I'm going to be quiet for a while so that we can enjoy each other's company, but I won't leave you, my darling. I'll never leave you, I promise."

Through a spy-eye, Erasmus saw Anna smile as she stared out at the swamps. Then he shunted his awareness to the Headmaster's office.

GILBERTUS STARED AT the exposed gelsphere and its faint glow. During his years on Corrin, he'd been able to watch the robot's flowmetal face. Although Erasmus had never been good at mimicking human expressions, Gilbertus could at least interpret his mentor's mood (though the robot insisted that he had no "moods").

"I've noticed recent changes in the behavior of Anna Corrino," Gilbertus said. "She talks to herself and smiles more often—something is different about her."

"I did that," Erasmus said. "She's a bright subject, but I've nudged her, guided her thoughts. One day, I even gave her sapho."

The Headmaster hesitated as he processed this revelation. "Sapho? I kept those samples locked in the medical dispensary."

"I had her remove one vial for an important experiment. Her response was enlightening, and I learned much about her past and her emotions."

"You shouldn't have done that. Did you harm her mind?"

"Of course not. The sapho enhanced her memories and allowed her to talk about difficult events that she had repressed. It was therapeutic, I'm sure. You saw yourself that Anna is happier, talks more. Sapho helped unlock her mind."

"Please don't give her any more." Gilbertus sat down at his desk, deciding to put the other sapho samples under tighter security to keep the robot away from them.

Erasmus said, "Why don't you use the remaining samples on other students? Study the effects. The drug enhances focus, which would be beneficial to Mentats."

"They can achieve that through the mental disciplines I teach."

"But sapho could create an even more intense focus. You should experiment with it."

"One day, perhaps. Right now it is critically important that I can give a favorable report about Anna's improvement to Roderick and Salvador Corrino. I want her cured—I want her normal." Gilbertus knew that if Anna Corrino's mind could be repaired, his school would forever receive the blessing—and protection—of House Corrino.

The robot remained silent for a long moment, then said, "I know how to cure her, but I have no intention of doing so. If she were to become *normal*, she would be far less interesting to me. I enjoy her as she is."

Gilbertus leaned closer to the exposed memory core. "But curing her has been our priority with her from the beginning."

The simulated voice was erudite and distant, exactly as it had been when Erasmus conducted his experiments with hundreds of human slaves at a time. "*Your* priority, perhaps, my son—but I see her as my very special laboratory subject, a unique window into the human mind such as I've never had before. Since I still have no physical body, I am unable to perform other experiments to satisfy my curiosity. I am left to conduct experiments that are within my capabilities."

Gilbertus flared his nostrils. "Anna is far more than a laboratory subject. We want her cured, and we need to keep her safe."

"At one time you were just my laboratory subject, but look at what you have achieved, thanks to me."

"Yes, and I could lose it all if we make a mistake and let them glimpse who we are. The Butlerians could easily retaliate against some imagined slight. Draigo Roget's visit affected me deeply, and I . . . I have always known my position is incorrect." He paused, feeling uncomfortable to admit that. "Manford isn't convinced that I am his ally. And I worry constantly about Anna Corrino's safety, for fear of provoking the wrath of her powerful brothers. This school has defenses, but not nearly enough to fend off an assault by Imperial military forces."

"I have suggested many times that we should vanish and start a new life." Erasmus paused. "And I would like to take Anna with us."

"We'd be hunted all over the Imperium."

Using his spy-eyes throughout the room, Erasmus assessed the flicker of emotions on Gilbertus's face, how he frowned, how his eyes flicked back and forth. The robot drew an obvious conclusion. "You resent how much attention I devote to Anna Corrino."

"That's not true," Gilbertus said, too quickly.

Erasmus manufactured a chuckle. "Your reflexive response indicates otherwise. I watch Anna, and I converse with her. I keep track of everything she does."

"I am not jealous, Father. Merely viewing the larger picture. We have to—"

The memory core suddenly interrupted him, blaring his words loud enough to stress his urgency. "Anna Corrino is in need of rescue. Summon your most physically capable Mentat trainees—we must save her."

Gilbertus erupted from his desk. "Rescue? What has she done?"

"She ventured out into the dangerous swamps, unchaperoned. She is all alone out there." The robot's voice sounded genuinely concerned.

"Why would she do that?" Frantic to get out into the hall, the Headmaster began to shut down the security systems that safeguarded his main office. "She could be killed!"

"It is consistent with her previous patterns of behavior. She knows that her fellow trainees test themselves in the swamps. Remember that Anna Corrino consumed poison at the Rossak School because other Sister trainees did so." As Gilbertus rushed to hide the memory core in its cabinet, Erasmus said, "My spy-eyes are widely scattered out in the swamp, but I can still see her. She has made her way deep into the sangrove thickets. I should have been monitoring her more closely. Anna Corrino cannot possibly survive out there for long."

"I'll send rescue teams." Gilbertus locked away the robot core, then burst out of his office, sounding the alarm.

THE SANGROVE BRANCHES were sharp, the curved roots like knobby knees, and the bark smooth and slippery, but Anna wove her way along like a human darning needle. It was challenging and gratifying. She didn't miss a step.

Bugs swarmed around her, some biting, others just flying in her face. Subconsciously, she counted and categorized the insects; she watched their drunken paths in the air and computed imaginary flight patterns for them. The bugs dipped and dodged aimlessly.

She worked her way through the thickets, ducking under branches, parting hairy strands of moss that dangled from above. These swamps reminded her of the fogwood tree back at the palace, Anna's beloved sanctuary—a place where only she could go. She used her mind as she touched the sangrove roots and trunks, but these swamp trees were deaf and stupid; they didn't respond to her thoughts as the special fogwood did.

She made her way through the thick network of roots, carefully balancing above the standing water, memorizing each step she took as well as every false path and dead end. It was simple enough to assemble her explorations into a map in her mind. When she finished, she would retrace her way to the Mentat School, and from then on she could move without additional complications.

She slipped on a smear of moss, but caught herself and breathed in a careful rhythm to restore her calm. The water beneath the sangrove roots wasn't deep, but she saw flashes of silver like swimming shards of glass. The channels were infested by razorjaws that would devour anything that fell into the water. When Anna's movements disturbed a nest of amphibious hoppers that leaped for other branches, some of them plopped into the water—which became a boiling fury as razorjaws devoured them.

Another person might have been frightened by the danger, but Anna wasn't worried. As long as she didn't fall from the roots, she had nothing to fear; therefore, she decided not to fall.

The reassuring voice of her friend reappeared in her ear. "Anna, it's time for you to return to the Mentat School."

"Not yet. I'm still exploring."

"I admire that you are a seeker of knowledge." The voice sounded like Hirondo, but she had eventually realized it wasn't truly him. This was her secret friend on Lampadas, someone much more faithful than Hirondo. "The Headmaster is concerned about you, Anna. The Mentats are searching now. They're coming close—you'll hear their voices soon. Respond to them. Help them find you."

She listened. For a moment, she could discern nothing more than the thrum of insects and faint ripples in the water, but then she heard distant shouts as Mentats worked their way through the sangroves.

"They shouldn't come out here," she said. "It's dangerous for them."

"They believe it's also dangerous for you."

"Then tell them I'm all right," she said.

The voice chuckled in a strange way. "I can't talk to anyone else the way I talk with you. And I . . . worry about you being alone here."

The shouts grew louder. Anna realized that the searchers were risking their lives to rescue her, even though she hadn't asked them to. She didn't want them to die. She let out a sigh. "You're right. Roderick always told me to think of other people. I'm not a selfish person."

"No, you're not," the voice agreed, and that made her feel good.

Remembering the precise safe path to take, avoiding her previous missteps and false starts, Anna darted through the sangroves, working her way back to muddy but more solid ground, where Mentat searchers could find her.

When they spotted her, they pushed forward with a surge of energy. One trainee slipped on a sangrove root, but nearby Mentats pulled him back up as the razorjaws swirled, snapping at their missed meal.

"I am here," Anna called as she made her way to the searchers, moving with more grace than they did. "I am safe."

Inside her ear, the friendly voice said, "And I intend to keep you safe for a long time."

*Every grain of sand in the desert is different, just as every planet in the Imperium is unique. But the more I see of offworld settlements, the more they look the same to me, like grains of sand.*

—TAREF, "A Lament for Shurko"

On his first arrival at the EsconTran spacedocks, fully trained for his new mission, in disguise and with a false ID, Taref quickly found employment as an interim worker on a planet called Junction Alpha. He had never heard of it before. Junction Alpha was not one of the worlds that evoked exotic images, such as Salusa Secundus did, or the glittering former machine stronghold of Corrin . . . or Poritrin, from which the Zensunni had escaped their slavery. There was no grandeur on Junction Alpha, just noise, smells, hard work, and no more satisfaction than he'd felt on Arrakis. Compared to his dreams, the young man found the rest of the Imperium rather disappointing. Junction Alpha was just a different kind of desert.

With his new background from Venport Holdings, Taref understood just how much wealth the spice operations generated—and by rights that wealth should belong to the free people of the desert, rather than to some offworld company. Instead, the Freemen chose to live like beetles under rocks, casting their gazes backward and not even trying to see the path ahead.

Taref and his friends had grown up cocky and aloof. They summoned sandworms to ride across the desert and returned to the sietch whenever they felt like it, surviving on their own, sabotaging the intrusive spice harvesters whenever possible. They had thought themselves wise in the ways of life—until the VenHold Mentat made his intriguing offer. . . .

At least now, each new planet Taref visited—even the dirty, noisy, industrial worlds—showed him how ignorant and naïve he had been all his life. In the desert, he had believed he knew everything important, but upon leaving Arrakis he had been overwhelmed by the breadth of subjects about which he knew nothing. He could never learn them all, even if he spent a lifetime trying. The horizon of wisdom was far, far beyond his reach.

At Junction Alpha, he had worked in the shipyards, keeping his eyes open for the right opportunity, as Draigo had instructed him. His first contract sabotage job had been the most difficult—not mechanically or technically, but because he was nervous, convinced that someone would realize his job skills were minimal. The entire Escon company was in turmoil, however. People whispered whenever ships disappeared . . . and EsconTran ships disappeared far too often.

Junction Alpha was a stopping-over planet, and many of the through-passengers were Butlerians. Taref had learned that their legless leader drove them into wild rampages. According to Josef Venport's vehement speech, Manford Toronlo was the greatest enemy of civilization, the most dangerous man alive. Any VenHold operative had unofficial instructions to kill him on sight, should the opportunity arise.

On Junction Alpha, Taref had altered the fuel flow in a large cargo ship and adjusted the feedback loop on a passenger craft filled with Butlerian pilgrims. The first vessel flew off and vanished somewhere in deep space. The pilgrim transport exploded in-system moments before the engines folded space. Escon-Tran couldn't hide that loss, and it was a dramatic embarrassment for the company. Since little wreckage remained, no investigator could determine that sabotage was the cause.

Taref had seen some of those fanatics board the ships, and he knew their bodies were now scattered across space. His sabotage was no longer theoretical, and a ship full of passengers had died because of his activities. He decided it wasn't his place to question.

Working alone gave him time to miss Lillis, Shurko, Bentur, Waddoch, and Chumel. After finishing their training, his friends had been separated and dispatched far away to work on spacedocks or at commercial spaceports where they could intercept EsconTran ships and complete their acts of sabotage.

After his third sabotage, Taref decided he needed to report to Kolhar. So, when the next VenHold ship arrived at Junction Alpha, he resigned from his work at the spacedocks, a common occurrence. Workers came and went quickly; for most, this was never expected to be a long-term job. Taref used one of his numerous disguises, with a corresponding ID card, and transferred to the Ven-Hold ship.

On Kolhar, he reported to the admin-tower to make his report to the Directeur. The young desert man had never met Josef Venport face-to-face, and the industrialist was an intimidating presence. Taref averted his eyes out of respect as he described his missions.

Draigo was present, remaining cool. Venport seemed happy with Taref's work, particularly the pilgrim ship that had exploded in full view of everyone. But beyond the Directeur's satisfaction and delight Taref saw a steely anger toward his competitor simmering just beneath the surface.

"Not only did your efforts remove an enemy ship, they also demonstrated how lax Escon safety is." A smile crept up beneath his thick mustache. "As an added benefit, we got rid of several hundred fanatics. You don't feel guilty about having blood on your hands, do you, young man?"

"In the desert we are no strangers to death."

"My Mentat assured me that you and your companions are not cowards. So far, your success rate has been commendable, with sixteen clean sabotages and only one loss of an operative."

Taref's head snapped up, suddenly worried. "Someone has been lost, sir?"

"Yes. One of your confederates was manipulating a navigation system, rigging a ship to become lost in the void, but somehow he got assigned aboard the ship as a replacement crewmember at the last minute. He couldn't transfer away without exposing the entire scheme, so he disappeared along with the vessel. Good man. Did his duty."

Taref's throat went dry. "Who was it?"

Venport frowned down at his desk as if searching for papers. The Mentat, standing at attention, said, "Shurko. One of the young men who came with you from Arrakis."

A chill invaded Taref's heart. Shurko, the one who hadn't wanted to come in the first place. Taref had wanted to show him the seas of Caladan, but now that imagined reward felt empty. He struggled to keep his voice firm. "So Shurko is dead? The loss of the ship is confirmed?"

"Yes, a major blow to EsconTran," Venport said, as if that made up for Shurko's death.

"Shurko," Taref whispered. He longed to see the rest of his companions, especially Lillis; they had so much to talk about, so many stories to share. And now Shurko . . . Maybe he should not have convinced his friends to come here with him. Maybe he should not have come himself.

Draigo said in an irritating monotone, "We have a new mission for you, Taref. Not in another Escon shipyard, but on Arrakis."

Distracted by his own thoughts, Taref wasn't sure he had heard correctly. "Arrakis? Why would you want me to go back there?"

Shurko would have wanted to return in a moment . . . but now he was dead, vanished out in space.

Directeur Venport tapped his fingertips on the desk surface. "You must have been glad to be rescued from that place. I hope you don't mind returning."

"I will return there if you command it," Taref said, though he felt reluctant. "What is it you need?"

"We're so pleased with your performance that we would like to recruit more Freemen. We want you to speak to the tribes on our behalf and present our offer. Find others who would like to join you in your work." The Directeur smiled. "I'm sure you can find young people eager to leave that dust pit. Aren't you glad you left yourself?"

Taref hesitated. Being away from Arrakis had opened his eyes, but many of his people would never imagine leaving the desert. If Shurko had stayed behind, he would have spent his entire life in the sietch, never straying from the desert, except maybe to Arrakis City on occasion. It would have been a small and unremarkable life, but a much longer one.

"I will ask them," Taref said, then admitted, "It will be good to feel sand beneath my feet again."

Standing beside the Directeur's desk, the Mentat touched his earadio, listened, and his normally flat expression broke into a broad smile. Josef Venport raised his bushy eyebrows, waiting for the report.

"Good news from the planet Baridge, Directeur," Draigo said. "The people have capitulated. They say they will tear up the Butlerian pledge if we trade with them again."

*If a person is properly instructed, yet continues to make mistakes, he must be severely disciplined. Such is the heavy responsibility every devout person must bear.*

—RAYNA BUTLER, last rally on Parmentier

I n his half-timbered cottage on Lampadas, Anari tended the Butlerian leader. She felt possessive of Manford and always made herself available, should he need her in any way. She wanted him to feel safe and protected, but not helpless.

In her efforts, she was aided by a meek and matronly woman who cooked meals, maintained the cottage, and performed chores. Ellonda was soft-spoken and sweet, without the slightest whisper of doubt about the Butlerian cause. The housekeeper accepted the holy teachings as a matter of course, not bothering with nuances, simply agreeing with Manford in all cases. She often hummed as she darned his clothes or helped him into bed, though Manford was perfectly capable of moving about his own quarters.

Anari passed Ellonda in the hallway, and without knocking she walked into the room where Manford was reading at his private desk. He promptly closed a book, startled. Anari noticed his jerky movements, the sweat on his brow, and immediately looked for a threat. "What's wrong?"

His tone was uncharacteristically defensive. "Nothing you need to worry about. I am merely . . . disturbed by what I just read."

Manford tried to hide the book—which, in itself, told Anari what it was, because she'd seen him with it before. "Why do you torture yourself by reading the lab journals of Erasmus?"

His shoulders slumped in shame, but he still held the volume close. "To understand our enemies. We must never forget how dangerous they are. This strengthens my resolve."

Anari sniffed. "We defeated the thinking machines. Our only enemy now is the weakness of human resolve."

"The thinking machines remain a danger. The robot Erasmus wrote, 'Given enough time, they will forget . . . and will create us all over again.' I cannot let that happen."

"I want to burn those books," Anari grumbled, "so no one can read them—and so you no longer have nightmares."

He placed the volume in a desk drawer and locked it. "I have more than enough nightmares—I've lived my life with them. They won't go away, whether or not you burn the journals in my possession. I . . . need to know what they contain."

Anari was disturbed to see him like this. He often read the laboratory journals in private, and she worried that he was increasingly obsessed with Erasmus, like a child playing with fire. Someday, for his own protection, she might slip into his office and destroy the volumes anyway. He would be angry with her, but she would be doing it for the proper reasons, to protect him.

He glanced at papers she carried, awkwardly changed the subject. "Something important?"

She placed a set of documents on his desk. "Despite your public blessing, it is clear that the ships of EsconTran are not divinely protected. You need to know just how bad it is, before you decide to travel offworld."

For weeks Anari had been studying schedules and actual witness reports of ship arrivals, as well as a complete accounting of which vessels vanished en route. There were far, far too many accidents.

He pushed the papers aside without reading them. "I'll be safe. You don't need to worry about me."

She remained firm. "You're wrong, Manford—I *do* need to worry about you. It's my main reason for existence."

Anari had read the documents carefully, a number of related reports that had been prepared for her. In one of them, Rolli Escon had admitted that some vessels had been lost due to "unforeseen difficulties," but he claimed the same thing occurred with any foldspace shipping company.

Ellonda bustled through the door carrying a tray with two cups and a pot of fragrant herbal tea. The old woman was more hurried in her movements than usual; she had been outside the office door arranging and rearranging the cups as Anari and Manford talked, waiting for an appropriate time to interrupt. Now she came in, smiling. "An evening tea to relax you before you go to sleep. You always talk about serious business, but you know it is best to settle down and not worry about everything, because God is on our side."

Even though Ellonda had cooked his meals for several years now, Anari intercepted the cup, tasted the tea, and waited for a few seconds before pronouncing it safe, finally passing it over to Manford. Ellonda did not look offended; it was a daily ritual. Anari did not fully trust anyone, when it came to protecting Manford.

He said, "Thank you, Ellonda. God is on our side, and I am His tool, with a sacred mission." He nodded. "Just as Anari's mission is apparently to worry about me."

"In all things," she said. Without question Anari would give her life for him—she would also give her *soul* to this man, and that was worth a great deal more to her. But whose side was God on? She was hesitant to point out that Ven-Hold ships had impeccable safety records. Why would God protect vessels belonging to the blasphemous Josef Venport?

Ellonda bustled around the room, setting up cups, straightening furniture, arranging pillows. She tried to remain unobtrusive, without success, but Anari turned her attention to the documents on Manford's desk. Spreading them open, she pointed to a summary page. "Until now, we feared that EsconTran's failure rate might be as high as one percent. Judging by the most recent information, I think their losses are many times that." She became implacable. "Based on my research into the matter, it is too dangerous for you to travel aboard their ships. Each time you take a foldspace voyage, there is a significant risk that you could disappear."

He shook his head. "Too many worlds need to hear my message and be reminded. Every time I speak to a wayward populace, it is *necessary*. I am required by God to make certain my people fight the temptation of machines. That is what Rayna Butler taught me, and I must show them how to be strong."

"You cannot teach them if you are killed!"

"And we will all lose if I don't press forward to complete my work."

Anari couldn't hide her frustration. "Send me in your place, then, if you don't absolutely have to be there yourself. Or send your double."

Manford frowned. "I will go where I need to go." He sighed, looking at her with great meaning in his eyes—not quite tears, but a reflection of his deep caring. "Your fears are misplaced. It is not my destiny to die a small and remote death."

THE ORTHODOX SISTER came as a gesture of good faith from Reverend Mother Dorotea at the Imperial Court, although Manford was certain Emperor Salvador knew nothing about it.

Sister Woodra arrived at dawn, dressed in conservative dark robes that concealed her figure. She was middle-aged, neither unattractive nor attractive—not that Manford bothered with such considerations. Woodra followed her faith and helped strengthen the unspoken alliance between the antitechnology Sisters and the Butlerians.

Upon arriving at Lampadas, she had convinced Deacon Harian to escort her directly to the leader's home. A scowling Anari Idaho answered the door at daybreak, not wanting Manford interrupted. The broad-shouldered Swordmaster stood in the doorway, wearing her weapon at her hip and denying them entry. "He is still asleep."

Deacon Harian bowed his shaved head in deference but refused to depart. "Apologies, but Sister Woodra comes on urgent business from Salusa Secundus. She has not adjusted to our time."

"Then she can wait. Manford does not accept intrusions into his private home, especially not at this hour. He conducts business in his headquarters offices in town. Tell her to come back later."

Though it was barely dawn, Manford had actually been up for some time, always troubled by nightmares when he slept and deep concerns when he was awake. Before the argument could escalate, he called from the back room, "Thank you, Anari. I will meet her now. She has traveled a long way."

He emerged walking on his hands. Pausing in the middle of the room, he looked up quizzically at Sister Woodra. "I've seen you on one of my visits to the Imperial Court. Your face is familiar."

She bowed formally, regarding the Butlerian leader with respect and, best of all, without pity. "We who serve there do our best to be unobtrusive, Leader Torondo. I was with Sister Dorotea when your Mentat defeated the mek in pyramid chess, and afterward when you announced the rampage festival."

Manford nodded. "Yes, I can place you now."

She bowed again. "I am here to offer my services as a Truthsayer. There are those who resist the Butlerian teachings and try to undermine your efforts at every turn."

"I am all too aware of that," Manford said. "And what, precisely, can you do for me as a Truthsayer?"

"Some Sisters have a heightened sensitivity to falsehood, which enables us to detect lies and concealments."

"A useful skill," Anari interrupted. "But you will find no liars here."

"I detect no falsehood in your voice, Swordmaster, nor in Deacon Harian's."

"And me?" Manford said. "What do you detect in me?"

"You are the most sincere person I have ever met. You believe in your cause without doubt or reservation."

With a quiet grunt, Manford turned himself about and told them to follow him into his sitting room. Without being asked, Anari settled him into a chair, where he could comfortably converse with his visitors.

Woodra's steady voice carried complete respect. "My Sisters and I understand the critical importance of your cause, Leader Torondo, but the battle is far from over. You need to know who is telling the truth and who merely pays lip service while secretly being Machine Apologists. Many have taken your pledge, yet they continue to purchase luxuries from Josef Venport."

Manford clenched his jaw, breathed in, and exhaled a long sigh. "Do not speak that man's name in this house." He noticed that Anari tightened her grip on her sword hilt.

Woodra nodded. "I would prefer never to speak it again."

Hearing that everyone was up, the housekeeper came in with a tray and proceeded to lay out a quick breakfast for the guests. "Sorry it's such an informal meal, sir, but this should hold you while I make fresh pastries."

"No need for pastries, Ellonda," Manford said. "My guests understand that a simple meal is enough, and a simple life is enough."

The old woman smiled and poured his tea first. Anari took the cup from Ellonda and tasted a sip before allowing Manford to drink.

The Butlerian leader spoke to his small audience, although he knew they were already convinced. "At first glance, we may look the same. Human beings have eyes and ears, minds and bodies. But all people don't hear the truth that is plain to the righteous. We don't all see the pure path that righteous people must follow. We don't all behave in the proper manner." His listeners remained so silent that it seemed as if they had stopped breathing. Manford gave a small nod. "Even I didn't recognize the perfect truth at first . . . until Rayna taught me. And the moment I heard it, I knew."

He closed his eyes and drifted into his memories. Humanity seemed comparatively safe now, though still scarred and weak—and struggling against the temptation of technology. Growing up, Manford had been desperately poor, and had run away from home, seeking *something*. He had no grandiose dreams, just wanted a truth to believe in. He didn't even realize he was searching until the first time he heard Rayna Butler. She was an old woman then, pale and ethereal, her skin like parchment. But she made holy pronouncements in the purest of words, reflecting her absolute purity of thought.

He heard Rayna tell a large audience that humanity's worst possible mistake would be to forget the dangers of technology. Ambitious humans had created Omnius in the first place, she said, and the cymek Titans had once been human. "Darkness lives within the human heart, and technology feeds it."

Young Manford had followed her from venue to venue, listening to more than a dozen speeches before she noticed him in the audience. She summoned the starry-eyed young man, talked privately with him, and he gave himself wholeheartedly to her cause, volunteering to be an assistant.

Though she was old enough to be his grandmother, Rayna was so beautiful and angelic that she captured his heart. He secretly scoured through archives until he located images of Rayna Butler as a young woman, and found that she had been as beautiful as he imagined. Soon Manford came to realize he was in love with her, in an unattainable way like the feelings that Anari now had for him.

After he learned what Rayna had to say, Manford built upon her teachings, and she added his contributions to her lectures, until together they developed the Butlerian philosophy into an all-encompassing way of life. Reliance on human skills rather than the crutch of machines, rigorous effort and strengthening rather than the laziness of computers. She had the charisma and passion to change the universe, to reshape the human race—until a madman's bomb tore her to pieces. Manford had thrown himself in the way, tried to protect her. In that moment, it did not occur to him *not* to give his life for her.

But he had not been swift enough, and Rayna died in his arms. He held her, barely conscious himself, not realizing that the lower portion of his own body had been blown off, and his legs were gone. . . .

"I can't do anything less than what Rayna's memory requires of me," he said now. "So many human souls are slipping through our fingers."

"Then we need to squeeze our fists tighter," Woodra said.

They finished their simple breakfast, and Manford realized he was glad to have the Truthsayer at his side. When it was time for Anari to carry him to his headquarters, a breathless young courier arrived at his doorway. "Leader Torondo! Directeur Escon has arrived with an important message for you. His ship just arrived in orbit."

Harian scowled. "That man always says he has an urgent message."

"Yes, but sometimes he really does." Manford turned to the courier. "Tell him to wait in my headquarters office. We will be there shortly."

The young man ran off down the street without catching his breath.

Anari settled Manford onto her strong shoulders, and in the early morning light she carried him through town to the Butlerian headquarters. Deacon Harian and Sister Woodra accompanied them, while Ellonda stayed behind to tidy the house.

When the party marched in, Rolli Escon was pacing Manford's office, nervous and flustered. He blurted out, "My Lord Torondo, I wanted—"

"*Leader* Torondo. I am no nobleman."

Anari Idaho deposited Manford into his high desk chair and asserted herself. "We know your vessels are unsafe, Directeur. Leader Torondo should not travel aboard them."

Escon was taken aback. "My vessels are not unsafe! I travel in them myself and will continue to do so." He looked dyspeptic at the reminder, then changed the subject to his urgent news. "I come here, sir, to tell you about Baridge! I just learned it myself. Deacon Kalifer and his governmental leaders have turned against us."

"How so?"

"The planet's population voted to set aside your pledge and bow to Josef Venport's ultimatum! They have requested an immediate shipment of supplies as soon as a VenHold ship can get there."

"How do you know this?" Anari said.

"My ships were there! We heard the deacon's transmission."

Anger welled up within Manford. "If we let Baridge get away with their hypocrisy, then other weak worlds will fall. We cannot let them change their minds! I must go to Baridge myself." He smiled tersely at Directeur Escon. "We may need to purge the entire planet—it'll be a thousand times more instructive than the lesson you saw at Dove's Haven."

Escon looked decidedly ill.

In a firm voice, Anari said, "As I said earlier, Manford, it is too dangerous for you to travel aboard a spacefolder until EsconTran improves their safety record. Let me go to Baridge in your stead. I'll take care of it personally."

Manford flushed. "No, this is too important. I have to be—"

Anari cut him off in front of the other listeners, which irritated him, but she would not sway. "I'll punish the hypocrites. And if Escon's ship should vanish with me aboard, then you can send another deputy. And another after that. But for the sake of our sacred cause, *you* must remain safe."

He did not want to argue in front of the others, nor did he want to seem petulant. "Then I'll send my double . . . just so they can see me."

"Your double is already delivering a speech on Walgis, Leader Torondo," Harian pointed out. "He was dispatched last week to hold a rally on—"

Manford waved his hand to silence the deacon.

Anari turned to Rolli Escon. "We must go to Baridge right now. Since you insist that your ships are safe, you will fly with me."

"My ships *are* safe!"

Sister Woodra watched him, then turned back to Manford. Her eyes had a strange glitter. "This man is not telling an outright lie, but he does doubt his own words."

Manford regarded the Sister. "I don't need a Truthsayer to tell me what is so obvious."

*The ideal form of mob behavior is controlled chaos.*

—MANFORD TORONDO,
comment to Anari Idaho

As a trained Sister, Dorotea did not normally dream, but when she did, the images often stuck in her mind like actual events. Sometimes she had trouble differentiating them from reality, especially with the distinct echoes from Other Memory.

She sat up in the darkness. Around her, the chamber was silent, as if holding its breath, but she had just experienced one of her more vivid, troubling dreams.

The Emperor had given Dorotea's followers austere quarters in a former military barracks near the palace. She had her own suite of rooms in an officer's section on the top level. After awakening, shaken, she rose from her bed and stood at the window, gazing across the grassy parade grounds, where she and her hundred faithful Sisters trained, along with the new acolytes they were now allowed to recruit. The parade grounds were empty, except for the night watchman's silent vehicle as he made his rounds.

She opened the window to feel a cool breeze. The air was moist and clean, suggesting that rain had fallen while she'd been deep in her dream. Moisture still clung to the air . . . just as the dream clung to her awareness, trying to send her a wordless message. Dorotea felt the dream forming a sharper reality in her mind, sculpting an opening for itself, a place for it to remain.

Before going to bed, she'd been thinking about one of the Sister Mentats back on Rossak, an aged Sorceress named Karee Marques. Before the schism, Dorotea had liked the old Sorceress, and had tried to learn from her. Karee had investigated Rossak plants and fungi, preparing poisonous distillates that could be used for the Agony. Though Dorotea assisted Karee in her pharmaceutical

work, the old Sorceress had always been reticent, leaving Dorotea to wonder what she was hiding. Karee had also been one of Raquella's closest confidantes.

*Did Karee know about the forbidden computers, the hidden breeding records? Did she know Raquella is my own grandmother?*

These questions still lingered, even now, but by voicing her suspicions to Emperor Salvador, Dorotea had touched a spark to kindling. She hadn't meant to cause such a disaster at the Rossak School. She had merely wanted to bring the Sisters back to the proper, safe path. The turbulence had gone out of her control—the massacre of the Sister Mentats, the disbanding of the Rossak order.

Now, she was determined that her orthodox Sisters would rebuild the order here on Salusa, correctly, with the full support of the Imperial throne.

The recent dream was sharper in her mind now, as if those other thoughts placed it in context, giving it a framework. While sleeping, Dorotea had seen herself talking with old Sister Karee about the important secrets Josef Venport was harboring—a conversation that was impossible, because Karee was dead, cut down by the Imperial soldiers. . . .

Nonetheless, the Sorceress was there in Dorotea's dream, very much alive and talking about current events after the breakup of the Rossak School. Sister Karee explained that VenHold continued to operate profitably, that their ships flew safely in direct contradiction to so many tragic losses from other shipping companies. In the dream, Karee used her Mentat skills to counsel Dorotea, outlining circumstantial but convincing evidence that suggested Josef Venport had more than good luck on his side. Not only did his ships use the skills of mysterious Navigators, they might also be taking advantage of forbidden computers.

Without proof of his twisted dealings, though, Dorotea could not expose Venport. She had already made a grave error in voicing suspicions about the Sisterhood's illicit computers, without having actual evidence. Many of her Sisters had died because of that. She would not make premature accusations again.

The dream-Karee wore the customary white robe of a Sorceress, giving her an air of mystery and secret knowledge. After the conversation, Karee watched Dorotea like a wise counselor while the younger woman ran a series of questions about Venport through her mind, as if she were using Truthsayer abilities on herself, rather than on someone else. Now her conscious mind asked questions of her subconscious, interrogating herself to get both sides of the truth.

Dorotea wore the black robe of a Reverend Mother, and somehow she was looking at herself as she spoke to herself, as if there were two versions of her at the same time—an older, wiser one and a younger version who still had much to learn. The older one acted as the Truthsayer.

"Speak to me of VenHold and of Combined Mercantiles," the older Dorotea said. "Tell me what you know."

The younger person hesitated, then said, "Directeur Venport has cut off the delivery of vital Combined Mercantiles products to any planet that supports the Butlerians."

"And what is the most valuable product that Combined Mercantiles delivers?"

"Melange, of course. Combined Mercantiles is the prime supplier, and they run their own spice-harvesting crews on Arrakis. After Directeur Venport's recent announcement, his Spacing Fleet will be the only distributor of spice. Aboard his own ships, Venport's Navigators consume enormous quantities of melange. VenHold and Combined Mercantiles are inextricably connected."

"What else? What about the spice?"

"Spice is increasingly popular across the Imperium. It extends life, it promotes health. Many people are addicted. With the VenHold embargo, the inhabitants of Butlerian worlds are unable to get their spice by any means, and they grow more desperate. Venport expects this unrest to weaken their faith in Manford Torondo. The deprivation may drive them to break their pledge—as Baridge just did."

The older, more sagacious version of Dorotea nodded. "Is it just political, or is Josef Venport using the embargo to increase profits as well? Speak to me of Ven-Hold and the major banks. What do you know of the flow of money?"

Wrestling with her memories, the hints as well as actual data that seeped into her mind, Dorotea was aided by Other Memory. Information surfaced from all directions.

"In addition to the shipping embargo, there are credible reports that the major planetary banks have acted in collusion to freeze the assets of planets that took the Butlerian pledge." She paused, followed another thread. "The planetary banks have also refused to grant financing to VenHold competitors, such as EsconTran. Nalgan Shipping nearly went bankrupt and was forced to sell its fleet to Venport. Meanwhile, the banks grant generous terms to Venport Holdings—and also to Combined Mercantiles."

The dreaming, younger Dorotea blinked as pieces clicked into place.

"And what have you seen that you don't know you've seen? Josef Venport is the Directeur of Venport Holdings. Who are the officers of Combined Mercantiles? Who are the officers of the major planetary banks?"

"I—I don't know their names."

"The names do not matter. You are missing the heart of the question."

The words were heavy as the younger Dorotea lifted them out of her mind. "Venport Holdings and Combined Mercantiles are one. Venport Holdings and the planetary banks are one. The puppet strings all go back to Kolhar."

The older Dorotea nodded like a wise teacher. "And the connections are likely to go farther still."

Off to the side of the dream, white-robed Karee Marques folded her gnarled hands in her white sleeves. She listened, nodding as the student dissected the problem.

The younger Dorotea remembered Venport's wife, Cioba, a powerful Sister from Rossak, someone else with Sorceress blood. Cioba and Josef had two young daughters, who were also being taught by Mother Superior Raquella. And Venport fostered and funded the new Sisterhood school in exile on Wallach IX.

She thought of Raquella's Sisters and Cioba Venport . . . which led her thoughts to Josef Venport, then Venport Holdings, the planetary banks, Combined Mercantiles, the embargo of Butlerian planets. It was all a web, with a single nexus.

Dorotea saw the old Sorceress nodding with a rueful smile on her lips. Then she faded away, leaving Dorotea awake in the darkness, feeling very much alone and troubled by these astonishing revelations. . . .

SHORTLY AFTER DAWN, armed with her realization, Dorotea awaited the Emperor outside his office in the Hall of Parliament. It was far too early for Salvador to receive visitors, but she felt a sense of urgency now that she had pieced together the broad strokes of Josef Venport's spreading plan. Without any doubt, the powerful Directeur had extended his web throughout many aspects of the Imperium, with no regard for the Corrinos.

More importantly, Manford Torondo needed to know, and she would send word to him on Lampadas. The linchpin seemed to be the Combined Mercantiles operations on Arrakis, the dependence on spice being the vital link in an ever more oppressive chain. Yes, Manford needed to know . . . but first she was obligated to inform the Emperor.

After revealing the fraud of House Péle and publicly humiliating Grand Inquisitor Quemada, Dorotea had been much more welcome in the Emperor's presence. She was Salvador's official Truthsayer, and her newest revelation would make her even more valuable to him. The Emperor would never again doubt what she had to say.

It might even make up for her disastrous fumbling of the situation on Rossak, which had destroyed the school there and broken the Sisterhood. . . .

The repercussions of Quemada's confession still reverberated through the palace. The apprentice Scalpel torturers had performed their work with precise efficiency. In a particular, but unsurprising, irony the Grand Inquisitor had not survived his own interrogation, and his organs were sold to a research group.

No one in Zimia would see Empress Tabrina again either. One of the most surprising revelations that spurted like blood from Quemada's mouth was that Tabrina had been aware that the Grand Inquisitor sold his victims' organs on the black market. Rather than exposing the scheme, though, she had blackmailed the torturer, forcing him to become her lover—surely not because she had any fondness for the man, but in bitter retaliation for all of Salvador's concubines. Maybe she liked Quemada's sense of power, or the lingering scent of blood on his skin. . . .

When confronted with the accusation, Tabrina had crumbled, begging not to be thrown to the Scalpel apprentices. Only Prince Roderick's hard and rational insistence had saved her. Grim and still grief-stricken after the death of his little daughter, Roderick insisted that the Imperium could not tolerate an expanding scandal. The Corrinos had already drained House Péle of its wealth, and Tabrina was sent into exile. Salvador had no need for her anymore—she had not given him an heir.

Dorotea knew Salvador would never have a child, not by any lover. The Sisterhood on Rossak had seen to it that he was secretly rendered sterile to cut off his flawed bloodline. It was one of the few matters on which Dorotea and Mother Superior Raquella had agreed. . . .

While she waited, listening to the palace stir, Dorotea heard a guard escort march down the tiled corridors. She rose to her feet, presented herself, and faced forward as Salvador and Roderick arrived together. She bowed, and when she straightened she said, "I have something you both must hear."

The balding Emperor looked as if he might panic at the thought of another crisis, but Roderick remained calm. He opened the door to the Emperor's main office and gestured them inside. "Your insights are always useful, Reverend Mother Dorotea."

Suppressing her nervousness, she followed them. Whispers at the back of her mind clamored for attention, the ancient voices that were much more real than a dreaming revelation. She knew her conclusions were valid. "I am not a Mentat, but as a Truthsayer I can detect falsehoods. I observe, I look at subtle threads, and during a particularly deep meditation I accomplished an analysis on a very large scale. . . . My conclusions are troubling."

Dorotea sketched out her discovery. "Venport Holdings is more than just a shipping fleet, and Directeur Venport's plans extend through all portions of our lives. He has created a vast invisible network, like a cancer working through the Imperium—he owns the largest spacing fleet, the only one with access to Navigators for safe transport. He secretly runs Combined Mercantiles and controls commodities, transportation, the spice industry. He is the power behind the largest interplanetary banks, and he transports the majority of Imperial Armed Forces on their maneuvers. In short, he is *everywhere*, Sire. We cannot even gauge the extent of the net he has woven around us."

The Emperor's eyes shimmered with surprise and anger. He fussed and fidgeted in disbelief, and looked to his brother for confirmation. Prince Roderick seemed more circumspect. "I will look at your records, have our own Mentats and accountants analyze the connections you suggest . . . but I suspect you're right. I was concerned when Directeur Venport recently announced his acquisition of Nalgan Shipping, giving him a virtual monopoly on foldspace transportation. His stranglehold tightens on the Butlerian planets, and the recent defection of Baridge is only the first of many, I suspect."

"He means to smother the Butlerian movement!" Dorotea was unable to hide her alarm. "If he allows thinking machines to return, we could all be enslaved again—"

While Salvador stared at him, unsure of what to do, Roderick lifted a finger to silence her. "There is a vast gulf between *allowing* the use of a machine and becoming *enslaved* by a computer overlord. Manford Torondo's 'slippery slope' warnings hold more hysteria than reality."

When Dorotea attempted to argue and defend the Butlerian position, Roderick's voice took on an edge. "Directeur Venport is clearly dangerous and ambitious, but *he* doesn't incite mindless riots in the streets . . . mobs that kill little girls."

Dorotea swallowed, listening to the sharp slap of his words. She had made her point, and the Corrino brothers did see the extent of Venport's schemes, but Roderick had no love for the Butlerians either. And the Emperor would do whatever his brother advised.

After a long silence, Roderick added, "Although I have no fondness for the Butlerians, if Sister Dorotea is correct, the influence of Manford Torondo pales in comparison to Directeur Venport's. We may have to force both of them to their knees."

*And how will you get the power to do that?* Dorotea thought, but did not dare to speak aloud.

Salvador was exasperated. "Is the whole Imperium going mad? Venport can't do these things without my permission! Where will he stop? Does Josef Venport want my throne, too?"

It sounded like a joke, but Dorotea nodded. "Perhaps so—if you get in his way."

*Those Sisters flock together like birds—carrion birds!*

—EMPEROR SALVADOR CORRINO,
comment overheard in the Imperial Court

Sister Arlett spent years out in the planets of the Imperium doing mission-ary and recruitment work for the Sisterhood, and when she returned she made her way to their new school on Wallach IX. She wasn't exactly exiled, but Arlett had been encouraged to do her work far from Rossak, searching for candi-dates who would benefit from Sisterhood instruction.

Of the dozens of missionaries, Raquella kept particularly close watch over Arlett's activities, because Arlett was her own daughter. And Dorotea, now the Emperor's Truthsayer, was Arlett's daughter, although Arlett didn't know it. A tangled web of DNA strands . . .

As such, the Mother Superior felt that Arlett might be useful. Even though Arlett had never attempted the Agony, had never become a Reverend Mother, perhaps she would make an effective, unofficial envoy to the orthodox Sisters on Salusa Secundus. Maybe Arlett could be the first step to healing the schism.

Years ago, Reverend Mother Raquella had sent Arlett away when she refused to choose the good of the Sisterhood over love for her new baby, Dorotea. Raquella knew she was loyal to the Sisterhood, in her own way, and she had al-most—*almost*—forgiven Arlett after her remarkable success in recruiting the talented Valya Harkonnen on Lankiveil.

But the old wounds were reopened when Dorotea survived the Agony and learned the truth of her own bloodline from the voices in Other Memory. Arlett did not know that Sister Dorotea was her long-lost daughter . . . but Dorotea knew. Maybe one of her internal voices was that of her own mother. . . .

So, when Arlett presented herself to the ancient Mother Superior in her

Wallach IX offices, Raquella felt unexpected joy to see her. She had no room in her busy life for love, though, especially now when the Sisterhood was so diminished and her own time so short.

With a glance, Raquella assessed the dark-haired Arlett, noting that she had her mother's lanky frame, upturned nose, and pale blue eyes. After so many years away, the missionary Sister had changed—but the Sisterhood training was so ingrained in her that it could never be taken away. If that were true of all Sisters, then even Dorotea might be salvageable.

Arlett sighed and sat in the proffered chair, but she remained tense. "I've seen so many worlds that I have fallen behind in the changes at the Sisterhood. I need to know what happened on Rossak, why some Sisters are now in the Imperial Court while others are here."

Raquella nodded. "You will receive a full briefing before I send you on your new mission."

"And I would love to hear about the progress of all my recruits—especially Valya Harkonnen."

"Once they join the school, acolytes are no longer your concern." Raquella heard the sharp tone in her voice and softened it, because this was not the time to antagonize Arlett. "Reverend Mother Valya has gone to Ginaz to assess the fighting techniques of the Swordmasters. I suspect by now she has thrown the entire combat school into turmoil."

Arlett looked relieved. "I watched her in combat against her brother Griffin. She had great talent even when she was young and uncontrolled. Without doubt, she will teach the Swordmasters a few things."

"Valya brought her sister, Tula, to our school. The girl showed promise, but left us for a personal matter. A severe disappointment."

A troubled expression crossed Arlett's face. "The Sisterhood is not for everyone, and recruiting is more difficult than it has been in the past. There are so many new schools for the ambitious to join, and ours has obviously fallen into disfavor."

"We may no longer be in our old complex on Rossak, but Emperor Salvador allows us to continue our training here. We will grow strong again."

Arlett frowned. "Or the orthodox Sisters on Salusa will grow strong. Apparently, Reverend Mother Dorotea is training new acolytes." Raquella heard no special intonation in Arlett's voice when she spoke her daughter's name.

"*This* is the true Sisterhood," Raquella reminded her. She stood up from her desk and gestured for Arlett to follow her to an instructional house where, seated in a circle on the cold floor, Fielle and five other Sister Mentats pored over bound volumes of family histories, bloodline trees, and genetic descriptions dating back to Mating Indices developed by the Sorceresses of Rossak.

Seeing them enter, Fielle rose to her feet, smiling as she greeted Raquella, while giving Arlett barely a glance. Now that Valya was gone, Fielle seemed even more eager to impress the Mother Superior. "We have collated and accessed enough data now, Mother Superior, that we have Mentat projections for many generations ahead—and we foresee a glorious pathway, one we will take to create the pinnacle of human development and consciousness."

"Every breeding plan must have an ultimate goal." Raquella felt a trace of hope. She had insisted that these women do the memorization work, although more comprehensive data was contained in the secret computers.

The wounded Sisterhood could begin to grow truly strong again . . . but that would not be enough for Raquella. Before dying she had to bring the two factions together again and choose a worthy successor. After carrying such a heavy future on her shoulders, she could not wait to pass the load to a younger leader.

Fielle continued, "We cannot be certain what lies ahead, Mother Superior. Our projections do not show faces or forms, only a tremendous potential for humankind, in which we create humans far superior to us now."

Arlett had been away from the main school for so long that she seemed alarmed by the idea. "Is it the Sisterhood's business to plan for that? What if our own plans turn against us? Is there not a risk?"

Raquella frowned at her daughter's ill-considered comment. "I have countless past lives in my head. They advise me, scold me, pressure me. Rarely are they unanimous, but Other Memory is clear that there's an even greater risk if we do *not* pursue this grand genetic scheme." She nodded to Fielle, then to the other Sister Mentats, who had paused to listen. "Proceed with your work."

Raquella was content to see all the myriad pieces of her Sisterhood working together, looking so far into the future, like a ship guided across stormy seas but by a steady hand on the helm.

How could these immense and complex plans proceed without her? Would any of the the squabbling voices of Other Memory surface for some other Reverend Mother to provide guidance and more detail? Who was qualified? Who had the experience, the maturity, the temperament? Raquella had lived far too long—if she had let herself die decades ago, during a more stable time, perhaps the new leader would already be seasoned. But she didn't have such a luxury. Her bones ached; her body felt fragile and tired.

Her two best students were Dorotea and Valya. Should her choice be Valya Harkonnen? She had undergone the Agony herself, all alone, and returned to the school. That in itself showed a measure of strength and dedication no one else could match. Valya was fiercely devoted to Raquella, although her temperament often provoked conflict, rather than resolving it. The young woman was intense and ambitious, but didn't have the wisdom a Mother Superior required. Still, as a Reverend Mother now, Valya had countless generations of memories within her, generations of wise advice.

Dorotea, though, had betrayed her fundamental loyalty to the Sisterhood, turning a philosophical difference into a personal one. The ancestral memories had revealed to her how Raquella had forcefully separated Arlett and baby Dorotea. Was that reason enough for her to expose her fellow Sisters to Imperial retaliation? Or, by throwing in her lot with the Emperor, did she have a painful but visionary insight into how to preserve at least some of the Sisterhood's teachings, right under the Emperor's nose? What if Dorotea had done the right thing after all?

Raquella didn't know, but if she could somehow co-opt the Salusan Sisterhood into her own and bring the two factions back together, then she could be content. What if choosing Dorotea as her successor healed the breach?

While the remaining sands of her life trickled through the hourglass, Raquella Berto-Anirul found herself increasingly tempted to join the voices inside her head. She could become part of the collective Other Memories, the sea of past lives.

But not yet. Neither she nor the human race could afford for her to go too soon.

Raquella knew what she had to do. As she and Arlett emerged from the teaching hall into the cool, gray morning, the Mother Superior turned to her daughter. "I want you to go to Salusa Secundus. Initiate a secret connection with Sister Dorotea so that we can resolve our differences."

Arlett was surprised. "She is the Emperor's Truthsayer. Why would she listen to me, Mother Superior? I doubt if she even knows who I am."

Raquella covered a small smile. "She will know who you are. Trust me."

Arlett seemed perplexed, but she drew herself up, ready to begin her assignment. "And what am I to say to her?"

"This schism has caused too much damage. Be my liaison and soften her heart toward me. Ask her to come to Wallach IX and speak with me—while there is still time."

Arlett seemed startled. "While there is time, Mother Superior? What do you mean?"

"Inform her that I do not have long to live. She is a Truthsayer, and will know you are not lying. Tell her that I want to talk with her before the end."

*Successful people sort through priorities and act upon them, while the unsuccessful see only a fog of chaos.*

—DIRECTEUR JOSEF VENPORT, instruction to business trainees

I n hand-to-hand combat, Valya Harkonnen had found only one true match for her skills—her brother Griffin, and he was dead.

Each time she practiced fighting now, each time she went through her lethal yet graceful moves, she remembered what she and her brother had taught each other. More recently, during Tula's training, her sister had shown quick advancement, too, almost fighting at Valya's level. But Tula was no match for Valya, as Griffin had been. She and her brother had shared something indefinable, had saved each other's lives, and forged a remarkable closeness.

Perhaps Valya would have that connection with Tula one day, after her sister had Atreides blood on her hands. . . .

For her other goal, the advancement of the Sisterhood, she would continue to instruct the Sisters on Wallach IX. Armed with specialized muscular and reflexive training to give them superior control of their bodies, as well as other fighting skills, the Sisters would become formidable fighters.

But first, Valya meant to acquire even more skills of her own.

The Ginaz School had been established during Serena Butler's Jihad. For more than a century, skilled Swordmasters had wrought great destruction on combat meks and fighting robots. Now, long after the defeat of the thinking machines, Ginaz still produced the best Swordmasters in the Imperium. Some worked as mercenaries for noble houses; many espoused belief in the Butlerian movement, since a true Swordmaster needed no advanced technology, only a sword and the ability to use it.

On the first day of instruction on Ginaz, Valya wore a sleeveless white combat suit. That morning in one of the simple, open huts where students slept, an aide had tied a black bandana around her head. The aide, an aged man who had never completed his training but remained at the school, called himself Rissar. Before sending her out to the training field, he had looked at Valya's outfit, nodded at her with a smile. "You are dressed like Jool Noret, the founder of the school. Now prove yourself worthy of that garment."

Rissar said the same to each of the other students as he prepared their headbands and fitted short training swords at their waists. Then the old man sent the candidates out to stand on a rocky promontory above the sea, facing away from the water. "Remain completely silent. And wait."

Perspiring in the tropical heat of the training island, Valya stood with the other students. As they waited for their instructor, she considered the legendary fighters who had been here before her. As soon as Valya incorporated their techniques with the skills she had acquired as a Reverend Mother, she could be more formidable than the heroes of Ginaz—and there had been many. With her already-honed skills and natural abilities, she expected to advance quickly here.

During the long, restless pause, Valya had time to study the other students standing in the sun: four women (including herself) and ten men, some anxious, some calm, all wondering when the lesson would begin. Valya endured the delay, annoyed that the school was wasting her time. She wanted to learn everything she could and return to Wallach IX as soon as possible.

A hot ocean breeze blew strands of dark hair around the sides of her face, though the headband held most of it in place. Ever wary, she kept watch over her shoulder, in case someone climbed the rocks. She began to suspect that the instructor might make some sort of dramatic entrance and leap into their midst.

As she assessed her companions in silence, she noticed some of them doing the same with her. At the far end of the line, a small, sinewy man stared straight ahead, not moving a muscle. His headband, combat suit, and sword-in-scabbard were the same as everyone else's, but he wore them differently; his stance was more prepared, as if he knew something they didn't. Supposedly all fourteen students were equally matched for the training, but Valya wondered if this one already had some training at the school, or—

Defying Rissar's instructions, she broke formation and walked over to him, meeting his steady blue-eyed gaze. He had a small mouth and broad nose; she noticed a pale scar on one cheek. "You've been in combat before."

"And you as well," he replied in a high voice, both amused and interested. "I can tell by the way you move and the way you survey your surroundings."

She had all the information she needed to know. "You are our instructor."

While the other students reacted with surprise, the man gave her a thin smile. He made a quick move to his right and darted around her, while she went into a defensive posture and spun to face him.

He landed on the balls of his feet, but did not attack. Instead, he faced the line of students. "I am Master Placido. I was only ten when the Swordmaster School accepted me, and over the past nine years I have collected plenty of experience. I intend to give a small amount of it to you—if you are ready."

With a sudden movement, he flourished his thin sword, then tossed it high in the air and caught it by the handle, before sliding it smoothly back into the scabbard. Valya was not impressed by the acrobatics; it was all braggadocio, effective for intimidating an average opponent or a class of green students, but Valya could easily have disarmed him while he was showing off.

She slipped back into formation, intentionally taking the spot where Master Placido had stood moments ago. He seemed amused by her behavior, but she was not amused by his. She used her training and observation techniques to measure his movements, attitudes, and abilities, so that she could defeat him.

"Only one of you proved observant enough to notice that I was different," he said. "Defeating an opponent depends on more than your ability to handle a weapon. Any fight begins with an accurate assessment of your adversary, to ascertain weaknesses and strengths."

Placido walked down the line of students, pausing in front of each, but he ignored Valya. Was he trying to irritate her? She made a point of controlling her emotions.

"Break into pairs and demonstrate your fighting abilities against each other, so that I can assess where the starting point should be for this class. Use your swords or not, as you prefer."

Valya was paired with a tall, thirtyish man who identified himself as Linari. She could tell from the way he moved and his muscular build that he'd been in fights before, but they had probably been brawls; he relied on strength and intimidation rather than finesse. Linari wore a sneering expression as they circled each other; both of them kept their swords sheathed. Valya knew she wouldn't need hers, and Linari refused to draw his own as a matter of pride.

As she and her opponent remained wary, evaluating, she heard other students wrestling or punching one another. She did not take her eyes from Linari's. When she decided she'd given him enough time, Valya lunged to the right and leaped up to strike Linari with a fist in the temple, stunning him long enough for her to go low and slide around him. She kicked his knees from behind and sent him tumbling down onto the rocky surface.

As Linari rose to his feet, his expression changed from haughtiness to respect. "Good move," he said, with a toothy grin. "Thank you for teaching it to me."

After each combat, Master Placido changed the pairings, and Valya rapidly proved herself to be the elite fighter in the class. In each case she took down her opponent with enough restraint to prevent injury, though she could easily have killed or disabled every one of them.

Placido watched her, measured her. He seemed to know Valya was holding back. As she dispatched one classmate after another, Placido and the other students gathered around to watch. Valya turned from the last defeated student, who hunched over, wheezing, and then she stood crisply in front of the youthful instructor, appraising him again. Her dark headband was damp with perspiration, but she did not feel tired. A breeze from the sea cooled her skin. She heard the waves, the movement of feet around her, the rustling of garments and sheathing of swords—and the awed whisperings of the students.

"Perhaps you would like to instruct this class?" Placido's body was rigid, his mouth a tight line, one hand near the handle of his sheathed sword.

"I have been instructing them. And now I would like to instruct you as well, Master Placido." Some of the students gasped; others watched in intent silence.

Placido smiled. "I am always eager to learn." The two faced each other and began the combat dance. Valya kept her knees slightly bent, her hands and arms relaxed and in front of her, watching his every move.

Even as tension built in the air, the Swordmaster continued to lecture the others. "Notice her precise muscle control, and the way her eyes absorb their surroundings. She draws information from every available sense, which enables her to adapt to changes in the combat situation."

Valya considered attacking, then decided not to, because Placido would expect her to do that. He gave a faint nod as he recognized what she was doing.

"She's wondering what I can do," Placido announced to the others. "That is good. Notice that her earlier aggressiveness has changed, and now she is in a defensive, wait-and-see mode."

In a lightning-fast maneuver, he somersaulted instead of walking, becoming a blur as he continued to circle her, sometimes on his hands, sometimes on his feet, sometimes sliding past her. A short sword suddenly appeared in his hand, and Valya realized that he had taken it from *her* scabbard, like an acrobatic pickpocket. When he stopped moving, Placido had a sword in each hand. He dropped both weapons onto the rocks with a metallic clang.

Valya turned, still alert, just as he blurred into motion again. She felt a hard thrust in her midsection that knocked the wind out of her and dropped her to her knees. When she looked up, and around, he was no longer there. Linari and several other students rushed to the edge of the precipice, staring down.

Catching her breath, forcing control on her body, Valya rose to her feet and fought back the after-echoes of pain. Far below, she saw Master Placido bounding along the beach at the base of the cliff.

"He must be afraid of me," she said, eliciting laughter from the others.

Moments later, Placido returned, after climbing the outcrop from a different side, and he presented himself, not breathing hard at all. He faced Valya. "You still have a great deal to learn, but I find you interesting."

Valya took care to maintain a nonthreatening posture, with her arms folded across her chest. "And I find you interesting as well. Perhaps I can learn from the Swordmasters after all."

His assessment of her went deeper than she expected. "You have fire in your eyes. There is someone you wish to kill. Not me, I hope."

"It is not you, Master."

He continued to stare at her. "Swordmaster training is not designed to create murderers."

She avoided a direct answer. "I have no vendetta against my fellow students, but I need to fight them as part of our lessons. While I train, I find it useful to think of someone I despise, so I can raise my skills to a higher level."

Placido nodded slightly. "An unusual technique, but you use it effectively." He looked at the other trainees. "For those of you who have hatred to spare, you might wish to do the same, while keeping the secret of your enemy's identity. I will teach you fighting methods, and you may customize them to your own abilities and needs. And hatreds."

*Every person has a powerful urge to return home. We go there to find meaning in our lives, even if our memories of home are filled with sadness.*

—VORIAN ATREIDES, private journals

Lankiveil was behind him now, and sometimes Vorian Atreides wondered how many miles—how many light-years—he had traveled during his long lifetime. Then again, maybe he didn't want to know. It would just be a number, and the memories of all those places, all those journeys, mattered more than the distances traveled.

After arranging to provide the financial lifeline House Harkonnen needed to solidify its position, Vor had traveled again, wandering from place to place. He bought his own passage, called no attention to himself, and made his way across the Imperium in a slow hopscotch until he finally found himself back on beautiful Caladan. Though he had taken his time to get there, even now he wasn't sure he felt ready to be back. *Caladan* . . .

Vor had endured more than two centuries of being uprooted and moving on, of leaving people he cared about, watching Time steal away his wives, lovers, children, grandchildren, and friends. Out of self-defense, he tried not to let himself grow too close to anyone, yet out of his own humanity, he often failed. Sometimes he left loved ones of his own volition, but too often events forced him to leave—such as when he departed from Mariella and their family on Kepler. And so many decades ago, he had left Caladan as well.

Over the years there had been wars, politics, and death—far too much death. Through it all, Vorian Atreides was still alive. For the first time, he was going in the opposite direction, heading back to a place where he'd known love once, and where he still felt deep roots, despite the long time away.

The blue gem of the ocean world of Caladan beckoned him from the windowports of the shuttle that took him down from orbit. Through the veil of clouds, Vor identified the major continents. He remembered his life there with Leronica and their two sons. Estes and Kagin had never been close to their father, resented his remote and aloof lifestyle. He had chosen to give his life to the endless Jihad, rather than settling down in a small house on the seashore. Leronica understood that, but Estes and Kagin never had. They were all long dead now, but Vor thought of the grandchildren he'd never met, and the great-grandchildren, an entire extended Atreides lineage on Caladan. It made him sad that he wasn't part of it.

Once, he had been happy on Caladan, at least as happy as he'd been on Kepler. He hoped he could recapture some of that now. Most people's lives were too short to atone for all the things they regretted, but Vorian Atreides had a lot more time than other people, and he wanted to spend it making up for what he'd done wrong. He doubted the Harkonnens would ever hold anything but hateful thoughts toward him, and he could live with that—it was a price he had to pay. He had helped them, though, whether or not they ever knew it.

Now he was on a new mission, going back over a different portion of his past. He had never met any of his remaining family on Caladan. Perhaps he could reclaim a family here.

THE MOMENT HE saw Caladan's rocky shoreline and grassy headlands, it all felt comfortable and familiar. As he made his way along a foot-worn path to the fishing village where he had spent so many years, this place seemed right to him. He needed to be here, needed to take care of matters that were long overdue.

The path ran along the top of a rugged cliff, with the ocean sprawling toward the horizon. Carrying a duffel bag of belongings, Vor paused to inhale the salty air. The blue-green sea looked like a placid lake, but in the distance he saw fast-moving clouds on the leading edge of a weather front.

More than a century ago, while on a scouting mission for the Jihad, he'd met Leronica in a tavern and was smitten by her playful personality and beauty. He could never forget her heart-shaped face, dancing brown eyes, or how he had picked her out in the crowd of locals. She had shone like a candle in the dark. . . .

Now, with a wistful sigh, he continued into town, pausing for a moment to look at a statue on the outskirts, depicting *him* as Supreme Commander of the Army of the Jihad in a heroic pose, gazing into the distance. But there were inaccuracies in the statue. The uniform was all wrong, and the face didn't look like Vorian at all, with a nose that was too broad, a chin too prominent. It was also a statue of an older man, not the man in his apparent thirties who led the human military forces to victory against the oppressive machines.

As he reached the main street that ran along the water, Vor saw fishing boats heading back to port ahead of the storm. He watched crews secure the boats and off-load their gear and cargoes, assisted by townspeople who rushed to the water's edge to help.

A pair of grizzled fishermen made their way along the main dock and onto a cobblestone street where Vor stood, watching. He hailed them. "I'm new in town. Can you recommend a place to stay?"

"With or without vermin?" said the older one, a gray-bearded man with a dark knit cap. His companion, a tall man in a heavy sweater, laughed.

"Preferably without," Vor answered with a ready grin.

"Then don't stay anyplace around here."

"Try Ackley's Inn," the taller man suggested. "It's clean enough, and old Ackley makes a great fish stew. Good kelpbeer, too. We're heading that way ourselves if you're anxious to buy a round."

"Not anxious, but willing—if it comes with some conversation?"

Vor accompanied them to an old, freshly painted building with a wooden sign swaying in gusts of wind. After checking into a small room on the second floor, he returned to the main hall to join the two fishermen at a corner table, buying them the promised round of beer.

"New to the coast, or new to Caladan?" asked the bearded man, whose name was Engelo. He had a smoky voice, and quickly finished off his pint.

"Neither, just haven't been back here in a long time. I'm traveling around, looking for distant relatives. Do either of you know of any Atreides?"

"Atreides?" asked the tall man, Danson. "I know a fisherman named Shander Atreides, and he has a couple of young men living with him—nephews I hear, though I'm not sure what their names are. Both boys work for the Air Patrol Agency, doing search-and-rescue missions at sea."

Engelo sipped his beer. "Shander Atreides lives up the coast a couple of kilometers, big house on a private cove. His nephews are Willem and Orry—Danson knows that, but he pretends to be stupid."

Danson sniffed, taking some offense, then chuckled. "The Atreides family has money, earned it in the fishing business after some distant relative sent them a financial stake to get started."

"The money came from the most famous hero of the Jihad," Engelo said. "Vorian Atreides."

Vor concealed his smile. He liked hearing that his money went to good use.

"Shander's a good man, runs a business mending nets now—likes to keep busy, even though he invested well. He took the two boys in after their parents were killed in a hurricane."

Danson picked up the story, as if to prove he wasn't really stupid. "The tragedy happened eleven or twelve years ago. Willem just turned eighteen, and Orry is twenty—but Willem's the one who looks older and acts older. Nice, polite young men, both of them. I hear Orry's due to get married soon, a whirlwind romance with a girl from inland."

"Thanks." Pleased that he already had a lead to follow, Vor paid and left a half-finished beer on the table. He was anxious to meet his relatives. Shander, Willem, and Orry were undoubtedly descended from Estes or Kagin. He felt ashamed that he didn't know any details of their lives. But that would change.

Engelo called out to him, "Say, you never told us your name."

Vor acted as if he hadn't heard as he strode up the stairway to his rented room. He had used one of his aliases when checking in, but intended to reveal who he truly was to his own descendants, and then word would surely spread. He was caught between desiring to hold on to the anonymity he'd enjoyed for so long and wanting to reunite with his family on Caladan.

Sitting in his room, he thought of how much history had passed since he'd last visited this planet—and how little had changed here. He opened the window to let in the cool breezes and gazed out at the rugged village. Long ago he'd had many fine years here—hauling in the fresh catch, sharing good times with family and friends, surviving storms at sea. *Living life.* It seemed like so long ago, partly a dream. As time passed, his recollections faded. In Vor's overfull memory, the faces were dim, but at least the personalities were brighter. He missed all those people he'd known here, but they were long, long gone.

He heard a sharp rap at the door of his room, and felt his pulse quicken. He was alert for danger, wondering if someone had hunted him down. Or maybe it was just the innkeeper with an innocuous question. He opened the door, smiling as if to greet an old friend he'd been expecting, but ready for anything.

An older man stood before him; he wore stained work clothes and tied his shaggy gray hair in a ponytail. Something about him looked familiar . . . perhaps the patrician nose or the deeply set gray eyes with a sparkle of impish intelligence.

"I'm Shander Atreides," he said. "The innkeeper sent a message that you were asking about me. I don't know why I'd be interesting enough for you to buy rounds of kelpbeer for the information, though. . . ."

They went down to the bar, and Vor couldn't stop smiling. "I'll buy a second round if you'll talk with me a while longer. I have a story to tell you, though I doubt you'll believe it."

"I've heard plenty of unbelievable stories," Shander said. "But I'll take that kelpbeer."

The two men spent hours at their table chatting, trying to sort out the complicated web of their relationship. Vor attempted to trace the generations, following Shander's parents and grandparents back to Vor's own son Kagin, and learning that Willem and Orry were from the line that descended from Estes.

Even after revealing his true identity to Shander, Vor felt a sense of serenity about his confession. The old fisherman laughed and refused to believe him at first, but as Vor told more and more stories, long into the night, Shander began to change his mind.

"You're really Vorian Atreides?" he said, with a slight slur of his words. "*The* Vorian Atreides?"

"That I am. Pay no attention to the face on that statue outside of town. The details aren't quite accurate."

"I never thought about it, just assumed the features were right. I have to admit, you do look a lot more like me than that statue does."

Reaching across the table, Vor clasped the fisherman's muscular arm. "We're Atreides through and through, both of us."

Shander's gaze sharpened. "I believe you're telling the truth."

"Usually I don't tell anyone who I am. I've been working at various jobs around the Imperium under assumed names, even checked into this inn under another name."

"And you need to check out of this inn," Shander said. "Come stay with me and the boys in my house. We have plenty of room."

"Not yet." Vor shook his head in determination. "I don't want to intrude, and besides, I'm an independent sort. I can be difficult to get along with."

"Aw, you're just saying that, Vor. I never met a man I liked more than you, and I can tell that right off."

Vor grinned. "Give me time, and I'll wear on you. Thanks for the generous offer, but no, I'll stay in the inn for now. I've got plenty of money. You know I do, because I sent you the stake to get your fishing business started."

"That was decades ago!"

Vor just nodded.

"Then my house is really yours. Or at least, you hold a mortgage on it."

"No, Shander, you earned the house. Any money I have is for my family, and that includes you. If things work out for me here, I'll build my own place. But first let's see how things go."

*I keep my eyes open and observe. And when I peer into hearts and souls, I see evil much more often than I see good—because I know exactly what to look for.*

—SISTER WOODRA, Truthsayer to Manford Torondo

By the time the VenHold supply ship arrived at Baridge, ending the embargo to wild cheering and applause, Anari Idaho was already there, lying in wait with her faithful Butlerians.

Anari and a hundred volunteers had arrived a full day earlier on the Escon-Tran ship, rushing to Baridge before Venport Holdings could deliver a bloated cargo of rewards and bribes for the weak-willed. She came unobtrusively, telling her Butlerian fighters to remain quiet. They wore normal Baridge clothing, filtering fabrics that provided some protection from the solar radiation.

During the VenHold embargo, Manford had maintained his contacts with Baridge residents who were dedicated to his cause. Much of the planetary population remained true to their pledge, even though the weak deacons allowed themselves to be tempted by Venport. Anari knew who the loyal ones were, and she moved surreptitiously throughout the city, organizing them to bolster the force she had brought with her. She did not make contact with the turncoat Deacon Kalifer, whom she despised for having been seduced by the temptation of imported luxuries.

The locals were pleased to see Anari, glad someone was there to tell them how they were supposed to react, now that their own leaders had broken under pressure. Yes, the people of Baridge needed medical salves and cancer treatments due to the upswing in the solar cycle, but above anything else they needed *faith.*

Her first night on Baridge, Anari met in secret with a core group of true followers. They talked under the open sky, because night was the safest time to venture outside, when the radiation flux was diminished. Overhead, the auroras looked like silent scarves of fire, shimmering colors draped across the darkness.

Many of the faithful showed her the skin lesions they had suffered after Ven-Hold criminally cut off their medical supplies; some displayed cancerous growths on their faces, noses, and arms, which they wore like badges of honor. Seeing what these people were enduring, Anari admired them for not listening to the silky promises of Josef Venport and his lapdog Suk doctors.

Anari spoke with an intensity that demanded attention. "I wish God would just force everyone to do the right thing, and then we wouldn't need to be so vigilant." She shook her head. "It's both the gift and the curse of humanity that we are allowed to make our own decisions—even wrong ones. And Deacon Kalifer made the wrong one here, which forces us to do the right thing and punish him. More importantly, we have to ruin Venport Holdings. If we cut out the serpent's tongue, then weak men like Deacon Kalifer will not hear tempting words. Thus, we save others from their own folly."

"We could kidnap Deacon Kalifer now," said the local leader of Manford's dedicated followers. "*That* would prevent him from accepting the VenHold shipment."

"No, he is beyond saving," Anari said. "Better that we spread the word among the faithful. I brought a hundred fighters, but we'll need a thousand more to accomplish our goal."

The local leader had a purplish, S-shaped lesion under his left eye. He squinted. "What do you have in mind?"

"I want to set a trap for that ship."

SINCE THE FIRST Butlerian planet to renounce Manford's antitechnology pledge was an important milestone, Directeur Venport wanted the cargo ship to arrive with tremendous fanfare. Everyone had to see Deacon Harian tear up the agreement and "rejoin civilized society."

Sealed in an onboard tank, the Navigator—Royce Fayed—interacted closely with the crew that operated the foldspace engines. Their skill was precise enough that the VenHold ship emerged in the sky directly over the city, as if by magic, with a thunder of displaced air.

The sigil of the VenHold Spacing Fleet was prominent on the hull. As the ship lowered itself toward the vast city square, people streamed out of the way to create a landing zone. Large cargo doors opened and smaller ships flew out to disperse across the city with medical supplies, luxury items, and melange.

Anari watched, her jaw aching from clenched teeth.

Deacon Kalifer had set up tall speakers for the event, and now he appeared at the head of the crowd to welcome the VenHold spacefolder. Anari observed the man as he mounted a speaking platform, and she hated him for his weakness. Ignorant people could be forgiven their mistakes, but Kalifer was a Butlerian *deacon*, indoctrinated in the truth, a man who knew the dangers and delusions of technology, yet he had still changed his allegiance and gone over to the enemy. Anari couldn't understand why. Did his soul mean so little to him?

Kalifer's voice resonated through the speakers. "I hear your cries of pain. I know how you suffer."

Anari felt icy inside. What did this man know of suffering? He still looked pudgy and pale. Every day when she cared for Manford, she witnessed the leader's resolve to continue fighting despite his cruel injuries, despite the loss of his legs. She thought of the many hundreds of thousands—*millions*—of people who would line up to give their lives for him.

The turncoat deacon raised his hands. "I did what was necessary to save us. I obtained the supplies we so desperately need, and now Baridge will survive and thrive. I reaffirm that we will never use thinking machines—but that doesn't mean we have to return to medieval squalor. Manford Torondo asks too much. Thanks to this agreement, we can all be happy, healthy, and productive. We will create our own new golden age."

As the smaller cargo ships opened their doors and VenHold workers dumped out crates of much-needed supplies, the people cheered, though Anari heard an undertone of uneasiness. Not everyone here was convinced. More than a thousand of Manford's faithful were surreptitiously sprinkled throughout the crowd, awaiting her signal.

Under the shimmering sky, drenched with solar radiation that filtered through the planet's weak magnetic field, Anari's vision blurred. When she stared at Deacon Kalifer, an image seemed to appear before her, obscuring the deacon. The vision was of an ethereal-looking, hairless woman, the legendary founder of the Butlerian movement, Rayna Butler. She had pale skin, white robes, and a voice that sounded like beautiful music. "Anari Idaho, you know what to do. Do not let this man destroy what so many people have suffered for, what I suffered for—and died for. Manford knows, and you know Manford. Save me. Save my dream!"

Anari's throat had gone dry, and she gasped as the image shimmered. "Rayna? Rayna Butler?"

But the image faded, and she saw only Deacon Kalifer on the platform, grinning smugly, announcing a festival to celebrate the happy times that had come to Baridge again. He told the people they should rejoice that their days of deprivation were over. "Enough suffering!" he shouted, to pockets of cheering and applause.

The Swordmaster pulled a red banner from her jacket and raised it high, so that it waved in the breeze. One of the nearby Butlerians saw her and also raised a red banner. As crimson cloths fluttered through the crowd, it looked like a spreading fire. Then her people surged forward with a mounting roar.

Although this was not a coordinated attack, the mob knew what to do. Anari raced along with them, pushed others out of the way. She had her rugged body and fighting skills, and the faithful who ran with her had their own collective ferocity.

The Butlerians swarmed the landed VenHold ship, overrunning the workers who were still unloading the cargo. They smashed the crates, scattered the contents on the ground, and stormed aboard the vessel to continue the orgy of destruction. Victims screamed; some of the attackers laughed.

Anari had plenty of volunteers to trigger the violence, and as soon as the riot began, more in the crowd joined in, unable to resist the tide. Perhaps they were showing their true feelings, or perhaps they simply did not want to be seen as an enemy and fall victim to mob violence. Either way, they were fighting on the correct side.

Unfortunately, the people got to Deacon Kalifer before Anari could reach him. He tried to fight them off, but his efforts proved useless as they beat him unconscious. They hacked off his legs in a twisted parody of Manford, then dragged him through the streets. He died of blood loss in a matter of minutes.

Across the city, the newly arrived supplies and ships were being destroyed. Deacon Kalifer and his entire government council were slain. Any citizen who tried to stop the mob from ransacking buildings also became a target. It was a necessary cleansing, since too many citizens of Baridge had forgotten the truth, forgotten who they really were.

Anari led the charge into the main VenHold spacefolder. The larger vessel was a former robot battleship, full of sharp lines and intimidating angles that were designed to trigger instinctive fear. Anari had been aboard such vessels before, when she and Manford destroyed any derelict thinking-machine ship they found.

Bloody corpses in VenHold uniforms lay in the corridors. Anari kept shouting commands even though her voice went hoarse. She knew how to find the control deck of the old robot ship, and led some followers there, while others spread out through the decks, looking for frightened crewmembers to kill.

She wished Directeur Escon could see the glory of these devout followers doing their holy work, but maybe it didn't matter. The shipping magnate was weak and made too many excuses; he remained aboard his own ship in orbit, not wanting to go down to the surface of Baridge until the matter had been resolved. Anari didn't really need him for this work.

After the Swordmaster gained some control over her wild anger, she realized that Manford could incorporate this vessel into his defense fleet—with the expanding conflict, he needed to gather all the ships he could. She issued orders to be passed among the swarming Butlerians: Capture or kill any traitors found aboard, but inflict no more damage on the ship. "Leader Toronto requires it," she said, and that was enough reason. In a matter of minutes, her followers mitigated their violence, although their continued shouts and howls sounded like war cries as they ransacked cabins and corridors.

Anari and a group of wild-eyed fighters reached the control deck. Two human pilots gave up without a fight, but she refused to accept their surrender, and slashed them to pieces herself.

When the bodies of the VenHold pilots were dragged away from the controls, she realized to her horror that *computers* were part of the navigation systems. It was like discovering a nest of scorpions. Even though she had advised the others not to cause further damage, she told them to smash the navigation calculators anyway. No sane person could have any use for those.

She heard a shrill yell. "Swordmaster! It's a monster!"

Two of her followers gestured toward a lift platform. When she reached the higher deck, she found a plaz chamber filled with orange-brown gas and a *creature* inside with an enlarged head, amphibious eyes, and webbed fingers. Its arms and legs hinted that it might once have been human. It had to be one of VenHold's mysterious Navigators, the prescient things that guided the ships.

"You must stop!" said a voice through the speakers. "You have caused enough damage. You do not understand."

Anari did not wish to hear any of this, had no tolerance for computers or monsters. She found the tank's hatch and released it, thinking she would climb inside and slay the twisted Navigator. But the internal pressure was explosive, and rich melange gas boiled out. The creature in the tank flailed, and his words were filled with alarm. "Stop! You will never comprehend the secrets!"

He spoke more words, but she stopped herself from hearing them by smashing the speakerpatch. Together with the others, she hammered at the tank until the plaz wall shattered. More gas spilled out, reeking of spice. *Spice . . .*

She watched the creature inside gasping, weakening. This VenHold ship had been loaded with melange, a gift for the weak people of Baridge. The Navigator thrived on spice, and now it seemed to suffocate without it.

She knew that Venport Holdings had been heavily involved with spice production on Arrakis. The clue felt like an irritating pebble in her shoe. Did Josef Venport depend on spice to create these horrendous monsters? The humanoid thing gasped, sucking in useless breaths, but its words were incomprehensible. It seemed to be pleading, trying to explain something.

Anari turned away. "Pull that creature out and drag it through the streets so all can see what sort of monstrosity allies itself with Josef Venport."

Coughing, her eyes stinging from the pungent spice gas, Anari watched them draw the slippery-skinned figure out of the tank, not caring that the jagged edges tore through its flesh. The creature would not live long, but its body would serve a purpose.

Manford would be pleased at what Anari had accomplished—and what she had discovered. The existence of this deformed *thing* changed everything. If Josef Venport's Spacing Fleet required great supplies of melange to keep functioning, then maybe she would have to take a trip to Arrakis. . . .

*Sometimes the best way to see the familiar is to go far from it.*

—wisdom of the desert

When he returned to Arrakis City under orders from Directeur Venport, Taref felt as if a dust storm had passed from his mind, and he saw the city clearly for the first time. Though he was sure it had not changed, this wasn't the same place he had left.

While growing up in the sietch, he'd thought of the city as a huge metropolis filled with strange noises and smells. In those days, he and his friends could journey for days across open featureless dunes and still find their way home, yet they could get lost in the city's tangled streets. There were so many tall buildings, confusing alleys, crowds of strangers, and unexpected perils.

Now, however, Taref realized that Arrakis City was small in comparison to other offworld population centers. Buildings that had once seemed magnificent were rather low and weather-beaten. The streets were dirty, the people huddled. Though large numbers of VenHold spice haulers lifted off daily, the Arrakis spaceport operations didn't compare with those on Kolhar, or even Junction Alpha.

He'd been gone from the desert for only a few months, but he'd grown accustomed to bathing and feeling clean. His flesh had gained an unsettling soft flexibility; he could now pinch it between his fingers instead of feeling the stiff tautness of a desert-adapted body. Naib Rurik would consider that a weakness.

Poor Shurko would have felt that way as well, Taref knew. Even on planets with an abundance of moisture, his stern young friend had rationed his water intake, afraid that he would forget the basics of simple existence, that he would grow soft and weak. Taref would never forget the core of the desert within him—

nor would he ever forget his dead friend—but he was open to learning and experiencing new things as well.

Yet the wondrous new places had not been so wondrous after all, and his work had been little different from what he had done when sabotaging spice-harvesting equipment—except that it cost a great many lives. And now Shurko would not be returning to the desert, would never need his desert knowledge again.

No, this had not been what Taref expected when he joyously convinced his friends to join him on a great adventure.

Taref's sietch brothers and sisters felt they already knew everything they needed to know, but now that he had been to other places far away—and he still had so much more to see—he could tell his people that so much more awaited them out there. He would extend Directeur Venport's offer, inviting them to see the things he had seen. Some might feel the same pull of dreams, though he'd always been a misfit in his own sietch. . . .

Before Taref set out on the new mission to Arrakis, Draigo Roget had given him a brand-new distilling suit, claiming that the old one wasn't worth repairing, even though Taref had meticulously maintained it for years. The young man checked over the new suit, noting the improvements that had been implemented, how the seams were double-sealed, the inner lining reinforced, the filter pads made more efficient. This stillsuit was finer than anything he had seen in his old sietch, better even than the one worn by a Naib. Taref would claim that this was just a hint of the rewards volunteers might receive if they joined him in working for Venport Holdings.

He wished his fellow saboteurs could come back with him, but Draigo had shaken his head. "They have their own assignments for VenHold, dispatched to deal with various EsconTran operations." His friends missed the dunes, especially Lillis, and the loss of Shurko had hit them all hard.

Taref's heart ached to know that his friend would never return to the desert, that he had vanished somewhere out in space where his body's water would not be recovered. Offworlders did not think about such things; water meant nothing to them, and sometimes their lives were cheap, as well. . . .

HE TRAVELED DOWN to Arrakis City, where he mingled with surly workers who'd come to join the Combined Mercantiles spice-harvesting operations. Taref was going home, but these workers saw the desert planet as their last chance. Most of them would never leave here.

Pretending to be one of the spice crew volunteers, he left the spaceport for the Combined Mercantiles headquarters. Most of these new workers had no experience at all in desert operations, and some wouldn't survive the first year. They reminded him of himself, and his friends, leaving what they knew for what they imagined would be a better life elsewhere, far away. He'd never thought much about the offworld workers before, and now he felt sorry for them.

Taref carried a special, coded dispensation from Directeur Venport that guaranteed him a spot on any crew he chose. He presented his credentials, a recorded message from Draigo Roget, and a VenHold-backed credit chit. One of the Mentat workers recognized him from his initial recruitment, sized him up. "You have matured and adapted, young man."

"I've learned much in my time away. Now my assignment is to recruit other Freemen so they can have the same opportunities as I did. For that, I need to go into the deep desert."

The Mentat nodded. "I hope you haven't forgotten how to survive out there. The dunes will always be a perilous place."

After Taref identified the general location of his sietch, the Mentat checked schedules and assigned him to a spice crew that would work in the vicinity. Taref could stay with the crew as long as he liked and draw a regular paycheck; whenever he felt it appropriate, he could leave to find his people.

He spent a week with the spice operations, readapting himself to Arrakis, and found that his fondest memories of the desert were now discolored by reality. As soon as he returned to the arid wasteland, smelled the spice-cinnamon air, and felt the grit in his teeth, Taref realized he had forgotten much, and changed much. He felt like a pair of stiff new boots that needed to be broken in again.

Before reappearing at the sietch, he remembered what it was like to live out here. He had never noticed the daily details before, since they had been part of his routine existence. By the time he left the spice crew, Taref still hadn't regained his sharp edge, but at least he was no longer so soft and rounded, and he did not perspire so profusely into the distilling suit.

His own people had no knowledge of what had happened to him or his companions, because no one had sent any message back to the sietch. Young Freemen often took solo journeys on unknown adventures; many didn't come back. No one would have guessed that Taref and his friends had traveled to distant planets. He had little to show for it, except for his own tales . . . which they probably would not believe.

Trudging away from the rocky camp as night fell and the desert cooled, he left the spice operations and struck out across the open dunes with his well-practiced random walk. Taref could have summoned a sandworm, which would have been a spectacular way to return: riding one of the huge creatures up to the cliffside, dismounting with a flourish, and running to the rocks before the leviathan could devour him. But he had no companions, no spotters, and only rudimentary equipment. He would have needed to plan better for such a grand entrance. Instead, Taref walked at night with irregular steps, found shelter during the day, and moved on again at nightfall.

His first sip from the suit's catch-pocket tasted flat and foul, and he thought something was wrong with the new stillsuit. But he realized that was the way reprocessed water had always tasted. He calculated how long he could last alone in the desert, and hoped he could reach the sietch in time. He had only a guess of the distance involved because he didn't know the exact position of the spice-harvesting operations. If he arrived at the warren settlement parched, dying, and begging for mercy, then his argument about the advantages of Venport Holdings would sway none of his people.

He crossed the desert for four days, picking up the pace, fighting back his thirst. He drained all the catch-pockets in his distilling suit and hoarded the last literjon of water he carried with him. In a few days he would have to worry about survival rather than discomfort.

Taref shuddered with relief when he saw the familiar cliff wall on the horizon, much closer than he had expected. A miracle! He arrived with enough water left for a day and a half, a great luxury, so he took the time to rest, drink, and refresh himself before climbing the hidden but familiar trail. Finally he picked his way up the rocks and presented himself at the moisture door. The guards were astonished to see him.

He had thought much about what he would say, how he would deliver his offer to the sietch—if Naib Rurik even allowed him to address the tribe. He faced the guards. "I have returned with an opportunity."

"Where are your companions?" asked a young male.

"They are having remarkable adventures on faraway worlds," Taref exaggerated, not wanting to tell them about Shurko just yet.

They opened the door to let Taref in. "The Naib will want an explanation from you."

"Everyone in the sietch will want to hear my story. It could change our way of life." Taref was smiling, but the hardscrabble people who emerged from their quarters and workshop rooms seemed more unsettled than happy to see him. They acknowledged the young man's return, but without a warm welcome. They had always looked askance at him, considered him odd. They had never been his close friends when he lived with them, but he at least expected them to be curious. He could tell them stories about water from the sky, white snow that piled up on the ground, and lakes so immense that it would take days to walk around them.

The Naib and Taref's two older brothers sat together in a cool chamber, drinking spice coffee, discussing politics and marriage prospects, planning a response to a petty feud with another desert tribe. As Taref listened to their conversation, their concerns sounded small to him, especially now that he knew of much vaster conflicts out in the Imperium involving Manford Torondo's Butlerians and Josef Venport, the fleet of EsconTran and the ships of VenHold.

Naib Rurik looked at his youngest son. Rather than showing elation at Taref's return, he sniffed. "You've been gone a long time, you and your friends. You left the rest of us in the sietch to do your work."

"I did work of my own while I was away, Father. *Important* work."

His brother Modoc said, "If it wasn't work for the sietch, then it was not important work."

His brothers had often ridiculed him, making Taref feel small, but that would not be effective against him now. "I don't care what you consider important. I have seen the vastness of the Imperium."

His brothers chuckled, and Rurik said, "What happened to your suit?"

"I have a superior one."

His father said, "You always want to change things."

"Yes—I dreamed about changing life for all of our people, for the better. We'll change the history of the Imperium. My friends and I have gone to various planets, we've done work for a great shipping company."

"What does offworld politics matter to us here?" asked his other brother, Golron. "You abandoned your responsibilities."

"'A man's responsibility is to the sietch and to his people.'" Taref flung the Naib's oft-spoken words back in his face. "I would like to speak to the sietch, call a gathering. I have come with an opportunity that will improve life for anyone who volunteers to join me. I've been to worlds where water falls from the sky, and where the temperature is so cold the droplets freeze and lie on the ground in white drifts. On many worlds, water is so plentiful that it just sits in natural basins in the ground. Lakes and seas!" He raised his chin, challenging them to deny what he had seen and done. "Directeur Venport asked me to recruit others, because he thinks Freemen are superior operatives. Anyone who comes with me can see these places for himself, and be well paid in the bargain."

Naib Rurik slurped his spice coffee. "I don't believe in worlds like that."

"And where are your friends?" Golron pressed. "Why haven't they all come back with wild tales like yours? Or did you lose them in the desert?"

"I lost *one*." Taref lowered his voice. "Shurko perished on a mission—but he destroyed an enemy ship, as he was ordered to do."

Naib Rurik's face formed a sour expression. "Freemen should not take orders from an offworld businessman."

"Did you bring Shurko's water back to the tribe?" asked Modoc. "It belongs to us."

"He was lost with the ship, out in open space. His water is gone."

"Then you failed your friend and you failed the sietch," said the Naib. "And you want to convince others to replicate your folly?"

"I want to give them the same opportunity I had. Directeur Venport pays extremely well. After we finish our service, we will bring many items of advanced civilization to the sietch, to make life better here."

"And why would we want anything to do with offworld civilization?" Golron asked. "Have you forgotten your own people's history? We were enslaved by that civilization. We have a far better life here."

"How do you know what's out there? You hide in your caves and insist this is the best of all possible worlds, without ever having seen another one."

Rurik shook his head. "You reek of civilization, of offworlders. You were always strange, Taref, yet I claimed you as my son because I did not want to shame you, me, or your mother." His expression darkened. "Leave now—you do not belong here anymore. Go back to your insignificant life in Arrakis City. You will not spread your nonsense here in the sietch."

Taref snapped, "You're holding back our people."

"No, I anchor them and give them stability. Your brothers will resupply you and send you out into the desert again. Don't bother to come back with wild stories or offers. Go!"

Modoc mocked, "Do you require us to carry you on a palanquin, so you can get safely back to your civilization?"

Disappointed, and wondering how he would explain this complete failure to Directeur Venport, Taref turned his back on them. "I still know the desert, but I also know many things you will never experience."

He had felt so saddened when he heard his friends complain about being homesick for the dunes and the old sietch. Now, though, Taref had no regrets about leaving here.

*How many people can be told a secret, before it is no longer considered a secret?*

> —Mentat conundrum (to which there is
> more than one correct answer)

Drawing upon more than a thousand years of memories, Erasmus had a wealth of stories to whisper into Anna Corrino's ear. He stopped speaking to her in the simulated voice of Hirondo when he discovered that she had never believed he was actually the disgraced young chef. Regardless, she considered Erasmus a true friend who would not abandon her, and he experienced an odd pleasure in hearing that.

Erasmus encouraged her attitude, along with the corollary that *he* was a far closer and wiser friend than Hirondo had ever been. As a companion, he was always with her, and Anna could rely on him for excellent advice. Erasmus had tailored this line of reasoning to achieve a specific goal, but the more he conversed with the young woman, the more he actually believed it himself. He really had become her friend.

Anna lay back on her bed, staring at the ceiling. "Tell me more about the terrible thinking machines."

She spent more time in her quarters now. Even though he could accompany her everywhere, thanks to the silver transceiver in her ear, she preferred to converse with him in private. Erasmus had advised her not to call attention to herself, but her increasing isolation was also drawing notice. With his numerous eavesdropping devices, he could listen to conversations among the Mentat trainees, and they talked often about the peculiar girl.

Erasmus promised himself he would do what he could to protect her. Yes, Anna Corrino was odd, but she was also a special young woman, just as Gilbertus had been special to him. And after nearly two centuries, Erasmus was glad to

"I have a name, but it would frighten you."

She chuckled. "You can't frighten me. I know you too well."

Erasmus went through countless calculations, following decision tree after decision tree with the techniques that he himself had taught Gilbertus. "How do I know you can keep a secret?"

"Because you know me. Who would I tell, anyway? I have no friends here. Even at the Sisterhood school on Rossak, Valya was the only one I was close to, and she's gone now. You're my last remaining friend. If you tell me a secret, I couldn't possibly discuss it with anyone but you."

The chain of reasoning was a human sort of logic, but Erasmus believed her. She was so earnest. Though he completed his calculations in a fraction of a second, he hesitated intentionally so that she would understand how carefully he weighed the decision.

"There's something I need to show you," he said. "Follow my instructions carefully."

WHEN HE HEARD about the uprising on Baridge, Gilbertus Albans was appalled, though he let himself show no emotion. A quick report had been rushed back to the Butlerian headquarters while Anari Idaho tied up the loose ends, and Manford Toronto transmitted his victorious news across Lampadas. He was actually proud of what his mobs had accomplished.

Gilbertus remembered Draigo urging him to stand up and expose the folly of the Butlerians. It would have been suicide, of course—and certainly the end of the great Mentat School. Nevertheless, being forced to maintain a meek silence rather than condemning the actions disturbed him. Gilbertus wanted to set an example for humanity, but his inaction in the face of such atrocities seemed cowardly.

Maybe Draigo and Erasmus were right. He should pull up stakes from Lampadas and just leave, change his identity and appearance, go back to a quiet bucolic life on Lectaire. Maybe eventually, in a century or so, he could form a new school somewhere else, possibly on Kolhar.

He was aware that many of the Mentat trainees—maybe even most—held the same mindset as he did, a tolerance of technology as long as it was properly controlled, yet they remained quiet because of the many vehement Butlerian students among them.

The Headmaster finished teaching his class, then gave the Mentat trainees hours of intense exercises under the supervision of his administrator Zendur. Gilbertus returned to his office, deeply troubled. Before making any major have another friend and confidante. He felt a strange sense of responsibility toward her.

"I will tell you about the thinking machines," he said, "but you have to decide for yourself whether or not they were evil. Let me give you a different perspective on history not told in official Imperial documents, and certainly not details that the Butlerian fanatics would share."

As Anna Corrino listened, Erasmus talked about Serena Butler, the girl's own distant ancestor. The robot didn't have to lie when he described his admiration for the strong woman who had led humanity in an astonishing uprising against the machines. And all because of the silly little death of an unremarkable child? He'd never understood that part. Why had that been the cause of such an uproar?

Serena was the first human Erasmus had ever seen as a real person, not just a specimen. She'd made him reconsider the potential of humanity, which had eventually led to him taking the feral boy Gilbertus as a ward.

When he finished that story, Anna wanted to hear more about the Butlers, so Erasmus told her how Serena was finally martyred by Omnius in a great bonfire—and how that horrific death had further galvanized the doomed humans into a furious, illogical energy. "And that gave them the irrational confidence that actually defeated the thinking machines. Otherwise, they would not have had the resolve."

Erasmus considered that an important object lesson, and he would never underestimate the power of human fanaticism.

When he recounted the fall of the Synchronized Empire, Erasmus managed to make her feel sad for the loss of the machine civilization. Tears actually ran down her cheeks! In vivid detail, he described the chaos when the Army of the Jihad overran the last Omnius stronghold, ruthless and savage in their destruction. He did not reveal that he had witnessed that mayhem himself.

Anna was so excited that she picked up the story herself. "And after the Battle of Corrin, Faykan Butler changed his surname to Corrino and became the first Emperor. My grandfather."

Erasmus didn't remember any of that, since by then he had gone into hiding with Gilbertus. Some former machine captives surely knew that the independent robot kept a pet human, but he had vanished among them. Fortunately, enough time had passed that virtually no eyewitnesses remained alive, though there were still some old images.

Anna startled Erasmus by saying, "I feel so close to you, stronger with you." She let out a long sigh. "I wish you were real."

"I am real, Anna. Very real."

"Then what is your name? Why don't you have a name?"

decision, he would discuss this with Erasmus, hoping to find some bastion of sanity.

When he opened his office door, he found Anna Corrino standing there. Inside.

Gilbertus stopped in astonishment. To his great dismay, he saw that she had found the secret wall panel behind his bookcase—and was cupping the Erasmus memory core in her palms as if it were a magical talisman!

He was so stunned he couldn't find words. When he realized any passerby could see the secret cabinet and the gelsphere, he quickly stepped inside, closed and locked the door. His mind raced through a series of Mentat projections, trying to determine how best to respond.

Anna smiled at the memory core, then looked up at him, her eyes sparkling with an expression of childlike awe. "He's beautiful. Erasmus is my best friend."

"How did you . . . how did you know where to find him?"

"He told me. It's our secret." Her brow furrowed, and she looked at the Headmaster. "He said we can trust you not to tell anyone."

The idea that *Gilbertus* might be a threat took him aback. He had rescued the robot and kept him safe ever since the fall of Corrin. "Of course I won't tell anyone." He did not like the sudden precariousness of the situation, now that his greatest secret was known by an unstable person.

The gelsphere thrummed, activating the small speakers. "We needed another ally, son, so I told her where to find me. Anna Corrino is the Emperor's sister. She can help us."

"And I need you." Anna looked lovingly at the glowing sphere, then at Gilbertus. "No more secrets among us. You can both tell me everything now."

"This is extremely dangerous, Father—if she lets slip any word, any hint at all . . . Alys Carroll watches her, and the other Butlerian trainees are always looking for me to make the slightest mistake." The possibilities continued to unfold for him in a series of disastrous Mentat projections. "And Manford Torondo might decide to take Anna as a hostage, in an attempt to control the Emperor. What would she tell the Butlerians?"

Anna sounded indignant. "I would never tell anyone."

"She needs to be involved in our dilemma," Erasmus said, "especially if we have to escape and find another sanctuary—just as Draigo Roget suggested. You should have listened to him when he was here."

"I haven't decided to leave," Gilbertus said.

"But I've decided that we can't stay. Look at the data, Mentat! You realize how great the danger is becoming. I am not confident the school's defenses will be sufficient if the Butlerian mob comes. What if someone discovers your true identity?"

Gilbertus thought this over. The old and harmless Horus Rakka, a former machine sympathizer, had been lynched because of what he had done eighty years before. . . . Considering the recent outrage on Baridge, as well as the frenzied rampage festival in Zimia, and the earlier battle at the Thonaris shipyards, Gilbertus could not deny that the antitechnology movement was growing increasingly out of hand.

But if he simply fled in order to save himself and Erasmus, who could quench the flames of fanaticism? He had to do something to protect the school.

"I have analyzed the mind of Anna Corrino with great attention to detail," Erasmus said, "and I understand how to repair and nurture her thoughts. I realize now that if I cure her, the Corrinos will be beholden to us. Then *they* will defend us against the Butlerians. A perfect solution."

"The Corrinos may not be as strong as you think," Gilbertus warned, though he very much wanted the young woman's mind repaired. "And the Butlerians may be more volatile than we can possibly imagine."

> *Evil is apparent to all who have eyes to see, yet evil also has insidious*
> *roots that plunge deep out of sight, like those of a noxious weed that must*
> *be uprooted and destroyed wherever it tries to spread.*
>
> —MANFORD TORONDO, *Lampadas rallies*

After the uprising, Baridge was suitably chastened—Anari Idaho had seen to it, and she sent a report back to Manford. Even now, the faithful on Lampadas would be celebrating. And when she returned, she would tell Manford in person what she had discovered about Directeur Venport's monstrous Navigators and the true reason for his stranglehold on spice.

Anari would have preferred to make a more drawn-out example of Deacon Kalifer, forcing him to endure a long trial and public humiliation before his execution. But the people had been too eager. The mayhem surrounding the deacon's demise, as well as the spectacle of the mutant Navigator's body, were satisfying enough.

Directeur Rolli Escon, who had kept himself sheltered from the violence, did not venture into the smoldering city until after the riots were over. Anari faced him in the town square in the shadow of the giant captured VenHold spacefolder. "Our people hold their beliefs in their hearts and are not afraid to act on them," she said. "Baridge is a good lesson for all to see, a message from Leader Torondo, reminding all loyal planets of their pledge."

Escon straightened, eager to show his dedication. "My ships will deliver the message everywhere Leader Torondo wishes."

She indicated the ransacked spacefolder. "Have your foldspace pilots ensured that the captured vessel is ready for its journey to Lampadas?"

"We have to check the foldspace engines and repair some of the piloting controls." Escon sounded uneasy. "Part of the control deck was torn apart. Your followers impaired some of the systems in their . . . enthusiasm."

"They killed a mutated monster, and I myself destroyed computers there. We don't need those things to fly a spaceship. The mind of man is holy."

"Of course, Swordmaster." He didn't sound entirely certain.

The following afternoon, when the systems were pronounced ready, Anari watched the scattered crew board the seized VenHold vessel. Of the hundred followers that had come with her from Lampadas, she selected two Swordmaster comrades and five fervent Butlerians, along with one of Escon's pilots, to send aboard the spacefolder back to Manford, where it would be added to his fleet.

Anari Idaho and Rolli Escon watched the massive ship lift off from the square. As the giant, angular shape hovered above the city, Anari and her avid followers chanted a loud prayer into the smoke-filled air. Then the pilot activated the fold-space engines, and the ship vanished with a thunderous boom.

ANARI REMAINED ON Baridge for several more days to continue the work, while the Butlerians hunted down enclaves of Machine Apologists, supporters of Deacon Kalifer, or anyone who simply didn't seem passionate enough about Manford's cause. Some nervous shopkeepers smashed their own businesses just to demonstrate their priorities and to avoid extreme retaliation.

At night the auroras blazed brighter, as if in a celestial celebration of the righteous victory. By daylight, the air of Baridge seemed to crackle, but Anari's followers weren't afraid of harmful solar radiation. God provided them with better protection than any technology could.

Rolli Escon prepared his own ship to return the Swordmaster to Lampadas. He claimed he was anxious to spread Manford's message, although Anari suspected he merely wanted to get away from Baridge. But she, too, needed to get back to see Manford. She worried about him when she wasn't there to protect him, and she had important news for him.

THE CAPTURED VENHOLD warship never arrived at Lampadas. Eventually, as days dragged out into a week after it was due, the conclusion grew inescapable: The seized spacefolder had vanished en route, as so many EsconTran vessels did. Anari was disappointed at the loss of the ship, which she considered a spoil of war, but she had other priorities.

When she arrived back at the capital city, she hoped for a private debriefing with Manford, and time to catch up with him, but the Butlerian leader wanted the rest of his inner circle to hear her report about Baridge. Manford called a meeting in his home, and the housekeeper, Ellonda, bustled around to prepare the main room, then attended the guests.

Deacon Harian refused to sit, and Anari was happy to let the bald man stand there and be uncomfortable. Sister Woodra listened to the Swordmaster's every word with narrowed eyes, assessing and analyzing her report for accuracy. Anari lifted her chin, ready to slaughter this haughty Sister if she so much as suggested that she was shading the truth.

Focused only on Manford, Anari described the mob uprising and the punitive actions she had taken. He approved of everything she'd done, as she knew he would. The only image she brought to show Manford—and the other curious onlookers, including the horrified old housekeeper—was of the humanoid Navigator.

"It's a demon!" Deacon Harian said.

"Worse than that. It was human once," Manford said. "This creature shows the vile pact Josef Venport made. Look what he has done to this poor being." He touched his forehead, said reverently, "The mind of man is holy."

Manford looked so disturbed that Anari wanted to hold and comfort him, and give him all of her strength, should he need it.

"Appalling," Harian said. "How can they create such monsters?"

"It lived in a tank filled with concentrated melange gas," Anari said. "No human could survive that much spice exposure, but the Navigator relied upon it, immersed himself in it. The VenHold ship was also carrying a cargo of spice from Arrakis. Half the Imperium is addicted to it, and I believe Deacon Kalifer was more interested in maintaining his access to melange than to any medical supplies. That was the bribe Venport used."

"Spice is an insidious drug," Manford said. "Even the Emperor uses it."

Woodra looked intense, distracted. "I received a message from Reverend Mother Dorotea on Salusa Secundus. She has uncovered remarkable connections to Venport Holdings, including the secret but absolute control of spice production and distribution—right under the Emperor's nose."

Ellonda picked up the dishes, clattering cups on the tray and dithering about the room. Frowning at the noisy interruption, Anari said, "EsconTran can provide necessary commodities to our planets, but he can't get supplies of melange. Combined Mercantiles has an exclusive arrangement with VenHold."

Sister Woodra said, "Melange has seeped into many aspects of life throughout the Imperium. It is a popular additive to beverages and foods, a stimulant, and it's said that those who consume it on a regular basis live longer, healthier lives. Other companies have tried harvesting spice on Arrakis, but Venport Holdings and Combined Mercantiles have a ruthless monopoly."

She narrowed her gaze, looked at Manford. "Now we know that Venport needs spice—a lot of it—for his Navigators. And he has a great many Navigators. If we break that monopoly, we severely weaken him."

Manford followed the argument, nodding slowly. "Then I must make a journey to Arrakis and convert those spice workers to our cause, deny Venport what he needs most."

"It is too dangerous for you to travel there," Anari said, putting her foot down.

He dismissed her concern. "All important battles are dangerous. But we must not fear."

"You cannot go, Manford. We discussed this before—EsconTran's safety record is too poor. We just lost another ship in foldspace. Until the navigational problems are solved, it's too dangerous for you to travel."

Manford admitted he was deeply troubled by the loss of the commandeered vessel. He shook his head. "It would have made a satisfying trophy, but it was a demon ship."

"I destroyed the computers on board, Manford," Anari said. "It should have been safe."

"But you couldn't destroy the taint of thinking machines. Maybe a hidden computer presence rose up from within the machinery and threw the vessel off course."

Deacon Harian said, "So many EsconTran ships have disappeared. His company must be cursed."

Anari couldn't argue with that, but she drove home her main point. "Let me go to Arrakis first, to reconnoiter. I will be your eyes, and I will report back. You know you can trust me."

Manford resisted. "They need to hear my words, see my face."

"They can't hear you or see you if you disappear into empty space!" She crossed her arms over her chest. Finally she said, in a small compromise, "Write your speech and rehearse it with your double. I'll take him with me and carry him on my shoulders. The people will never notice the difference, but *I'll* know you're safe. With that confidence, I can do a better job."

Manford's shoulders slumped in acquiescence. "Very well, take my double to Arrakis and report back. It is critically important for us to learn how we can destroy all Venport operations there."

*I am an educated, rational businessman, not prone to emotional out-
bursts, and yet I despise the Butlerians with every fiber of my being. I
hate them more than any apparatus can measure.*

—DIRECTEUR JOSEF VENPORT, *to his wife, Cioba*

When the news about Baridge reached Kolhar, Josef couldn't find an appropriate outlet for his disgust and outrage. The murder of more than a
hundred VenHold employees and forty Suk cancer doctors, the destruction of
cargo shuttles as well as a massive spacefolder . . . and the slaughter of a priceless
Navigator, Royce Fayed!

In his office tower overlooking the spaceport, Josef met with Cioba, who had
let her long hair down so that it trailed past her waist. Draigo Roget wore a stony
expression that did not entirely mask his inner anger.

"I have no words for this." Josef prowled about with unreleased rage. "The
thinking machines were our enemies, but at least they were comprehensible.
Who can explain this? *This!*" He hammered his hand down on another report
that glowed up on his desk screen. "After the rampage festival in Zimia, I expected Emperor Salvador to crack down on the Butlerians . . . but again, they
launch their barbaric insanity on another planet. Against *me*—with impunity!"

This had gone far beyond profits and power. As Norma Cenva had warned, it
was now a war of civilizations. Josef struggled to understand the Half-Manford's
fanaticism. How did he get all those people to follow him blindly, questioning
nothing he said? Josef had watched video recordings of the leader's speeches, dissected his demeanor, the way he spoke—and the man was not that charismatic.
Aside from having no legs, Manford seemed rather ordinary, which made his
mass appeal even more baffling.

Draigo spoke up, his normally flat voice uneven, an indication of how unsettled he was. "Manford Torondo sent out a call, and his planets are reaffirming

their commitments to honor their pledges. He also sent a delegation to Salusa Secundus to insist that Emperor Salvador take aggressive action against you: new tariffs and restrictions on VenHold trade."

Josef frowned. "Emperor Salvador is as ineffective as he is indecisive, a ruler who does nothing but collect fees and sit in pompous glory on his throne. The Imperium is being torn apart between pro- and antitechnology supporters, and he does his best to appease two sides while making no movement at all." He let out a scornful noise. "Like a trained monkey, balancing on a ball." His heart pounded, and the ache in his skull grew greater. "If the Emperor won't impose punishment, then it falls to us. We have resources. We can do something."

"The first planet to issue a statement reaffirming the oath to Manford is a small backwater world called Lectaire," Draigo pointed out.

"Never heard of Lectaire. Does it have any economic significance? Is it even on our trade routes?"

"It's a small agricultural world with minimal resources, no strategic importance, population under a million. Two primary cities, numerous scattered farms. No defenses whatsoever. VenHold ships have serviced Lectaire over the years, though not on a regular basis, since it isn't cost-effective. Lately, the planet has been on our embargo list." The Mentat blinked. "Other companies have recently made several runs there, but on the whole Lectaire is insignificant."

Josef sat down, still trying to control his anger. "It *is* significant because it is the first planet to reaffirm the Half-Manford's manifesto. We can't let these fanatics have any victory at all. They can dance around their cave fires, but they must not be allowed to think that they've won."

"Royce Fayed was a valuable asset," Cioba said. "Norma Cenva was close to him. She'll want to help us."

Josef considered his options. A direct military strike against Lectaire or any other Butlerian world would certainly be traced back to him. Even if the Imperial Space Fleet and House Corrino were seemingly ineffective, he didn't want to provoke outright war or nudge Salvador into making the wrong decision.

But he had a weapon that no one in the Imperium knew about: All of the new cymeks from Denali, guided by the brains of failed Navigators. He could give Ptolemy the opportunity for a real demonstration.

Josef realized he was smiling for the first time since the news had arrived. "The cymeks were impressive on Arrakis. They won't have any trouble against a small farming world. We will leave no evidence behind of what hit Lectaire, and no trace of the human settlements there. It'll be just like the Time of Titans—except this time we have a just cause."

⟨⟩

EVEN ISOLATED ON Denali, Ptolemy reviewed reports of the latest atrocities committed by the Butlerians. He didn't need further incentive to despise the savages. He still had nightmares of Dr. Elchan's screams, and of the calm, even amused expression on Manford Torondo's face when he watched Elchan roasted alive. . . .

Though seven of his best cymeks were lost on Arrakis, Ptolemy had been building his army all along. And they were ready to be sent into action.

The enormous robot walkers trudged across Denali's bleak landscape, impervious to the corrosive atmosphere. Still building up the new group, he'd installed many more failed Navigator brains into canisters, connected the thoughtrodes to the engines and motivators of new walkers. These cymek candidates were still practicing their reactions and learning how to unite their brains with their new artificial bodies.

And they were terrifying.

When plotting revenge, some people could wait for years and years, arranging tiny pieces in such a way as to set up an enemy for complete downfall. Josef Venport was not such a man. He felt gravely insulted by Butlerian tactics. The business interests of Venport Holdings had been hurt by destructive mobs, and a Navigator had been murdered. Josef demanded a swift and devastating retaliation. Like a viper that had been stepped on, he struck back immediately.

Ptolemy was pleased to be Josef Venport's fangs.

A VenHold hauler came to Denali to retrieve the cymek assault force. To demonstrate the importance of the mission, Norma Cenva herself guided the spacefolder.

Ptolemy worked with Administrator Noffe to load eighteen of his best cymek attackers aboard, for secret transport to Lectaire. Though he knew they would perform well, Ptolemy insisted on going along. He wanted to observe his shining examples under real conditions, a genuine victory rather than the proof of concept.

Noffe looked very proud as Ptolemy prepared to board the shuttle. "We have already accomplished tremendous things, my friend." The pale blotches on Noffe's skin were more prominent when he flushed with excitement. "But be careful. I want you to return safely—we still have a lot of work to do together."

"The cymeks will protect me from the barbarians," Ptolemy said. "And after this mission, we'll have fewer barbarians to worry about."

He had begun as a pure researcher, a man of science and ideas. On the planet Zenith he had devoted his life to research projects, discovering new methods to help humanity after the Jihad. He had never been bloodthirsty, never imagined harming another human being.

But such pacifism had been burned out of him by the fires that consumed his research laboratory . . . and his friend.

As the spacefolder traveled to Lectaire, Norma Cenva remained alone up on the pilot deck. When they reached orbit over the bucolic planet, Norma finally contacted him and also sent her message to the new cymeks. With her vastly expanded intellect, she seemed more in tune with the failed Navigator brains than with Ptolemy. Out of deference, it seemed, she included him.

"I understand the causality of revenge," Norma said. "Butlerian ignorance harms our future." Her warbling voice hesitated, and then she added, "This sad mindset killed Royce Fayed."

Ptolemy spoke to the Navigator brains as well as to Norma, although he doubted they needed encouragement. He had tremendous faith in his creations. "We will punish them. Butlerian superstitions can't protect them from superior weapons and superior minds."

Norma said with great portent, "Ignorance is a powerful armor against the truth."

The eighteen walkers dropped down in landing pods that split open upon impact. They landed near the main town just as dusk was deepening. The new Titans emerged from the landers like spiders from eggs, with their claws extended, cannon arms telescoped into firing positions, and flame jets fully primed. Each combat body had a different configuration, because Ptolemy wanted to test a variety of designs.

First, the walkers descended upon Lectaire's primary farming and market city, where the natives didn't know how to react, except with terror. These towering cymek walkers were the embodiment of their worst nightmares.

Ptolemy did not bother with any recorded warning or explanation. There would be no survivors here, and he would be careful to leave no evidence behind that might identify the attacker. The new Titans charged through the town, and weapons fire from their bodies and arms exploded buildings and mowed down fleeing villagers.

In his observation room aboard the spacecraft, the screens were arrayed like the interlocked facets of an insect's eye. The new Titans had visual and auditory pickups, and they transmitted the screams, crackling flames, and explosions. Ptolemy reveled in the murderous destruction for a while, then finally became numb. He muted the sounds, although he continued to watch the screens in fascination.

Carefully coordinated with the help of their superior Navigator brains, the eighteen Titans annihilated everything in the town, then spread to the outskirts, where they laid waste to surrounding farms.

Up in orbit, Norma Cenva's ship deployed sensors to watch for any incoming ships, but Lectaire was rarely visited. Ptolemy knew the cymeks would have as much time as they needed.

"Magnificent," he whispered, watching the impressive forms obliterate agricultural fields, farm buildings, storage silos. The mayhem was quite thorough.

From orbit they were mapping and targeting the location of every small settlement on the sparsely populated planet. Ptolemy had developed the methodical plan, though he was sure the Navigator cymeks would do an excellent tactical job. According to his best projections, they would complete the punitive scouring of Lectaire in seven days or less.

It was going to be a long but gratifying week.

*Symbols are powerful motivators of human behavior. And symbols can be destroyed.*

—DIRECTOR JOSEF VENPORT, "Memo on Extrapolations
of Business and Power"

Turning his back on the sietch that did not want him, Taref worked his way across the desert back to Arrakis City.

The week-long trek was arduous, and the desert austere and uncomfortable, but he endured the deprivation. When he reached the city, he would find other Freemen who had left their sietches, Freemen who might be tempted to join him. He vowed to himself he would not return to Directeur Venport empty-handed.

If he'd been able to recruit eager volunteers from the sietch itself, Taref would have summoned a sandworm to transport them swiftly across the open dunes. He would have stood tall atop the head of the monster, feeling the sun and grit on his face.

At the moment, though, he had no cause to celebrate. He didn't care about the father and brothers he'd left behind; he'd known that they would sneer at the idea, because they were ignorant and closed-minded. He had been reminded of how squalid and backward his tribe was, and yet the glorious promises and shining visions he had once believed in now also tasted like dust.

When he and his friends had left poverty behind, they'd been so excited for the opportunity, especially him. Taref tried to take comfort from the fact that Shurko had lived more in his brief months working for VenHold than he would have experienced in a lifetime out in the desert. Surely his friend had seen and enjoyed some wonders on his travels.

Knowing what Kolhar, Junction Alpha, and all those other run-down spaceport worlds were like, should he bother to go back at all? If Taref were to vanish here, Directeur Venport and Draigo Roget would chalk up his loss to an unspecified desert hazard. He could easily find a way to survive, even here on Arrakis, maybe joining another spice crew.

But he didn't want to do that, didn't want to hide. No, Taref would go back to Directeur Venport, because he had promised. With the authorization he carried, he could have flown to Kolhar on the next spice hauler, but first he had to do what he had agreed to do. He would find volunteers, somehow. . . .

On the way to Arrakis City, Taref was surprised at how the desert environment now grated on him as much as the backward desert mindset did. His still-suit was scuffed and dusty, but it still looked different with its obvious offworld modifications. He had a few coins, a Maula pistol, his stillsuit, a desert cloak, and his VenHold ID. His demeanor was no longer that of a furtive, ever-wary sand dweller. Reaching the city, he noticed the people regarding him as if he were an outcast here, too.

For a while Taref observed the spaceport operations, watching the vessels load up with melange and take off from the landing field. Before, when he'd worked on spice crews, Taref had never given much thought to where all that spice went after the haulers departed from Arrakis. Now he knew so much more. Seeing a small freighter take off, he remembered dreaming about those romantic, far-off places—Salusa Secundus, or Poritrin, or the ocean-drenched world of Caladan, a planet he still hadn't seen. Surely there were other people here willing to leave.

He watched the freighter ascend into the lemon-colored sky, and decided he had put off his work for too long. He would convince others to join him, promising them wonders that he now doubted existed. He would find young men or women with sparkling eyes turned toward the skies imagining a far better life elsewhere. Taref would tell them everything they wanted to hear, everything *he* had wanted to hear. . . .

Then a miracle occurred in the streets.

A muscular female Swordmaster strode through Arrakis City with the stump of a man riding on her shoulders. They were accompanied by an entourage of defiant, disheveled followers, each wearing the badge of a machine gear clenched in a symbolic fist—the badge of the Butlerians.

Taref stared. This was the Butlerian leader, the man whom Directeur Venport loathed, the fanatic who had caused such turmoil . . . the man Venport wanted dead, by any means.

He knew immediately what he had to do.

Although he had no personal interest in politics, he owed his loyalty to Josef Venport, and Venport wanted to cut off the head of the barbarian monster that was destroying humanity's future. The Directeur's enemies were Taref's enemies.

Manford rode high on Anari Idaho's shoulders, a perfect target above the throngs around them. Taref could never fight the Swordmaster, not even with a precious wormtooth dagger, but he did know that none of the Butlerians would be wearing a body shield. They abhorred technology, foolishly expecting their faith to protect them.

Taref didn't make a plan, didn't think about his possible escape. He merely reacted. He already had the blood of many thousands on his hands from the spaceships he had sabotaged. This one man, though, counted for more than all of them together.

Taref drew his Maula pistol, aimed, and fired.

The projectile struck Manford in the head, shattered his skull, and splattered brains and blood over his shocked supporters. The Butlerian leader jerked backward, his legless form knocked out of the padded leather socket that secured him to the Swordmaster's shoulders.

A sudden startled hush fell on the streets. All eyes had been watching the marching Butlerians. The Maula pistol had made only a whizzing *clack* from its spring-loaded mechanism.

Manford tumbled to the ground, twitching but obviously dead. The Swordmaster wailed.

Taref dropped the weapon and melted back into the crowd. Though numbed by the knowledge of what he had done, he forced himself to keep moving. Fortunately, his dusty desert garb looked commonplace in the streets. He heard gasps. People reacted with shock and dismay, and he glanced from face to face, mimicking their horror as he pretended to search for the source of the danger.

The Swordmaster scooped up the legless body and bounded away, carrying Manford Torondo like a limp doll. Other Butlerians screamed, but they could not find who had shot their leader. Some of the offworlders even gave water for the dead, as tears streamed down their dusty cheeks.

Taref didn't stay to watch, but slipped under a sheltered overhang, and then away. He knew Directeur Venport would reward him for this one act far more than if he had brought a hundred avid recruits.

He decided to use the VenHold line of credit for a nice meal and a room after all. Then he would depart on the next spacefolder.

ON KOLHAR, WHEN Taref reported to the administrative towers without his promised volunteers, Directeur Venport's face soured in disappointment. "No one else wishes to join our cause? You could not convince any of your desert people?"

Taref could barely contain himself. "You might not need any more volunteers, ever again." He blurted out, "I assassinated Manford Torondo on Arrakis!"

That claim seemed to freeze time itself. Draigo Roget turned to him, his dark eyebrows raised in disbelief. The Directeur straightened behind his desk. "What?"

Taref was breathing quickly. "I saw him and his Swordmaster in Arrakis City. I don't know why they were there, but I remembered your orders. I had a Maula pistol, so I shot the Butlerian leader in the head. I saw him fall. He's dead, Directeur Venport."

Josef looked at Draigo, struggling to conceal elation behind his thick mustache. "Is he telling the truth, Mentat?"

"I am not a Truthsayer, sir, but I will verify the facts as soon as possible."

"I saw it with my own eyes, Directeur," Taref insisted. "Half of his head was blown away, his brains splashed on the people around him and the dirt of the street. He's dead—no question about it."

Venport began to chuckle. "If you're right, this almost makes up for the Baridge debacle. Without their pathetic half-leader, the barbarians will scatter like rodents." Directeur Venport stepped over to Taref in a single stride and clapped a hand on the young man's shoulders. "Good work."

⚜

*A threat works only if the recipient believes you are willing to carry through with it.*

—REVEREND MOTHER RAQUELLA BERTO-ANIRUL

I t was not a good time for the Mother Superior to die.

Prior to the crisis, Raquella had been quite healthy despite her advanced age, and now, only a year later, she felt decades older. Sorrow, despair, and the stress of rebuilding the Sisterhood school on a different planet would have taken its toll even on a much younger woman.

In order to maintain herself, she consumed frequent doses of melange supplied by VenHold, as well as other drugs, but they were rapidly becoming insufficient. Even melange only stretched her already-long life like a rubber band. Now her lifeline was almost to the breaking point.

Early each morning, locked in her private quarters, she went into a trance and analyzed her internal chemistry and cellular structure. With her skills and control as a Reverend Mother, she could observe each biological detail as if projected on a screen in her mind.

After analyzing the tiniest cellular nuances, Raquella used the information to determine what adjustments were necessary to sustain her for one more day. But tiny errors and failures had been mounting, and she'd been in crisis mode for a long time, just trying to stay alive. Her rate of decline was increasing, and she knew she could not maintain the biological façade for much longer. And the Sisterhood was still broken.

Raquella would have preferred to orchestrate her passing much differently. She had to save the Sisterhood, choose her successor. Otherwise there would be more turmoil, more arguments, maybe even further splits. Valya Harkonnen seemed the obvious candidate, but there was also Dorotea. Each woman had certain advantages, and obvious flaws. If only Raquella could combine the best of both, fuse the factions, *heal* them.

The other Sisters on Wallach IX didn't notice the extent of the Mother Superior's deterioration. They had seen the old woman for so long that they turned a blind eye to her mortality. Raquella's followers didn't know about the effort she expended just to keep standing upright. If she made the slightest slip, the house of cards that was her body would collapse. She didn't know how much longer she could keep this up.

Now, on a bright morning under a clear sky, she walked out on the steep trail, climbing high Laojin Cliff as she often did. To demonstrate her health, Raquella continued to go for long walks. The wooded path was familiar to her, and she liked being high up, where she could look down at the cluster of buildings that constituted her new school.

Fielle accompanied her this morning, listening more than talking, as she often did. The large-boned Sister Mentat was in good shape and could actually walk faster, but was holding back. Raquella appreciated the company. She missed conversations with her dear friend Karee Marques, who had also been a Mentat, with the capacity to offer objective, well-reasoned advice.

Fielle was not an appropriate choice to become the next Mother Superior, but if Raquella were to die tomorrow—with Valya away on Ginaz for Swordmaster training, and Dorotea ensconced on Salusa Secundus—who would lead the Sisters? Raquella needed to decide on her successor.

Continuing to walk, the old woman remained silent, but her mind was not quiet; the rattling voices of Other Memory, dead Sisters from her bloodlines, clamored for her to join them. Raquella was not quite ready—but it had to be soon. She felt dread and anticipation.

They reached a sunny overlook on the steep trail, one of Raquella's favorite spots. There they could sit on a flat stone and gaze out on the trees, lakes, and mountains of Wallach IX. A chill wind blew across the treetops and ruffled their robes.

Bundling up, the two sat for a long, contemplative moment. Fielle's brown eyes were filled with compassion and concern. "Are you feeling well today, Mother Superior? You seem to be keeping something inside. Would you like to share it with me? I'll do whatever I can to assist you."

Raquella felt weary in every aged muscle and bone of her body. "It is no secret—I'm dying."

The Sister Mentat did not react with denial; instead, she just gave a sad nod.

"Fielle, you are one of the most selfless people I've ever met, and I admire you for that." Raquella smiled. "And for other fine traits. But you are so young, dear, so very young."

"And I have much that I still want to learn from you. Is there any way I can help? For all of us, please find a way to keep going, Mother Superior."

"The *Sisterhood* must keep going. I have already lived long past a normal lifetime, and I worry not for myself but for the future of this school, and these Sisters. I don't want it all to die with me."

Fielle raised her voice. "We would never allow that, Mother Superior!"

"I have often said that emotions get in the way of our tasks, that love is a dangerous distraction, but maybe I was wrong about that, Fielle, because I'm buoyed by the love you show for me, and I appreciate it more than you can possibly realize. But among other Sisters who will outlive me—those here and others on Salusa Secundus—there is such enmity that I don't see a way to bring them together. We are too fragmented."

"There may be a way, Mother Superior. I have run Mentat projections." Fielle rose to her feet and paced the promontory, as if it were an office. "Without you, there would likely be a civil war among the Sisters, a power struggle, perhaps even further Imperial intervention. Reverend Mother Valya could instigate it, or maybe Dorotea—but it would happen for certain. Each side would view your loss as a vacuum that must be filled."

Raquella's eyes burned with emotion. "Unless I fix it first. I have asked Dorotea to come here so I can speak with her, beg her . . . but I suspect she will not listen."

Fielle sounded more optimistic now. "A crisis broke us apart, Mother Superior. It will require another crisis, not mere diplomacy, to bring us back together. My Mentat projection suggests a method to reunite the estranged factions, but I hesitate to tell you. It is perhaps too radical."

"I need a solution, so give me the raw information. Let me decide." She rose to her feet and stood with her arms folded across her chest, trying not to shiver in the breeze. "What do you have in mind?"

The younger woman avoided making eye contact, as if ashamed of what she was about to suggest. "They still love you, regardless of politics, Mother Superior. All the Sisters on Wallach IX do, and I am convinced Dorotea and her orthodox Sisters do as well. Use that."

"How?"

"Demand that the factions put aside their differences and find common ground—now. You do not have the time to craft a gradual peace. If they fail to do so, then shock them into doing what they must. As has been proved time and again, never underestimate the power of a martyr."

"You mean, threaten to kill myself?"

"You may have to do more than threaten. If logic doesn't make them solve their differences, maybe guilt will."

Raquella thought for a moment, and nodded. "Sister Arlett has already departed for Salusa Secundus with a message for Dorotea. I'll dispatch a coded letter to Ginaz recalling Valya. I need them both here immediately, so I can give them my ultimatum. If they refuse . . ." She shrugged. "My life is at an end anyway. Maybe my death can accomplish one last thing."

The pair began walking back down the trail, moving at the old woman's pace. Raquella was slower than usual. Although now she had a glimmer of hope for the Sisterhood, she felt the deep fatigue of a long lifetime.

↬

*There is beauty in the eyes of the youth who dreams of a bright future.*
—wisdom of the Ancients

Though Caladan was quiet and bucolic, it boasted an impressive Air Patrol Agency. The scattered fishing fleets, the occasional sea storms, and the creatures out in the deep oceans—all required the locals to be ready to mount a rapid and efficient rescue when necessary.

Vor smiled when he studied the history of the Caladan Air Patrol and their years of service. No one knew that the rescue organization had been established and funded well over a century ago through an anonymous foundation set up by Vorian Atreides. Yes, he still had many ties here.

Though they were still young, his great-great-grandsons Willem and Orry had made themselves important pilots in the Patrol. Both young men had a love of fast and dangerous flying in their blood, but Vor decided this was a much better profession than piloting warships against robot vessels in the Jihad.

After that long, late-night confession and conversation with Shander Atreides, Vor felt relieved. He rarely got a chance to shed so many secrets. Even so, from Shander's raised eyebrows and uncertain chuckle, he wasn't sure the wealthy old fisherman—actually Vor's great-grandson—completely believed him. Shander was aware only that one of his ancestors had been a great war hero, as attested to by the statue in the town square; but that was far back in the days of the Jihad, and the fact meant little to their daily lives. Nevertheless, Shander accepted Vorian's friendship, seeing him as a curiosity and a spinner of tales. Good company overall, regardless of his past.

In a broader sense, Vor wanted to reconnect with the tapestry of his family, his roots, and to apologize for the aloof way he had treated Leronica and their two sons . . . generations ago. Although no one on Caladan even remembered the slight, Vor needed to do it for himself.

His openness and candor surprised some on Caladan who heard his story, while others simply assumed he had a wild imagination. Vor didn't mind; he intended to stay on beautiful Caladan for a while—for quite a while, in fact. Willem and Orry were strangers to him, but he could hardly wait to meet them.

On the third day after Vor arrived on Caladan, Shander Atreides offered to meet him for lunch to introduce him to the two young men, who were due back from a long patrol. At the last minute, Shander had to respond to an insistent customer, some kind of urgent repair order for fishing nets, and so Vor went to the landing-field café himself. He had faced greater challenges before.

Walking in, he felt tense but eager to meet Willem and Orry. Vor found them sitting at a table by a window that overlooked the Air Patrol field, where seaplanes took off and landed. He was startled when he caught his first glimpse of the two laughing young men. Even in their flight suits, they looked very much like the twins Estes and Kagin. He caught his breath, felt a pang, and then smiled as he stepped forward.

The brothers rose in unison to greet him; each shook his hand with a firm grip. Willem was taller than his older brother, with blond hair, while Orry's was black like Vor's. "I'm glad to finally meet you both," Vor said.

They were polite, formal, although neither seemed to quite understand who he was. Willem said, "Uncle Shander told us you're a surprise visitor. Some long-lost family member that we need to meet?"

Vor sat back, surprised. "He didn't tell you my story?"

"We've been out on patrol for a week," Orry said, "filling in at another airfield."

"My name is Vorian Atreides." He saw that they recognized the name but couldn't quite place it. "I'm your great-great-grandfather. I spent a lot of time here on Caladan, long ago during the Jihad. I met a local woman named Leronica Tergiet, and we had twin sons. One of them was your great-grandfather."

Willem and Orry blinked, then chuckled, but their laughter fell into silence when Vor continued to regard them with a serious expression. He explained the life-extension treatment he had received from his father, the cymek General Agamemnon. He was sure they must have been taught the history of the Jihad.

Orry said, "This is impossible. This really sounds impossible!"

Willem sat back at the table, looking skeptical. "We've heard of you, of course, at least the name. But . . . that's all ancient history, and whatever you did all those centuries ago doesn't affect us here. Not anymore."

Vor frowned. "It's been a very long time, but that doesn't mean the past can't find you here. I'd just like to get to know you both."

Orry grinned. "I'll bet he has some amazing stories."

With a nod, Willem said, "As long as he pays for the meal."

The boys showed no animosity toward him, just friendly curiosity. It appeared that any disappointment Estes and Kagin might have felt toward Vor had not lasted over the generations . . . unlike the bitterness House Harkonnen felt toward him. He could start fresh with these young men, earn their friendship without any preconceptions.

Their meals arrived, a local specialty of dark bread baked with meats, cheeses, and fresh vegetables.

"If you're a member of the family, then you have to come to my wedding," Orry said.

Willem explained, "My brother's been in such a rush since meeting this girl—and he's gone a little dizzy over her—but we can add an ancient war hero to the guest list."

"Sounds like I arrived at just the right time. I'd love to attend." Vor remembered all the family promises he'd broken in the past and vowed not to do it again. "When is it? Tell me about her."

Once encouraged, Orry seemed unable to stop talking about his fiancée, while Willem just rolled his eyes. Orry had met a beautiful, charming young woman from an inland village, and they'd immediately felt sparks between them. "She swept me off my feet."

"She *knocked* him off his feet." Willem wore a long-suffering expression. "I've never seen him so love-struck. It happened so fast that no one's had much of a chance to get to know her—except Orry, of course." His tone was teasing.

"From the moment we met, we were two pieces that fit perfectly together," Orry said, then turned to his brother. "Someday you'll find a woman as perfect as . . . Well, *almost* as perfect, because there isn't anyone to match her."

Willem sighed. "I don't believe in love at first sight."

"I knew if I didn't make my move quickly, you would have been after her," Orry said, smiling. "And you know it, too."

Willem gave an embarrassed chuckle. "You might be right."

"I'm looking forward to meeting her," Vor said. "And to spending more time with you two. Does the Air Patrol have room for another volunteer? I was a crack pilot once, and I've got experience—centuries' worth, in fact."

Willem seemed thrilled with the suggestion. "Want to go out with us after lunch? Our multiwing tiltplane can hold a third passenger—there's even room for famous people."

"I'd rather not be famous," Vor said. "I prefer to be treated as an ordinary man for a change."

Orry laughed. "We can do that. Most people won't believe your war stories anyway. But they beat the wild tales our fishermen tell."

They finished their meal, eager to head back to the airfield. As they left the café and walked out to the landing area, Willem said, "We can't offer any combat missions against robot battleships, though. You might find it boring."

"I'm perfectly happy with a boring mission. I risked my life enough times." Vor had nothing to prove to anyone. He felt glad he had decided to make his way back to Caladan.

An alarm klaxon sounded from the airfield, and Willem and Orry looked at each other before bolting toward a patrol craft. "We're on call," Willem shouted as Vor hurried to keep up with them. "It's an emergency."

Orry jabbed his finger toward a long, thin aircraft that had a red light pulsing on top. "That's our plane." The craft had rotors and a complex arrangement of wings to operate as a helicopter, airplane, or watercraft. Vor had never flown that exact model before, but it looked similar to many he had used.

An attendant was refueling the tiltplane for immediate takeoff. He looked up at the trio running toward the craft, said, "A man's been caught in an undertow taking him out to sea. Report came in from a woman harvesting anemones by Gable Cliff." He closed the cap, rapped the side of the craft. "You're ready to go. I ran through the checklist."

The tiltplane's cockpit was barely large enough to accommodate the three men; Vor crammed into a jump seat behind the two younger Atreides. From his days on Caladan, he recalled instances of dangerous riptides and unexpected currents near the shore. Any victim swept out to sea would not last long.

Willem took the controls, and as they taxied for takeoff, Orry went through his own quick checklist and adjusted his headset. "Report came in ten minutes ago, but the victim isn't far. We might make it in time, if he's a strong swimmer."

"First we have to find him out in the big water," Willem said, then glanced back at Vor. "Your extra set of eyes could come in handy."

They soared over the high promontory of Gable Cliff and turned out to sea, dipping down to fly low over the waves. Another patrol plane joined them, and they spread out their search patterns. Whitecaps licked the rough sea, and a brisk breeze buffeted them. Vor leaned against the side windowport and pointed. "I see something at two o'clock."

They circled back for a closer look, and a human figure came into view, a gray-haired man floating in the water. Operating the controls to shift the tiltplane's wings, Willem hovered over the area while Orry worked his way to the back and pulled himself into a sling. Clipping his supports into place, he slid open the access door to a roar of wind and aircraft engines, then pushed himself out, pulling the rope taut as the sling lowered. Vor clipped himself into place with a safety harness and helped guide the rope down.

Even with the sharp breezes, Willem held the craft in perfect position. Orry rode down on the sling, and maneuvered into position until he could grab the floating man. Orry's motions were urgent as he wrestled with the victim and strapped him into the sling. He kept shouting into the comm, but Vor could only hear the wind, engines, and static.

Willem's face was pale and grim as he raised the winch, hauling both Orry and the victim back up to the open hold. Vor leaned out in his harness and reached down to guide them aboard.

Orry seemed to be crying as he clung to the dripping old man. Vor hauled them both inside and secured the sling. The victim slumped forward, facedown and motionless on the deck. Orry tore himself free of the harness, crawled over to the body, and rolled him over.

Vor grabbed the first-aid kit, but he could tell the man was dead—he had seen enough death in all his years. The old man's eyes were open, his head smashed, his face badly swollen and bruised, almost unrecognizable. *Almost.* His heart sank.

It was Shander Atreides.

The hatch closed and the tiltplane flew over the water as Willem raced back toward shore.

Orry was sobbing as he tried to resuscitate his uncle, and Vor helped, even though he knew it was useless. Still, he had to let the young man do what he needed to do. Shander had raised the boys.

"It looks like somebody beat him," Willem said, his voice breaking.

"I was thinking the same thing," Vor said. Shander's death was clearly not an accident.

> *In hand-to-hand combat, even the most formidable opponent can be defeated. You must find an inner calm and visualize the path to victory.*
>
> —JOOL NORET, the first Swordmaster

For weeks, Valya trained hard at the Ginaz School, learning what she could from the Swordmasters, adding their specialized knowledge to the already lethal fighting arsenal she possessed.

Despite his challenge to her on the first day of instruction, Master Placido took a liking to Valya. He gave her a great deal of personal attention, both during the classes and outside them, making himself available for questions and additional demonstrations. "One must be open to receive wisdom from any source at any time," he said, which reminded Valya of Sisterhood instruction.

The instructor was attracted to her, but she calmly, firmly, put him out of her mind. With the Other Memories awakened inside her, she had more recollections of sexual encounters than she could possibly review.

And she had other priorities.

As dusk settled over the archipelago on Ginaz, she practiced alone on a rocky expanse outside the simple open-air student dormitory with its palm-frond roof. Fighting against imaginary opponents that she saw vividly in her mind, Valya ran through a combination of her Lankiveil sessions with Griffin, the Sisterhood training she had undergone on Rossak, and the skills she had learned at the Swordmaster school.

She drew her short practice sword and attacked with ferocity. Out of the corner of her eye, she saw Placido watching. In his arms he carried a long case. He observed her in silence, waiting for her to pause and catch her breath.

He finally asked, "Would you like a real opponent? I could give you a more advanced lesson than you've had before."

During their sparring and instruction, she had noticed Placido observing her techniques, seeing what he could draw from her, because Valya's fighting methods were quite different from those that the legendary Jool Noret had developed for his Swordmasters. The instructor had given her brief demonstrations with foil, épée, and saber swords, and even once with a stiletto.

At the moment, though, Valya wanted solitude so she could perfect her moves, increasing her speed, angles of attack, and precision. The Swordmaster would only distract her, but he continued to press. Trying to ignore him, Valya centered her concentration, using her skills as a Reverend Mother to control her pulse, her metabolism, her muscular movement . . . and her temper.

But he was not going to leave. Exasperated, Valya turned toward Master Placido and extended her short sword, then pointed it at a slight angle upward, awaiting his approach.

Grinning, he set down the case and knelt to open it, revealing four long swords. "No training blade tonight. Select your weapon from these."

She tossed aside her dull practice sword and stepped forward. With a nod, she studied the offered blades, picked each one up for a brief test, and then selected the dueling sword that had the least ornamentation on the hilt, but the best balance.

"Ah, I have won many duels with that fine weapon," Placido said. "Even killed an intruder with it when he broke into our headquarters on the main island. That was a year ago." With a confident smile, the teacher selected one of the other swords and swished it through the air with a sharp, whisking sound.

"Shall we don masks and vests?" she asked. "It is tradition."

"Not tonight." He swished his sword again. "I am paying you a compliment."

She understood. "You believe that I can protect myself."

He smiled. "And I also believe you can restrain yourself from harming me."

Valya considered her answer. "Perhaps I'll do so."

"Your techniques are still rough, and you have a great deal to learn. Becoming a Swordmaster requires years of instruction."

"And there is a great deal I could teach you." She gave him a hard stare. "But I don't have time for that."

He began the attack, and she countered with an easy defensive move. Aware of her own relative inexperience with these weapons, Valya knew better than to press an attack against a master, so instead she concentrated on a series of parries to stop every blow he made. Placido lunged and thrust, using moves that she had not seen before. Even so, she countered him each time.

From past experience, she knew he would grow increasingly aggressive as the engagement continued, providing her with more difficult challenges. She kept herself calm. Her goal was to hold him off for as long as she could.

"You have excellent natural instincts," he said with a tight smile, "an ability to adapt to gambits I know you've never seen before." She noticed uncharacteristic perspiration on his forehead. "Tell me truthfully, Valya—were you ever instructed by a Swordmaster before you came here?"

"No, but I observed." As a Reverend Mother, she carried memories of other women in her past, and some had been skilled fighters. She drew upon their subconscious reflexes as a secret resource. He didn't need to know about that.

She realized that half a dozen Swordmaster students had emerged from the dormitory and gathered to watch. Valya blocked them out and focused her attention on Master Placido.

He gave her a thin smile. "Now let us see how you react to my next series of moves."

The teacher barely had the words out when he thrust his blade toward the left side of Valya's chest and then swooped the point up, just enough to nick her cheek and create a tiny spot of blood. She was amazed at his precision, and just as amazed that he had slipped through her defenses so easily.

She sliced viciously in an attempt to throw him off-balance, but he ducked under her response, then surprised her again by springing into a roll and bounding up with the tip of the blade just under her chin. If he had not exhibited perfect restraint, he could have killed her. Of equal concern, if she had not moved exactly as he expected, he could also have killed her by accident.

Placido filled the brief moment of her realization by switching his sword to the other hand, then followed through with a series of seemingly unrelated moves. She defended herself, using techniques she and Griffin had developed, forcing Placido to react, while she made no attempt to cut him. She used all her concentration, all her focus, and held him at bay with a composite-parry defense that surprised and delighted him.

Valya needed to do something he would not anticipate. She veered to her right and away, opening the distance between them. He began a flèche move, darting toward her with a running attack, blade extended. His eyes gleamed.

Though he had surprised her moments ago, she was getting to know his emotions, his mindset. She had not only been studying his fighting methods and sword techniques, she had also been studying *him*, attempting to take his complete measure so that she could use her developing power of manipulative voice against him. She remembered commanding Sister Olivia and the other women down in the Rossak cenote when they retrieved the hidden computers. Valya called upon that knowledge now, focusing it into a remarkable new weapon. Her voice.

As he charged toward her, Valya stood her ground and said in a compelling, throaty articulation that summoned a core of command, *"Halt!"*

Master Placido froze as if she had felled him with a club. The tip of his extended blade stopped a hand's-breadth from her chest. She drew tremendous satisfaction from seeing the gleam in his eyes replaced by shock. He stood there, paralyzed.

Smiling, Valya said with all the force she could put into her voice, *"Do not move."* She walked around him, as if he'd become a statue.

His eyes twitched as he tried to follow her movements. She took a step back and moved her blade around his frozen weapon. Her pulse pounded, adrenaline flowed, and a part of her wanted to kill this man. She touched the flecks of blood from the small cuts he had dealt her.

Instead of killing Placido, though, she used the edge of her sword to draw a thin red line across his brow. Not a deep wound, but enough to leave a fine white scar to remind him of his defeat.

The students watching were aghast.

Valya slid her dueling sword back into its scabbard. "During a real fight, even an instant's hesitation would have proved fatal."

She could see him struggling, and finally after several seconds he began to fight off the compulsion. He gasped, touched the flow of blood on his forehead. "How did you do that?"

She answered him with no more than a secretive smile. She didn't fully understand the new technique herself, but it might well be as dangerous a fighting method as the best skill with a sword.

Valya turned her back on him and strode calmly toward the dormitory.

AS SHE PASSED through the school grounds, the rest of the students regarded her with awe. She could hear whispers and could read even more from their flickers of glances, a sudden turning away.

At dawn, a courier from the main island arrived, rushing to the student dormitory with a message for her—from Wallach IX. She felt a sudden dread. Had Mother Superior Raquella died? Perhaps she should not have come here to Ginaz after all.

She unsealed the letter to read a coded message hidden in the arrangement of the characters, and saw that the note itself came from Raquella. So, the old woman was still alive:

> Return to Wallach IX immediately. I can wait no longer. I
> must announce my successor.

Manford shook his head. "Harian will take care of it. No one can know there is a body here. I must be seen as unharmed, perfectly healthy."

As the serving woman set out the tray, unable to tear her gaze from the corpse, Manford turned to his companions. "When I get to Salusa, I will demand that Emperor Salvador seize all spice operations on Arrakis. We showed our power during the rampage festival, and he will do whatever we ask."

"If the Imperium absorbs spice operations, there will be an advantage to the Emperor as well," Sister Woodra pointed out. "Given the huge profits in the melange industry, that planet should be under Imperial control."

Manford conceded the point. He was surprised at how calm and controlled he sounded, even as a great storm raged inside him. He couldn't erase the image of Josef Venport from his mind. "Venport tried to kill me! We will go to Salusa Secundus, and I will file my formal complaint with the Emperor." He glanced at Anari. "And this time you won't talk me out of traveling. I am *not* a coward, and I need to go there in person."

"What if Roderick Corrino orders you arrested and makes you pay for the death of his daughter?" Anari asked.

"I wield far more power than the Emperor's brother does. If he were to arrest and accuse me, he would unleash a storm he could never control." He smiled. "No, he will not do that."

Deacon Harian cleared his throat. "Your second body double has been ready for more than a year, just in case. We had to search several planets until we found a satisfactory look-alike. He still needs to have the final surgery, of course."

Manford nodded. "Let me see him and thank him before his metamorphosis."

As Ellonda scurried away, uncomfortable to be near the dead body, Sister Woodra scowled after her.

Harian summoned the volunteer from town; the other look-alike had been kept behind closed doors where others couldn't see him. The man entered now, with short dark hair, squarish face, handsome features—objectively five years younger than the real Butlerian leader, but his features were similar. From a distance, as a showpiece, he would look sufficiently like Manford Torondo.

The volunteer glanced at the corpse, drawing conclusions, then focused his gaze on the Butlerian leader. "I have been summoned by truth and destiny. I am ready."

"Know that I appreciate your sacrifice," Manford said. "I had no choice about my legs . . . but you do. And you still made the right decision, the courageous decision."

"This is no sacrifice, Leader Torondo. It is one small way that I can help save us all."

Harian stepped close to the volunteer. "The surgeon is ready. You should undergo the procedure as soon as possible. Your recovery might take a few weeks, and there's no telling when we might need you."

"I'm ready now," the man said.

Manford wanted to apologize in advance for the pain this volunteer was about to suffer, both mental and physical. But pain was a very human thing. Pain separated mankind from the thinking machines. Pain was a blessing. He would have to remind the volunteer of that, after his legs were amputated.

MANFORD'S ANGER FESTERED as they waited for an EsconTran ship that would take them to Salusa. *Josef Venport ordered my assassination!*

Unable to resist, he dipped into the Erasmus journal again, pondering the nature of evil. The independent robot was fundamentally damned, with no possibility of redemption, but Venport was a human being, and he had *chosen* his own evil. Manford was still horrified by the robot's thought patterns, but he learned from the appalling "medical" studies that read like a textbook in sadism. He made notes of certain torture procedures developed by Erasmus that he would like to use on Josef Venport, then locked away the vile journal, afraid someone might find it and become seduced by the evil robot's thoughts.

But that was distraction and fantasy. He had a more important case to make. Manford took time to outline and write the speech he would deliver to Emperor Salvador Corrino. His threat could be subtle. Everyone at the Imperial Court was aware of how much damage a Butlerian mob could inflict. Manford Toronto could either control them or unleash them. Emperor Salvador couldn't possibly say no to his demands.

Yes, Venport was going to pay dearly.

At his desk, Manford looked up as Deacon Harian barged in with Anari beside him, her face dark with anger. They hauled a struggling old woman between them—Ellonda, whose modest dress had been torn. Her hair was loose, her eyes wild.

Confused, Manford asked, "What are you doing to her?"

Sister Woodra appeared behind them in the doorway. "I detected dissonant notes in this woman's voice, flinches in her expression, moisture on her forehead and palms. I watched her, questioned her." Woodra paused. "She is a spy for Venport Holdings."

Manford nearly lost his balance on the padded chair. "Impossible! She has been with me for years."

"It is proven, Leader Toronto," Harian said. "After we brought back the body of your double, she slipped away to send a transmission to another operative here on Lampadas. She revealed our plans! That's when we caught her. She has been reporting your moves to Josef Venport for some time now."

"She has tended me, cooked my meals, been in my house. Venport wants me dead—surely she could have found some opportunity to kill me. This makes no sense."

Anari lifted her chin. "I taste all your meals for poison, Manford. I watch over you and make certain no assassin would ever have such an opportunity."

"But you were away on Arrakis with my body double. You are not with me every moment."

"Perhaps Ellonda simply didn't have the resolve," said Harian. "Not everyone has the spine to commit murder." He made it sound like an insult.

The panicked woman struggled to break free. "None of this is true, sir! I've always served you faithfully. I am loyal to the Butlerian cause—you know that!"

Sister Woodra said, "Lies continue to drip from her lips."

Manford felt gooseflesh on his skin. "Even I can hear it in her voice." He watched as Ellonda slumped, knowing it was hopeless to say anything more.

Anari said, "Shall I interrogate her, find out why she turned against the truth?"

Manford just shook his head, warring with his emotions, fighting back the rage he wanted to unleash. "What does it matter *why*? Her reasons would be incomprehensible to us. Did you capture the other operative?"

"Yes," Deacon Harian said, "but Ellonda transmitted a broad message packet. We don't know how many others might be involved."

Manford felt a slow boil. "Interrogation is one thing, punishment something else entirely." He thought of the exhaustive, sickening records the robot Erasmus had left behind, the myriad experiments and imaginative tortures. Perhaps he should put some of them into practice now. "I will provide instructions, Deacon Harian. I have some . . . ideas." He angrily gestured for the wailing woman to be dragged away. Then he drew a deep breath.

"Meanwhile, I need to plan my immediate departure to Salusa Secundus. We must finish this." He shook his head. "The crisis is upon us, and there can be no further doubts about loyalty to our cause. I have to know who is with me, who is against me. Everyone must choose a side—publicly. No one can be neutral. Our entire population will reaffirm their loyalty to me, or face death."

"We should require individual oaths, Leader Torondo," Harian suggested. "Not just communities and planets promising general allegiance. *Each person* must swear before a trusted official that they believe technology is evil." His voice gained vehemence. "Any advanced machinery, electronics, or other insidious devices must be discarded on pain of death."

Worked up by the deacon's vehemence, Manford took a deep breath. He did not look at the squirming Ellonda as she was pulled out the door. How many more like her were hidden among the faithful? He intended to root them out.

"Agreed. Anari and Sister Woodra will accompany me to Salusa, but while I am gone, Deacon Harian, you will institute a new planet-wide oath to be sworn by all individuals. No exceptions, no excuses on any grounds. Everyone must declare allegiance to me." He let out a long sigh, looked at Woodra. "If only we had enough Truthsayers to test every person who claims to be my ally."

*We are human not because of our physical form, but because of our underlying nature. Even when fitted with a machine body, a man may have a heart and soul . . . but not always. People made of flesh can be monsters, too.*

—PTOLEMY, *Laboratory Sketches*

Yes, it was time for his Titans.

Ptolemy felt exhilarated by his increasing successes, beginning with the dramatic (though costly) demonstration on Arrakis, followed by the glorious eradication of the cowering savages on Lectaire. Dr. Elchan would have been pleased, he knew it.

Energized by Ptolemy's work, other Denali researchers redoubled their efforts to create imaginative weapons for use against the Butlerians. In one noteworthy example, Dr. Uli Westpher was ready to ship his first "crickets"—thumb-sized devices programmed to skitter across a landing field. The small machines could slip through the tiniest crannies of external engine ports, where they dismantled fuel lines and spilled volatile chemicals. Then the crickets would scritch their roughened mechanical legs together until they struck a spark and ignited the fuel. The crickets were too small and too fast to be seen, and even a small package of them could cause immense devastation to an EsconTran shipyard.

Meanwhile, Ptolemy continued to modify his work to improve thoughtrode linkages with machine systems, assisted by Administrator Noffe, who brought his Tlulaxa sensibilities to the work.

A new group of Tlulaxa specialists had been brought to Denali, continuing research that the Butlerians had forbidden. While other engineers built immense mechanical walker bodies, the Tlulaxa team grew biological body parts, reinforced with flowmetal enhancements. Soon enough, they would be able to grow entire replacement bodies—but humanitarian work was not their main priority . . . not until after Manford Torondo's barbarians were defeated.

Ptolemy found the Tlulaxa work interesting, although he thought the basic human body was already too weak. He himself had been too weak to stand against the raving hordes that destroyed his facility and killed Elchan. If he were going to accept a new body, Ptolemy never wanted to feel weak again. He wanted something powerful and impressive. . . .

When a shipment arrived from Kolhar bearing the medically sustained brains of ten more failed Navigators, Ptolemy was glad to have new candidates for his expanding ranks of Titans. The other proto-Navigator brains available to him were already ensconced in preservation canisters, so they could be installed into any cymek walker. Now he had even more specimens to work with.

When the cargo ship was ready on the loading dock, workers carried the Navigator brains on suspensor pallets, and Ptolemy sent them to his laboratory. The ship also brought two of VenHold's private Suk doctors, specialists who had extracted the brains from the spice-saturated bodies on Kolhar. They had come to Denali to observe Ptolemy's work firsthand.

With his lungs still scarred from exposure to Denali's caustic atmosphere, Ptolemy coughed while greeting them. "I'm grateful for the assistance and advice from graduates of the Suk School. My new thoughtrodes are adaptive, easily connected to the living tissue of an aware brain. Our work is far superior to—" He had to fight back an intense fit of coughing, then wiped away an embarrassing smear of blood from his lips. The guest doctors fussed over him, but Ptolemy brushed them aside. "I already have my diagnosis. It's not relevant to our discussion here." And he pushed on.

Inside his main development chamber, he was proud to show the Kolhar team his preservation tanks and test beds, while assistants prepared the new Navigator brains. Ptolemy was well practiced in how to install them into his cymek walkers, but he was always creating and testing new modifications in an effort to perfect the advanced machine bodies. His special Titans might not be powerful enough to fight an Arrakis sandworm alone, but they were sufficient to slaughter any number of Butlerian cowards.

And that, Ptolemy knew, would be good enough.

INSIDE THE HANGAR dome, Administrator Noffe took a detailed inventory to ensure that the proper demonstration models were aboard the shuttle for transfer back to Kolhar. Directeur Venport would be eager to see the latest creations from his captive scientists.

In the years since his rescue after a Butlerian purge, Noffe had worked here, hoping to advance human capabilities and help bolster civilization against anti-technology phobia. He wanted the Imperium to grow, colonies to expand, humans to live longer and achieve greater things. Years ago on Thalim, Noffe had regarded the blight of Butlerian ignorance as a troublesome, distant thing . . . until the barbarians surged onto his world, ransacked his laboratory, and marked him for death because of his "unacceptable investigations."

Uneducated, superstitious fools! How were they better qualified to choose the future than he was?

Admittedly, the Tlulaxa people had committed crimes during the long Jihad, selling black-market organs, falsifying death records, experimenting with clones. Yes, his people had cringed with racial guilt for many years, but after Directeur Venport rescued him, Noffe cast aside that guilt. He and other Tlulaxa researchers could accomplish tremendous things—and here on Denali, they had done just that. Noffe knew that once these technological miracles were delivered to VenHold, the future of humanity was in good hands. So long as the Butlerians did not win. And those savages must not be allowed to win.

Now, as Noffe supervised the activity from inside the shuttle's cargo hold, workers loaded carefully packed prototypes along with new explosive mixtures and pulse scramblers that could incapacitate a barbarian army. The administrator made a notation of each crate as it was loaded; in the manifest he included a personal message that explained each of the new deliveries. Directeur Venport always demanded reports.

When Noffe studied the crate containing the first hundred of Dr. Westpher's mechanical crickets, though, he found damage on the bottom, a small crack that had been . . . enlarged? He saw a tiny form dart into the shadows of the cargo hold, disappearing between the crates. Then three others scuttled after it. Squinting, he bent down, saw movement—and knew what it was.

He yelled to the workers in the bay. "Some of Westpher's mechanical crickets have escaped! We need to clean them up here."

On the other side of the hangar, he heard a man shout, "There's a fuel spill under the shuttle—the lines are leaking. Get a repair tech right now!"

Noffe glanced into the shadows, where the crickets had vanished. "Fuel spill?" He hurried down the ramp. "If that's a fuel spill, we'd better—"

A tiny robotic insect skittered into the puddle of volatile fuel. Noffe watched in horror while the cricket rubbed its back legs together as it was programmed to do, striking, striking, striking—until a spark appeared.

The spark became a wall of flame that engulfed Noffe and hurled him backward.

IN THE INFIRMARY dome, when Ptolemy saw the charred Noffe, the blackened and oozing red wounds that made his friend's flesh look like badly cooked meat, he couldn't stop thinking about how Dr. Elchan had burned alive.

Somehow, Noffe clung to life—at least for now.

The visiting Suk doctors worked desperately, using all of their techniques, pumped him full of fluids, connected him to life-support machines. Though awash with drugs in a medical coma, Noffe writhed in tremendous pain.

Ptolemy hovered in the infirmary, but could do nothing to help the doctors. He had studied science and engineering, but was no medical expert. Once again he felt so powerless! Even with all of Ptolemy's accomplishments, like the titanic machine walkers he had built, he couldn't help another friend in his time of terrible need.

Overcome with emotion, he touched Noffe to reassure him he was there—and even in his coma, the burned man recoiled in pain.

"We can do very little to help him," said one of the doctors.

But Ptolemy had been considering possibilities. Previously, he had delayed taking the next step, but now he had no choice.

He coughed, and his lungs burned. He controlled the spasms with shallow breaths until he could form words again. He looked down at the bandaged, suffering patient. "There is one more thing we can do—and I need you to help me."

◁─◆─▷

*One of my primary tasks in advancing the cause of the Sisterhood is to think of human society as a whole, rather than in terms of small family units. We are much bigger than that. A first step is to break the natural bond between mother and child, to expose a girl from infancy to her larger role in humankind. That powerful, but limiting, emotional connection must be diverted and rechanneled, so the energies of both mother and child are devoted to the future, rather than to petty personal concerns.*

—MOTHER SUPERIOR RAQUELLA BERTO-ANIRUL, private remarks

The Imperial Court sparkled with ladies in jeweled gowns and dashing noblemen in exquisitely tailored uniforms, sashes, and caps. For the evening festivities, the courtiers and Corrinos were entertained by exotic performing artists, including talented musicians and dancers.

Reverend Mother Dorotea and Prince Roderick sat in smaller chairs beside Salvador on his immense throne of green crystal. Together, they watched a young woman perform a baliset ballad from her homeworld of Chusuk, a romance set during the time of thinking-machine brutality. The singer sat on a stool in her colorful native costume, holding the streamlined instrument so Dorotea could recognize the work of the master artisan Varota. At first glance, the Chusuk girl seemed too young to be entrusted with something so valuable, but she had an extraordinary talent, delivering a full range of tones with the baliset to accompany her haunting voice.

The Emperor, however, was not interested in the performance. Despite the beauty of the music, the Chusuk woman was rather drab, especially in this setting. Salvador seemed bored and irritable, consuming more than his usual amount of red wine mixed with melange. The nervous Imperial sommelier stood by, ready to call for another bottle from the palace cellars, should the Emperor require it.

Dorotea studied Salvador; he was overly concerned with his imagined physical ailments and had been increasingly uneasy and impatient after executing his personal Suk physician a year ago. Salvador was too nervous to allow another Suk until they could guarantee their new Imperial Conditioning, which was supposed to make them unbreakably loyal. Dorotea did not know which paranoia would win out—his fear of a conspiratorial doctor, or his chronic hypochondria.

Dorotea observed that the Emperor's excessive consumption of wine and melange did not mix well with his edgy temperament. He had grown more volatile in the weeks since Empress Tabrina's banishment from court after the scandal. Despite his long-standing marital problems, Salvador seemed oddly gloomy without her around.

With a wave of his hand, the Emperor interrupted the entertainer during her song, and she was so startled that she jangled the baliset. A robed protocol attendant hurried the Chusuk girl away. She was replaced by a storyteller, supposedly an authentic native of Arrakis who would recite traditional Zensunni fire poetry. With creased, weathered skin, the storyteller wore a desert cloak and a black distilling suit, but to Dorotea's careful gaze, his garments and filter tubes did not appear properly fitted, making it look more like a costume than authentic attire.

In a sonorous voice the man told the timeworn tale of two children—a brother and sister—who ran away from their sietch and rode sandworms to the farthest reaches of the great Tanzerouft, never to return. They became the stuff of legend, reportedly seen for centuries afterward riding the great worms, remaining children forever, never growing into adults. While the story had some appeal, Dorotea found the man's voice shallow, his tale-spinning abilities mediocre.

"Thank you." Salvador interrupted the man as he was about to begin a second story. "That will be enough of that."

The storyteller bowed and hurried away while the Emperor took another sip of wine. Salvador looked crossly toward a doorway where even more entertainers awaited their turns. Three jugglers in whimsical costumes glided across the floor, but had barely begun their tumbling before the Emperor dismissed them. "No more jugglers for the rest of this month! This is an Imperial edict. I'm not in the mood for such frivolity. If I see another juggler, I will run him through with a sword."

He chuckled as the frightened entertainers tripped over one another to exit, while Roderick looked at him with concern. During a moment of confusion about who would perform next, the Emperor lounged back, obviously uncomfortable. "All right, that's enough foolish entertainment for this evening. A man of intelligence and culture can only take so much of this sort of fare. I shall have more wine and spice instead, and a little serenity."

Glancing past the throne, Dorotea met Roderick's gaze. She could tell they both wished the evening would end quickly. Perhaps Salvador would go distract himself with his concubines.

Despite the Emperor's words, the members of his court continued chattering

"Yes. How can you forgive Raquella for what she did to us?"

Arlett summoned surprising inner strength. "I am a loyal member of the Sisterhood, so I understand their reasons. I always do as our Mother Superior commands."

From Arlett's demeanor, Dorotea could see that she had not forgiven her mother, but remained loyal nonetheless. She used the tension to put the missionary Sister in her proper place. "What is your errand, *woman*?"

Arlett struggled to compose herself. Her eyes burned with pain, sadness, and anger. She took several calming breaths, and the blue eyes softened as she looked at Dorotea, then became unreadable and distant. "I am here to appeal to you. This schism weakens the Sisterhood, and Raquella would like to remove the fences between us."

"Her use of forbidden computers weakened the Sisters of Rossak and brought about their downfall. Your downfall."

Arlett forcibly controlled the tone of her voice, did not continue the old argument. "We have our minds and abilities, and we are not alone. The two groups of Sisters have much in common. We all want to help our race reach its potential. The VenHold Spacing Fleet is developing Navigators, unlocking the *human* abilities of their minds, as are the Mentats at their Lampadas school. Do we not all want to improve humanity without thinking machines?"

Dorotea wanted to nod, but remained wary of being guided to a conclusion that she hadn't reached on her own.

Arlett pressed on. "You understand the need for mapping and monitoring human bloodlines, with or without computers. When our Sister Mentats were killed on Rossak, the entire Sisterhood was weakened, and this in turn weakened the human species. You had a part in that. Don't deny it, *daughter*, because you know it is true."

Dorotea felt personal guilt over her role in Salvador's overreaction, but knew she could not go back. "I wish it had been different. I did save the Sisterhood from being completely erased—at least a part of it."

Arlett shook her head. "You sought personal advancement with the Emperor, no matter what your selfishness did to the core of the Sisterhood. It is time for you to repair the damage you caused." She lowered her voice to a husky whisper. "I plead with you, and I *demand* it of you. Mother Superior Raquella summons you to see her at Wallach IX before it is too late."

Dorotea saw something strange on her mother's face. "Too late for what? What more aren't you telling me?"

Arlett's eyes were suddenly full of compassion. "The Mother Superior is dying, and she will soon announce her successor. You must come immediately—we have very little time."

〜❧〜

*All power bases are made of flesh, and must eventually decay and crumble.*

—ancient admonition

After his ship arrived at Salusa, Manford Torondo sent a courier to the palace, demanding an Imperial audience. Not bothering to wait for an answer, he and his entourage moved through the capital city with a crowd of earnest followers massing behind him. The palace would never have enough time to prepare, but Manford made sure the Emperor had time to panic.

As usual, Salvador turned to his brother for advice. Prince Roderick, unable to forget the tragedy and violence the Butlerian leader had caused on his last visit here, felt an icy chill go down his spine. Recently, the antitechnology mobs had struck Baridge in a bloody riot that they called "holy." Roderick saw nothing even remotely holy in their work, and Manford had never atoned, never apologized for, never even seemed to *notice* the death of Nantha or any of the others killed in their reckless fervor.

And now he was returning to Zimia as if nothing had happened.

All around the capital city, government employees assigned to the Committee of Orthodoxy remained at a heightened state of readiness, to demonstrate that they were always watchful for any technology that Manford had declared unacceptable.

Roderick wished his brother could outlaw the whole movement and render them impotent . . . but that would be like playing with explosives. Nevertheless, he blamed Manford Torondo for Nantha's death; that could not be forgiven, regardless of politics or risks.

As the Butlerian delegation made its way through the city, Roderick increased the number of security teams around the palace, granting them quiet permission to use lethal force if a riot began. Meanwhile, court functionaries organized a reception as quickly as they could. They rushed about to prepare the Audience Chamber, setting up drinks and hors d'oeuvres on gilded tables. Salvador suggested that the formality of the reception would force Manford to behave like a diplomat; Roderick didn't think the man deserved any amenities. He kept his anger in check and decided to make certain his brother wasn't bullied into additional foolish concessions.

Salvador sat sweating on his throne, dreading Manford's arrival. He had already consumed several goblets of wine mixed with melange. His spice consumption had increased dramatically of late, and he kept powdered melange in its usual place in a little jeweled box on the armrest of his throne. The stimulating effect of spice made the Emperor's eyes shine.

Even in the midst of his aching grief over Nantha's death, Roderick was perceptive enough to realize that Salvador was also depressed, a gloom that began after the exposure of Empress Tabrina's affair with the Grand Inquisitor. She was banished, and Quemada executed by his own Scalpel torturers, the entire affair kept quiet from the public on Roderick's insistence. But still . . . even though Salvador had openly despised his wife—and the feeling had been mutual—he showed unexpected misery at her absence. Salvador wanted Roderick to comfort him, although his pain could not possibly match the pain of losing an innocent daughter.

A lesser man might have sought to capitalize on his brother's shortcomings, especially in a time of personal crisis. With all the turmoil in the Imperium, the out-of-control Butlerians and the ruthless commercial war VenHold had launched against them, Salvador's rule was unsteady. Roderick was loyal to the Corrino throne, a moral man. He was the second-born, and his role was clear. He had never wanted more.

Leaning close to the throne, Roderick suggested, "Allow me to remove your wineglass and the melange box, just for a little while? Leader Torondo is entering the palace now, and we don't want to show him any weakness."

Salvador appeared reluctant before he gestured in acquiescence. "Of course, of course. I don't need it." The Prince whisked away the two items, handing them to a uniformed man, who hurried out a side door.

One of Dorotea's orthodox Sisters, Reverend Mother Esther-Cano, entered the chamber, followed by a team of functionaries that Roderick had assigned to record the proceedings. He wished Dorotea were here because he trusted the Truthsayer's wise counsel, but she and several companions had just departed for Wallach IX on a mysterious, urgent mission.

Esther-Cano led Sister Woodra, who had offered her Truthsayer services to

Manford Torondo. Did the Butlerian leader suspect that Salvador might lie to him? Roderick stiffened at the thought. He would have to make sure his brother was careful about whatever he said, whatever he promised. . . .

Sister Woodra looked around the vaulted chamber, nodded, and sent an all-clear signal. With a buzz of activity, Manford Torondo entered, riding on the shoulders of his Swordmaster.

Roderick narrowed his gaze while remaining close to the Emperor. He kept his hand protectively near a hidden weapon. Roderick had always disliked the fanatics, but after Nantha's death, he felt deep revulsion, resentment, and distrust toward Manford Torondo.

Anari Idaho approached the throne, carrying Manford as if she were a beast of burden. Sister Woodra stepped away from Esther-Cano and joined the Butlerian delegation, apparently to demonstrate where her loyalties lay.

Salvador tried to hide his nervousness with formality. "Greetings, Leader Torondo." His voice was steady and dignified, showing hardly any slur from the effects of alcohol and spice. "Your arrival is unexpected." He cleared his throat. "How can I be of assistance to you, my good friend?"

Roderick felt a burn of anger at these words. Friend?

"Friendship has nothing to do with my visit." Manford's face showed more than a little irritation. He glanced around in displeasure. "Hors d'oeuvres? And wine? Do you think we are here for a party?"

Roderick tensed at the blatant disrespect, but Salvador was quick to sound ridiculously conciliatory. "We have more than wine and treats, of course. We simply wanted to extend courtesy. If this is not enough, a banquet in your honor can be arranged."

"There will be no rampage festival this time," Roderick broke in, raising his voice. "We have security teams in place. Crowds of your followers will be vigorously dispersed if you attempt to incite them to violence."

"Your security teams can try to do so. . . ." Anari Idaho muttered.

From his place on her shoulders, Manford turned to look at the Corrino Prince. "Why would I incite my followers to violence? I abhor unnecessary violence. In the last festival, my followers were overly enthusiastic. We apologize for the inconvenience we caused."

Roderick wanted to rage at him, *My daughter's death was not an inconvenience!*

But the Butlerian leader had already turned his attention back to Salvador. "I'm not hungry, Sire—except for *action*. Not long ago, you disbanded the poisonous Sisterhood school on Rossak because they conspired against you. Now you must do the same to Venport Holdings. Josef Venport is creating monsters to navigate his ships, corrupting the human form and the human mind. His ships use computers, too—we have proof, because we captured a foldspace vessel he sent to Baridge."

Roderick's eyes widened. Concrete evidence that VenHold ships used computers in their navigation systems? The banned practice had long been rumored. "And where is your proof?"

The Swordmaster lifted her chin. "I saw it with my own eyes."

Manford added, "The ship was unfortunately lost in transit, as so many have been."

Salvador sat up on the throne. "Then you have no proof."

"We went to Arrakis to uncover Directeur Venport's schemes—and his thugs tried to have me killed." The Butlerian leader gestured to Sister Woodra, who removed a small holoprojector from her robes. Roderick frowned; no device should have slipped past security.

Woodra fumbled with the recording crystal, installed it in the player, and activated the image. She made an adjustment and projected a series of blurred images of dusty streets, a yellow sun and sky, people running.

"On the streets of Arrakis City," Manford said, "a man in the crowd shot a crude projectile pistol. I was his intended target."

The next image showed what appeared to be Manford Torondo dead, with half of his skull blown away. His body lay sprawled on the floor of a fire-illuminated room. Anari Idaho looked furious to see the images again.

"I narrowly escaped with my own life."

Emperor Salvador regarded the images with faint amusement. "You seem to have recovered rather well." Without being told, Roderick realized the victim must have been the body double Manford used for some of his public appearances.

Manford lowered his voice to a growl. "The assassin was convinced he had hit the mark. Josef Venport ordered my murder—I know it!"

"I believe you've called for *his* death as well," Roderick pointed out. "You reap what you sow. As I understand it, Venport barely escaped with his life when your ships attacked the Thonaris shipyards. And your followers have shown a great capacity for bloodshed. Perhaps Directeur Venport should be the one here asking for our protection?"

Salvador added, "I wouldn't put too much stock in the attack. Arrakis is a rugged, dangerous world, and that city is not a place for civilized men. People are murdered there every day. How do you know it wasn't just a random act of violence?"

"Because I know. I demand that you condemn Venport for this act, just as you must condemn him for the continued use of thinking machines. His crimes are inexcusable. The penalty must be death."

Salvador looked to his brother for help, and Roderick raised his voice. "You *demand?* Leader Toronto, you do not dictate Imperial policy."

"And *you* do? You are the Prince, not the Emperor." He obviously intended for his comment to sting more than it did.

Emperor Salvador looked irritated. "What am I to do about this? The squabble is between you and Directeur Venport—I wish you wouldn't put me in the middle of it."

Manford scowled. "If you had the moral courage to choose the proper side, you would not be in the middle. Venport Holdings has been strangling any world that takes our pledge of purity. Some of the faithful are weakening, but I've commanded that all must renew their oaths in no uncertain terms."

Holding on to Anari's shoulders, Manford leaned forward, staring at the Emperor. "My followers can fight with their faith, and we will win. But it is not enough—we need your help, Sire. As the ruler of the Imperium, you have a weapon that can hurt him financially. Strike him where he is vulnerable—and enrich yourself at the same time."

Salvador blinked at Roderick. "What does he mean? What financial weapon do we have?"

The Swordmaster stepped closer to the dais, and Manford ignored Roderick. "Economics. All he cares about is profit, and Venport's key vulnerability is spice! Combined Mercantiles is just a front for Venport Holdings. He set up a widespread network of melange harvesting and distribution, created his Navigators by saturating them with spice. And he has addicted a large portion of the Imperium, through which he can control populations."

Salvador looked away, his eyes frantic. "My Truthsayer recently made the same claim."

Manford said, "As the Emperor, how do you allow one man to wield so much power?"

Roderick clenched his jaw, muttered, "We could ask the same question of you, Leader Torondo. . . ."

Sister Woodra crept forward, stood on her tiptoes, and whispered to Manford. The Butlerian leader nodded. "You recently annexed all the assets of House Péle, Sire, including your wife's personal holdings, in retaliation for a treacherous scheme. Directeur Venport's crimes are far more serious to the Imperium, and he commands a near monopoly on all spice operations right under your nose. Shouldn't such a vital industry be under *Imperial* control? Not in the hands of a private citizen? What if Venport decides to place an embargo on melange shipments everywhere, the way he has embargoed Butlerian worlds?"

Salvador frowned as he considered. "I consume spice myself, for my own health. As do many of my subjects, whose supplies I do not want cut off. That would increase discontent. There could be riots in the streets."

Although Roderick did not approve of Butlerian tactics, he felt a chill as he began to realize just how wide a net of dependence Josef Venport had spread. Sister Dorotea had laid out her suspicions of the connections Venport Holdings had not only with Combined Mercantiles, but to planetary banks, along with a monopoly on safe shipping. . . .

Manford said, "Josef Venport is a temperamental, vengeful man who wields far too much power. With his stranglehold on so many critical services, this *one man* has created suffering and unrest across the Imperium. Do you see the knife he holds to your throat? Salvador Corrino, *you* are the Emperor of the Known Universe. Why do you let that man control you? Why are you letting him make the Imperial throne *irrelevant?*"

Roderick added in a cautious tone, "Before you cause too much disruption, Sire, remember that much of the Imperial military fleet is carried aboard Ven-Hold haulers. Some of our ships have Holtzman engines, yes, but no Navigators. Others still have old-style faster-than-light engines, which require weeks or months to travel from system to system. If the VenHold Spacing Fleet were to block critical foldspace routes, the Directeur could force even the throne to capitulate. He might even overthrow House Corrino and crown himself the next Emperor."

Sister Woodra added, "Perhaps foldspace travel should be under Imperial control as well."

"I shall exert control over all spice operations, for a start," Salvador said, not looking at his brother for confirmation. "I *am* in fact the Emperor of the Known Universe, so I should control the only known source of spice."

Roderick was startled by the drastic, provocative suggestion. "We should consult further, brother, before taking rash action. This is a dangerous situation. I fear the widespread reprisals VenHold could launch if you attempt to seize melange operations."

Manford focused a withering gaze on Salvador. "The people can decide this matter if you do not. If they decide you are in collusion with the demon Venport, I would never be able to control them. Maybe *they* would take your throne, rather than Venport."

"I do not need more time to consider such an important matter," Salvador snapped. "I am tired of being made irrelevant." He leaned forward and raised his voice. "I hereby declare that spice operations are strategically vital to the Imperium and by law must be operated under direct Imperial control. As Emperor, I shall take charge of Arrakis and mobilize the Imperial fleet to enforce my will.

My trade advisers will inform Directeur Venport and prepare the necessary documentation for a smooth transition."

Roderick stared at him, aghast, but Salvador just waved a hand casually. "You worry too much, brother. VenHold will be fairly compensated. In fact, I'll go there myself with a small force of soldiers to oversee the transition."

Roderick felt disturbed, but could see that his brother was buoyed with excitement. Salvador grinned as if he had made a good decision. "Spice will be Imperialized. It is time to show who is really in command!"

A cold heaviness settled in Roderick's stomach, but he forced a brave face. Salvador didn't often make his own major decisions, and when he did, they rarely went well.

*I prefer to celebrate my decisions, whatever they are, rather than regret them.*

> —JOSEF VENPORT, VenHold internal memo

News of Manford Torondo's death traveled slowly across the Imperium, especially with so many interdicted worlds and rerouted spaceship schedules. For weeks now, the Butlerians had been oddly quiet about their loss.

After assassinating the leader, Taref was treated better than a Naib at the Kolhar space complex. He was considered a hero, and he told the story repeatedly, describing how he'd seen the opportunity and taken the successful shot.

At night, though, he felt qualms as he remembered the *whizz-clack* of the Maula pistol projectile, the splash of blood as the man's skull shattered, and his body tumbling to the streets. A powerful leader of a terrible movement, killed so easily . . . and so much more personally than all those who had died when Taref sabotaged EsconTran ships. With his own eyes, he had seen the blood, the falling body. . . .

Reports from other operatives on Arrakis verified the news of the kill. As a reward, Directeur Venport offered Taref a large bonus, but the desert man asked for nothing more than a chance to meet with his friends and wish them well whenever they came back to Kolhar. If he could get them all together again, maybe they would travel to Caladan, as Venport had promised them.

Then Taref learned that one more of his desert friends, Waddoch, had also been killed, caught committing sabotage on an EsconTran ship. Other engineers had discovered his false identity, and seized him, but Waddoch took his own life before he could be turned over for questioning. As a matter of honor, the young man had done the only correct thing.

The loss opened another deep wound in Taref. . . .

Lillis was the most like Taref, the person who most closely shared his dreams and imaginings. She had spent her youth fancying what lay beyond the stars and cultures other than her own. She even seemed interested in finding Zensunni remnants who still lived on distant planets—ancestors of the desert people of Arrakis. Like him, Lillis had always thought about more than going on desert raids to sabotage spice harvesters, or playing tricks on offworlders. Few young women turned their backs on sietch life, and he knew she had grand dreams.

Taref could not deny that their imaginings were far different from the missions Directeur Venport had assigned them. He and his companions weren't being sent out to find the roots of their culture, nor were they exploring exotic places that would make wonderful tales back on Arrakis. Instead, they were destroying a rival's ships and killing everyone aboard without regard to guilt or innocence. And Venport rewarded them well for doing it.

That wasn't how any of them had expected it to be, certainly not what he had promised them when he pressured them to follow him on a grand adventure. . . .

When Lillis returned to Kolhar from another mission, Taref hurried to greet her. He felt joy in his heart again to know she was back. The weather was gray and windy. Cold raindrops and hail pellets whipped across the sky, spattering their faces as they stood outside the main barracks. When he saw her face, though, he could see she was miserable and shivering, her eyes downcast.

"It's so cold here, Taref," she said. "So cold everywhere compared with home. And the moisture in the air makes it hard to breathe. So much water." Her dark eyes still showed the deep blue of a lifetime of melange consumption. "They have a word for it—*drowning*—when one is submerged in the water until the lungs fill."

Taref tried to summon excitement in his voice, for her sake. "But remember, we're on another *world*. I thought you wanted to get away from Arrakis, just as I did. One day we'll go to Caladan together and see the oceans."

She extended her hand, palm up, and it trembled as the drizzle came down. "I don't want to see those places, not anymore. I'd rather be . . . home."

Taref's heart went out to her. "I'll arrange it so you can return to Arrakis, if that's what you really want. Directeur Venport told me to ask for any favor I wish. Go back to our sietch—will that make you happy?"

Lillis sighed. "I feel like a hatchling taken out of a hawk's nest. Even when it's put back, the other birds never accept it. They kill it."

He didn't know how to help her. "I have been back there," he said. "You will see the desert differently."

"I see the whole universe differently, Taref." Her voice sounded so empty.

"My dreams are gone. And my home is gone. All I have is this. . . ." She looked up at the gray skies, held out her palms to the cold sleet. "And I don't want it."

AT DAWN THE next morning, Taref emerged from the barracks and found Lillis lying on the pebbled ground outside the building, face up, arms spread at her sides. Not moving.

Taref rushed to her, picked up her shoulders, and cradled her head. With tears streaming down his cheeks, he whispered her name. Lillis's eyes were open, but she was covered with a light dusting of snow. She had no body warmth left. Sometime during the night, she had lain down on the ground, and just *died*.

Taref groaned, holding her stiff, cold body, rocking her back and forth. Lillis would never go back to the dunes now. She had perished far from home, far from the sunshine and golden sands, the pungent smell of melange, and the majesty of the giant sandworms.

Both Shurko and Waddoch had died on their missions, and now Lillis had simply surrendered. He would have joined her in a trip back to Arrakis, would have accompanied her to the sietch, or wherever she wanted to go—but it was too late for that now. He pulled her body closer as a hard sleet began to fall, and he felt the impenetrable cold.

He would go to Directeur Venport and demand passage back to Arrakis, would take Lillis's water and deliver it to the sietch, as he should have delivered the water of Shurko and Waddoch. It was the way of the desert.

In that small matter at least, he would help Lillis go home. Home . . .

LATER THAT DAY, astonishing news came in on a spacefolder from Salusa Secundus: Manford Toronodo was alive and well, and had just appeared at the Imperial Court. Worse, he had convinced the Emperor to seize all spice operations on Arrakis.

Directeur Venport didn't know which piece of information disturbed him the most.

The Half-Manford had somehow survived the assassination in Arrakis City, and emerged without a scratch. Young Taref had been easily fooled, and Venport's other observers, too.

Josef wondered why he had not heard the news sooner. His operatives had long been in place on Lampadas, some quietly observing for years. He should have received a message.

Then the Butlerian leader sent one of Josef's carefully infiltrated spies back to Kolhar—an innocuous old household servant named Ellonda. She'd been cut up in small pieces and sent in seventeen separate packages, each one personally addressed to Directeur Josef Venport.

It was shock on top of shock.

But the greatest outrage was the Emperor's acquiescence. Cowardly Salvador had let the barbarian leader bully him into making his ridiculous power grab for Arrakis. According to a sweeping Imperial decree, the spice from the desert world was a "treasure for all humankind," not for the profit of one man. By signing the order, Salvador annexed Combined Mercantiles, the spice fields, storage silos, processing plants, factories, and even the cargoes already aboard VenHold ships.

Filled with fury, Josef and his wife and his Mentat walked out to the temple-like structure that surrounded Norma Cenva's spice tank. "If the Emperor thinks he can do that, we'll topple his throne and show him where the real power lies. Norma's spice supplies will not be cut off or restricted!"

VenHold's demand for spice production had increased month after month as the Navigator conversion program expanded. Even after the mutated humans finished their transformation, they required extensive amounts of melange to maintain proper saturation levels. Josef refused to tolerate any disruption in the flow of melange—neither by the barbarians, nor by the Emperor.

It had been more than eighty years since Faykan Butler, a great hero of the Jihad, renamed his family House Corrino and established the new Imperium. But in those years, the throne had lost effectiveness. "Perhaps it's time for a major change," Josef muttered. "If Salvador means to declare war, then we will be forced to fight back."

"The Imperium is already crumbling," Draigo said. "I have run projections, and it matters surprisingly little who sits on the throne. The strands that bind the government are laid down by transportation and communication. Interaction among the worlds is what knits a multiplanet civilization together."

"We need someone better than Salvador Corrino," Josef said.

As they arrived at Norma Cenva's tank, Cioba was troubled. "That is a very ambitious plan, husband. An overthrow of the Imperial government would create as much havoc as the Butlerian mobs do now. Maybe there is a less extreme way, a more focused way?" She raised her eyes and looked into Josef's.

Draigo seemed distant, running calculations through his head. "Norma Cenva told us the conflict will be wide-reaching, and now is the time to draw lines, take sides—we need powerful allies." He paused, gathering courage. "We need my mentor Gilbertus Albans more than ever. I know he is torn. Let me speak to him again, and plead with him as a Mentat—he needs to choose the side of reason. If Mentats would all fight on the side of civilization, we could not lose."

Josef nodded. If he had hundreds more like Draigo Roget, the opportunities would be incalculable. "Very well, return to Lampadas and get that alliance. I hope you have a better result this time, for we are more desperate than ever. Go immediately—before it is too late."

Inside the swirls of thick mist, Norma drifted close to the curved observation plates. Even with her distorted face, she looked troubled. Before Josef could explain anything to her, she said, "Our supply of spice is threatened. Politics and turmoil must not be allowed to disrupt our great tapestry."

"What do you foresee this time?"

"I foresee patterns—the large plan, not precise details. The ripples of my prescience are very strong now. We face great peril." She blinked, and Josef looked into her face, trying to read her emotions.

"Salvador is the problem," Josef said. "He is weak and indecisive, a poor leader. We all know that Roderick would make a far better Emperor, a rational person who wouldn't be so afraid of the barbarians."

"His daughter was killed in a Butlerian riot," Cioba said. "He holds no love for Manford Torondo."

Norma continued, "Nothing can be allowed to stop the delivery of spice."

"I won't let it happen. Emperor Salvador announced he will go to Arrakis and take formal control of all spice operations. I will pretend to welcome him and invite him to see the harvesting operations in person. In fact, I'll escort him into the desert myself."

Cioba seemed discouraged. "I doubt you can convince the Emperor to change his mind, husband."

"Nevertheless, I'll try to make him see reason. And if not . . . I'll deal with the problem some other way."

*Truth is an amorphous thing, not quantifiable. There is no such thing as Pure Truth, because any attempt to understand this ideal involves a mental journey through shades of meaning and shades of purity. Does any form of truth reside in spoken words? In demonstrable actions? In supreme exercises of logic? Or does it lie in the secret places of the human heart?*

—Annals of the Mentat School

With Manford Torondo away to meet with the Emperor, Deacon Harian and his deputies were determined and ruthless in carrying out their leader's edicts on Lampadas. In the capital city people flocked to raise their hands in front of officials, swearing their vows in the names of the Three Martyrs.

Even at the isolated Mentat School, Gilbertus Albans learned of the harsh oath that Manford now required all individuals on Lampadas to swear. "The oath collectors are on the other side of the continent," he grumbled in his office, knowing Erasmus was listening. "But they will be here soon enough."

"I do not doubt it," the robot replied. "The actions of the Butlerians are both predictable and irrational. I continue to study and analyze them, even though Anna Corrino is a more interesting subject. She and I have grown close, don't you agree?"

"Too close," Gilbertus said. "She has started to mutter and make comments to you where other students can hear. Alys Carroll watches her intensely, suspecting she is possessed by a demon."

Erasmus chuckled, but the Headmaster found no humor in the situation. He was afraid of what Anna might say aloud, what revelations she might blurt out about the existence of the robot's hidden memory core.

"Manford's deputies will demand that every trainee at my school take the oath." Gilbertus had a copy of it in front of him, and he grew increasingly disturbed as he read it. He wondered if Manford had written the phrasing himself. "This pledge is even more bombastic and paranoid than the usual Butlerian vehemence. Condemnation of any form of advanced technology—although they don't define exactly what that might be."

Erasmus said, "I expect the definition will change according to Manford Torondo's convenience."

Before the latest flurry of activity, the Imperial Committee of Orthodoxy had already been making revisions to the old lists of banned technology. Gilbertus knew that once a device appeared on the Unorthodox list, it would never be removed. No one was allowed to appeal without facing suspicion and censure.

He regarded the printed notice with contempt, tossed it aside. "I won't encourage my Mentats to swear allegiance to this. They're not blind sycophants who agree without thinking."

"You are asking for trouble from the Butlerians," the robot said. "Why don't you simply do as humans do—lie? Repeat the oath when asked, even if you don't believe it. That will take care of the matter, and they will leave us alone. You must not end up like Horus Rakka, murdered because of your past. If anyone finds out who you were on Corrin, we will both be in terrible danger."

In his recent nocturnal visit, Draigo Roget had made a great impact on Gilbertus, causing him to doubt the choices and compromises he had accepted. "As the founder of the Mentat order, as the Headmaster of this great school, I teach students to use logic to arrive at the truth. It is something to strive toward, not to muddy, and certainly not to run away from. I intend to make a stand against this oath."

"Don't be silly. Rise above your moral objections for the greater good."

Gilbertus shook his head. "It's more than that. Even if I could be convinced to set aside my moral objections for a larger purpose—such as my own survival and the survival of this school—the Butlerians could bring a Truthsayer with them. I cannot lie about something this important. I just won't do it."

Ever since Draigo had confronted Gilbertus about his alliance with the Butlerians, he had questioned his implicit acceptance of antitechnology fanaticism. The Headmaster had cooperated with Manford because he didn't want to draw unwanted attention to the Mentat School, but he'd been a willing participant in too many questionable Butlerian activities.

Draigo had done what an excellent student should do—challenge the educator and make him *think*.

Gilbertus Albans had lived a long life full of accomplishment. He had worked hard to maintain a balance, to bridge the gap between humans and thinking machines. After nearly two centuries of life, how much would he give up to ensure his personal survival? Shouldn't he be thinking of his *legacy*, instead of prolonging his life at any cost?

The answer seemed clear to him, no matter the dangers involved.

Manford Torondo was exuberantly leading human civilization toward a new dark age, and Gilbertus had paid lip service to those beliefs to keep himself out of danger. But through his inaction, he only enabled the fanatics in their destruction. If he mouthed the words of this new oath without challenge, he would be condoning continued extremism, even promoting it.

"You have been silent for a long time," Erasmus said. "That suggests you are troubled."

"I am troubled, Father, and I have a big decision to make, the most important one I've ever made."

DEACON HARIAN'S PARTY arrived days later than Gilbertus expected them. Since the Butlerians insisted on an overland journey rather than taking a swift aircraft, their travel was slow and uncertain, especially when they reached the treacherous ground near the school. The public road through the swamp was intentionally circuitous to hinder the progress of anyone who approached.

Harian arrived at the thick barricade wall with six other Butlerians in his group, all haughty and energized. Seeing them, Alys Carroll flung open the high gates, even before word reached the Headmaster. A group of the Butlerian-picked trainees, including Alys, greeted the delegation with bristly familiarity.

Erasmus's spy-eyes warned Gilbertus before his administrator Zendur ran up to tell him the news. "Alys Carroll let them inside the walls!"

Gilbertus was disturbed by how quickly she had allowed the delegation through the defenses into the secure perimeter. He had no justification for keeping the Butlerians out—at least not yet—but the walls and the gate, as well as other less-obvious security systems, had been erected for a reason.

"I've been expecting them," the Headmaster said, keeping his feelings to himself. He sent Zendur away. Then, breathing calmly, he took a few moments to touch up his makeup, put on his spectacles, and adjust his formal robes before hurrying to the main gate.

When he met the delegation at the wide courtyard deck in front of the main lecture hall, Alys was already uttering the words of Manford's new oath before a deputy, as if reciting a sacred prayer. She was the fourth student to swear individually in front of the oath-deputy, and others were lined up behind her.

Deacon Harian had a hard countenance, and he looked dyspeptic today. No doubt he had spent days listening to thousands of oath-takers who asserted their devotion to Manford and professed abhorrence of technology, and he looked worn down and not inclined to exchange pleasantries when Gilbertus Albans faced him.

The bald deacon had always regarded the Headmaster, and everyone else, with a shadow of suspicion, as if he saw machine ghosts out of the corner of his eye. "Headmaster, summon the rest of your students in organized groups to line up. One by one they will recite the words to affirm their loyalty to Leader Torondo and the sacred Butlerian cause."

"You can't ask them to swear an oath they have not had time to read or consider."

Harian arched his eyebrows. "What is there to consider?"

"A person should fully understand the words of any oath before he swears to it—otherwise the promise means nothing. That is simple logic."

"This oath means a great deal, Headmaster," interjected the oath-deputy. A tall beanpole of a man, he had a pointed jaw and tiny eyes. He wore a badge with his title and name: Deputy Rasa. "Everyone must take it."

Gilbertus didn't move. "All the more reason that it should be duly considered first, so that each person knows exactly what he or she is swearing to before uttering the words."

"The *words* have been properly vetted by Leader Torondo himself," Harian said.

"Good, that means Manford knows what he is demanding, but my students are trained to think and make their own decisions. I cannot throw out a key tenet of Mentat instruction. You have my permission to leave the text here, and we will thoroughly discuss the matter among ourselves. Return in two months. By then, we will have completed our analysis and discussion, and will give you our decision."

Harian blinked, as if Gilbertus had just struck him in the face. Alys Carroll stepped up. "I have already taken the oath, Headmaster. It's plain enough, and states the truth we all know. What is there to discuss?" Her fellow Butlerian students muttered in agreement, as did the entourage accompanying Deacon Harian.

Gilbertus glanced at the printed words—which he had already reviewed in his office—then waved the copy in front of the deacon. "With only a quick glance I can see that this wording is too broad and not thoroughly thought out. It states unequivocally that anyone who uses computers must die, but what if someone accidentally finds and uses old technology? The thinking machines had a penchant for imitating human behavior. What if a person doesn't *know* he is interacting with a robot?"

"Any person of faith will instantly recognize the difference," Harian said.

"According to your oath, *any* person who uses advanced technology receives the penalty of death, but Leader Torondo recently flew aboard a foldspace ship to

Salusa Secundus. Does that mean he has condemned himself to death, by his own terms?"

"The ships of EsconTran have received a special dispensation," said Deputy Rasa. This was an old argument, one with no clear solution.

"There may be exceptions to the use of advanced technology in the further-ance of spreading our message," Harian explained. "But that exception does not permit the use of forbidden computers in navigation systems or other aspects of space travel. Anyone who uses computers must die."

Gilbertus turned to his gathered students. "And yet, my trainees proudly call themselves 'human computers.' On Rossak, Emperor Salvador declared ten Sis-ter Mentats to be 'computers,' and murdered them all—an action that was con-demned afterward by many members of the Landsraad. Are you asserting that anyone who uses a Mentat is therefore using a computer and must be executed? That would be highly unusual, since Manford Torondo uses my services. Could he, on that charge alone, be subject to the execution decree?" He swept his hand out, indicating the students. "These young people have spent a great deal of ef-fort learning to become human computers. How can I possibly have them swear such an oath, knowing they would be signing their own death warrants?"

He turned to Alys Carroll and her companions. "And what of these very students before you, who just swore your oath—do you now expect their im-mediate, irrational suicides? Or will you execute them yourself, since they *are* considered computers?" Gilbertus formed a polite smile. "As you can see, it is a slippery slope."

Alys scowled at the Headmaster. Several trainees chuckled at the logical co-nundrum, which only made Deacon Harian and the oath-deputy angrier.

Gilbertus, though, remained calm. "My prior actions in cooperation with Leader Torondo prove my long-standing faithfulness and reliability. Did I not just challenge and defeat a thinking machine at the Imperial Court? My past record of cooperation is evidence enough of my loyalty." He crossed his arms over his Headmaster gown. "Your insistence on this oath is offensive to me, as it should be to any person of intelligence."

Anna Corrino drifted forward among the trainees with a distant smile and sparkling eyes. "Omnius used to force human captives to do things against their wishes. That's just what Manford Torondo is doing now."

Harian's eyes bulged. "Thinking machines are demons! Leader Torondo pro-tects us all from that trap—Headmaster, make her retract the statement!"

Gilbertus pushed the spectacles up on his nose. "You would have me com-mand the Emperor's sister? I doubt Salvador Corrino would be pleased with that." He put a paternal hand on the young woman's shoulder, pressing hard and hoping she understood that he didn't want her to speak further. Erasmus could whisper in her ear as well, and he hoped the independent robot would warn her to stay silent.

Gilbertus maintained his cool smile. "You see, Deacon? Anna Corrino is a perfect example of my hesitation about forcing others to take your oath. She suffered grave mental damage and now studies among us in hopes of regaining the normal use of her mind. As her comment suggests, she is not capable of taking such a pledge."

Harian narrowed his eyes as he studied her. "Leader Torondo decreed that *all* people on Lampadas must swear the new oath—including the Emperor's sister."

"Leader Torondo does not decree what members of the Imperial family must do," Gilbertus said. "By implication, do you suspect the Emperor's own sister of disloyalty?"

"I suspect that while she is vulnerable, her mind could be corrupted," said Harian.

Deputy Rasa added, "She once attended the Sisterhood school on Rossak, which was disbanded after accusations that they used forbidden computers. Now it appears obvious you are providing a bad example for her, Headmaster Albans. The girl is at risk. Maybe we need to take Anna Corrino with us now for safekeeping."

Gilbertus's heart skipped a beat. "Anna was placed with *me* for protection, so she will remain here. I gave the Emperor my word." This was a matter of honor, not of intellect, and he had a firm—even *emotional*—need to do the right thing. "My other students will not swear to this oath. It's too vague, too draconian, and most of all, completely unnecessary."

As a supreme irony, Gilbertus's *emotions* had provided him with the key to an eminently logical conclusion, opening the gates to his own learning. He needed to make an ultimate counterpoint to Manford's destructive emotionalism— opposing it with an act of supreme logic and human heroics that would be remembered and would ultimately bring down Manford. Gilbertus wanted to become a human ideal for others to admire, the opposite of the Butlerian leader's terrible example.

A chill ran down his spine, as he remembered that the founder of the movement, Rayna Butler, had become a martyr. Perhaps Gilbertus would have to martyr himself in order to diminish her legendary image, push it out of the human psyche. Logic must trump hysteria. Humans should be creative and giving; they should achieve everything possible with their minds, using their mental powers for good works, not for mayhem and violence. They should build, not destroy.

His assistant Zendur and the gathered Mentat trainees watched the Headmaster's defiance with varying degrees of fascination, support, and terror.

"I am Headmaster here, and I choose what is best for my students. Leader Torondo may discuss the matter with me in person when he returns from Salusa Secundus, but this school will retain its autonomy and its honor. Now, please leave."

Harian, Deputy Rasa, and the small entourage looked as if they'd unexpectedly fallen off an easy path. "You just made a great deal of trouble for yourself, Headmaster Albans," the deacon growled.

"And yet, my decision remains unchanged," Gilbertus said. When he repeated his demand for them to leave, the group turned away, filled with obvious plans for retribution.

Gilbertus didn't need to converse with Erasmus to know that he had, indeed, placed both of them in grave danger.

*The wrongful death of a child is something a parent can never forgive,*
*but I fear for the safety of my husband if he seeks reprisals against the*
*Butlerians.*

                              —HADITHA CORRINO, private diary

T he consequences of such a brash action against VenHold will be like an
      avalanche, Salvador," said Prince Roderick. "More than we can handle.
It's not a good idea, and it's not safe for you to go to Arrakis—not while the situation is so volatile."

He and the Emperor walked with Reverend Mother Esther-Cano, who had
taken on the Truthsayer duties while Dorotea was away on Wallach IX.

Salvador sounded defensive. "I will have Imperial soldiers with me. In fact, you
should come along—we'll do this together. We won't be using a VenHold transport, and the faster-than-light engines on the Imperial Barge are perfectly safe."

Normally, the Emperor and his contingent traveled aboard a perfectly safe
VenHold spacefolder, but since the Emperor's edict had such drastic implications
for VenHold's business operations, Salvador did not feel comfortable riding on
one of Directeur Venport's ships, nor would he accept the services of a rival
transport company with an atrocious safety record.

"The non-Holtzman engines are safe, yes," Roderick agreed, "but the trip to
Arrakis will take three weeks, which means I have to stay on Salusa. You'll be
gone at least two months, and someone reliable has to run the Imperium until
you return."

They entered the palace hangar where the Imperial Barge was being prepared for the Emperor's forthcoming trip, a grand old vessel that traveled
the old-fashioned way, as all the ships in the League of Nobles had before Tio
Holtzman's invention of foldspace travel. Roderick agreed that the journey
would be safer than risking foldspace travel without a Navigator, but that wasn't

what he worried about. He thought his brother's entire plan to seize spice operations would provoke one of the most powerful men in the Imperium.

Salvador would not be convinced otherwise.

Echoing noises of tools and voices filled the hangar's cavernous space. The barge was more than large enough to hold an entourage of Imperial guards, along with staff and servants. They all anticipated having a marvelous journey, filled with pomp and circumstance.

Salvador looked up at the gilded hull. "It will be fine, brother. Directeur Venport sent a message accepting the edict. He is not happy about the transition, but he agreed to show me the spice operations personally."

Roderick lowered his voice. "That doesn't sound right to me. All the profits and power you're asking him to surrender? He's not the kind of man to surrender to your decree so easily."

"On the contrary, it's refreshing when a subject actually heeds the orders of his Emperor. You can be sure we'll hear plenty of complaints—a veritable army of VenHold attorneys will descend on Zimia to thrash out the details, and I do not for a moment believe he won't profit from the change."

Roderick made a noncommittal sound, unable to forget the image of the Manford Torondo look-alike assassinated in Arrakis City. He lowered his voice. "This might be an excellent time to test your stand-in. Your new double looks so much like you that he might almost fool me."

"But he wouldn't fool you, brother, and I doubt he would fool Directeur Venport either. My double would have to keep up the charade for weeks, in close quarters. No, this is something I must do for myself. I am the Emperor, and no one would dare harm me."

Esther-Cano listened to both men. Even though she was a pureblood Sorceress with Sisterhood training, she had proved herself reliable to Roderick's satisfaction. She had close-cropped black hair, small intelligent eyes, and an air of command, as if she had experience and wisdom far beyond her years. Now she interjected, "Sire, the Prince is wise to suggest caution."

The Emperor shook his head. "I've already made my decision. We will depart as soon as the barge is ready and my entourage has been gathered." He turned and issued orders to whomever might be listening, assuming that someone with authority would hear him. "Make certain the vessel is supplied with everything we need. Oh, and add some extra troops, just to keep my brother happy."

Roderick let out a slow, uneasy sigh, didn't argue further.

Workmen scurried along a webwork of scaffolding around the ship, inspecting the hull and taking measurements by hand, rather than using automated metal-lattice scanners, which the Committee of Orthodoxy had recently forbidden.

Reverend Mother Esther-Cano looked up. "Away from the scaffolds—*now!*"

She rushed them to the side an instant before a heavy seam welder crashed to the hangar floor where Salvador had been standing. Above, the crew cried out in dismay; guards raced into the hangar, yelling for all work activities to stop.

Rather than being outraged by the accident, Salvador was fascinated by the Reverend Mother. "How did you know that? Are you prescient?"

"Just observant, Sire."

He gave her a paternal pat on the back. "Well, I'm glad of that." He shouted back up to the crew. "Interrogate the clumsy worker, but I want no delays. We have a long journey ahead of us."

More cautious now, they continued the inspection, staying at a safer distance from the work area.

The barge was an elaborate and antique construction in the shape of a teardrop. Even though it would travel using old-style FTL engines, the aft compartment had been expanded to carry backup Holtzman engines as well, for folding space if necessary. The hull gleamed with an amalgamation of rare and valuable metals; the ship had a style and class of fine workmanship that had not been seen since the start of the Jihad. The Emperor especially liked the opulence of the interior, fitted with tiny jewels from a variety of planets around the Imperium.

The vessel was one of the treasures Salvador had acquired from the renegade House Péle, and he was eager to show it off. Several pilots were specially trained to operate the craft. When the fittings and preparations were completed, the barge would be ready, and its systems given rigorous shakedowns before the journey to Arrakis.

Salvador looked up at the barge, smiling. "I shall arrive with great fanfare and put an end to this matter. With spice operations under Imperial control, I shall reassert my authority and elevate my position as Emperor . . . and I will not have to worry about melange supplies. I'll plant the Corrino flag and establish a desert palace on Arrakis." He chuckled. "On an *oasis*, even if we have to import the water. It will be done, because I have commanded it."

Filled with pride, Salvador made the whole Arrakis venture sound fabulous and romantic. Yet Roderick doubted his brother would ever want to return to the desert planet after he experienced what Arrakis was actually like. There would be no desert palace, no royal oasis.

The balding Emperor paused beneath the bulbous front end of the craft and admired the golden-lion Corrino emblem, shiny and polished, which had recently replaced the flame symbol of House Péle.

Despite his reservations, Roderick did not dispute the concerns Manford Torondo and Dorotea had raised about the overreach of Venport Holdings; he was more worried about the volatile Butlerians, however. Manford was a bully, a loose cannon, and not afraid to use his followers as a threat. Though Roderick wanted to hamstring the reckless mobs, he knew that House Corrino was not strong enough to survive a widespread Butlerian uprising across the Imperium.

The power and influence Directeur Venport wielded were just as great as Manford Toronodo's, but he had not been openly hostile to the throne. Much of the Imperial Armed Forces even depended on VenHold ships for transport. The man had built his own commercial empire, made his own rules, while paying little more than lip service to the Emperor. At least he was reasonable, Roderick thought. The lesser of two evils . . . unless Venport was provoked too much.

Salvador said, "I will be glad to be done with this. I have grown exceedingly tired of the petty feud between Venport and the Butlerians. *I* am the Emperor, and by taking over Arrakis I intend to show *both* of them who rules the Imperium."

"Directeur Venport won't see it that way—he'll know you're still doing what Manford wants," Roderick said. "By bowing to Butlerian demands and seizing the spice business, you may well be creating a much more dangerous enemy."

"Nonsense! Despite Manford's suggestion, Arrakis was my world to begin with. We are only formalizing what already exists." He smiled stiffly. "This will be like our triumph on Rossak. We broke the Sisterhood, got rid of the corrupt part of it, and kept the best Sisters here, close to the throne. We'll do the same with VenHold."

Esther-Cano stood quietly next to the two men. "Sire, our orthodox Sisters will be watchful and warn you of any retaliation Directeur Venport attempts to impose. Leader Toronodo is correct—Josef Venport is dangerous, and for the sake of our souls, you must see that he is defeated, or at least controlled."

Roderick held his tongue, because the Butlerians needed to be controlled as well. Thinking back, from the time of Faykan Corrino I, to Emperor Jules, and now Salvador, he saw the Corrino throne growing weaker and weaker. Unless Salvador ever had an heir of his own—which seemed increasingly unlikely—Roderick's own son, Javicco, would become the next Emperor. Would Javicco only be a figurehead, presiding over an empire with an ill-prepared military force at the mercy of a group of antitechnology fanatics while beholden to a powerful business magnate?

Roderick knew that both Venport Holdings and the Butlerian movement needed to be drastically weakened before the Corrino throne could regain its rightful level of power. And with that goal in mind, perhaps Salvador's action was a step in the right direction to diminish Directeur Venport's power. After that, the Butlerians had to be neutered.

Better, Roderick thought, if the two great forces could bloody each other. . . .

*I long for something that has always eluded me in my centuries of life: an enduring sense of family and home.*

—VORIAN ATREIDES

V or stood on the aft deck of the sport-fishing boat, watching as a reticent Willem Atreides organized the nets, traps, floats, and other gear. The young man worked silently, going through the motions with efficient familiarity.

It was a modern craft and well maintained, with teak decks, custom storage lockers, and polished brass fittings. The boat glided through moderate seas, with Orry at the helm inside the cabin. The skies were gray, the air chilly.

"I've got years of experience on the sea," Vor said to Willem. "Can I help?"

"No, thanks," the tall blond man said as he yanked a knot tight. "This was Uncle Shander's boat, and I know where he liked to keep everything, exactly how he wanted the lines rolled." Willem drew a breath, let it out in a long sigh. The old man's mysterious death still hung above them like a heavy storm. The coroner had verified that Shander had been struck in the head and then swept out to sea, but no one could prove it was a murder.

Vor didn't think the young man intended to hurt his feelings with the remark, but it reminded him of how much he'd missed in his years away from Caladan. Family relationships were fraught with countless details, unseen threads, and tiny puzzle pieces of the past that formed a series of everyday events. The two brothers had spent most of their lives with Shander Atreides, building a comfortable nest of existence with untold thousands of interactions. Vor couldn't just step into that and expect to be treated as part of the family even in the best of times, and now after the tragedy everyone was off-balance.

He could tell how much the two young men had loved their uncle. Willem and Orry had experienced devastating losses when their parents were killed in a monstrous hurricane that tore up the coastline, but they had been young at the time. The inexplicable, unexpected death of a kindly old man who liked to repair fishing nets seemed beyond their comprehension. Over more than two centuries, Vor had been through every possible emotional permutation of grief himself. . . .

He felt a gentle breeze on his face, heard the drone of the boat's twin engines, and smelled the familiar salt air that he remembered from so long ago. The scent refreshed his memories, and he pictured the first time he'd seen Leronica Tergiet in a seaside tavern. The town had changed so little over the generations. . . .

Orry worked the controls, and Vorian felt the engines vibrate harder. They glided around foaming water and the shadows of submerged reefs, then picked up speed as the boat headed out to open sea.

Life was unpredictable, with some delightful surprises, but also shocking events. Vor had returned to Caladan in search of an anchor in his life, trying to regain a part of the happiness he'd left behind. Maybe he was naïve in that wish. He had been back only a short time before Shander Atreides died. It was a silly superstition to think so, but perhaps he carried the shadow of bad luck with him.

Unfortunate events occurred everywhere, to everyone—life just happened. Shander's family might never learn the exact details of how he had died, or who might have been responsible, but Willem and Orry would mourn him and remember him. And eventually, they would move on. Orry was about to get married, Willem had a chance to be promoted in the Caladan Air Patrol . . . and Vor could try to forge the bonds he'd never had with his own sons.

He could never take Shander's place, but he could be Vorian Atreides. He had battle ribbons from his service in the Jihad; Imperial coins had been minted with his face on them, but none of that mattered anymore. He would rather be recognized for his ability to *love*. He wanted to care about other people, about his family—however far estranged they might be—and have them care for him in return.

That would require a different type of commitment and endurance. He had found that for many years with Mariella on Kepler, but had been forced to leave it all behind in order to save his family. He wasn't certain if he could reestablish a sense of family here on Caladan, but he vowed to try.

The boat continued chopping its way through the small waves, bouncing hard enough to jar Vor's teeth. He gripped the side rail to keep his balance. Young Orry seemed intent on the boat's controls, accelerating. Willem stood at the bow and let the spray and wind whip his face and hair. He closed his eyes, as if drinking it all in.

With a whirring noise, long, thin stabilizers extended outward on either side of the hull. Orry increased the speed even more. Vor peered over the rail, then looked up to shout at Willem. "What kind of a rig is this?"

Seeing his tight grip, Willem laughed as he shouted back. "Uncle Shander let Orry tinker with the engine compartment, making a few crackpot enhancements."

From the cabin, Orry yelled at his brother, "They're not crackpot modifications! You've seen them work."

Vor knew about Caladan's large sea animals—some predators, others passive. "Speed is always a good thing to have, when you need it."

Orry pushed the controls forward, and Vor straightened, then laughed aloud as he shared the exhilaration with both young men. The bow lifted off the water, and spray flew like a rain shower all around them.

Willem said, "We don't usually go this fast, so he must be showing off— maybe even trying to scare you."

Vorian grinned. "I've told you about my record in the Jihad. Only a fool says he's never scared—but it'll take more than a fast boat to worry me as long as the engines can take it." He watched Orry at the controls. "We don't want to break down out here."

Willem came closer so he didn't have to shout over the roar of the wind and engines. "I could ask him to slow down, but he wouldn't pay attention. I told him to slow down with his fiancée, too—see how well he listens? Now we've got a wedding in a few weeks."

"I look forward to meeting her," Vor said, and then felt a stuttering vibration in the hull. The engines sputtered; first one went off, then the other, and the boat coasted along in sudden silence. Orry tried to restart the engines, but they only made disturbing clinking noises.

Red-faced, Orry emerged from the cabin and opened a cooler-locker. "Time to stop for lunch anyway." He handed out packets of sliced meats and cheese, which the three ate as the boat drifted on the open sea. After they finished, the two brothers each took toolkits and climbed into the cramped engine compartment while Vor remained on deck to watch the water. He listened to the clanking tools and the young men discussing what could be wrong, replacing parts, arguing at times, and laughing.

On deck, Vor saw the rolling curve of a large marine animal that surfaced not far off, then descended. Moments later, the back of another creature rolled through the water, extending a triangular fin the size of a warehouse door, before gliding back beneath the surface. Vor didn't recognize the species.

He called down into the engine compartment, "We have visitors—several animals. Big ones."

Willem and Orry climbed back on deck, saw the large humps on either side of the stranded boat. "Not good," Willem said. "That's all one animal—an Alada sea snake, the largest I've ever seen."

"They usually stay deep." Orry ran inside the cabin and returned with three rifles. "I've heard they can drag down whole boats."

"Let's hope that's not true." Vor took one of the rifles from Orry, and Willem took another. As they watched the curves of the dark sea snake ripple up and down, part of the beast's back lifted to buffet the boat, and Willem fired two rounds at it.

Puffs of blood spurted from the thick hide, and the serpent's body flinched away, then struck the hull again more aggressively. Off the port side, Vor saw the monster's head surface—it seemed impossibly far away to be part of the same body. He fired at it several times, but the animal snapped its plated head back, and the shots missed.

The serpent collided with the boat and nearly capsized it, but the extended stabilizers kept the vessel afloat. The beast then curved around, its head cutting a wake as it churned closer. Smelling the fishy stench of the creature, Vor continued to fire the rifle, hitting it this time, but not deterring the beast. Orry and Willem also peppered the sea snake with bullets. The serpent recoiled, but still circled the boat.

Vor heard a distant buzz in the sky and saw two aircraft approaching. Willem looked at his brother. "You called in the Air Patrol? We could have fixed the boat ourselves."

Orry seemed embarrassed. "I thought I'd give the search-and-rescue some practice. Besides, we don't have the parts we need for the fuel system."

The wounded sea snake lunged at the boat again, ramming the hull with its armored head. Vor heard wood splintering. "Put your pride away. I'm glad they're here."

The planes buzzed overhead and dropped concussion charges that made loud splashes in the water. The sea snake writhed and finally dipped beneath the waves to get away.

Feeling a wash of relief, Vor let himself grin. "Thanks for an exciting outing, boys."

THE AIR PATROL arranged for the fishing boat to be towed into port for repairs. When Orry and Willem stepped onto the dock, they found half a dozen of their flight comrades ready with teasing remarks.

"We spotted you on the sat-screen cruising so fast that we thought you were a low-flying plane," a young redhead said. "We decided the pilot was insane—and that's how we knew it must be Orry Atreides."

"Didn't know if we'd have to shoot you down or rescue you," said another man.

"Glad you helped drive that sea snake away," Willem said. "Though we could have handled it on our own."

"Yes," Vor said. "Given a few months we probably could have paddled or drifted back to the coast." Everyone in the group laughed.

He saw a pretty young blonde hurrying toward them with a bright smile and a gleam in her eyes—her gaze was directed entirely at Orry. She had a hypnotic way of moving, as if she had mastered the technique of drifting over the ground.

Orry lit up and pushed his way past his comrades to greet her. The others gave knowing smiles and lifted their eyebrows. She rushed forward to hug the young man. "I'm so glad you're safe. I was worried about you!"

Willem just rolled his eyes.

Orry grabbed her arm and pulled her toward Vor. "There's someone I want you to meet." He seemed proud and love-struck, like a man showing off a great prize. "This is Vorian Atreides, my . . . distant relative." Vor thought her face looked vaguely familiar, though he knew he had never seen her before. "And this is my fiancée, Tula. Tula Veil."

Tula was indeed beautiful, but her eyes had an odd intensity when she looked at him. She extended her hand, and her grip was cold. "Vorian Atreides—I am very glad to meet you."

*Inflexible convictions are powerful things. But are they a suit of armor
or a prison cell? A weapon or a weakness?*
—EMPEROR JULES CORRINO, strategic briefing
on unrest in the former Unallied Planets

Gilbertus knew the school's situation would only grow more dangerous by
the day. The Butlerians had proven themselves to be volatile and prone
to violence, and with his refusal to take the oath, he had just jabbed them with
a sharp stick.

Nevertheless, he approached the crisis with cool logic. An hour after the
Butlerian delegation left in a huff, he called the entire student body and addressed them in the main lecture hall. This was the same auditorium where
he had dissected thinking-machine brains and human brains; here, he had also
debated the merits of computers while some students listened in horror. That debate had provoked an extreme reaction from the Butlerians, who forced him to
retract his statements and destroy all robot specimens stored at the school.

All of the robot specimens they *knew* about.

"Many people on Lampadas have already sworn the new Butlerian oath without giving it a second thought, and they are welcome to do so," Gilbertus said to
the students in the auditorium. "But I expect you to be deep thinkers and understand the nuances involved." He paced in front of them. "I comprehend why
Manford feels the need for such an oath, but I make an important distinction,
not merely an esoteric one. An oath should neither be reactionary, nor taken in
haste. A commitment is a serious matter."

He paused to look at them all. "This school is vital. Our teachings are vital.
We teach you *how* to think, not *what* to think. The mind of man is holy, as the
Butlerian mantra says. It cannot be battered into submission by threat of vio-

lence. Absolute rules are for unthinking people. Sheep require fences—humans do not."

Gilbertus saw remarkable courage on the faces of most students, and he was proud of them. With emotion welling up, he continued, "I understand, however, that some of you may disagree with my stance. Therefore, anyone who wishes to depart from the school may do so right now. I will not make you listen to my words or abide by my teachings. You have all the data necessary. Consider your decision and follow your conscience." He raised his hand. "But if you choose to stay here and stand by me, then I expect you not to change your mind."

Alys Carroll and twenty-two others departed promptly, saying that if they hurried down the narrow swamp road, they might even catch up with Deacon Harian's departing entourage. Watching the Butlerian-trained students go, Gilbertus felt a sense of relief. He had been forced to accept them in his school in the first place, and had never wanted them in his midst.

The more he observed the dangerous collective mindset of the antitechnology fanatics, the more he appreciated Draigo Roget's abilities. And the more convinced he was that he should have stood up to Manford long before now.

Unfortunately, the departing students also carried knowledge of the Mentat School's physical layout, perimeter, and defenses. As a practical matter, Gilbertus immediately assigned his remaining trainees to shore up and alter the defenses, providing additional physical and electronic barriers on the lake side, as well as strengthening the gates and walls. The security codes would be modified.

He sensed the changing mood among his students as they ran Mentat projections of their own—undoubtedly realizing that they were in the midst of a serious and deadly conflict. For his own part, Gilbertus had spent a great deal of time studying Manford's followers, and he expected the fervor to grow worse than even his most concerned students feared, or projected. Manford's retaliation against the school would be swift and brutal—as it had been at the town of Dove's Haven.

But Gilbertus and his Mentats would not be taken unawares.

The Headmaster circulated the complete text of the new oath and, as an exercise, requested that his students compile a list of the document's flaws, contradictions, and loopholes. "When one swears on one's life, the agreement should be absolutely clear, without equivocation, and without gray areas."

In ensuing days, led by Zendur as if this were no different from any other class, the students discussed, documented, and presented the Headmaster with more than five hundred weaknesses in the one-page oath, many of which even Gilbertus had not considered. It was valuable ammunition for his debate with

Manford Toronto . . . though he doubted the Butlerian leader would be in the mood for open intellectual discourse when he arrived.

Next, as a strategic exercise, Gilbertus asked his students to develop scenarios of how the Butlerians might respond—and to consider the very real possibility of deadly violence. He wanted to make certain they were loaded with all the mental ammunition they needed in order to make their decision about the oath.

Erasmus also understood the danger. He urged, "You must prepare a way for us to escape! You should have made plans earlier."

Shaking his head, Gilbertus said, "You sound emotional, Father. Are you afraid of dying? I'm not afraid for myself."

"I fear the destruction of all of my knowledge and ruminations. The loss to the universe would be extreme. Therefore, it is my duty to survive."

"I have a similar devotion to my school. This institution is my life's work, and it needs to stand for something." He drew in a deep breath. "If I simply abandon them and run, it would be like watching a house burn without lifting a finger to extinguish the flames."

Before retiring for the night, when Gilbertus knew the robot would be deep in his private conversations with Anna Corrino, he decided to check the school's private hangar to make sure he still had his escape shuttle. If the worst happened, the shuttle might be the only way for him to save his beloved Erasmus.

He was shocked to discover that someone, perhaps the zealot Alys Carroll, had dismantled the flyer's engine and smashed several vital components before departing. He did not have the spare parts to repair such damage.

Now Gilbertus had no way out.

WHEN MANFORD RETURNED from Salusa Secundus, he was both disturbed and disappointed to learn how the Headmaster of the Mentat School had defied him. He had considered Gilbertus Albans an ally, and Mentats were certainly useful, but he had always felt an ember of doubt. The very idea of creating humans that emulated computers made him uneasy.

He fell silent, pondered what to do.

Deacon Harian's face reddened, and his voice rose. "He betrayed you, Leader Torondo! I always suspected that man was secretly a Machine Apologist."

"Headmaster Albans knows what our people could do to him and to his school. What reason did he give for his refusal to take the oath? Does he have some esoteric concern about the wording—a concern that means nothing to anyone except himself and his students?"

"That is what he claims," Harian said, "but I do not believe him."

Sister Woodra paced the floor of the headquarters office. "I want to go there and see the Headmaster myself, and observe whether he tells the truth."

Manford narrowed his gaze. "I doubt he poses an outright threat—unlike Directeur Venport."

"Do not underestimate him! Even now, he is corrupting the minds of those trainees—and that makes him a threat," Harian insisted.

Anari Idaho was not convinced either. "Regardless of the man's motives or objections, we cannot allow him to defy a clear order. Manford guides us. Manford thinks about what needs to be considered, and Manford draws the conclusions that are right for all of us. If we allow Headmaster Albans to express *doubts*, even as an intellectual exercise, then he may encourage others to doubt. They may draw conclusions that differ from the approved canon. I agree that the man is dangerous." She grabbed the hilt of her sword. "We need to go to the school, strike him down, and capture the other Mentats for retraining—or kill them. Then we'll sink the buildings into the marsh lake. It is the only way to be certain."

Sister Woodra added, "And we need to take Anna Corrino under our protection, until the Emperor has followed through on his commitment to take over VenHold's melange operations."

Manford knew they were right, but he was hesitant. Gilbertus Albans had proved useful in the past, and destroying the Mentat School would not be like killing the weak and gullible people on Baridge, who chose their own comforts over the austerity of true faith. He shook his head slowly. "I still respect Headmaster Albans, and I am saddened it has come to this. I must confront him with these accusations."

"The man is a traitor and a spy," Harian said, "just like your household servant was."

Manford made up his mind. "We will bring a Butlerian army to the Mentat School and resolve this, but our main battle is not here on Lampadas against a group of scholars who seek to make computers irrelevant. I want all of our supporters in harmony so we can fight the true threat of Directeur Venport. I would much rather secure the Headmaster's cooperation. Maybe I can still convince him to swear the oath."

Anari, Harian, and Sister Woodra shook their heads at this optimism, but Manford raised his voice. "I've seen the worth of Mentat trainees. Alys Carroll and her comrades survived the seduction of technology, and now they are better for it . . . but the graduates must think properly. The Mentat academy must only teach appropriate lessons. No matter what happens, I'll need to impose changes."

"We'll bring the whole population of Lampadas to besiege the school. That will make the Mentats quake behind their walls," Anari said, and he had no doubt that she could do exactly that.

"No need for that yet. Such a huge group of followers setting up camp in the swamplands would be . . . unwieldy," he said. "Bring your Swordmasters and five hundred Butlerian soldiers. That should be more than enough."

"We'll set out within a day," Anari promised.

Manford realized that this crisis could be a pivotal point for his movement, and he had to mitigate the damage that had already been done. If weak spots appeared among the faithful, some of his followers would lose their resolve when VenHold kept dangling the so-called advantages of forbidden technology in front of their faces. Manford didn't dare fail.

Gilbertus might have to serve as an example. A lesson.

"We'll take over the school and salvage what we can," he said. "We shall re-program the errant human computers."

Mentat student picked her way forward, and the Swordmasters copied her steps, forming a line across the expanse of water.

Carroll was ready to take her next step, but Anari called for her to pause, and gestured for everyone else to stop. She pointed at floating black forms, mostly submerged, in the water nearby. Anari counted four. "Those are not fallen logs."

Alys Carroll's eyes widened. "Swamp dragons."

The shapes drifted aimlessly. One floated closer to the Butlerian Mentat, who had frozen in place. But as the monster came close, Anari pounced onto the stepping-stone next to Carroll and thrust with her sword. When she stabbed the armored creature, it did not resist.

Anari plunged her blade again, looking for blood, sure that the struggle would attract the other swamp dragons. But the shape simply bobbed and drifted away. Anari snagged it with the point of her sword and pulled the thing closer.

It was indeed a swamp dragon: a hideous, scaled creature with powerful jaws and long fangs . . . but it was already dead, a preserved specimen, dissected and stuffed.

"Merely a decoy to frighten us," Carroll said. "A trick from the Headmaster."

Anari nodded. "A stalling tactic. But it won't work for long."

Carroll turned forward again, scanning the starlit water ahead. "Follow me." She moved to the next submerged stepping-stone, then jumped to a third and a fourth. Another fake swamp dragon drifted toward them. Anari stabbed it with her sword just to make sure, and the stuffed specimen floated away.

The Swordmaster commandos followed on the precise stepping-stones. Anari watched the placement carefully and imitated Carroll. The other woman moved ahead, jumping confidently until they were halfway across the width of the waterway. Then she gasped in surprise and fell in. Splashing and flailing around, she tried to locate the stepping-stone. "It was *here*! The Headmaster must have moved the stones. He—"

Anari swung her head, alert. "Look out!"

One of the floating swamp dragons was not so listless after all, but had been lying in wait for its prey to make a mistake. Struggling to pull herself out of the water, Carroll turned as the creature surged out of the brown slurry, lunging for her. The monster hooked its powerful jaws on to her torso and crunched down, barely giving her time for a whimpering scream before she vanished underwater.

Anari didn't know where the next stepping-stone might be, and she couldn't fight that creature in the murky water. The other commandos, poised on unseen stepping-stones, watched the swamp dragon attack, then began a swift retreat. Many of them missed the hidden stones and slipped into the water, which only increased their panic. Then someone imagined he saw razorjaws swimming around them and yelled out. If the nearby swamp dragon hadn't already had its meal, Anari's followers would all have been killed in their frenzy to escape.

Anari remembered her Swordmaster training clearly, focused her thoughts, and made herself calm. She forced herself to recall where the stepping-stones were behind her, and jumped from one to the next to the next. She barely caught the last one on its edge, swayed to catch her balance, and heaved herself onto solid ground again while the rest of the scout party splashed and crawled to the shore.

Disgusted with herself, Anari looked back at the still-untouched Mentat School.

GILBERTUS REMAINED ON the battlements far into the night. Flickers of light, splashing, and screams on the sangrove swamp side told him that the Butlerians had made an ill-advised sortie. He hadn't needed to lift a finger to respond. The swamp and the marsh lake provided all the defenses the school needed for now.

Next to him, Anna Corrino gazed into the darkness, listening to the sounds. "Our little trick worked. That is comforting." They were the only two who knew that the decoy swamp dragons had been Erasmus's idea.

Gilbertus pondered whether he should lie to reassure her, but decided to be honest and forthright. "This is only going to get worse, Anna. Much worse."

*As a human being, I was born on the brink of personal destruction, and*
*I have spent my life dancing along the edge of that cliff.*
—MOTHER SUPERIOR RAQUELLA BERTO-ANIRUL

Despite her increasing infirmity, Raquella felt a burst of energy, fueled by anger. Gripping a curl of message paper in her hand, she walked at a brisk pace through the plant- and statue-lined portico that had been set up in one of the new school buildings. Her shoes made sharp reports on the tiles, sounds that grew louder as she rounded a corner before coming to a wooden door.

She rapped sharply and stood staring at the door, as if willing it to move. Finally the door opened, and Reverend Mother Valya stood before her in a new black robe.

"I ordered you to attend the reception for Dorotea and her companions from Salusa Secundus." Raquella waved the message paper under the younger woman's nose. "Why did you decline?"

Valya had been on Wallach IX for less than a day since returning from Ginaz, but she arrived before Sister Arlett, who was bringing Dorotea from the Imperial Court. Now the transfer ship from Salusa Secundus was about to land at the spaceport, and Raquella didn't have the time for squabbles or stubbornness. This had to end now!

Valya's dark eyes hardened. "How can I welcome Dorotea when she is responsible for the murder of so many Sisters? She teaches a heretical group of women that pander to the Emperor and swoon whenever Manford Torondo mutters a command. To invite Dorotea back here, even to suggest that she is still one of us—"

Raquella did not try to quell her emotions. "I am the Mother Superior, and this is *my* school. I made it clear to everyone—Acolytes, Sisters, and Reverend

Mothers alike—that I want the two factions to reconcile before I die. Valya, you must set aside your feelings for the sake of the Sisterhood . . . for *my* sake."

Valya squirmed, obviously fighting her dislike. "I will never trust a turncoat, Mother Superior. On Rossak, you asked me to pretend to be Dorotea's friend so I could spy on her—I have seen her heart, her unbridled ambition."

Raquella's voice was sharp, like a weapon. "As I have seen yours."

Valya looked at the floor, then raised her gaze and seemed to summon her courage. "I left my Swordmaster instructor and came back at your urging, but what is all this talk of reconciliation? How can you forget our Sisters who were cut down by the Emperor's troops?"

Raquella's voice was quietly reassuring. "I'm not ignoring anything, but I must make compromises, for the future of the Sisterhood. When I am gone— and that will be soon, Valya—my work could be torn apart by a civil war, and I don't want that to happen. All Sisters follow the same basic teachings and believe in our plan to improve the human race. It is best for us not to be divided simply because we disagree about the tools we use. It is *essential* for us not to be divided."

"And who is to replace you?" Valya pressed. "Your message said you had chosen your successor."

"I will tell you when I tell all of the Sisters. My choice will assure the best chance for the Sisterhood's survival."

"Is it to be Dorotea, then? The woman who abandoned us? Your own granddaughter?"

Raquella gripped Valya firmly by the arm and guided her out into the corridor. "My decision is forthcoming. And you *will* attend the reception."

THE TWO WOMEN entered the austere reception hall, one of the first large structures built by VenHold workers. The school had expanded greatly in the initial year, but the women wasted no time or effort on unnecessary amenities or furnishings. The hall thronged with black-robed Sisters and a small number of white-robed Acolytes.

Just inside the doorway, Raquella said, "It would please me to see you and Dorotea spend time together. Make the initial effort. You used to be friends."

"I pretended to be her friend."

"Then pretend again. The Sisterhood is at stake." The Mother Superior flowed away into the crowd of women, leaving Valya on her own.

Raquella eased herself into a seat and poured a glass of springwater from a pitcher. Going into a deep analysis, she felt her nerves crackle with misfires, her metabolism strain, her cellular chemistry struggle to continue functioning. Any normal woman would have died decades ago, but Raquella used her extraordinary bodily control to keep herself alive. She closed her eyes to dive deep into an inner trance where she worked within her own cells, monitoring the biological machinery.

Just a little longer . . . Maybe tonight she could surrender and be done with her work, with her life.

She returned to awareness when Sister Fielle spoke to her. Raquella realized that she had drifted off for longer than she expected. "Dorotea has arrived, Mother Superior."

The young Sister Mentat extended her arm and helped the elderly woman to her feet. "Thank you." Raquella resented her own increasing weakness, and she drew upon energy reserves to steady herself so that others would not see.

Valya stood off to one side, surrounded by a group of Sisters. Raquella realized that they were the commando women who had gone to retrieve the hidden computers from Rossak; they were also the Sisters most dedicated to Valya's personal combat training. Of course, she should have realized that Valya would gather her own allies at the school. . . .

When the main doors opened, Sister Arlett strode into the reception hall, introducing the guests she had brought from Salusa. Dorotea followed her, a lanky figure wearing a black robe that was of a different cut from traditional Sisterhood garb; hers even included a Corrino lion crest. She was accompanied by six other women who also served in the Emperor's palace. Raquella remembered all of the prodigal Sisters, wished they had never left.

Dorotea and her entourage looked around the hall to assess the Mother Superior's new headquarters. Raquella caught hints of . . . haughtiness? Superiority? Disappointment at these workmanlike buildings, which were far inferior to the ostentatious spectacle of the Imperial Palace?

The orthodox Sisters mingled with their Wallach IX counterparts, showing no reservations. It was either a sign of submissiveness, or perhaps arrogance, since they had the Emperor's favor.

From across the large room, Dorotea's eyes met her grandmother's like weapons systems acquiring targets. The voices of Other Memory became a loud whisper in the back of Raquella's mind, a gathering storm. The other woman regarded her as if they were equals . . . and perhaps that was how Dorotea felt.

The old woman used well-honed techniques to control her blood pressure, her metabolism, her pulse. She had to remain calm and fully alert, using her last energy reserves. Most of all, she had to be ready to do what she must, the martyrdom solution—it was a tremendous gamble, but Raquella knew it was the best move she had left to her.

As Dorotea came forward with gliding steps, the Sisters gave her a wide berth. More and more Sisters congregated around Valya, facing Dorotea and her smaller entourage. Raquella wondered how many seeds Valya had already planted among the Wallach IX followers, how much of a personal power base she'd been building. Dorotea and Valya exchanged glances, but neither showed any emotion.

Now the Mother Superior gripped Dorotea's hands warmly. "Welcome back, Dorotea. The Salusan Sisters are still our Sisters, though we have traveled different paths. Those paths are converging again."

Reverend Mother Dorotea held the old woman's hands formally, then squeezed tighter, but just for a moment. Was she trying to communicate some sort of message? "It is good to see you, Grandmother. We are both far from Rossak."

"In distance perhaps, but we are not necessarily so separate. At least, it doesn't have to be that way."

Raquella was aware of all the women listening in on the conversation, not saying anything. Many of the Wallach Sisters shot questioning glances at Valya. The Mother Superior needed to seal this matter of opposing loyalties.

Raquella hoped that Fielle's risky solution would succeed.

The Mother Superior had to stage a dramatic, emotional event that would likely result in her death. She had spent years demanding that her students learn to rein in their emotions, but now the future depended on both Valya and Dorotea *caring* about her.

DURING THE TENSE reception, the Wallach Sisters treated Dorotea and her companions as if they were made of cold glass.

The Mother Superior seated herself at the head of a long dining table and instructed Valya to sit on her right, Dorotea on her left. The two younger women kept themselves in separate pools of moody reticence, speaking only when spoken to, constantly on the alert for their rival's every move, gesture, and word.

Through a high window in the hall, Raquella could see the fading outlines of nearby hills as darkness set in. She turned to Valya and Dorotea. "Back on Rossak, you two were comrades and learned from each other. You both endured the Agony, though you took separate paths to pass through to the other side."

The two younger women seemed ready to interject, but Raquella held up a hand to silence them. "I know your disagreements, I know your beliefs—but I hope that both of you will understand that the Sisterhood is more important. The things we have in common are more fundamental than our differences. We know from history—written in documents and told to us by our ancestors within—that since the beginning of civilization countless societies have warred over nuances, while forgetting the commonality of their basic beliefs. We must not let that happen to ourselves."

"Others have tried and failed," Valya said sourly. "The Commission of Ecumenical Translators sought to find common ground among feuding religions and produced the *Orange Catholic Bible*. That didn't turn out well at all."

Dorotea snorted, agreeing with Valya. "We could ask the members of the CET, but most of them were murdered. The only ones left are in deep exile."

Mother Superior Raquella gave them each a stern glance. "The final success or failure of the *Orange Catholic Bible* remains to be seen. In the Sisterhood, we must take the long view—thousands of years, hundreds and hundreds of *generations,* not just a few decades."

She paused for breath. "I am ancient and should have died long ago. Now I must anticipate what will happen to the Sisterhood when I am gone—*my* legacy." She nodded toward Fielle. "Our Sister Mentats have run extensive projections, and I know what must be done. . . . I also know the dire consequences if I fail. When I die, it is up to you, and to all of my Sisters."

"We can never forget that Dorotea betrayed us," Valya said.

"I was not the betrayer. Your use of computers was a betrayal of the Imperium, and of humanity itself!"

"An unproven charge," Valya said, "which you made with no thought of the consequences. Because of you—"

Raquella cut them off. "Enough!" It seemed hopeless, but she had to proceed with her plan. She had to force a rapprochement, and her final alternative would require her remaining energy. If she failed, she would be dead. "I grow weary of this. I grow weary of life."

With all the dignity and energy she could muster, she strode out of the hall.

RAQUELLA WAS ON the edge of despair about the crumbling future, and every one of the Sisters needed to understand why she felt that way. The Sisterhood no longer matched her vision; perhaps it was appropriate for it to end with her, if the factions could not work together.

Bitterly, she wrote several identical farewell notes with subtle yet clear nudges and a deep sadness. Raquella explained in the letters that she had decided not to appoint a successor, that she had surrendered to the inevitable crumbling of her work. She said there was no sense in lingering longer. She made certain that the messages were delivered simultaneously to Valya, Dorotea, and several other close Sisters.

In any case, the die was cast.

Then the old woman left the school buildings and walked off by herself, wearing only a thin robe in the chill night. She carried a small handlight as she toiled along the familiar trail up the slope of Laojin Cliff. She made her way up to the crest of the promontory, where she would await the sunrise. The wind was cold, but she didn't think much about it as she stood on the edge.

When day broke in a few hours, she would see bright sunlight spilling over the school buildings, and she would see the sheer cliff edge . . . just before she flew off it. Raquella had enough control over her body that she could simply shut down her organs and die quietly in bed, but that would not provide the drama she required. Fielle had been right about that when they had formed the plan, Raquella's last chance. . . .

She hoped that the shock would be enough to force Valya and Dorotea together, and that the two quarreling women cared enough about *her* to set their differences aside. If not, the Sisterhood was already too broken anyway and would degenerate into a civil war. She would not allow that.

Her body seemed to be strung together with spiderwebs, ready to fall apart at a moment's notice. Yet when Raquella finally stood on the very edge of the cliff, looking into the abyss of deep shadows, she maintained her balance despite the strong gusts and updrafts.

Other Memory gave her an infinite encyclopedia of experiences from human history, but her own long life provided enough memories to surround her: her younger years working with Dr. Mohandas Suk on Parmentier, before they were forced to flee riots when machine plagues raged across that world; her years on Rossak, helping the Sorceresses in their fight against thinking machines; Ticia Cenva's efforts to catalog the bloodlines of humanity, even as the machines did their best to make humanity extinct.

With the night making her numb, Raquella's eyes fluttered closed. The past was all around her, and she swayed on the edge of the cliff, but did not fear the plunge. She and Death were old companions, who had dueled several times before—with Raquella winning each of those matches.

But this time it would be different. Her female ancestors in Other Memory were ready to welcome her.

Long ago, while tending to the plague-struck people on Rossak, Raquella had caught the dread disease. She would have died, if not for the healing properties of the cenote waters. She had defeated Death then, and again shortly afterward when Ticia Cenva poisoned her. In the process of surviving, Raquella had altered the poison, changing *herself* to become the first Reverend Mother.

For eight decades she had tried to teach others what she had learned, to build something lasting—an order of powerful, enlightened women who would guide the destiny of the human race. Now she knew it had been a false hope if the Sisterhood could not last even one generation. The squabbling proved that her Sisters were no better, and no more visionary, than other people.

Daylight leaked over the horizon, rising like rays of hope. Raquella opened her eyes and saw the huddled rooftops of the school buildings below. She heard voices, shouts—and saw the shadowy shapes of women rushing up the trail to the top of Laojin Cliff.

Good, they had received her message.

She heard Dorotea's pleading voice, which brought comfort as well as urgency. "Mother Superior! Please come back."

With a warm surge of relief, she also heard Valya calling out. "Dorotea and I will find a way to work together. The Sisterhood can't stay broken."

As the daylight brightened, she saw Dorotea and Valya leading a group of Sisters toward her. Raquella did not move from her position, but remained standing on the edge of the cliff.

At the top, Valya pushed her way forward. "We read your message, and it brought us to our senses. Dorotea and I have come here together—and we promise to do whatever is necessary to heal the wounds." Then Valya's voice shifted, and she said in a throaty, emphatic tone, "You will not jump, Mother Superior. Step back from the edge, *now*."

Raquella had noticed a subtle shifting in the younger woman's voice previously, when she spoke with other Sisters. The Mother Superior had always ascribed this to Valya's intense personality, but now the voice seemed different, and the old woman felt something tugging at her, impelling her to step away from the edge.

"*Step back from the cliff,*" Valya repeated, with the same coarse edge to her voice. It was not a request, and Raquella felt the power of the words immobilize her body. She struggled against the strange power—or what seemed to be a power. Then she relaxed her muscles and just stood there, not wanting to jump, but uncertain if she should step back.

Valya moved closer and said in a softer tone, "We *need* you, Mother Superior. Both Dorotea and I are desperate for your wise counsel."

"We'll look for common ground and build on that," Dorotea said. "I promise, we will find a way. You need to know that the Sisterhood will live on."

Fielle and dozens of others—including the visiting Sisters from Salusa—rushed to the top of the cliff. Despite the cold wind that swirled around the promontory, Raquella felt increasing warmth inside. Tears streamed down her face, and she could not stop them.

But she refused to step to safety. "How can I be convinced you won't simply return to your quarrels once you've lured me away from the edge?"

"You have our sworn promise," Dorotea said. "Hear the truth in my words."

"I swear there will be no further conflict between Dorotea and me after we resolve this," Valya said.

Dorotea stepped closer to her rival. "My truthsense tells me that Reverend Mother Valya speaks honestly." She extended her hand to the old woman, beckoning her. "Let us fulfill your dreams and visions, Grandmother. Let us build on your example, rather than on a tragedy."

As the wind whipped around them, Raquella heard an upswelling of internal voices in her female ancestry, a chain of voices telling her in a strange harmonics, "This is not your time to die, Raquella. Not here, and not today. You need to live and inspire others—for as long as you can."

At last, she turned away from the precipice and faced the gathered Sisters of Wallach IX and Salusa, all crowding together, beseeching her. Raquella said, "The voices of Other Memory tell me to believe you. They are normally a background murmur, but they speak to me now—clearly, and in complete agreement."

The women whispered, looked at one another. Their eyes were wide, desperate. She saw both factions standing resolved, ready to cooperate.

The old woman stepped away from the cliff and into the arms of Valya and Dorotea, who both embraced her in a moment of shared emotion.

*An Emperor's grasp can encompass a million worlds, and his decisions can bring down entire civilizations. Even so, the day-to-day activities are tedious.*

—EMPEROR SALVADOR CORRINO,
*Expanded Memoirs*, Volume VII

When the Emperor arrived at Arrakis to assert Imperial control over spice operations, Josef Venport intended to be there waiting for him. Salvador Corrino was so naïve!

Departing from Kolhar on one of his fast spacefolders, Josef took the desert man Taref, who had served him well, despite being duped by the Half-Manford's supposed death. The Freeman saboteur had been of little use, though, since finding his female friend dead in the snow; all he could talk about was returning to Arrakis. Josef couldn't understand the workings of the desert man's mind.

Initially he'd been convinced that once the primitive nomads saw other planets and tasted as much water as they could drink, they would never want to go back to their original poverty. How could they not be grateful? But for some incomprehensible reason, the squalid desert life beckoned Taref again.

Too often Josef was disappointed by irrational human beings, the bad decisions they made, their self-destructive behavior. He mourned for the species.

Showing considerable sympathy, he had even offered the young man a furlough on Caladan to recover and get his wits together, since the desert people seemed to have an obsession with that ocean world. Taref had insisted that he wanted to return home—though he couldn't explain what he expected to find there. He had made it clear he had no place in his old sietch. Nevertheless, Josef granted the request, knowing he would gain nothing by arguing.

When they reached Arrakis City, however, Josef delayed releasing the young man from his service. "I have one final task for you, something only you can do. I will pay you well."

Taref looked away. His melange-blue eyes were eerie and hard to read. "I don't require any additional payment, Directeur. You have returned me to Arrakis, as I requested. Now, I wish to be on my own."

Josef frowned, scratching his mustache. "But where will you go? What will you do here?"

"I do not know . . . but at least I am back on Arrakis. The path of my life has vanished like footprints in the sand. I cannot entirely retrace my way."

Josef had little patience for Zensunni mysticism, nor for gloom and malaise. "But I still require your services. Do one last thing for me—and then I will send all of your friends back here, if that's what they want."

"Why would you do that?"

"If they don't want to continue to do their jobs, then your companions are no good to me anyway. I'll send them back here, provided they go to the deep desert and never reveal what they've done for me."

Taref considered for a long moment. "I am confident they will want that. But I am surprised you would release us so easily."

Josef narrowed his eyes, as if the young man were questioning his sense of honor and gratitude. "I don't put loyal, competent workers to death, young man. Unlike some leaders, I believe in human nature. I treated all of you fairly, and I've always kept my word. In return, I expect continued honor from you."

"Honor, yes. The honor of saboteurs." Taref shook his head, then squared his shoulders again. "Very well. But when I finish this task, I will be gone, with no further obligation to you, to my people, or to anyone else. What do you require of me?"

"The Emperor is taking a long, slow passage with old FTL engines. As soon as he arrives, I need you to find a way aboard his barge with the regular spaceport maintenance and refueling crew." Then, to Taref's astonishment, he explained the mission.

THE IMPERIAL BARGE took its time getting to Arrakis, on a leisurely, luxurious voyage the way the old League of Nobles members used to travel.

Meanwhile, Josef spent three days in Arrakis City receiving reports from Combined Mercantiles, inspecting spice-harvesting records and assessing the numerous losses, including expensive machinery as well as experienced crews who were killed in Coriolis storms and sandworm attacks. Salvador Corrino had no idea how dangerous a business it was.

The spice workers were proficient in mounting a rapid response every time a worm was spotted. The moment one of the monsters was identified in the distance, rescue aircraft would soar in, evacuate the crews, and whisk away the spice cargo in containers designed to be detachable. In dire circumstances, the armored spice containers could be jettisoned far enough away that they might be retrieved. Draigo Roget had dedicated an entire arm of VenHold manufacturing to producing replacement equipment faster than Arrakis could destroy it.

Through its many separate holdings, the company's investments were immense, as were the profits, which increased every year. For generations, the Venports had cultivated and improved the melange industry, inventing techniques and equipment, driving out poachers, securing and solidifying their claims.

And Salvador Corrino thought he could simply step in and seize it all with a personal appearance and the stroke of a pen? What a fool!

The Imperial Barge was a flying palace, complete with a throne room, audience chamber, functionaries, sycophants, and attendants, along with a ten-member military crew. According to his intelligence from the Imperial Court, the barge had fallback Holtzman engines, but relied on the slower drive that had been used before the discovery of foldspace travel.

Normally, the Emperor would have traveled gratis aboard a VenHold spacefolder, so by using his own transportation, he was snubbing Josef. Despite the intentional snub, the Imperial Barge would have to be serviced and refueled by an Arrakis City maintenance crew—which would provide all the opportunity Taref needed.

Through high-resolution surveillance satellites, Josef watched the gaudy Imperial Barge enter orbit. One of the Emperor's ministers sent a message to the Combined Mercantiles headquarters even before Salvador delivered his pompous declaration of arrival and formal intent, which followed minutes later.

Reading the transmitted decree, Josef shook his head at its verbosity and folly. Such a waste of his valuable time. He knew the Half-Manford was behind this absurd action, but the Emperor should know better—as should Roderick Corrino. Had everyone lost their sense of reason?

Before Salvador could make too much of a spectacle of himself—he seemed to expect the hard-bitten desert workers to bow down and weep with joy in his presence—Josef transmitted a welcome on a direct-line transmission.

"Emperor Corrino, we are honored that you would grace this humble world with your visit. Our desert operations are complex and difficult, as you must have been briefed. VenHold attorneys are already meeting with Imperial representatives on Kolhar, and I hope you are aware there will be a lengthy transition period as we turn over administration to Imperial control. In the meantime, please allow me to welcome you in person."

On the screen, Salvador shook his head. "I'd rather not come down to that dirty and insecure place. Manford Torondo was nearly killed in Arrakis City when he visited."

Josef flinched. "Mere rumors, Sire—but your concern is merited. Arrakis is a harsh world with rough people. Should I join you aboard your Imperial Barge instead, to discuss matters?"

The Emperor looked relieved. "Yes, that would be preferable to getting dirty."

Josef took his own shuttle from the Arrakis City spaceport up to the barge, bringing a routine team of company maintenance workers. Dressed as any other VenHold employee, with appropriate papers and credentials, Taref melted into the work crew.

In his climate-controlled Imperial chamber, Salvador was in a good mood to receive a presumably cooperative Directeur Venport. Josef tried to put the conversation on the correct track from the start. "Your offer of compensation is fair, perhaps even overly generous, Sire. I understand the power of the throne, so magnanimity is always welcome. You rule the Imperium, and my company is a valuable resource. I look forward to a much closer alliance with you." He bowed. "My Mentat lawyers inform me that it would have been within your powers under the rules of eminent domain to simply seize the operations without compensation. I appreciate your willingness to work with me for a mutually acceptable solution."

With a sniff, Salvador said, "Yes, I could have used an iron fist, as I did with House Péle, but VenHold administers many resources for the Imperium, and you have demonstrated your ability to manage your company quite well. I want us to be on friendly terms. The Imperium and the Imperial Armed Forces depend on your ships for many things."

Josef struggled to suppress his anger. "As Emperor, you have a very difficult role, Sire. I understand the narrow path you must tread, balancing the sensible needs of businessmen like myself against the wild and extreme demands of the Butlerians. I'm confident our representatives can negotiate mutually acceptable terms on the Arrakis contract and subsequent House Corrino control. We can all profit from this situation."

Salvador's eyes were sparkling. "I'm relieved you've decided to be reasonable, Directeur. I only wish Manford were so tractable."

Some of the Imperial functionaries chuckled, but their laughter had a nervous edge.

In a dining chamber that seemed too ornate to be inside a spaceworthy ship, the Emperor served a fine banquet while they orbited Arrakis. The meal included braised game hens, chocolate-mist desserts, expensive wines, Salusan fruit juices, and artesian ice water. On Arrakis, this water-extravagant dinner—the drinks alone—would have cost more than a spice crew supervisor's annual salary, but Josef didn't comment on this. Salvador wouldn't care, anyway.

*The universe does not always allow victory, not even for the most tal-
ented. There are times when one must accept the reality of defeat.*

—GILBERTUS ALBANS, Mentat School decree

Though the Mentat trainees were not warriors, they understood the theoretical basis for warfare and how to defend against a siege. In preparing for
the arrival of the Butlerians, the students had developed and installed many in-
novative defenses, booby traps, and deceptions, many of which incorporated the
natural hazards of the marsh lake and swamplands to keep the enemy at bay.

They held out against Manford Torondo's forces for six days, until Deacon
Harian arrived with a thousand reinforcements, supplies, heavy amphibious vehicles, and artillery. The expanded army picked their way across the rough
swamp and floated out into the murky water of the lake.

The initial besiegers erupted in a cheer, and Gilbertus saw the flurry of activity, heard the rumble of engines as the armored amphibious vehicles entered the
water and took up positions around the defensive walls.

In any modern military sense, the Mentat School was vulnerable, and had
lasted this long only because the Butlerians avoided high technology. A sophisticated aerial attack would have brought them down easily. Gilbertus regretted
that he hadn't installed shield generators to protect the entire complex, but
he had not wanted to provoke Manford by flaunting the technology. Now, he
wished he had.

Gathered on the walkways and observation decks, the trainees muttered in
dismay when they saw the new Butlerian troops, twice as many as had previously
encamped there. The heavy cannons they brought were primitive, but could still
blast the school buildings and slaughter hundreds of students. Gilbertus didn't
want that.

"The important first step, Sire, is for you to witness the melan[
with your own eyes. I've made arrangements for you and your ent[
taken under utmost security out to the deep desert, where you will
our biggest spice-mining operations. The factory moves from day to [
ters find new concentrations of melange. That way, you'll see for yo
the spice is gathered, and why the operational expense is so high."

"That sounds interesting and informative." The Emperor nodded,
his functionaries nodded as well.

"Because bandits often prey upon our operations, it's best if we d
nounce the location or timing of this expedition."

"Is it dangerous?" A hint of alarm crept into Salvador's voice.

Josef smiled. "I'll be right there with you, and we will be surrounded
powerful paramilitary force. You'll be far from the dangers of a confined p[
tion center such as Arrakis City. As for the Tanzerouft, where we'll be, th[
incidents of harassment came from unruly Freemen who resented our intru
into their lands. We have that fully under control now, so it's nothing to w[
about. And you will see more spice than you can possibly imagine, tons and t[
of it just lying on the ground!"

Josef had noticed that although his visitors consumed the wines and delic[
cies with avid abandon, they only took small amounts of melange, treating it a
if it were in limited supply.

Salvador visibly relaxed. "We look forward to that, Directeur." He lounged
back in a large chair at the banquet table, not exactly a throne, but more ostentatious than the other seats. "And now, for the second main course!" he called.
Servants rushed forward from the galley.

As the ship continued to orbit the arid world, they all dug into the feast.

Manford Torondo remained out of view during the arrival of the additional forces. When they were in place, he finally came forward to the main gate at the edge of the sangrove swamp. He sat on his Swordmaster's shoulders and used a bullhorn to shout toward the school towers. "Headmaster Albans! Out of courtesy for our past alliances, I give you one hour to run Mentat projections, but the conclusion is plain to anyone. At the end of that time, I expect your unconditional surrender. We will take Anna Corrino for her own safety."

Gilbertus listened from his observation platform, but he didn't capitulate. His administrator Zendur and four senior trainees stood alongside him, their expressions grave. Gilbertus turned to them, said, "Now we know the parameters," and retreated to his office.

HE ASKED ANNA Corrino to join him, locked the door using the old-fashioned key in his pocket, then activated the full array of impenetrable security systems. Anna seemed disturbed, but at least she was lucid, showing an awareness of the gravity of the situation.

"I don't wish to be used as a pawn, Headmaster, but I would rather be a pawn for you than for Manford. Offer to turn me over if he agrees to withdraw his forces. The Butlerians would never allow harm to come to me."

"Is that what Erasmus suggested to you?" Gilbertus activated the sliding panel, opened the secret locked cabinet, and withdrew the memory core.

The shimmering gelsphere glowed blue, showing the independent robot's agitation. "I would modify your assessment, dear Anna," Erasmus said. "I do not believe the Butlerians would ever accept the *blame* if you were harmed . . . but we are cut off here on Lampadas. Salusa Secundus is too far away for them to learn what is happening in a timely manner. If Manford Torondo destroys the school and eliminates all witnesses except for his own, he can make whatever report he wishes, fabricate any explanation. I . . . worry about you."

Gilbertus experienced a sinking sensation. "Manford's priority is to further the Butlerian movement: He will rationalize whatever he needs to." The Headmaster shook his head. "You might make a useful hostage, Anna, but if you were killed in an attack on the school, Manford would call it a terrible tragedy and then blame me."

"An unacceptable resolution. We need to escape," Erasmus said with uncharacteristic urgency. "You and Anna should take my memory core and slip out through the swamp at night. I will map a route using the spy-eyes implanted in the sangroves."

Gilbertus slumped into his chair and regarded the pyramid chessboard as if this were any other day; the set was waiting for a diverting round of intellectual play. With a sideways motion of his hand, he swept the tiered game and pieces aside, scattering them to the floor.

"No! If I flee, my whole school is forfeit, and this is my life's work. The trainees will be murdered, just as Manford killed everyone at the Thonaris shipyards. He'll burn the buildings and sink them into the lake. I won't let my great accomplishment be destroyed." He flexed his hands, folded his fingers together. "The Mentat School has to survive. Our methods of training, the creation of human computers, will have an impact far beyond our individual lives . . . far beyond even yours, Father."

The Erasmus core shimmered and flashed, as if in disagreement, but he said nothing.

Unable to forget Draigo Roget's invitation to join forces, Gilbertus raised himself from his chair. "For decades I maintained a low profile, bending where I needed to bend, raising no suspicions. In the process, I let my honor bleed through my fingers." He shook his head in dismay. "If there's a way to save this great institution of learning, then I must do it."

He looked at the glimmering golden clock on the shelf next to the books, its springs and gears turning with smooth precision. His hour was nearly up, and Manford would demand his answer. "I will go out and negotiate with Manford Toronto, leader to leader. He needs me—or at the very least he needs Mentats. If I can find a way to keep what I must, even if it entails my personal surrender, I'll consider it a victory—a small one, perhaps, but survival is a victory in itself. The continuation of my Mentat school would be a victory, so that my independent-thinking students can carry on after I am gone."

Lovingly, he cradled the robot's core in his palm. He thought of how he had traveled with this priceless and dangerous object hidden in his possessions while pretending to lead a normal life on Lectaire. For more than eighty years he had kept Erasmus safe—they had kept each other safe.

"This is the most precious possession I have ever owned." Gilbertus turned to Anna Corrino. "If anything happens to me, you have to protect Erasmus."

Anna accepted the memory core with awe. "Thank you, Headmaster. I will keep my friend safe at all costs."

FROM HIS OBSERVATION platform above the main gate, Gilbertus shouted down to the Butlerians, calling for Manford Toronto. "The mind of man is holy, but the heart of man is violent." He gestured toward the hundreds of fighters and heavy artillery pieces. "Civilization depends on rational discussion. A disagreement should be settled with brains, not with weapons and bloodshed."

The Butlerians jeered at him, but a sharp word passed among them, and they grew quiet. Manford approached the school, riding on Anari Idaho's shoulders. "Headmaster, for years I thought our causes were aligned. Didn't you establish your school to prove that thinking machines are unnecessary? It pains me to see your defiance now."

"Then perhaps you don't understand the heart of our disagreement," Gilbertus called back. "Shall we reason this out like men? I'll come speak to you, on condition that you give your word—in an oath as sacred to you as the oath you tried to make us swear—that your followers will not pillage and ransack the school, that my students will remain unharmed, and that you guarantee my personal safety."

The Butlerians muttered angrily. Manford hesitated before he said, "What do you have to fear, if you have done nothing wrong?"

"What I fear, Leader Torondo, is that your followers will take matters into their own hands, as they did in Zimia and on Baridge, and in countless other instances."

Manford nodded. "Regrettably, they can be overly enthusiastic. As Headmaster of the Mentat School, you shall receive my full protection. I promise that no harm will come to you during our negotiations."

"Not good enough," Gilbertus shouted back. "I require your word that your followers will not harm this school, or its trainees who have merely followed the instructions of their Headmaster. Only then will I come out and speak with you."

Gilbertus knew he had to press the matter now, for he had no real leverage. The large artillery pieces could blast the school buildings to splinters at any moment, and a prolonged bombardment would wipe out every person inside the complex.

When Manford accepted the proposal, many of his followers cried out in dismay, but the Butlerian leader ignored them. "Very well, Headmaster. It's in both of our best interests to end this confrontation. No one will harm your school or your students, and you have my personal guarantee of protection."

Gilbertus continued to stare at the forces arrayed against the school. At his side, Zendur said quietly, "I don't believe him, sir. He could promise anything, and then do whatever he wants."

"I know that all too well, but these are the best terms we're going to get." He straightened his robes and prepared to parley with the Butlerians.

*The happiest moments can be a heartbeat away from the saddest.*
—ancient wisdom

After a few weeks, Vorian Atreides felt that Caladan was his home again, that he belonged here. He wanted to put down roots in this place and recapture what he had lost so long ago. How different his life—and the *Imperium*—would have been if he had never left this world. . . .

Vor had fallen into the pleasant routine of taking a midday walk along a rugged hilltop trail with spectacular views of the ocean. As the trail descended to the seaside village below, he reveled in the sunshine broken by puffy clouds, and the smell of moist, salty air. On a stretch of grass just above the village, preparations were under way for the outdoor wedding of Orry Atreides and Tula Veil, featuring pavilions and tables, even a small stage for musicians to play.

Tula was unquestionably beautiful, with blond hair and sea-blue eyes, but Vor kept remembering how her eyes had flashed at him when they first met. He had detected a hint of hostility that he didn't understand.

Maybe she resented something from the legends of Vorian Atreides and his military career, although most locals seemed disinterested in ancient tales. Caladan, far from the Synchronized Empire, had been on the outskirts of the destructive battles of the Jihad, and its inhabitants had suffered little from thinking-machine attacks. More than eight decades after the Battle of Corrin, Caladan seemed aloof from Imperial politics. Here, the locals were more preoccupied with preparations for the wedding, which was only a few hours away.

The girl's background was mysterious, and Vor had heard rumors in town that Tula had run away from an abusive father. Vor hoped she'd find happiness here with Orry. Everyone seemed to accept her and care about her. He looked forward to getting to know her himself. Someday, perhaps Tula would explain what, if anything, she held against him.

Vor hoped Orry would have a happy marriage and a good life. He looked forward to spending family times with them, acting as a surrogate grandfather (ignoring how many times the word "great" should appear before the title). He needed to make up for the lost time and lost relationships in his own life. Someday soon, Willem would find a wife and form a family. And Vor planned to be there, as well. . . .

The weather couldn't have been better, though it had rained the night before, leaving the land green and sparkling in the sunshine. With the sweet sharpness of memory, Vor recalled taking Leronica out on a picnic at the top of this very same hill.

Reaching the grassy expanse, he paused to watch men and women as they arranged seats on the lawn, set up bouquets of bright flowers, and strung pastel ribbons on the marriage arbor.

He spotted the town's wedding planner, a fussy little man in a black formal jacket, who was already dressed for the ceremony. The man waved his arms and shouted directions and kept glancing at his pocket chronometer, telling everyone to hurry up. The event would begin an hour before sunset, so the couple could take their vows as the sky cast spectacular colors over the sea.

Knowing that he had to get ready, Vor returned to the village. In his room at the inn, he took out a clean but simple gray suit he had purchased from the town's tailor, along with a black ruffle-front shirt. It might have looked dashing to wear his old uniform from the Army of the Jihad, but he had left the garment, and the obligations, behind him long ago. Besides, he didn't want to dredge up the past—especially not such an ancient past. Orry and Tula were getting married, and they were the focus, not him. . . .

When he was formally dressed, Vor looked as if he could have been the young man's father . . . or another kindly uncle, like Shander Atreides. He returned to the grassy site, where townspeople had already gathered, smiling and chatting. Vor knew only a few of the villagers by name, but many recognized the exotic offworld stranger. Not wanting to call attention to himself, though, Vor simply drank in the murmur of conversations and shared the anticipation.

Willem stood near the wedding arbor, dazed but happy to stand as his brother's best man. He had worried about Orry's impetuosity in falling for the young woman, but Vor remembered how swiftly he had fallen for Leronica. Since Tula Veil came from an inland village and knew few people here, she had no special friend to stand at her side.

The seats around the arbor filled. At the appointed time, musicians struck up traditional music with pipes and stringed instruments, and everyone turned their heads. Behind them, a proud-looking Orry Atreides came up the path, his dark hair ruffled by the breeze. He wore a blue formal jacket, and Tula followed him in a long, sea-foam-green wedding dress. By ancient Caladan tradition, the bride followed her husband-to-be in the symbolic expectation that she would follow him in all things during their marriage. Vor smiled to himself: Regardless of the ceremony, reality would set in soon enough when the couple found their own balance of responsibilities.

Tula's golden hair was pinned back, but the curls fluttered in the wind. She was a picture of loveliness floating down the aisle in her long dress. She seemed to have a hypnotic hold on Orry.

Next came a procession of eight village children ranging from a pair of tow-headed little girls to a black-haired boy of perhaps ten or eleven. Vor saw the boy's patrician features, especially in the gray eyes and prominent nose. Atreides markers. He wondered how many people in this town were related to him. Once he settled down here, he would try to get to know all of them.

The traditional music was so hauntingly beautiful that it brought tears to Vor's eyes. It seemed essentially *Caladan*, making him think of waves lapping against the rocky shoreline and a fisherman's life on the sea.

Under the arbor, Orry and Tula faced each other, holding hands, while Willem stood behind them. The couple said their vows aloud, swearing their commitment before all those who could hear. They had chosen to perform a local "open sky" marriage, without the intervention of the village priest, a corpulent man who stood nearby holding a copy of the *Orange Catholic Bible*.

Instead of rings, the couple exchanged small gifts. Smiling as if mesmerized by his bride's beauty, Orry slipped a golden bracelet onto Tula's wrist, and she draped a simple medallion over his neck. He seemed pleased with the present, but she surprised him by taking his hand and looking into his eyes. "I have another gift for you—something that I have saved for later, in private."

An amused chuckle rippled through the audience, and Orry reddened in embarrassment, but Tula flashed a quick glance around them; something in her eyes silenced the laughter. "It is a special gift that my family has held for generations. The whole town will know what it is tomorrow."

The priest cleared his throat and made his only official contribution by announcing the marriage complete and blessed. The sun set out on the ocean, causing flares of color to stream across the sky; according to sailors' tradition, a bloodred sunset indicated fair weather ahead.

During the reception, Orry and Tula danced together, whenever the attendees would give them the space. Vor kept a respectful distance, just watching. Orry Atreides had grown up among these people, so they should be closest to him on this special day.

Looking over her new husband's shoulder, Tula caught Vor's eye and abruptly whispered something in Orry's ear. The young man looked disappointed by whatever it was, but then she whispered again, and he smiled.

When the dance was over, Orry raised his voice and spoke to the guests. "Since my wife has a special gift to give me from her entire family—and I am as intrigued by this as the rest of you are!—we'll be taking our leave to begin our new life now. I insist you all stay here and enjoy yourselves. My brother will entertain you—he's got nothing else to do."

Willem looked surprised. Some guests murmured, but others chuckled or whistled as Orry and Tula hurried off to the home the two brothers had shared with Shander Atreides, which the couple would use as their honeymoon cottage. Willem had temporarily gotten a room at the local inn, so his brother and new wife could have their privacy

Vor was sorry that he'd had no opportunity to talk further with Tula, but there would be plenty of time for that later, and he didn't want to intrude now. In fact, he made up his mind to help the young couple whenever he could, maybe even using part of his fortune to establish their new household, similar to the help he'd given to House Harkonnen on Lankiveil.

A spark of memory came back to him, and he tensed. The youngest daughter of Vergyl Harkonnen . . . Griffin's other sister. Wasn't her name Tula? Orry's new wife did have a hint of Griffin's features, but Vor wasn't convinced. He had never met either of Vergyl Harkonnen's daughters. Although he had seen a family portrait inside the Harkonnen household, he couldn't quite remember what the girls looked like. It must just be a coincidence, similar names.

He set such thoughts aside and went to join Willem as the dancing and music continued.

AFTER THE WEDDING festivities, Vor returned to his room and fell into a deep, satisfied sleep, thoroughly reminded of his fondness for good Caladan wine, as opposed to mediocre kelpbeer.

Orry's wedding had been different from others he recalled, but all of it had been pleasant; the music, the laughter, the camaraderie, and the warmth of the people. Willem had showed himself to be quite proficient at the traditional dances, and he had no trouble finding partners. Vor had done his best to keep up, and found some of the women flirtatious, some in awe of his history, and all vastly younger than he was. None could hold a candle to Leronica. Or Mariella.

When he drifted off to sleep in his bed at the inn, he was enfolded in a satisfied happiness, with the buzz of wine in his head and the ringing echoes of music. He had long since learned the folly of wallowing in regrets and second-guessing his decisions, but he did regret ever leaving beautiful Caladan. The weight and obligations of Serena Butler's Jihad had made him think beyond his own personal interests.

All that had been over for such a long time. Even if he let himself put down roots in this place, he was not ready to start another family of his own. There were too many reminders of his beloved Leronica here, and he didn't yet feel enough distance from Mariella and his other family on Kepler. . . .

He awoke in darkness, feeling that something was wrong. He sensed a stir in the silent shadows of his room, felt a creak of movement, heard a rustle. He remained utterly still.

A breeze whispered through the open window . . . yet he was certain he had closed it before going to bed. Through narrow-slitted eyes, he saw a figure dart through the faint shreds of starlight—and the silver glint of what appeared to be a knife blade. He still felt a little groggy, wondered if it was a dream.

But his instincts, honed by years of facing danger, kicked in. Vor rolled to one side on the large bed even before he grasped what was happening. He heard a quick expulsion of breath, an abrupt outcry, as the blade streaked down where he had been only a moment ago, slashing into the blanket. He flung his pillow at the indistinct figure, pulled off the blanket and threw it over the moving arm to snare it. He bore down with a steely grip, grabbing the wrist.

It was a small wrist, but the attacker had wiry strength, and writhed and thrashed. Vor felt an explosion of pain as the intruder struck him hard just beneath the left eye with what seemed to be a fist, but he didn't release his grip on the wrist, and thrust up with one knee, after shifting his body to gain more leverage on the bed.

Fully awake now, he saw more details—blond hair, gleaming eyes filled with hatred. Another sharp blow from the intruder's free hand bloodied his nose, and Vor released his grip. "Tula!" It was Orry's new wife.

She recoiled and sprang backward, pulling free of his grip and the blanket with which he had tried to entangle her. Then, with barely a pause, Tula hurled herself upon him again like a rabid panther. She slashed with the dagger, this time ripping open his nightshirt and cutting a fiery line across his chest. He felt blood and burning pain, but he fought back.

"What are you doing here?" he demanded. The nightstand crashed to the floor and he leaped free, gaining room to maneuver.

Tula fought with a ferocity he had rarely seen before, and he struggled to keep the knife away from him. "I had to change my plans," she said, not even out of breath. "I came here for Orry, but you were always our target, Vorian Atreides. You killed my brother Griffin. You ruined House Harkonnen."

Vor didn't bother to respond, certain that conversation would make no difference. Tula—Tula *Harkonnen*—meant to kill him, not talk with him. She fought with techniques similar to the ones Griffin had demonstrated when he dueled with Vor in the desert sietch.

She flung herself at him again, but Vor used his right hand to snatch a water pitcher from the dresser. In a swift arc, he smashed it against her head, sending the young woman reeling. Her knife clattered to the wooden floor.

Now he heard pounding on the door, shouts of people roused by the disturbance. "In here!" he yelled.

In the low light he saw Tula glaring at him, blood dripping from her hair. As the door burst open, she dove out the window like a killer eel into a dark underwater lava tube.

Willem charged into the room from the hall, looking flushed, dressed in his nightclothes. "What's happening?"

Vor grabbed him by the arm and raced out into the corridor. Tula had said she had come here seeking revenge, stalking Orry. "We have to check on your brother!"

Willem was confused. "Wait—you're bleeding."

Vor touched his chest. "It's nothing. Come—we have to hurry!" After sounding an alarm, they raced off to what should have been the quiet, happy nuptial cottage of the newlyweds.

IT TOOK SEVERAL agonizing minutes to secure a groundcar, and by the time the two of them were speeding over a rough road with Willem at the controls, dawn was beginning to brighten the sky.

Shander's cottage was just outside the village on a pristine sandy beach; it had been specially decorated for the newlyweds. A caterer had crafted a lavish traditional dinner and left a bottle of vintage wine, contributed by Vor himself. Orry and Tula were alone there with the roar of the surf, undisturbed by pranks or good-natured harassment from the locals.

Just ahead, Vor saw the cottage bathed in golden sunlight to herald the first full day of their marriage. A serving woman was knocking on the door, carrying a gourmet breakfast that she was ready to set up. When no one answered, she let herself inside, tiptoeing, calling out—only to run back out, screaming.

Vor and Willem jumped out of the vehicle and rushed past her, through the open cottage door. The air inside smelled sour and metallic, and Vor immediately identified the stench of blood—a great deal of it.

Young Orry Atreides lay dead on the wedding bed, his throat cut. The sheets were soaked in blood. There was no sign of Tula.

Willem let out a loud, raw scream, and Vor, trembling in horror, felt the dead boy's arm. Orry's skin was cold, his dull eyes staring up at the cottage ceiling.

Willem dropped to the bedside and pulled his brother toward him in a sad, macabre embrace, unable to understand what had happened. Vor felt icy and alert. A deep fear settled into his stomach.

He was the first to notice the bloodstained note left by the bedside—nineteen lines written in a style that looked psychotic, forming an odd shape on the paper:

*The last words Shander and Orry Atreides heard,*
*Tula Veil is Tula Harkonnen of Lankiveil.*
*The price of Atreides treachery*
*Is Harkonnen vengeance.*
*We have only begun*
*To hunt you down.*
*First Shander,*
*Then Orry*
*Then all*
*The rest*
*Of the*
*Vermin.*
*Never enough*
*To compensate for*
*The murder of our beloved*
*Brother, son, friend, and companion;*
*Griffin Harkonnen, we loved you dearly!*
*Take flight, Atreides cowards, and try to hide, but*
*You must flee for all time, because we will never forget.*

*Every Mentat knows there is no such thing as the future. As the ancient philosopher Anko Bertus said, there is a range of possible futures, and each has its probabilities. Mentat projection can sort them, to guide the creators.*

        —GILBERTUS ALBANS, instruction to students
        at the Mentat School

The weak sun rose over Wallach IX the following morning, and Dorotea hurried across a courtyard filled with meter-high greenhouse structures where the acolytes grew fresh vegetables. Mother Superior Raquella had summoned her to her private chambers. It was not a casual request. The red-faced Acolyte runner said it was urgent.

After the silvery-purple jungles of Rossak, and glorious Salusa Secundus, Dorotea did not like this cool, plain planet, and she looked forward to returning to the Imperial Court. The orthodox Sisters who had accompanied her were also anxious to get back to their duties in the palace.

But Raquella had terrified them all the night before, forcing them to see the destructive nature of their factional differences. The Mother Superior had nearly flung herself off the cliff in despair, but stepped back from the brink in exchange for the promises of Valya and Dorotea. Dorotea meant her promise that they would find common ground, would work together.

In her heart, she understood that the two factions still had philosophical differences, particularly regarding the use of advanced technology. But there didn't have to be a permanent, fundamental difference. The breeding-record computers—which Dorotea had never been able to find—were either destroyed or abandoned. The argument didn't matter anymore. Both parts of the Sisterhood believed in developing innate human skills, watching and guiding the evolution of the human race.

The details of a new coalition would be the most difficult part, but Dorotea felt confident that she and Valya could negotiate terms acceptable to both factions. Dorotea wanted to fashion the combined Sisterhood into a legacy Mother Superior Raquella would be proud of.

If the new Sisterhood resolved to turn its back on forbidden computers, Dorotea was sure she could convince Salvador Corrino to forgive the women who had strayed. Then all Sisters could follow the correct path together, with the blessing of the Emperor. . . .

To her credit, Valya also seemed to be making genuine efforts to reunite with Dorotea, for the good of the order. Even so, the other woman's reluctance still simmered beneath the surface, and Dorotea was sure that Valya had deceived her in the past, pretending to be of the same mind when she joined their quiet conspiracy. Valya was powerful and talented, a Reverend Mother now, just like Dorotea. And the aged Mother Superior considered her to be one of her most reliable confidantes.

Dorotea already had her hundred orthodox Sisters on Salusa, as well as more than a dozen new Acolytes. They filled significant roles at court, basked in their importance. But after Raquella's crisis on the cliff, Dorotea had removed the Imperial insignia from her black robe, indicating that she considered herself a Sister first. Her six companions had done the same.

And now she had received an urgent summons to the Mother Superior's quarters. After all these years, the old woman—her grandmother—was on her deathbed. Dorotea felt a sinking in her heart.

She climbed a wooden stairway in one of the prefab buildings and hurried down a hall to the second door, which was half open. She pushed her way inside.

The Mother Superior's apartment consisted of three modest rooms, one of which she used as a private office, cluttered with files from ongoing projects. Dorotea saw papers strewn about. "Mother Superior?" she called out.

Valya appeared in the bedroom doorway, her face drawn and gray. She motioned for Dorotea. "Mother Superior is increasingly feeble. She asked to see us both right away. I believe she has chosen her successor." She shook her head in dismay. "Yesterday's ordeal drained the rest of the life from her."

After a cold shudder, Dorotea straightened her posture. "Whatever her decision, we must abide by it and work together. My orthodox Sisters are prepared to do what is necessary for the Sisterhood."

Valya rushed her inside. "Hurry!"

Inside the dim, stifling room, Raquella sat propped up in her bed, surrounded by pillows, and she looked *ancient*, as if years and years had been heaped on her overnight. Her eyes appeared to have sunk deeper into her skull than the day before, and her skin looked translucent, showing age spots and blood vessels. A medical Sister leaned over her with a handheld scanner to monitor vital signs. A worried Fielle stood nearby, looking very unlike an emotionless Sister Mentat.

Raquella dismissed the medical Sister in a breathy voice that sounded like crackling papyrus. "Leave us." The doctor hurried out of the room and closed the door.

"Sister Fielle has made an important Mentat projection," Raquella said. "We all need to hear it for the good of the Sisterhood. After she speaks, I will announce my successor." The ancient woman drew a long breath, which required great effort. "I am nearly finished with this life. But I want to make certain my work goes on."

The Sister Mentat gave a somber nod. Her short hair looked wilder than usual. "Some time ago I warned Mother Superior that a civil war might occur among the Sisters without her leadership. I suggested that either of you might instigate it." She looked first at Dorotea, then at Valya. "My Mentat projection told me that the only way to bring the factions together was for Raquella to make a martyr of herself, like Serena Butler, to force the factions to reconcile.

"When I told Mother Superior of my projection, I did not inform her that I knew exactly what she would do—that she would take it to the brink, but that you both would make it unnecessary for her to kill herself after all."

Raquella was surprised to hear this. "I fully intended to leap off the cliff if necessary."

"You may have thought so, Mother Superior, but my projection told me what would happen. I'm ashamed to admit that I withheld this information from you, but you needed to be absolutely convincing. Valya and Dorotea had to be certain you would actually plunge to your death."

Raquella said in her weakened voice, "I was ready to leap, and would have done so if I didn't believe Valya and Dorotea would work together, rather than at cross-purposes."

Dorotea found the sincerity in the old woman's voice moving.

Raquella's weak laugh was barely more than a spasm of exhaled breath. "All things considered, I'd rather let myself die here in bed, surrounded by all of you." She raised her eyebrows at Fielle. "Even though you did deceive me. I would have done what was necessary regardless."

The Sister Mentat looked away. "My projection told me it was necessary."

"In the future, you will reveal all details of your projections to the Mother Superior. *All* details."

Bowing her head, the young woman agreed.

Raquella patted her hand, spoke to the other two women. "Fielle is young and headstrong. She will be a challenge for the Sisterhood's new leadership, but her intentions are true and good. This one is a gem to be polished."

Fighting impatience, Valya asked, "Who is to be your successor, Mother Superior? I want to be sure you have peace, that you rest easily."

Adjusting herself on the pillows, Raquella said, "My choice is a nonchoice—as it must be. Dorotea and Valya, you both bring strengths and advantages to our future, and you each know what they are. I want you to lead the Sisterhood together—merging the orthodox Salusan school and the Wallach IX school. Find a way to intertwine all Acolytes and Sisters, take the pieces and forge a stronger whole. Work as partners."

Dorotea bowed, accepting the decision, but Valya's dark eyes remained wide in disbelief.

"There is more than enough for both of you to do," Raquella continued. "Cooperate. Repeat that word over and over in your minds, and act it out. *Cooperate.* You are both Mother Superiors. Establish a division of responsibilities. Repair our splintered Sisterhood and make it strong again."

Valya nodded slowly. "We will do our best, Mother Superior."

Dorotea straightened at the old woman's bedside, let out a long breath. "Agreed. Henceforth we will fight external enemies, not internal ones."

A broad smile formed on Raquella's creased face, and she suddenly looked less weary. "Now that the conflict is resolved among my Sisters, I am content." She breathed a sigh of relief and appeared to be near tears, as if she could finally let go after a lifetime of hard work.

Raquella beckoned Dorotea closer. "Before I go, there is something I want to share with you, Granddaughter." She pressed a forefinger against her own temple. "Lean close, very close, and touch your forehead to me . . . here. You have Other Memories, but you don't have all of mine."

Dorotea hesitated, then complied. As their skin touched, she felt a sudden flash, like the opening of a floodgate. Information and memories rushed into her mind in a transfer of vast knowledge, a wealth of past lives and experiences. She received her grandmother's hopes and dreams for the Sisterhood—all of the information Raquella had withheld—and now she learned with a certainty that there *were* computers here on Wallach IX! She nearly recoiled at the revelation, but before she could pull back, the Mother Superior pressed a gnarled hand against the back of her head, holding her in place with surprising strength.

With the information came a broader understanding, astonishing conclusions . . . until the flow of data gradually stopped. Thoughts flashed and dimmed, then faded—as Mother Superior Raquella herself faded. Moments later, she was gone.

Dorotea blinked her eyes, then raised herself from the bed to find Raquella dead, looking peaceful but *empty.*

Dizzy with the terrible loss, Fielle held on to the wall for support as she stumbled out of the room and slammed the door shut behind her.

Valya, still in disbelief, stared at the Mother Superior's body, then at Dorotea. She seemed numbed by the shock of the tremendous loss.

But Dorotea now had *everything.* She grasped the fantastic scope of Raquella's work—her dreams, her ambitions, her complex plans. Despite her previous horror of computers, Dorotea reluctantly vowed to respect her grandmother's wishes, and focus on what was needed to fulfill Raquella's vision for humankind. She understood so much more now! Dorotea possessed the information, and the strength, to build the Sisterhood into the grand and powerful organization it deserved to be—united and far-reaching.

But if she and Valya were supposed to be partners, each a Mother Superior sharing the responsibility for leadership, why had Raquella given only *Dorotea* her full life and memories? In order to be equals, she and Valya should have the same resources, the same knowledge.

Had the Mother Superior sensed something . . . perhaps that Sister Valya was not quite as trustworthy?

Reeling, Dorotea delved into her new knowledge, trying to decipher the ancient woman's thought processes, but there was such a wealth of information that she would need a great deal of time to sort it out and ponder it. Perhaps during the long flight back to Salusa Secundus to inform the orthodox Sisters at the Imperial Court, she could make sense of it all.

Their reverie was interrupted by Dorotea's own internal turmoil of Other Memory. The ancestral voices became chaotic and clamorous. The awakened voices of her ancestors—including Raquella herself—were screaming at her. A warning!

Dorotea became aware of Valya standing there at the dead Mother Superior's bedside, looking at her in a most peculiar, unsettling way.

VALYA STRUGGLED WITH what the Mother Superior had just decreed. After all this waiting, all the years of proving herself, she was supposed to share power with the woman who had wrecked the Rossak school?

It made no sense at all. And Raquella had clasped Dorotea close in some strange final embrace just before she died. *That* had not been equal at all, and Valya had no faith in the traitor Sister, regardless of the platitudes they had exchanged. She was poison.

Dorotea seemed dazed as she reeled back from the deathbed. Valya could hear a distraught Fielle weeping out in the corridor through the closed door.

Valya would have to act quickly. She had the correct goals, and the determination to complete them. Only as the *sole* Mother Superior could she achieve everything she desired, both for the Sisterhood . . . and for House Harkonnen. Now was the time.

Dorotea looked up at her from Raquella's silent body, drew a long breath. "The future of the Sisterhood is up to us now."

"You are mistaken. It is up to *me*."

Valya had taken Dorotea's measure, her physical reactions, her reflexes . . . her weaknesses and anticipated resistance points. Dorotea was an especially strong person, and a Reverend Mother Truthsayer. Sharpening her Voice into a well-honed and perfectly aimed weapon, she spoke with all the power she could summon. *"Don't move!"*

The words froze Dorotea. Valya knew this would be harder than when she had paralyzed Master Placido on Ginaz or directed the commando Sisters on Rossak. For an instant, Dorotea could not move a muscle except for a slight, alarmed widening of her eyes. The traitorous Sister could do nothing more than watch in surprise and horror as Valya calmly removed a knife from her own robe, and raised it like a viper preparing to strike. She said, *"Take this from me."*

Like a puppet, Dorotea accepted the knife, fumbling her fingers around the hilt. She had never encountered such an assault before, had no experience in resisting it.

Valya felt a flush of excitement. She remembered thinking that her compelling Voice might be boosted by the power of Other Memory she carried within herself, all those other experiences, that wisdom, that power. It was a visceral feeling she had, because the throaty sound was so similar to a background rumble she often heard in her mind. So far, Valya seemed to be the only Sister who could do this.

*"Now drive it into your throat!"*

Dorotea struggled with herself, and her arms trembled as the knife lifted up and wavered, its point targeted on the hollow of her neck. She tried to yank the blade away. Regaining some control, she took a lurching step toward Valya, her eyes ablaze, sweat pouring from her brow. She managed to turn the blade away and shove it toward Valya, but despite the effort, Dorotea's hands turned the blade back toward herself.

Valya leaned close and commanded, *"Drive it into your throat! Now!"*

Dorotea fought back. The knife wavered in the air; the hilt was slick with sweat. Finally, with a gasp as if something had broken inside her, Dorotea let out a despairing cry and rammed the knife deep into her neck.

With only a thin gasp as the blood gushed, she collapsed across the body of Raquella Berto-Anirul and died—granddaughter and grandmother dead within moments of each other.

Valya stood over the treacherous Sister, thinking that this was but a small repayment for all the damage the woman had done on Rossak. All those Sisters dead . . .

The blade was lodged in the base of Dorotea's throat, her dead fingers wrapped securely around the hilt. Poor Dorotea, overwhelmed by grief and unable to face the huge responsibilities placed upon her, had committed suicide. It was obvious to anyone who looked.

Valya was the Sisterhood's Mother Superior now.

Valya *Harkonnen*.

*Some of us carry a portion of our past hidden inside us like a small time bomb, ticking, ticking away, waiting to explode.*

—GILBERTUS ALBANS, private journals
(not included in Mentat School Archives)

In the siege camp outside the Mentat School, Manford Torondo's headquarters tent was sensibly protected from the elements. Its raised floor kept it dry on the soggy ground, and the fabric walls coated with water-repellent film blocked out rain, wind, sun, and persistent insects.

The Butlerian leader asked for no special amenities—only a camp desk to do his work and cushions to sleep on—but Anari insisted on making him comfortable, wanting the tent to be more of a home than a battle headquarters. Whatever his Swordmaster didn't provide, his followers brought for him: blankets, rugs, pillows, and lovingly prepared camp food that was as good as his meals back at home. He didn't need the pampering, but gratefully accepted the gifts and love that his followers presented. His graciousness made them love him even more.

All that mattered to him at the moment was that his tent was a good place to parley with the intractable Headmaster of the Mentat School.

When Gilbertus Albans emerged alone from his towering school walls, he looked proud and not at all disheveled. Manford gave Deacon Harian specific orders that the Headmaster was not to be harmed or harassed in any way. "I gave him my word in front of my followers, and I won't have it broken."

Harian looked angry—as he often did—but he assented with a clipped nod. From observation platforms on the defensive walls, curious and intimidated Mentat students watched Gilbertus emerge from the gates and walk into the unfolding crowd of antitechnology supporters.

From the murmuring resentment in the air, Manford could tell that his own followers had already made up their minds that the Mentat Headmaster had betrayed them, that he was teaching his students heretical, forbidden techniques. His people wanted to fire artillery projectiles that would shatter and sink the school buildings in order to prove their implacable faith and demonstrate the futility of opposing the Truth. The Butlerians had shown that iron resolve at Dove's Haven, in Zimia, and on Baridge. But in those places, only the guilty had suffered; this time, the entire Mentat School had defied him. Given the simmering, mounting rage, Manford wasn't sure if he could control his own followers. But he had given his word.

As Harian pushed aside the tent flap and led the Headmaster inside, Gilbertus stepped past the deacon, paying him little heed. Harian continued to stare at the Headmaster as if he'd caught him doing something. Even Manford didn't know why the bald deacon showed such hostility toward the calm and studious man. But Manford intended to put Gibertus Albans in his place, in his own way.

Manford didn't offer any refreshment; this was no social visit. "You've caused me a great deal of trouble, Headmaster."

Gilbertus gave a polite bow. "And your new oath has caused me and my students no small amount of consternation. It is ill-advised and unconscionable."

Glowering, Anari Idaho placed her hand on the hilt of her sword, but Manford gestured for her to desist. The air around them was brittle with tension. Sister Woodra stood inside the command tent at Manford's request, watching the Headmaster's every gesture and expression, analyzing the tone of his voice.

Gilbertus didn't acknowledge anyone other than the Butlerian leader. "If you had consulted me beforehand, Leader Torondo, I could have explained our concerns before this became a crisis. If your lackeys"—now he nodded toward Harian—"had listened to reason, then the matter need not have escalated."

Manford spoke over a muttering of discontent from his aides. "And what do you find so objectionable about an expression of faith, Headmaster? Why will you not reaffirm your stance against thinking machines? Surely, you must see that your refusal raises suspicions. How can I be expected to tolerate it?"

Gilbertus remained standing. "I object to the new oath both on principle and because of its wording. I prepared a list of six hundred thirty-seven specific flaws, contradictions, and ambiguities." He frowned at Harian. "Your deacon confiscated the document I carried with me out of the school, but I can recite the flaws from memory, if you wish."

Even though he was not invited to do so, the Headmaster began to rattle off details. Manford was neither interested nor impressed. What sort of man was this Gilbertus Albans? He was most perplexing and irritating—but also, in a strange way, admirable. The Headmaster managed to list more than twenty specifics before Manford silenced him.

Gilbertus did not seem upset at being cut off, but said, "It's not possible to debate the merits of an issue if one side stubbornly refuses to listen."

"If the opposing side has no merits, one doesn't need to listen," Manford countered.

"Then why am I here?"

Manford glanced at the avid expressions of Deacon Harian and Anari Idaho. Sister Woodra looked calculating, her eyes bird-bright and attentive. He dismissed them all, telling Anari to stand guard outside his tent while he and the Headmaster discussed important matters.

After Manford shooed them away, Gilbertus took a seat across the camp table. The Butlerian leader hardened his expression. "You know I cannot allow your Mentat students to deny me with impunity. Everyone on Lampadas is aware that you refused the oath, and I *will not* ignore your defiance."

"This matter could have been dealt with quietly. I am not the one who spread the news around Lampadas and sent a force against the school." Gilbertus looked maddeningly calm. "Your oath was unnecessary. You had every reason to assume my Mentats were loyal, while I, personally, have done everything you asked. I spoke out against thinking machines, assisted you on the Thonaris raid, and defeated a robot in chess for your spectacle at the Imperial Court. My loyalty was already plain—you did not need to force the issue. But you did . . . and this is where we now find ourselves."

With a deep sigh, Manford said, "Perhaps you're right, but make one of your Mentat projections now. You know what has to happen next: Your students must all surrender and promise to follow the Butlerian path. They must take the new oath, because if I make an exception in your case, others will demand the same. I can't have that."

"You also need Mentats, Leader Torondo. We provide a valuable alternative to thinking machines, and we show the Imperium that society doesn't need computers anymore. You can't destroy our example." The Headmaster paused, and added, "Maybe I could rewrite the oath for you, clarify the terms and add definitions, caveats—"

"No! One exception leads to another and another. You don't understand my followers—they are not deep thinkers who understand nuances. They must have black-and-white choices. Your tampering would only open up room for doubt."

"Then send my school away from Lampadas as a punishment. Exile us. All my trainees will go elsewhere."

Manford shook his head. "We could never allow you to leave." *Especially not with Anna Corrino.* He sighed again. "I'm granting a great courtesy in discussing this with you at all. Your Mentats have enjoyed small victories during this siege, harming some of my scouts with your defenses, but you can't last for long. We will overwhelm you."

Gilbertus's eyes flashed. "You swore you would not harm my school or my students."

"I won't need to do anything. We can merely stay here and wait until you all starve or surrender."

"That would still be harming my school, albeit indirectly."

Manford shrugged. "You waste too much time on minutiae. In my mind, the matter is clear-cut—just as the new oath is."

Outside the tent, he heard Deacon Harian's voice. "I must see Leader Torondo. Let me in—I have the proof we need!"

"Then I hope your dead lips can speak it, because you will not enter the tent," Anari said. "I am commanded not to allow any interruption."

Manford had no doubt Anari would give her life before allowing the deacon to pass, but he also knew that Harian would continue his ruckus until he was finally allowed in. He called out, "Anari, let us see what the deacon has discovered." He added a warning edge in his voice. "You can slay him if he wastes my time."

Deacon Harian did not balk, nor did Manford expect him to; if nothing else, the man was resolute. Anari opened the tent flap, and the bald deacon strode in, carrying a tome. Sister Woodra accompanied him, as if she served as his personal Truthsayer rather than Manford's.

Harian glared at Gilbertus Albans, who sat straight-backed at the table. With the delicate touch of a forefinger, the Headmaster pushed his spectacles higher up on his nose.

Harian thumped the heavy book down on the camp table, then turned to a page that featured the image of a face. "This was brought to my attention by one of our loyal followers, an archivist who found this volume in his large collection. It was published shortly after the Battle of Corrin." He pushed the book forward onto the table, demanding that Gilbertus look at the image.

Manford had seen the picture many times: the historical record from the climactic battle of the war against thinking machines, when the Army of the Jihad rescued the hostages that Omnius placed in harm's way, using them as human shields at the Bridge of Hrethgir. In the image, frightened people crowded together, liberated from their long nightmare.

Harian continued, "The book includes details of humans who collaborated with thinking machines, the demon robots—and how some of the turncoats escaped in the confusion by mingling with refugees."

Gilbertus looked at the picture, then back up, showing no apparent interest.

With his eidetic Mentat focus, he had probably memorized every detail with a single glance.

Harian stabbed his finger at one of the figures, a face that was plain on the high-resolution image even after all these years. "This is *you*, Headmaster Albans.

Manford stared down in disbelief. The image showed a man who was perhaps in his midthirties, with facial features that appeared to match those of the Mentat Headmaster.

"There is a resemblance," Gilbertus said, "but it proves nothing."

Harian smiled cruelly. "Nevertheless, it *is* you. I've had my suspicions about you for some time now, Headmaster, and finally I have proof."

"How could that possibly be me? The person in that image would be . . ." He waved a hand. ". . . extremely old. Far beyond a normal human life span."

"An ancient machine sympathizer was recently caught and executed," Sister Woodra pointed out. "A man named Horus Rakka. He changed his identity, lived among normal humans, and hid from his past, but eventually he was found out and met the fires of Butlerian justice."

"Yes, I heard about that, but Horus Rakka was a very old man. I may have a few gray hairs, but I'm not decrepit."

Harian flipped open the tome, looking for the page he wanted. "This book also contains records of refugees who were saved from the Bridge of Hrethgir, those given passage from Corrin after the fall of the thinking machines. The archivist spent days poring over the long list of names."

"One of my Mentats could have done it in an hour," Gilbertus said with only a hint of a flippant tone.

Harian found the right page. Among the thousands of names listed in the book, he pointed to one specific entry. "That's your name, isn't it, Headmaster? *Gilbertus Albans*."

The Mentat glanced at Sister Woodra, then looked at Manford as he answered. "That name is the same as mine. Again, it proves nothing. If you examined all historical records, across all settled worlds, you will probably find other identical names as well."

"Ah, but the demon robot Erasmus had a special ward, chosen from the slave pens and trained specially. Gilbertus Albans was his name. Several of the refugees from the Bridge of Hrethgir recorded that fact to accompany their oral statements. But Gilbertus Albans was never found after the Battle of Corrin."

The Mentat's expression remained mild. "Corrin was leveled in the attack. Many humans were never found. Your story grows more absurd by the moment."

Harian leaned forward, raising his voice. "I believe that when you were raised on Corrin, the demon robot found some way to prolong your life. We know the thinking machines had that technology. I am convinced you slipped away during the confusion, posed as one of the refugees, and created a new life for yourself. You've been hiding here on Lampadas all this time, haven't you? Assuming no one would remember."

Manford couldn't believe what he was hearing. Anari looked ready to explode, her emotions boiling across her face.

Shaking his head, Gilbertus said, "Your evidence is circumstantial, and your conclusion strains credulity. You haven't even proved that the person in the image matches up with a name found on a long list."

Harian sniffed. "Your resemblance to the man in this image, and the identical name, *could* be nothing more than a coincidence." And now he smiled, as if delivering a coup de grâce. "But Sister Woodra is a Truthsayer. Speak now, Headmaster. Tell the Truthsayer that you are *not* the man in the image, that you're *not* the Gilbertus Albans who was raised by Erasmus. She will know if you are lying."

Sister Woodra stared intently at him. Gilbertus remained still, seemingly at peace and smiling slightly, whereas a guilty man might squirm and perspire.

"I'm not the man in the image," Gilbertus insisted. He stared calmly at the Salusan Sister.

"You're lying, aren't you?" she said.

"The fact that you have framed that as a question shows your uncertainty." A small smile worked at the edges of his mouth.

"You're probably the best liar I've ever seen, but you are lying. I hear it in your voice, a tremor so slight that no one but a Truthsayer would ever notice it. But it is there, nonetheless. And I see the soft glistening of your skin. Not perspiration, but a barely perceptible change on the surface of the epidermis. These things are even more apparent to me, Headmaster Albans, because I have watched recordings of you giving speeches and talking to your students—obtained by the Butlerian students in your midst. Your voice and skin were never like they are now, because you were not lying on those occasions." She looked even more intently at him. "There is something in your eyes, too. Fear, perhaps."

"I am not afraid of the truth," Gilbertus said.

"Fear for the fate of your school, then," she said. "Fear that Manford will destroy it because of your crimes."

After a long, tense silence that seemed like a void, Gilbertus said, "Manford has promised he will not harm the school or my students. But perhaps you are right, Sister Woodra, perhaps I am still worried for their safety."

"You are only worrying because of your true identity. You are the Gilbertus Albans from Corrin. You were the ward of the robot Erasmus. You are an enemy of humanity."

"I am not an enemy of humanity," he said, but pointedly did not deny the rest.

Manford stared. "This is not possible." His gaze intensified, like a scalpel cutting away the Headmaster's secrets, and he cut deep. "But I can see it is true."

Gilbertus remained silent for a long moment, and then turned to the Butlerian leader with a solemn nod. "Yes, I am the man in the image, and I am more than one hundred eighty years old."

*Even an Emperor must earn respect before he is entitled to receive it.*

—EMPEROR FAYKAN CORRINO I

When Taref arrived aboard the Imperial Barge, dressed in an approved maintenance uniform for servicing the FTL and Holtzman engines, the ghost of Manford Toronto accompanied him.

Not long ago, he had celebrated killing the Butlerian leader in Arrakis City, pleased to report his triumph to Directeur Venport. But afterward, Taref had suffered terrible, recurrent nightmares of the *whizz-clack* of the Maula pistol, the screams of the crowd, the legless body sprawled on the dusty street. *Dead.* The man's skull had exploded, his blood and brains spraying in all directions.

Dead!

It was *not possible* that Manford could have survived. And yet he was back, and very much alive. The Butlerian leader said he was blessed by God and indestructible, and Taref had seen the proof of that claim. His entire view of the universe had shifted.

Life was hard and cheap in the desert, and Taref had been familiar with killing . . . though he had never done it in such a personal way before. Even all those people lost aboard the pilgrim ship and the other EsconTran spacefolders he had sent off into the depthless nowhere of the universe . . . those were just distant casualties. Now Directeur Venport wanted him to do the same thing to the Emperor's ship. But this was personal, too—like killing Manford Toronto. Another important name and face, the leader of the Imperium, a man with so much power that he could simply annex the entire planet of Arrakis *on a whim.*

As the third son of a Naib, Taref had little status in his tribe, but he had always scorned status because it measured things he did not care about. Directeur Venport had offered him an escape from Arrakis—and now a return to it—which came with a price he was willing to pay. A price that was, in its own way, quite high. But one more mission and he would be free. Directeur Venport had promised to release him from any remaining obligations.

According to Venport's orders, the Emperor of the Known Universe must be irrevocably lost on his journey home.

Taking his diagnostic tools, Taref worked in the engine room of the Imperial Barge with two other mechanics, workers from Arrakis City he had never seen before. They didn't know about his special mission. Directeur Venport trusted only him, and he had impressed upon Taref how terribly dangerous, yet necessary, this mission was.

The ghost of Manford Torondo mocked him: "Once more you try to kill a great leader, and again you will fail, because God Himself does not wish it. You are a tool of God, not a tool of that evil man."

"You cannot speak to me," Taref muttered aloud. The hum of the resting engines drowned out his words. It was a large and complex engine compartment, crowded with both types of stardrives. The barge was practically empty, with the Emperor's entourage gone as Taref spoke aloud in the emptiness. "You are not even truly dead."

"Because you failed," said the voice. It was not really a ghost, couldn't be. It was just Taref's conscience, his own imagination.

He went to the FTL and foldspace diagnostic panels, the latter of which looked similar to the EsconTran panels he had serviced and sabotaged on several ships at Junction Alpha. He ignored the voice as he selected his tools, made adjustments to one of the engine couplings, then altered a programming flow. Regardless of which engines the pilots chose to use when departing, the navigational calibration was now corrupted.

"I serve myself," he said. "I make my own decisions."

Manford's presence found the comment amusing, and laughed inside Taref's head. "No matter how strong you think you are, if you try to do something God does not wish, you will not succeed."

Feeling a knot in his stomach, the young man reconsidered. He studied the engine control board, not wanting his conscience haunted by the Emperor's ghost, in addition to the other one.

What did it all matter to him? What did a lowly desert man know, or care, about interplanetary politics? Before leaving his sietch, he'd never thought much about the Corrino Emperors, nor had he ever heard of Manford Torondo.

The Butlerian movement had nothing to do with the timeless ways of the desert, nor did Emperor Salvador and the politics of seizing the spice operations.

Would Imperial control be any different from that of the offworld industrialists? Taref couldn't understand Directeur Venport's hunger for riches and power either. Once a person had everything, how could he keep wanting more?

Through all these thoughts, Taref decided he would no longer be a pawn, doing whatever he was ordered to do.

Anxious to get back to the purity of the desert, he packed up his tools, leaving his work only partially done, without the backup sabotage he customarily performed on each vessel. Even so, what he'd done should be enough to destroy the navigation system and send the ship careening wildly into deep space, with no way for the pilots to reach any inhabited world. Taref was the first to board the return shuttle. That was enough. He had one last message to send to Directeur Venport.

EMPEROR SALVADOR HAD made a string of poor decisions, and now he was asserting himself in a grand and irritating way. Josef could barely control his annoyance.

What might have been a simple expedition to the spice fields became an operation as complex and cumbersome as a planetary invasion. The preparations and sheer dithering made Josef want to scream, yet he maintained his smile through it all. It was one of the greatest challenges he had ever faced.

The Emperor had brought hundreds of people aboard his Imperial Barge, uprooting the Salusan court and hauling the bloated party to the desert planet. Josef hadn't expected the Emperor to take *most* of them on the tour of the spice operations as well, but Salvador left only a handful of pouting functionaries behind on the barge, probably the ones who had displeased him somehow during the weeks-long journey to Arrakis.

In addition to the court functionaries and advisers, more than a hundred armed Imperial soldiers joined them to protect against desert bandits. "A wise decision, Sire," Josef said. "This is an extensive spice operation, and while I have my own troops, your added force is always welcome."

Salvador patted him on the shoulder. "Not to belittle your protective measures, Directeur, but my security team is superior."

Yet from watching the Imperial guards for only a short time, Josef could see that they were not nearly as sophisticated as his own paramilitary fighters. "I'm sure you're right, Sire." And he thought for the thousandth time that Roderick would make a much better Emperor.

According to Cioba, the Sisterhood had identified a grave danger to civilization if this idiot were allowed to bear offspring, and they had surreptitiously sterilized him. But now Josef was in a position to solve the problem in a more permanent way and save the present as well as the future.

The desert expedition required a large overland shuttle, complete with refreshments and two young women who skillfully played balisets during the journey. The loaded shuttle flew across the expanse of dunes, bypassing Arrakis City and leaving no record of their passage, in accordance with Josef's orders. In orbit, the barge's skeleton crew remained in contact with the Imperial party, some clearly disappointed that they weren't joining this merry adventure.

"This looks like an awful place," Salvador mused as he stared out at the monotonous dunes.

Josef said, "We don't value Arrakis for its beauty, Sire, but for its spice."

A cross-shear from the fringe of a minor storm buffeted the shuttle, and the entourage gasped in sudden panic. With his face twisted in annoyance rather than concern, Salvador signaled the cockpit. "Pilot, use caution, or I'll find someone more competent to handle the controls."

The pilot meekly apologized and gave the small storm a wide berth, which further delayed their arrival at the spice operations. Fortunately, having anticipated the ponderous nature of the Emperor's entourage, Josef had not dispatched the spice factory until the shuttle was already on its way. Timing was crucial. Harvesters could only work a melange vein for a limited time before a sandworm forced them to evacuate. Salvador Corrino probably expected the desert leviathans to accommodate his schedule.

Josef fashioned a false smile to make himself appear pleasant; the muscles of his face ached.

He was surprised to receive a direct communication from his saboteur Taref, especially so close to the Imperial entourage. In fact, he had never expected to hear from Taref again, counting on the desert man to simply fade off into the dust and sand.

For security, the Emperor had private cubicles aboard the elaborate shuttle. Trying not to show his sweat, Josef took the communication off-line temporarily and smiled. "If you would excuse me, Sire? I have an urgent business matter."

Salvador gave him an indulgent smile. "Of course, Directeur. Always crises! It comes with your position of responsibility. You must be so relieved to be done with all the pressures of the melange industry."

Josef could not seal himself in the chamber quickly enough, and he demanded answers and reassurances from his Freeman operative. "Is it done? Where are you?"

The young Freeman sounded hesitant and sad. "I did not complete my task, Directeur. In fact, I refuse. I began to corrupt the ship's nav-controls, but I will not have an Emperor's spirit haunting me." The desert man's face looked haunted on the screen, his eyes hollow.

Josef felt chilled. "But you must! It is the only way—"

"I am done with this work, Directeur—and done with other worlds. It is in God's hands now." He terminated the transmission.

Josef wanted to scream. It was such a neat, simple, perfect plan—the Imperial Barge would simply vanish en route, along with the worthless Emperor and his worthless entourage, lost on their way back to Salusa. The spice industry, the future of Venport Holdings, Norma Cenva's precious Navigators—everything depended on it.

The Emperor *could not* return to the palace. He could not be allowed to continue his blundering damage to civilization—no matter how much the solution cost.

As the shuttle continued to fly across the desert, Josef felt his face burning with anger. His thoughts churned, then focused, and soon he had another solution. A more expensive plan, harder to cover up, but effective nevertheless. He hated to spend so much—but if he did not find some way to take care of Salvador, VenHold would pay a much, much higher price.

Fortunately, he had operatives on all spice crews, people who were paid well for their services. He could get rid of the Emperor, but he had very little time to make the arrangements. Still in the private chamber, he sent out another urgent communication. By the time he emerged to rejoin Salvador and the rest of his contingent, Josef had calmed himself, and no one noticed a difference in his mood.

A dust plume was visible in the air as sand grains and fine particles were exhausted through the chimney-mouths of the mobile factory. Like a bloodstain, a rusty smear from a recent spice blow marked the dunes. The machinery scooped the top sandy layers into separation chambers, where centrifuges and filters did the first-cut processing to pull out the spice and eject the debris.

Salvador sat in his padded seat, peering through the expanded central observation window, while his functionaries gathered at smaller portholes on the sides. "What huge machinery!" one of them gasped.

Spotter aircraft flew high, keeping watch. Salvador's own guards remained alert and wary, but Josef reassured them. "Those flyers are constantly on the alert for giant sandworms."

"Your harvesting crew is creating an awful mess, isn't it?" Salvador said. It wasn't really a question.

Josef saw the churning scar the mobile spice factory was leaving as it scooped melange-saturated sand. "They've been at full production now for only about fifteen minutes."

"Fifteen minutes?" said one of the baliset players.

"Spice operations are a race against the worms," Josef explained. "Sire, when these become Imperial operations, your workers will have to heed that as well."

Salvador raised his eyebrows, but it was clear that he really didn't care. "We intend to hire many of your own crew chiefs, and we'll bring in Imperial geologists, industrial managers, planetologists. If you like, we may even retain you as a consultant."

Josef wanted to strangle the condescending nobleman, but instead he chuckled. "Venport Holdings gives me plenty to occupy my time, Sire. My family has accomplished a great deal here over the generations, but spice harvesting is dirty and difficult work, with many losses as well as gains. Honestly, I won't miss it in the least."

Emperor Salvador seemed overly pleased with himself. "I love situations where everyone wins."

The shuttle found a landing spot in a flattened area marked off between dunes. Josef had given instructions to the spice crew to get ready for a secret high-level inspection, telling them to prepare a landing area, since he didn't think the Emperor's pilot would be skilled enough to land on the factory's upper deck.

The craft lurched from side to side as it set down, and the group made sounds of dismay. This time the pilot apologized for the rough landing before Salvador could scold him.

The party emerged wearing no protective clothing of any sort. They weren't going to stay here long, and they could always retreat to the Imperial shuttle if the heat and dust grew too uncomfortable.

A yellow glare reflected off the dunes. Several functionaries coughed in the swirling dust. Salvador blinked in the bright light. "The smell of spice is . . . suffocating," he said, then laughed. "I never imagined a person could smell too much spice!"

The factory crew chief, Baren Okarr, came forward to meet them. A weathered, squat man with a dust-encrusted face, Okarr showed little deference for the Imperial Presence. His pleasantries were cursory. "I have a quota to meet, Sire." He nodded to Josef. "Directeur, our operations are at full capacity. We hope to have another half hour of harvesting time before a worm comes."

"Will we see a worm?" asked Salvador.

"Oh, you'll see one," Josef said, "no doubt about that."

"But how close is it now?" asked a functionary.

"The vibrations of the factory will attract at least one," Josef explained. "It just depends on how far we are into the worm's territory, and where the monster is when it detects us." The entourage seemed nervous, so Josef urged them to

He'd given the spotters strict instructions, and a promise of huge rewards—enough for each man to retire—if they contacted him first, privately.

"We've got distant wormsign, Directeur, but have not informed the factory yet."

"Excellent. And have the carryalls been withdrawn?"

"Yes, sir. Are you sure you wish to do this?"

Josef thought about Emperor Salvador and how the ponderous, dallying fool had decided to take over these vast spice operations on a whim. "I'm positive."

He took off in the flyer, leaving the Emperor and his entourage vulnerable, along with (sadly) a qualified and experienced crew. And all that expensive equipment. VenHold was contributing both blood and treasure to this operation, but it was worth the cost.

With the remote-control device in his pocket, he triggered the focused limpet detonator he had planted, which exploded in a small puff, crippling the Emperor's shuttle. Then he opened the comm line again to the two spotter pilots. "Good enough. Go ahead and make your announcement."

The worthless Emperor might as well know what was coming.

hurry. "The crew chief will take you inside the factory for a tour, but it has to be quick. I want you to see the harvesting and processing." He gestured for the people to move forward, smiling and nodding, while he lagged behind. Even without the pounding machinery, the clumsy footsteps of a hundred people would have attracted a sandworm.

As the others chattered with nervous excitement, Josef slipped a focused limpet detonator into his palm and casually approached the shuttle hull, tossing the limpet up against the near engine socket, where it adhered. The placement didn't need to be accurate—the focused charge would do enough damage to the engines that the pilot would never take off again.

Inside the spice harvester, the operational noise was deafening, the smells offensive, the grit everywhere. Emperor Salvador kept his hands close at his sides, reluctant to touch anything. He frowned at the unavoidable brown-orange stains that marked his fine garments. Dirty desert crewmen rushed up and down the corridors, brushing past the visitors, hurrying about their tasks.

"This is an active operation, Sire," Josef said. "Every person has a duty, and very little time to do it in. If one person misses a deadline, then the rest of the operation fails—as you can see, this is a huge undertaking."

Salvador was struggling with his own discomfort. "Now I see why melange is so expensive."

The crew chief led them up to the main operations deck, where twelve men and women sat at their stations, shouting into radio links. They remained in contact with the spotters and ground crews, and with the dune rollers that mapped out the expanse of visible melange, sending probes down into the sand. The pounding racket and miasmic odors made the operation unpleasant, and Josef knew the pampered Emperor Salvador would not tolerate it much longer. He felt tense.

Finally, at the central communication station, a dusty older woman looked up at him. "Directeur, there's a message for you."

His heart leapt with relief. "Excuse me, Sire. I've been expecting an urgent communication. I'll deal with it quickly, and then we can continue your tour."

"But what about the sandworm?" said Salvador.

"No sign of one yet. Don't worry." Josef hurried away from the control deck, ostensibly to an office compartment. Instead, he climbed a metal ladder and opened a hatch to the roof of the factory, where he kept a small escape flyer on the upper deck. All around him, dust and sand blew, while mechanical scoops hammered into the dunes, sending an irresistible summons to any sandworm in the vicinity.

Minutes later, he sealed himself into the escape flyer's cockpit, activated the engines, and transmitted to the two spotter craft that had sent him the message.

＿＿＿

*When the weak become powerful, their former oppressors will tremble
in fear.*

—*Orange Catholic Bible*

At first, the visiting Suk doctors were afraid to do what was necessary, but
Ptolemy would not let them avoid their responsibilities. They were the
only ones who could help Noffe. The scientist commanded them, bullied them,
and hovered beside them inside the Denali surgical center as they completed the
work. This was not, after all, much different from what they had done many
times before to extract and preserve the brains from dying Navigator bodies.

For the first week after the surgery, Ptolemy rarely left the preservation tank
that held the administrator's brain, and the thoughtrodes functioned exactly as
he expected. He connected the speakerpatch first, along with the conversion
software that translated Noffe's panicked thoughts into words.

Initially, the responses were jumbled gibberish, but Ptolemy had infinite patience. He spoke calmly, giving explanations so that his disoriented friend wouldn't
be so lost and frightened. The input sensors converted his softly spoken words into
comprehensible pulses so that Noffe's disembodied brain could understand him.

Finally, as Noffe calmed himself enough to focus on a single thought, he kept
expressing, "Dark . . . too dark . . . too dark."

Ptolemy leaned closer to the tank. "That's because you have no eyes, my friend.
Those will come next—optic threads to give you a visual clarity beyond anything your human eyes could ever have. After you adjust, you will be able to see
all parts of the spectrum, and vast distances. Imagine the clarity. You will focus
and see things no one else has ever seen! I envy you, in a way."

In the speakerpatch, Noffe's voice fumbled, tried several times, and then finally said, "Don't envy me. . . ."

Several days later, once the optic sensors were installed and Noffe could "see" the laboratory around him, the administrator changed his dreary, disoriented gloom to optimistic marveling. Most importantly, he could now discern Ptolemy nearby, which he found reassuring; Noffe said he could even read an expression of concern and wonder on his friend's face. Ptolemy responded with increasing excitement. "I'll do everything to make this the best experience for you that it can possibly be, I promise."

Noffe's thinking was not as adept as an enhanced proto-Navigator brain, but with a week of practice he was able to control his thoughts and communicate clearly through the speakerpatch. Before long, he accepted and even embraced his new situation. "My old body was imperfect and weak, in need of repairs."

Ptolemy fell into a fit of coughing. Despite his own treatments, his scarred lungs felt as if he had inhaled embers that refused to be extinguished. The visiting Suk doctors had treated Ptolemy's damaged lungs, mitigating the worst symptoms, but even with the best medical attention, he would degenerate. "My body needs repairs as well."

Noffe seemed eager. "When might I have one of the new walker bodies?"

Ptolemy was glad to consider the possibilities. "One step at a time, my good friend. I've trained many failed Navigators, but their minds are more adaptable than yours. I don't want to rush you."

"I am excited about this, very anxious," Noffe said. "Don't wait too long."

Ptolemy let out a wistful sigh and tried to make a joke, but then squeezed stinging tears out of his eyes and struggled to hide his pain from Noffe's new high-acuity sensors. "You'll have all the time you could possibly wish," Ptolemy finally managed. "Some of the Titans lived for thousands of years."

"You should join me," Noffe said. "I would hate to have humanity lose your insights . . . and I'd hate to lose you as a friend."

Ptolemy had been thinking the same thing, daydreaming but not willing to succumb to the temptation. Even before his lungs were damaged, he had often looked longingly at the new cymek walkers, marveling at the strength of their mechanical arms and their protected body systems that allowed them to survive in the harshest environments . . . and gave them the ability to face hundreds of screaming barbarians.

"I have considered it, Noffe—many times."

TO START WITH, Ptolemy installed Noffe's brain canister in one of the smaller, old-model cymek walkers. The administrator reveled in being able to move about, and he gingerly tested his mechanical legs, growing more comfortable as he walked on them with increasing strength and balance.

In the meantime, Ptolemy's own modified walker had been repaired, the life-support systems checked, and the enclosed full-body cab reinforced against leakages or malfunctions. He rode inside, sheltered and safe. Though he still felt uneasy about how close he'd come to death because of a simple mechanical failure, he didn't want to miss the experience.

Ptolemy accompanied Noffe across the rough Denali terrain. Because he had practiced frequently in his manual-drive walker, Ptolemy was more comfortable moving the artificial legs, but Noffe quickly familiarized himself with the systems. Thoughtrodes linked his mind to the walker mechanisms, and he soon adjusted to a new rhythm as he moved across the ground.

"With my sensor eyes, I can see all the way to the horizon—even through this mist," Noffe transmitted. He bounded forward, using sharp claws to scuttle up a rock face that was dappled with alien lichen. His simulated voice exuded pure joy. "I can switch to different portions of the spectrum, find zones of transparency, and I can *see* so much more than I used to! And my hearing—with a slight adjustment I could hear a pebble fall kilometers away. In fact, I think I hear . . ." Swiveling his optic turret to face the west, he added, "Somewhere beyond those hills—ah, yes, it is the wind whistling through rocks."

Ptolemy worked the controls of his primitive walker, clomping along with a rocking gait, but he soon fell behind. "This is like dancing, my friend!" Noffe said. "I'm so limber now. I could never run this fast or jump this high before."

Ptolemy switched off the transmitter inside his life-support chamber when another coughing fit washed over him. He didn't want Noffe to hear him over the intercom. He had so many things to finish, so many ideas to pursue, so much to accomplish for Directeur Venport.

"Freedom, strength, and immortality," Noffe crowed. "We'd better keep this procedure a secret, or the entire human race will clamor to become cymeks."

New Titans with Navigator brains marched over the nearby terrain, performing exercises with their superior machine bodies. They were almost ready for battle. Ptolemy badly wanted to participate in the upcoming fight, but he had always been too fearful and queasy for personal combat. He remembered how shocked and impotent he had been when Anari Idaho used her sword to butcher the new bioengineered legs he had given Manford Torondo as a gift, and how he'd been too weak to stop the burning of Dr. Elchan.

With a Titan body of his own, Ptolemy could fight the barbarians, *and* he could still think at a very high level, could still perform advanced research. He would no longer be plagued by a maddening cough and chronic pain. He would no longer be weak in any sense of the word.

When he activated the transmitter again, Ptolemy weighed his words, then said, "You've convinced me. I have no reservations—I know now that it's possible."

"You'll join me?" Noffe sounded delighted through the speakerpatch. His voice was a reasonable imitation of the administrator's original voice.

Ptolemy swung his walker around and began the march back toward the glowing domes, working the legs in perfect sequence. At the research facility, the framework of a new landing chamber was still under construction after the explosion that had nearly killed Noffe. Unhindered by the poisonous atmosphere, a team of cymeks performed the work, making significant progress. They would have the dome rebuilt within days, and space transportation would resume as before. Then the Suk doctors would return to Kolhar.

Ptolemy had to act soon.

"I'm tired of being insignificant," he said. "I have lost too much already due to the frailty of human bodies and the brevity of human lives. I want to join you, Noffe—I want to take part in the upcoming fight . . . and I want to be alive afterward, so that I know how it all ends."

A strange sound came back over the comm speaker, and Ptolemy knew that Noffe was learning how to laugh with his thoughts. "We'll be there together."

Ptolemy increased his pace until they reached the airlock of the remaining access dome. Noffe chose to stay outside, saying that he wished to continue his explorations. "I can map portions of Denali that my human eyes have never seen, even though I've been administrator here for years."

Using the manual controls, Ptolemy lumbered his immense mechanical body through the access door and sealed the dome behind him. After the air had been exchanged, he stepped out of the life-support cab and fought down another racking spasm of coughs. He had no second thoughts, no doubts, only determination.

He marched into the infirmary, where Suk doctors were tending to a technician who had a minor chemical burn. They looked very bored. Ptolemy presented himself and said, "Now that you have practiced, now that you are experts, there is another surgery I need you to perform."

The doctors didn't understand what he was asking at first, until he crossed his arms over his small chest. "You'll need to become proficient at preparing new cymeks from human volunteers. This will be only one of many such surgeries."

*I now understand regret, loss, and sadness. These are all concepts—emotions—that previously eluded me, especially the emotion of love. Now I can fit them into a workable mental framework. For my progress in this, I owe a great deal to Gilbertus Albans.*

—ERASMUS, *Latter-Day Laboratory Journals*

The robot reviewed the entirety of his existence, fast-forwarding down the centuries of the Synchronized Empire, how he had become unique among thinking machines, a true counterpoint to the overconfident Omnius. Erasmus had never stopped trying to understand . . . everything. He wanted to know the entire universe, and had a specific interest in humanity, in what it meant to be a fully conscious, fully functioning *Homo sapiens*.

But that was not a simple problem, and there wasn't one clear solution. The complexity and volatility of humans unsettled him.

He had seen the extremities of human emotions, including irrational and self-destructive behavior, such as when Serena Butler had reacted so strongly to the simple death of her child; and those emotions also caused extremities of overconfidence and refusal to concede logical defeat—the humans had kept fighting the Jihad long after any rational being would have seen the futility. And yet they had won.

Erasmus realized that the study of their species would be an unending quest, and their quirks would require millennia to analyze. Even then, as the race evolved, he would have to reevaluate his theories.

Now, with Butlerians surrounding the Mentat School and his devoted ward their prisoner, Erasmus was discouraged to think that his noble and lofty quest might end here in such an ignominious way. He had become fascinated with Anna Corrino, but he still had much to learn from Gilbertus Albans.

Ever since founding the Mentat School, Gilbertus had been treading lightly around antitechnology sensibilities, careful to provoke no retaliation from the

Butlerians. He bowed to them, compromised with them for too long, implicitly endorsing their fanaticism by his silence. Now he had brought the current situation on himself because of his stubborn sense of honor and personal belief system.

Erasmus still struggled to understand.

Meanwhile, behind the protective walls, the Mentat students continued to keep watch. They evaluated the school's security measures, both from the lake side and the marshes and sangrove swamps; despite its defenses, the facility could not outlast the large Butlerian force. The faculty, students, and support staff had placed their confidence in the Headmaster's ability to negotiate with, or at least outthink, Manford Torondo. Erasmus monitored the siege through his remote spy-eyes, but could find no escape either.

With Gilbertus gone, Administrator Zendur was ostensibly in charge of the school. As a Mentat, the middle-aged man was swift in his calculations and talented at making projections, but he was not a leader. Though a skilled graduate of the school, Zendur was clearly out of his depth.

Since Gilbertus had charged Anna Corrino with the safekeeping of the memory core, she concealed Erasmus in her private chambers. Even though the robot could communicate with her through the implanted transceiver, she loved to hold his gelsphere in her hands and cradle it like a precious object.

"I suspect they are going to kill Headmaster Albans," she said, in an affectless voice that carried no fear at all. Erasmus knew that Anna's emotions were anomalous and didn't fit the pattern of the human norm. Earlier, she had been emotional, flighty, immature, and overreactive—that was why she'd been sent to the Sisterhood school on Rossak, where her impulsive consumption of poison had damaged her brain. On the other hand, that tragedy had turned her into such a remarkable specimen.

Even with her difficulty in expressing herself, Erasmus knew the young woman was disturbed by the plight of the Mentat School and its Headmaster. "I share your concern, Anna Corrino—I have run computer projections. Gilbertus will do his best to resolve the situation, but I believe the Butlerians will exact a terrible price on him."

"I'm worried about him."

Erasmus considered for a long moment, running the data again and again, and kept reaching the same conclusion. "I am worried about him, too."

No matter what Gilbertus negotiated, even after the price was paid, Erasmus didn't trust the Butlerians to keep their agreement. "Use your training and make your own projections. I have taught you how," he said to her. "With the Headmaster gone, what is the school's most valuable asset?"

She answered immediately. "You are."

"Thank you for that," Erasmus said. "But we must assume they don't know about me. I rephrase the question: Other than myself, what is most important?"

Anna pondered, then spoke without any pride. "I am, of course."

"Precisely. And the Butlerians will want that asset. Therefore, we need to keep you out of their hands."

"I agree," she said, and then her expression fell. "If they take me hostage, how can I possibly protect you? That is really the most important thing."

Erasmus didn't argue with her.

Anna had spent a significant amount of time on top of the defensive walls, studying the Butlerians, counting their campfires, their numbers, their weapons. Then she wandered into obsessive numeracy, counting how many people wore red in their garments, how many wore blue, how many wore brown. She counted the number of men and the number of women, as close as she could determine, though some muffled their features with hats and scarves. She provided the data to Zendur and the Mentat students for tactical planning, though the information was not necessarily useful.

Erasmus had observed. After going out to meet with the Butlerian leader, Gilbertus had been surrounded by their guards and taken into the main head-quarters tent. From a distance, using his spy-eyes from trees in the swamp, the robot watched closely. He detected anger and uneasiness in the besieging army.

He didn't trust the unruly followers. What if Manford couldn't control his own fanatics? An uproar could turn into a lynch mob—it had happened before. From prior analysis, Erasmus had determined that the legless leader maintained control of his followers by allowing release of their anger and tensions under certain circumstances, and when he saw them reaching critical levels, he didn't even try to control their emotions. If the Butlerians grew too outraged, Manford might need to ignore his promise and unleash them.

A flurry occurred in the camp as a rumor rippled among the followers. Erasmus recognized Anari Idaho, Manford's stubbornly loyal but decidedly un-imaginative bodyguard, stalking through the gathered fanatics. She led Gilbertus, obviously a prisoner, to another tent at the edge of the camp, where he was placed under heavy guard.

Analyzing the facial expressions acquired from high-resolution images, Erasmus determined that the fanatics were agitated and furious. Maybe Gilbertus had refused to strike a bargain with the Butlerian leader . . . or maybe it was something else.

Finally, at dusk, Manford approached the front gates of the school, riding on the shoulders of his Swordmaster. After sealing his memory core in a special hiding place in her quarters, Anna went to the battlements to watch, but Erasmus stayed with her anyway, speaking into her ear.

The Butlerian leader's voice carried through the air, and all the listeners fell silent, barely breathing. Even the swamp insects fell into a hush.

"I gave my word not to destroy the Mentat School if Headmaster Albans cooperated, and I will keep that word," he shouted up at the gate. "I also promised the Headmaster that no harm would befall him if he met me face-to-face. Alas, that particular promise cannot be kept, now that we know the true identity of Gilbertus Albans. We know that he is nearly two centuries old, that he lived on Corrin as a collaborator with the thinking machines. We know that the demon robot Erasmus trained him and extended his life."

The murmur of the Butlerian crowd grew louder, angrier. Behind their walls, the Mentat trainees remained silent, stunned and confused.

"His horrendous crimes long predate my promise. And punishment for a machine sympathizer who aided in the torture and murder of millions of human beings must take precedence over my agreement. That punishment is immutable. Gilbertus Albans will be executed at dawn, and then his school will be opened to us, even if we have to blast it open. All Mentat trainees will undergo careful reeducation." Manford raised himself higher on Anari's shoulders. "The mind of man is holy. The crimes of man must be punished."

Anna muttered to herself, as she often did, but she was speaking to Erasmus. "They know the truth about Gilbertus. Before long, they will probably find out about you. You are in danger."

The robot took little consolation in saying, "I doubt Gilbertus revealed that my memory core is hidden here, but somehow they did discover his past. This leads me to a difficult but necessary conclusion, Anna Corrino. You and I must escape from here—tonight."

~~~

*Is it better to make a vow to a person or to principles? Which is more important?*

<div align="right">

—Annals of the Mentat School

</div>

D raigo Roget arrived at Lampadas hoping to recruit Headmaster Albans, to bring him to the side of reason and civilization—only to find that the Butlerian world had gone insane.

Previously, Gilbertus had managed to keep his school isolated out in the inhospitable wastelands, but now Manford Torondo had roused his mob and laid siege to the school. Draigo was angry just to see it.

When he was a student here, Draigo had never revealed his loyalties to VenPort Holdings; he kept his political opinions to himself, but he had been unable to hide his talent. Headmaster Albans had acknowledged that Draigo was the best student at the Mentat School.

In addition to mental exercises, Draigo had passed the rigorous physical challenges: sprinting through treacherous sangrove forests, memorizing the submerged stepping-stones through the marsh channels, keeping track of every safe path, every devious trick and trap. He understood that danger and physical effort helped trainees to attune their minds, that adrenaline and risk pushed them to the edge of their capabilities. Now he realized that Headmaster Albans had been preparing all along to defend the school against the Butlerians, even as he tried to remain neutral.

Leaving the covert VenHold spacefolder in orbit, Draigo used his shuttle to descend to the surface. In the darkness, his shuttle's sensors mapped out a cluster of people camped in dry patches on the grassy marshlands. In spite of the natural defenses of the swamps, a horde of barbarian fanatics had surrounded the school, laying siege to the walled complex, with amphibious craft patrolling the marsh lake, tents and artillery posted on the moist ground.

Just glimpsing the scene infuriated Draigo. If he had brought a VenHold warship, he could scorch the Half-Manford's entire camp!

Activating the automated guidance systems, he landed at a safe distance out on the edge of the sangroves. Draigo had turned off any of the shuttle's external lights that the Butlerians might see. After stabilizing the craft on the water-logged ground, he changed into nondescript attire such as the common people of Lampadas wore. Butlerians also wore a badge of their movement, a human fist clenching a stylized machine gear, but Draigo would not go so far. He slipped a pulse-stunner into his shirt.

He made his way overland to the edge of the sprawling camp, and slipped in among the restless people without difficulty. The Butlerians were angry and suspicious, but the majority were simpleminded, as Draigo had always known. They directed their fervor toward the Mentat School, never imagining that outsiders might come to defend it.

The siege camp was fairly well lit. The barbarians made campfires out of whatever dry wood they could find. In addition, there were portable lamps near and inside the tents. Draigo approached.

INSIDE ONE OF those tents, Manford Torondo sat on the fabric floor, balancing his torso with his hands at his sides. He heard Anari speaking to a guard outside. Her constant presence was reassuring and allowed the Butlerian leader to concentrate on his important work, without concern for his personal safety.

In the low light cast by a lamp, he looked intensely at Gilbertus, who sat on his low bed-pad. The Headmaster looked much younger with his aging makeup scrubbed off, and his elegant robe was wrinkled and soiled. His face was half in light, half in shadow.

"You knew Erasmus better than anyone," Manford said, "so I want you to tell me about him, everything you can think of that might be useful to me in advancing the cause of humanity. What were his thoughts, his plans, his weaknesses?"

"You wish me to speak on behalf of a thinking machine from long ago?"

Manford's nostrils flared. "I want you to speak about him, not for him. You must reveal these things, after the crimes you have committed. They will not remedy your crimes, but they may be of help to me. Tell me why he conducted his cruel experiments on human beings."

"To *understand*. It separates some of us from those who wish to remain ignorant."

Manford's eyes flashed. "I have read the laboratory journals of Erasmus. I have struggled to understand the enemy. What was it like living on Corrin with the thinking machines? Is it true you considered Erasmus a father figure, and he thought of you as a son? How could such a bizarre relationship exist? He was a monster!"

"You cannot understand Erasmus, or me. The gulf between us is too great. You and Erasmus represent two extremes."

Manford pursed his lips thoughtfully. "And I will proudly keep to my extreme, for the soul of the human race depends on it. Spend your evening in contemplation, Headmaster, for tomorrow you will die."

DRAIGO WANDERED THROUGH the encampment, absorbing information. When he saw that many of the Butlerians sported crudely bandaged wounds, he wondered if some great battle had occurred. But after listening to conversations, he learned that the casualties had been inflicted by swamp creatures or the Butlerians' own ineptitude at living out in the wild. Draigo found the knowledge both ironic and insulting to those who turned their backs on the conveniences and safety of civilization.

"Leader Torondo should just execute the Headmaster tonight and be done with it, so we can go home," grumbled a man sitting by a fire. "Why wait until dawn? What's the point?"

Next to him, a younger man sorted through broken branches, discarding wood that was too wet for the blaze. The two men noticed Draigo, and he decided that ducking away would draw more attention, so he came closer. Although his heart pounded when he heard their conversation, he remarked in a casual tone, "I never question what Leader Torondo wants to do, or his timing."

The other two looked at each other and shrugged. The younger one discarded another wet stick. "He gave his word, though. A promise is a promise."

The older man disagreed. "Leader Torondo gave his word to keep the Headmaster safe, but the confession changed everything. The execution order against machine sympathizers was in place long before. The Headmaster tricked everyone. He collaborated with Omnius and the demon robot Erasmus!"

Draigo was startled. "Headmaster Albans is a collaborator with the thinking machines? What proof do you have of that?"

The younger man glared at him. "How could you not know? Have you been deaf all afternoon?"

"Not deaf—I was out hunting, but didn't have any luck." Draigo indicated his dirt-smudged clothes.

"Headmaster Albans was raised on Corrin, and Erasmus kept him as a pet. He escaped after the Battle of Corrin and has been living as a different person all this time."

Draigo turned his head to hide his astonishment. "That's not possible! Corrin fell eighty-five years ago. I've seen . . . images of the Headmaster. He's not old at all."

"Some sort of trick from the demon machines. Deacon Harian found his past in the old records. There is conclusive proof. When that Truthsayer caught him at his lies, he had no choice but to confess."

"I shouldn't waste any more time hunting, then," Draigo said. "If Leader Torondo is going to execute him in the morning, the siege is almost over."

"This won't be over until that machine sympathizer lies on the ground, with his head in one place and his body in another." The older one chuckled at the grisly image.

Draigo wandered away, so as to not look too interested, but he kept his eyes and ears open, and asked questions whenever he could do so without raising suspicion. He touched the pulse-stunner concealed in his shirt. If the Butlerians caught him with the weapon, they would know he was not one of them.

As he walked further into the encampment, drawing little attention and nodding dumbly whenever someone looked at him, he spotted the muscular female Swordmaster. Wearing a determined expression, she marched through the camp, making her way toward a large tent, where she took up a sentry position by the front flap. Anari Idaho's protection was always reserved for the Half-Manford, though, not Headmaster Albans, who was likely to be somewhere else. Draigo ducked back, keeping to the shadows, because she might recognize him.

The tent holding the prisoner was more isolated, as if the Butlerians feared Gilbertus might contaminate them by mere proximity to his thoughts. Draigo saw two nervous-looking guards standing in front of the entry flap, with a portable lamp burning beside one of them. Keeping his distance, Draigo prowled around the tent, trying to determine how he could approach and free his mentor. This was not a matter that needed Mentat projections; it was a matter requiring quick and efficient action.

In the rear, he saw the shadowy, squatting figure of a third guard. He could tell by the guard's posture that he was awake and alert, not dozing. Unfortunate. Draigo chose not to use his pulse-stunner, because it would make a faint but perceptible noise, and the two guards at the front might come running.

He approached the tent from the rear, moving as cautiously and silently as only a person with full Mentat awareness could. He knew he could defeat all three of them, but he couldn't afford to have them sound an alarm.

Draigo withdrew his small throwing-knife—a crude weapon and less accurate than the stunner, but at least it was silent. From this short distance it was simply a mathematical problem: calculating parabolic arcs, air resistance, gravity. In a flash, he checked and rechecked his calculations, cocked back his arm, and hurled the knife. The challenge was not in striking his target, but in how quickly he could kill the man. If the knife struck the wrong place and left the guard alive long enough to flail and gurgle, it would be a mistake.

Draigo Roget did not like to make mistakes.

The blade sank neatly into the hollow of the man's throat. The guard grabbed at the blade, but his jerking and squirming only drove the point deeper. One of his legs kicked out and just missed the side of the tent. Draigo darted forward and seized the man's head, slashing with the knife to cut the jugular. After that, the twitching was inconsequential.

He could have sliced through the tent fabric, but even that small noise might have alerted the two front guards; once inside he would also have to talk with Headmaster Albans, and their voices might draw attention. Draigo wanted to make this neat and clean, so that they would have the best chance of slipping away from the barbarian camp and back through the swamps to his ship.

No other choice: He had to incapacitate the other two guards.

Acting casual, he circled out into the shadows and sauntered up to the two guards at the front of the tent. When they saw him coming, he raised a hand in the traditional Butlerian salute, to which they responded.

"I've come to relieve you," he said.

"Not till dawn," said the man on the left.

The other guard narrowed his eyes. "Is that blood?"

Draigo recognized him as one of the Butlerian Mentat students, and the trainee recognized him as well, but Draigo was prepared. He slipped the pulse-stunner out of his bloodstained shirt and dropped both men quickly; though not dead, they fell like corpses cut down from a gallows. They would remain unconscious, but for an unpredictable amount of time.

A wise Mentat eliminated as many variables as possible. Not willing to take chances, he cut their throats with the knife he had retrieved from the first body and left the bodies propped outside the tent.

Slipping through the front flap, he stood up in the shadows and presented himself. His heart was pounding wildly. "Headmaster, I've come to rescue you."

Gilbertus Albans was awake, seated on a mat on the ground. "Draigo Roget—this is unexpected."

"It's meant to be unexpected. I have a ship. I can take you away from these savages."

Gilbertus didn't stir from his mat, but looked at Draigo, his eyes bright in the shadows. The Headmaster's spectacles were gone, but he didn't act as if he needed them. "I can't go, Draigo. While I appreciate your effort, I'm honor-bound to stay here."

"Honor-bound? I don't give a damn what promise you made to Manford. He intends to execute you at dawn. These people are irrational and won't be satisfied until they've killed you. They're even saying that you collaborated with Erasmus back on Corrin. They'll say anything!"

"That part, my excellent student, is true."

Draigo stopped. "What do you mean? The notion is absurd. You would be over a century old."

"Much more than that. I am one hundred eighty-six, by my best estimate. Since I was born in a slave pen among other feral captives on Corrin, the exact date of my birth is unknown."

Draigo, numbed by the revelation, reassessed and reprioritized his situation; this part of the discussion could take place at a later time, in safety. "You are also the Headmaster of the Mentat School. You were my teacher and mentor, so I am honor-bound not to let them execute you. Come quickly—we have to get away."

"I refuse. The consequences are too great. I gave my promise to Manford Torondo, and in turn Manford swore not to destroy the school. If I flee with you now, they'll blast all the buildings to pieces with artillery and kill every one of my students. You yourself told me I had to stand up for an important belief. I cannot run away. Better that I make the sacrifice for the greater benefit of my students."

"I have Mentat students of my own, and I've been training them with your methods," Draigo said. "Come to Kolhar with me. Directeur Venport would welcome an alliance with you. We can send other ships back here, a full battle group to rescue the rest of your students."

"They will arrive too late," Gilbertus insisted. "The moment Manford discovers I'm gone—"

"But I can't just leave you here!" Draigo realized his voice was getting too loud, and someone might overhear them.

"I haven't asked you to leave. There is something I need you to do, something more important than saving my life."

Draigo focused his thoughts, squared his shoulders. "I'm listening."

"I'm not the one who needs rescuing. I made another promise a long time ago after the Synchronized Empire fell, when I saved a mind more precious to me than any other. I promised to protect it."

"Who?" Draigo asked.

"I have no time to be subtle. It is Erasmus. The independent robot still exists, and he is far more important than I am. It was his idea to set up the Mentat School."

Draigo stared in disbelief, processing the information.

"Directeur Venport would find Erasmus useful," Gilbertus continued. "And there is also the Emperor's sister—I gave the Corrinos my word that I would keep her safe. I am certain the Butlerians mean to take her as a hostage, to force the Emperor to agree to even more of their demands. We have improved the school's defenses, but I can tell you a safe approach. I want you to get inside the walls and find Anna Corrino—she has Erasmus's memory core. Directeur Venport can protect both of them. There is hope for them, but not for me."

Gilbertus described the safe path into the school complex, the rearranged stepping-stones in the water, and an underwater access gate that he could reach after dark, without needing special equipment.

Then they heard a shout from outside the tent, a woman's deep voice. Anari Idaho. "Raise the alarm! Someone killed the guards! Quick—to the prisoner!"

Gilbertus's eyes widened in alarm. "You need to get away, or all is lost. Do as I told you. Help me to keep my promises."

Draigo hesitated for an instant. "All right, Headmaster." He took out his knife, slashed the back fabric of the tent, and dove through the opening. He leaped over the body of the third guard and raced into the darkness, melting away in the swamp as Butlerians surged toward the prisoner's tent.

Glancing back, he saw Anari Idaho charging through the camp like a juggernaut, her sword raised as she hunted for him. Draigo wished he'd had more of a chance to say goodbye to the Headmaster, but with his organized Mentat mind, he would always be able to recall every detail of Gilbertus's face with perfect clarity.

*There are far more pleasant places for an Emperor to visit than Arrakis,
but it is important for the sake of appearances that I go there in person. I
reign over my subjects on squalid worlds as well as those on magnificent
ones.*

—EMPEROR SALVADOR CORRINO, *Imperial Journals*

The spice crew chief received word from the spotter aircraft. "Wormsign,
chief! It's close—and a big one."

The Imperial entourage responded with a titter of nervous excitement. Salvador hurried to the dust-smeared observation windows on the control deck.
"Good. I've been wanting to see one."

The crew chief kept his attention back on the communication system. "Plot
its course. How long do we have?" The spotter transmitted coordinates, and the
location of the behemoth appeared on a grid-map of the surrounding dunes.
"Gods below, it's close! Why the hell didn't you spot it sooner?"

"It must have been running deep, Chief," the spotter replied.

"You should hire better spotters," Salvador remarked.

Crew Chief Okarr's drawn expression and gray complexion alarmed the Emperor. "This one is extremely close, Sire. *Too* close!"

Wondering what action was necessary, Salvador snapped a signal to his Imperial troops. "Be on high alert. We may need your protection."

The factory crew chief blinked at him in disbelief. "Sire, your guards can't do
anything against a giant sandworm."

Directeur Venport's voice came over the comm speakers, sounding scratchy
and distant, even though Salvador thought he had merely gone to an office in
another part of the spice factory. "Chief Okarr, prepare to jettison the spice—we
don't have much time." The Emperor was not impressed with the electrical systems aboard this big mobile factory. Static storms and dust must be playing
havoc with the circuitry.

"Yes, Directeur. I summoned the carryalls, and my crew is ready to evacuate. I'm trying to reach the rescue ships right now—they should be inbound momentarily." His hands a blur across the controls, the chief prepped the spice container and launched it.

The loud explosive report startled Salvador. "What was that? Are we under attack?"

"That was planned, Sire." Chief Okarr was flushed and tense, but he still answered the Emperor's questions. "All the spice gathered during our operations is packed into an armored cargo container, which I just jettisoned. In tight situations like this, we launch it with a locator beacon far from the spice factory. With the worm distracted by the greater vibrations from our operations, we can usually retrieve the container later."

"Interesting," Salvador said, but his nervous entourage did not seem interested at all.

The captain of the Imperial Guard picked up on the tension in the control room. "Sire, we should return to the Imperial shuttle. It's time to get to safety."

Salvador nodded. "Yes, let's leave these good people to their work. Spice mining is a complicated business, as we've seen firsthand. Good job, all of you."

The guard captain touched his earadio, listened, and recoiled. "Sire, there's been an explosion on the shuttle! I think it's sabotage."

The entourage gasped, looking to Salvador for guidance. He tried to be strong, for their sakes. Mustering a calm voice, he said, "We were warned of the dangers on Arrakis, but we'll be all right. Captain, arrange for us to get away."

"Sire! The shuttle *can't fly*! The engines are ruined."

"Ruined? You mean they can't be repaired?"

"*Ruined*, Sire! We're trapped here."

"Will we still be able to see the worm?" asked one of the baliset players, as if she were more interested in inspiration for a new song than her own safety.

"I'm sure we'll see the worm from the evacuation ships. Crew Chief, where do we go to board your rescue vessels?"

The chief was short-tempered, barking orders into the comm system. "We don't have enough escape ships for a hundred extra people!"

"Carryalls aren't responding, Chief—I can't raise them at all," shouted one of the workers. "They've *got* to be inbound."

Someone else yelled, "That worm will be here in less than five minutes."

Venport's voice crackled over the speakers on the control deck. "Emperor Corrino, my apologies, but urgent business has called me away. I would have preferred to tell you in person." He sounded flippant. "I've decided to reject Imperial seizure of my spice operations. Here on Arrakis, power doesn't come from a title or bloodline, but from actions, resources, and carefully laid plans."

Salvador didn't understand what the man was saying.

Venport continued, "Chief Okarr, the spice cargo has been jettisoned safely away. You and your men have served Combined Mercantiles well and generated a great deal of profit for us. It was your bad luck to be assigned here today, but rest assured that I will compensate your families generously for their losses. And Emperor Corrino . . . enjoy the rest of your tour."

The chief roared curses into the voice pickup. Imperial soldiers closed around Salvador to protect him, though he didn't feel any safer having them near. The factory workers were in a complete panic. Some curled up, muttering prayers, while others fled the control deck, but there was no safe place to go.

Outside on the dunes, a handful of ground rollers raced away from the harvester factory. Salvador wondered if he and his inner circle could commandeer those vehicles and get away across the desert, although apparently the giant worms pounced on any small vibrations.

He felt confused, frozen into inaction. Roderick would have known what to do—*he* would have issued the right orders to arrange an escape, might even have been able to prevent Venport's treachery in the first place.

Alas, his brother had always been a stronger, more competent person than he was. Many of Salvador's special guards and advisers were concerned that Roderick might assassinate his brother and take the throne, but Salvador had never worried. Roderick was his closest, most loyal friend.

No, his brother would have kept them all safe. In fact, Roderick had advised him against imperializing the Arrakis spice operations at all. It had been Manford Torondo's idea, and a very bad one. Roderick had advised him not to go to Arrakis, too. He bit his lower lip and muttered, "You were right, dear brother."

The guard captain withdrew his Chandler pistol and pointed the deadly weapon at the crew chief's florid face. "Tell us how to get the Emperor out of here, now! There must be a way."

Unafraid of the weapon, the chief bellowed back, "There is no way—I'd evacuate my own people if I could! We can't possibly call in any rescue ships in time. We have only minutes left."

At the observation window someone screamed—a thin, womanish wail, though it came from a stocky man, the Minister of Mining. Salvador shoved him away and pressed closer to look through the main window. Dust had blown in front of the plaz, obscuring the view.

The guard captain, still waving his ineffective pistol, took over the spice factory's comm systems, swiftly adjusting to a private frequency to transmit to the Imperial Barge in orbit. "Our Emperor is under attack! Convey this urgent message to Salusa Secundus. Directeur Josef Venport sabotaged the operations and abandoned us to be consumed by a sandworm. I . . . I do not believe we can survive. I have failed in my sworn duty."

Hearing this, the barge pilot should know to activate the foldspace engines and race away, returning to the capital world with the news. Roderick would learn the truth, and *he* would retaliate against Venport Holdings.

Salvador found that satisfying, at least. Everyone was screaming now. Looking through the observation window, he said in a peculiar, matter-of-fact voice, "There's the worm."

The eyeless monster burst out of the desert, its mouth a cave filled with sparkling crystal teeth that scooped tons of sand down its gullet as it swept forward.

"It's so close!" Salvador said, until someone said the thing was still at least two minutes away—the gigantic size made it appear much nearer. The worm hammered forward, the size of a starship. His brain went numb, frozen with terror and disbelief.

Maddened by the pounding vibrations, the worm careened forward, and Salvador had to admit that it was indeed very impressive.

LOOSE ENDS HAD a way of strangling a person. When making his assassination plans, Josef Venport had considered merely leaving the spice harvester to its fate, but he needed to see with his own eyes that the worm swallowed the factory, its crew, and the Emperor's entourage.

Taref's news of killing Manford Torondo had been premature, much to Josef's disappointment, and now the young Freeman had thrown the carefully orchestrated plan into chaos, but thankfully Josef had implemented an emergency backup plan. This was not the way he would have preferred to handle the situation, but it accomplished the necessary purpose anyway.

It was sad to lose the spice crew and crew chief, who had done nothing wrong. This was a high-risk profession, however, and everyone aboard the harvester had known the risks when they signed on. Even spice factories with experienced crews were lost in the desert all the time. At least these people's sacrifice would strengthen VenHold's future, as well as that of the melange industry itself, and therefore the economy of Arrakis—along with commerce across the Imperium.

Even more important, with Salvador Corrino gone and a more rational leader in place—someone who could stand up against the barbarians—Josef would prevent the looming dark ages that Norma Cenva had envisioned. Yes, the spice workers would understand his choice, and their sacrifice was unavoidable. He couldn't save them.

The two spotter pilots who had been paid to report the wormsign to him would be taken to Kolhar. They would remain under tight security and close observation. An evil man would simply have killed them to eliminate the last witnesses—the more cautious course—but these pilots had served him as he'd asked, and Josef always rewarded those who performed their jobs well.

He would keep the pilots alive on Kolhar, granting them their reward (though they might not immediately consider it a reward). Eventually, they would appreciate being sealed into tanks of spice gas and transformed into new Navigators. . . .

He hoped he had been able to get the message to Norma Cenva quickly enough. He could never tell when she was receptive, when she would just *know*. But he could always count on her.

Josef guided his escape flyer, looking down at the undulating ground as the sandworm circled the spice factory. On its approach, the worm offhandedly devoured several scout rollers that tried to escape across the dunes. The jettisoned melange container had landed more than a kilometer away in an adjacent valley; he would have someone retrieve it, once the dust settled around here.

Josef was startled and annoyed when Salvador's guard captain transmitted an urgent tight-beam message to the Imperial Barge, alerting them to the treachery. It would have been simpler to take care of the barge if the crew remained ignorant, but Josef had planned for that already. He sent a signal to orbit. "Grandmother, are you there and prepared?"

He activated a screen in his cockpit, a projection from a nearby VenHold ship in space that was tracking the Imperial vessel. Transmissions were picked up, alarms sounded. Only a skeleton crew remained aboard the barge, but they were already priming their engines and setting their mechanical navigation system to escape. Their old FTL drive would not be fast enough, and he wasn't sure they could activate the backup Holtzman engines in time.

"I am here," Norma said. "As are the rest of our warships."

With a shimmering wink, twenty fully armed VenHold vessels emerged from foldspace to surround the opulent Imperial Barge, weapons activated.

The barge pilot yelped into the comm line. "We've been betrayed!"

"Indeed you have," Josef muttered to himself.

Beneath him as he circled, Josef watched the whirlpool of sand. The giant worm rose up and crushed the spice factory, shearing away the metal plates. All the panicked transmissions ended abruptly. The worm circled back and struck again, then dragged the wreckage of the offending machinery under the surface.

On his cockpit screen, VenHold warships opened fire on the Imperial Barge.

But the Imperial ship, given the brief warning, had already begun its escape— and the crew proved to be unexpectedly swift in their reactions. The VenHold warships launched another volley of projectiles that blackened the barge's hull, but the pilot activated the emergency Holtzman engines and plunged blindly into foldspace.

Norma's voice came across the comm line. "They escaped, but they were clearly damaged."

Frowning, Josef said with a sigh, "A plan can have many prongs. That ship won't be going anywhere." He hoped Taref had indeed caused sufficient damage to their navigation systems.

Below, the worm retreated underground, leaving only a churned cauldron with a few rusty smears of spice. All the evidence was gone. And soon, with storms and other weather patterns, the excavation site would look as if it had never been disturbed by man.

*I only hope I have enough time and good fortune to do what needs to be accomplished.*

—VALYA HARKONNEN, to her sister, Tula

The Sisterhood possessed layer upon layer of secrets, and Valya Harkonnen was the sole custodian of the most important secret of all. *Mother Superior* Valya Harkonnen.

Explaining Dorotea's death involved meticulous choreography, and Valya attended to the details with intense focus. No mistakes. The scenario was obvious to the Sisters who ran into Mother Superior Raquella's chamber and saw the two women dead. And Dorotea's own Truthsayers were there to announce the veracity of Valya's account.

The following morning, she stood alongside Sister Fielle and Sister Olivia on the grass of the commons, watching as gray smoke curled from the top of the masonry crematorium structure. Dull gray clouds overhead matched the color of the smoke. Valya shivered as a chill wind cut through her robe.

Prior to her death, Mother Superior Raquella had left instructions that she wanted no funeral for herself and no mourning. Back on Rossak, the body of any dead Sister would have been cast into the jungle, for nature to reclaim. Here on Wallach IX she had asked to be cremated without fanfare, her ashes scattered in the central commons of the school complex.

Since Dorotea, overcome with grief, guilt, and despair, had purportedly killed herself after the Mother Superior's death, Valya seized the opportunity to suggest that they be cremated together. It was fitting, she said, since their bodies had fallen together in the end. She chose her words with great care to make the point without lying—especially in the company of the six orthodox Sisters who had come from Salusa Secundus. "It is a perfect symbol of what we agreed to do, to show that Dorotea truly and fundamentally rejoined our Sisterhood."

Since Valya was now the Mother Superior, the other Sisters did not challenge her suggestion. She watched the smoke continue to dance out of the chimney. Both bodies were fully consumed now, along with any lingering evidence of Dorotea's murder.

And what evidence could there be? Those last moments were locked inside Valya's mind. "Dorotea took her own life," she asserted, standing firm with her story. "Just before she died, Mother Superior Raquella did something to Dorotea's mind, changed her somehow. Dorotea was distraught, overwhelmed. She took the knife in her hands and plunged it into her own throat. I saw it myself."

The visiting Salusan Sisters were appalled and outraged at the turn of events, suspicious that Valya might have murdered her rival, possibly even the old Mother Superior, too. But three of Dorotea's companions were also skilled Truthsayers. They had faced Valya with their veiled accusations, scrutinized her as she repeated her story. "Listen to my words." She allowed just the right mix of anger and indignation to mingle with deep, heartfelt sadness, and added a customized edge to her powerful Voice. "Dorotea *took her own life. She stabbed herself with the knife.* I did *not touch her.*"

Even the most skeptical of the Truthsayers could detect no falsehood in her words—and Valya reminded them of the promises they had made to the revered Raquella Berto-Anirul. They must all accept Valya as the next Mother Superior.

Now, as the last smoke wafted out of the crematorium chimney, Valya said, "Although Mother Superior Raquella disdained emotional involvement, I can't help feeling great sadness. But she died knowing we had reached an agreement, that the schism was healed and the two factions of the Sisterhood could go forward united, stronger than ever. I intend to follow those wishes and do everything possible to ensure the extraordinary future Raquella envisioned."

Fielle and Olivia nodded, remaining close beside her. The other Sisters had lined up on the commons, including the six orthodox visitors, all enduring the cold wind.

Fielle said, "Mother Superior had faith that you would both do what is best for the Sisterhood. Dorotea must have had her own insight, a tragic one that led to her suicide. Was that a failure, or a radical decisive action? Maybe she knew that, despite the best intentions, having two Mother Superiors would eventually lead to division again."

Valya liked the sound of that. "I choose to believe Dorotea wanted to prevent further chaos."

Sister Olivia was shaking her head, deeply bothered. She kept both hands in the large side pockets of her robe, accentuating the pear shape of her body. Valya realized that the Sister Mentat was waiting to be formally recognized by her Mother Superior. "Yes, Olivia?"

"I was following a projection. Raquella was the founder of our order, and Dorotea led the other Sisters on Salusa. Now we've lost both of them, our best chance for reconciliation." Her expression grew agitated, and she fidgeted. "What will become of us now? I want to do as Mother Superior Raquella would have wished."

"*I* am the Mother Superior now," Valya said, firm but not angry. "And you are overwrought. I need you, as a Mentat and a Sister, to control your emotions. Only in that manner can we succeed against all of our challenges. We must work harder to master our feelings. Look what despair did to Dorotea."

A startled expression. Then: "Yes, Mother Superior! I'm sorry, Mother Superior. I shouldn't be worried about our Sisterhood, with you leading us. Perhaps I should go to the pharmacy for a sedative?"

"I'll leave that to you," Valya smiled gently. With a quick bow, Olivia hurried away.

"Your friend has a tendency to be nervous," Valya said to Fielle. "We cannot afford hysteria or rash decisions. Raquella worried about the survival of the Sisterhood when she chose her successor. That part is past now, and I have even bigger dreams. As Mother Superior, I will change the emphasis of our teachings, focusing on allied mental and physical disciplines. Sisters must learn how to fight and defend themselves on a personal and collective basis—but we can't let outsiders suspect just how powerful we are. We have a great deal of work to do, momentous challenges to face."

And Valya knew she would also have to keep the secret of the breeding-record computers from all but her inner circle of Sisters. It had been done before.

Fielle lifted her chin. "I will aid you with my Mentat projections. What do you plan, Mother Superior?"

"Our Sisters will train here on Wallach IX, and they will also serve on Salusa Secundus, all loyal to the Mother Superior. I would like to post them in each of the noble houses of the Landsraad as well. As our influence spreads, the Sisterhood will grow stronger. Those who remain at the Imperial Court will reassure the Emperor so that he continues to accept our order."

Fielle coughed in the dry, cold air. "I would like to be more than a Sister Mentat, Mother Superior. With your permission, I feel I am ready to face the Agony. If I become a Reverend Mother, the Sisterhood will grow even stronger."

Valya stared hard at her for a moment. "That is not a decision to make lightly . . . and even with the refined Rossak drug, many candidates still die in the attempt. Sister Fielle, in you I see not just a possible Reverend Mother, but a possible leader. I think Raquella saw that as well."

"But how could I lead other Reverend Mothers without being one myself?"

"You are a *Sister Mentat*, an essential element of our organization. I will depend on you for advice. I need Sisters I can rely on. You were there when Mother Superior Raquella died. You saw that she put her faith in me, and I put my faith in you now. The Sisterhood needs you, Fielle. *I* need you at this critically important time in our history."

"As you wish, Mother Superior." For a moment the Sister Mentat seemed disappointed, but she mastered her emotions, and Valya saw her features relax in acceptance. "I will do as you command."

As Valya watched the gray smoke dissipate, she thought of her own rapid ascension here. The library of ancient experiences and knowledge in Other Memories had made her wise beyond her years.

She also knew that the resources of the Sisterhood gave her a clearer path to advance House Harkonnen. She could accomplish both of the goals that had consumed her for so long. As she co-opted the Salusan Sisters, she would gain greater influence with the Imperial throne, find and expand opportunities, seek ways to increase Harkonnen participation in the Landsraad. Maybe find a place for Danvis, maybe use Tula as a breeding mistress . . .

Griffin would have been proud of Valya. She knew that her beloved brother would have agreed with what she intended to do next.

The last wisps of smoke from the crematorium washed away in the morning breeze. It was over now. Both Dorotea and Raquella had been reduced to fine ash. Valya inhaled a long, deep breath of cold air, but didn't allow herself a smile. She would continue to control her emotions.

"After we scatter the ashes," she said, "I will make preparations to go to the Imperial Court and inform the orthodox Sisters of the deaths of both Raquella and Dorotea, as well as the good news that we are once again unified, and that I am the new Mother Superior. The six Salusan Sisters who came with Dorotea will accompany me to vouch for what they witnessed here."

Fielle added, "And you must arrange for a new Truthsayer for the Emperor, now that Dorotea is gone."

Valya had already been considering possibilities, reluctant to let one of Dorotea's original followers take such an important role, though Salvador might insist on it. Valya needed her own loyal Truthsayers. "I will take Sister Olivia with me on this visit, and three or four other Wallach Sisters as well. I want you to remain here and manage the school in my absence."

Fielle lowered her voice. "We dare not share the knowledge of the computers with the Salusan Sisters. That would shatter the Sisterhood again."

"We kept that secret on Rossak, and we will keep it here, too." Valya took a deep breath, as she pondered the future of the Sisterhood before her. "We will be a long time recovering from what the Emperor did to us on Rossak, and we must take great care not to incite extreme reactions. We will not become fanatical Butlerians, but we will quietly demonstrate that our human abilities are superior. And after generations of carefully modeled, studied, and manipulated breeding, we will advance humanity even further."

When she visited the Imperial Court, Valya would take stock of the women there, assigning some of them back to Wallach IX, where they could be closely watched, while others might be more malleable and left on Salusa. She would also assign some of her faithful Sisters from Wallach IX to fill certain roles on Salusa. It would be a gradual process, requiring years, maybe even generations. Mother Superior Raquella had taught her how to think in the very long term.

"Our task will be easier, and far less dangerous, once the Butlerian hysteria quiets down," Valya mused.

"Without Manford Torondo, the movement will fracture and fade away," Fielle said. "I'm surprised he hasn't been assassinated yet—by Josef Venport or someone else."

Valya's voice was completely even. "Are you volunteering for the assignment?"

"No, Mother Superior! I didn't mean to suggest the Sisterhood would condone anything like that."

Valya arched her eyebrows. "You should make a Mentat projection on the possibilities and probabilities. We might be better off if the Butlerian leader were out of the way."

"Or worse off, if someone even more dangerous took his place."

Two black-robed Sisters emerged from the crematorium, each carrying an urn. The ashes would still be warm, reminding Valya of how a body's warmth lingered even after the heart had stopped beating. In time, the memory of the traitor Dorotea would grow as cold as her ashes that were soon to be spread on the ground. Valya would make sure that Dorotea was not revered, her actions not emulated. Perhaps even her name would be forgotten.

Raquella, though, was a different matter. There would be statues erected in her honor, and her memory would endure as long as the Sisterhood. And Valya Harkonnen would forever be known as her chosen successor, the bearer of her eternal torch.

Valya knew she was also much more than that. . . .

*The tangible expression of the human soul lies in the record of our thoughts and actions, and how we influence future generations.*
—GILBERTUS ALBANS, last letter to Erasmus, found and decoded by Mentat Zendur (never delivered)

By night, the tangled sangrove forest was eerie and threatening, but Anna made her way along instinctive paths. She wasn't afraid, because she had Erasmus with her—both the comforting voice in her ear, and the physical memory core that she had bound to her body beneath her clothing.

The gelsphere glowed through the material with varying degrees of brightness, providing faint illumination to light her way. Sometimes the orb went entirely dark when the robot's spy-eyes sensed that Butlerians might be nearby. Once, he whispered to her to stop moving, and she froze, in total darkness, listening while someone moved through the forest nearby. When it was safe, she continued to make her way from the besieged Mentat School.

Anna hadn't been instructed in physical combat. As the Emperor's sister, she had led a pampered life, and when she trained with the Sisters on Rossak as well as at the Mentat School, her studies had been devoted to focusing her mind.

Now, as she slipped through the forest murk, balancing on the upthrust roots and taking care not to slip into the water, Anna heard faint voices seeping into her thoughts from memory . . . but not her own memory. The danger to the Mentat School and to the Headmaster brought the ghost whispers frothing out of her personal turmoil. Those clamoring memories must be echoes of past lives—female ancestors whose spirits were imprisoned within the double-helix cage of her DNA. Yet how could they be? Though she had survived the Rossak poison, Anna was not a Reverend Mother, and could only hear the whispers of what it must be like to be one.

The most important, and clearest, advisory voice belonged to Erasmus. "I can guide you with my spy-eyes while we are near the school. Did you memorize the new path the Mentats made?"

"I know the path, and I know my own shortcuts."

"You're a clever girl," Erasmus said. "I am proud of you." His comment made her feel good, and he added, "We need to maintain a swift pace, to get as far as we can from the Butlerian camp before sunrise."

She felt distraught and wanted him to understand her urgency. "They're going to execute Headmaster Albans. Shouldn't we try to rescue him?"

At the thought of execution, Anna suddenly reeled as howling childhood memories surged back—her father forcing her to sit at his side while CET members were murdered in front of her. He had insisted that the experience would strengthen her, make her glad to see justice done. But it hadn't. Instead, the bloodshed had showed her the horror of harsh penalties.

She didn't want Headmaster Albans to face such a terrible fate, but felt helpless to save him. She wanted him to find some way to escape and flee into obscurity as Toure Bomoko had, while the rest of the CET members were executed in his stead. She wondered if the same thing would happen here. Gilbertus was a very smart man.

"If Headmaster Albans were to escape," she asked, "wouldn't Manford still want someone to die instead?"

"All of the other students, I expect," Erasmus said.

"I don't want them all to die, and I don't want the Headmaster to die either."

"All humans die. The only variable is timing. Come—we must hurry."

"Where will we go afterward?" Anna asked.

"I have not calculated that yet."

Anna picked her way around the tangled roots, careful not to fall into the water, where glints of silver showed night-prowling razorjaws, like reflections from shattered bits of mirror. Her progress was painstakingly slow.

"The water is not deep," he said. "It will be faster if you wade through the channels."

"The fish would eat me," Anna said.

The robot core said, "I can fix that." A pulse of blue light crackled through the water, a power discharge that lit the marshy streams with cold fire. Like bubbles rising in a cauldron, hundreds of silvery fish bobbed belly-up, dead.

"Gilbertus placed many defenses around the school, but I considered them insufficient, so I added more. The channel is safe for you now. I'll tell you when you need to climb back up on the roots."

Trusting him entirely, Anna dropped into the cold water and waded along. Now she made better progress through the sangroves, safe from razorjaws, but she knew there was still danger from Butlerian scouts who roamed the swamps.

As she sloshed along, a buzzing sound came close—a cloud of stinging night-gnats. Anna plunged her head underwater, trusting that the razorjaws were still incapacitated. The swarming insects swirled low, dusted the top of the water in search of blood, and then flew away. Finally, Anna raised her head and shoulders out of the water, dripping wet, and kept moving.

After several more minutes, Erasmus said, "I suggest you climb up on the roots now. I am recharging the pulse-batteries through the waterways, but more razorjaws may come soon."

Anna hoisted herself onto the suspended roots and climbed along, carefully choosing her footing. Around her, the sky began to brighten with the approach of dawn. Looking back in the direction of the Butlerian camp, she spotted a shadowy figure moving through the sangroves—and in the same instant the man saw her, too. He had broad shoulders, and a square of fabric was wrapped around his head. His eyes were bright in the swamp shadows.

"You're the girl Manford wants, the Emperor's sister." The man sprang toward her with a careful grace, bounding from one sangrove elbow to another. "Come with me, and you'll be in time to watch the Headmaster's execution."

Holding on to a branch, Anna scrambled backward and swung to another root. Sharp sticks scratched her, but she didn't feel the pain. Erasmus couldn't help her now.

The Butlerian man was swift and nimble as he chased her. He might have been an experienced hunter, accustomed to being outdoors, and he was in-tent on catching her. He grabbed Anna's arm, yanked her close. She started to scream, then bit it off, knowing the noise would only attract more atten-tion from the siege camp—and she didn't know how to fight such a muscular man.

She was about to ask Erasmus to save her when in her mind she heard a roar of whispering voices from generations of women, all long dead. They surged into her thoughts like a school of telepathic fish, showing her what Erasmus could not. Her muscles acted of their own accord, like loaded springs.

She ripped her arm free of the man's grasp. Moving as if another person were controlling her body, Anna planted her other hand squarely on his chest and shoved hard, knocking him off-balance. Surprised, he splashed backward into the channel. In a panic, he thrashed in the water . . . but when no razorjaws struck, he laughed. "I'm wet, but unharmed." He flashed his teeth.

In her ear, Erasmus said, "Allow me."

A wash of blue electricity exploded through the water, like an aurora distilled into the marsh. The Butlerian man jittered, convulsed, and fell backward into the water, belly-up like the fish.

"We need to keep moving," said the Erasmus voice in her ear. "Let me direct you now. My peripheral spy-eyes have detected an unexpected visitor who can aid us in our escape."

Anna didn't ask questions. "Tell me where to go."

IT WAS STILL dark, shortly before dawn, when Anari Idaho entered the tent. The three dead guards had been taken away, the gash in the fabric of the back wall stitched shut. Eight Butlerian guards now replaced the ones Draigo had killed, even though Gilbertus showed no inclination to escape.

"When the sun rises, Headmaster, you will meet your death at the blade of my sword," she said. "It was wise and honorable of you not to flee when you had the chance."

"I made a promise," he said. "I explained that to my well-intentioned student who tried to rescue me."

"He murdered three of the faithful. He is marked for death as well." Anari's face darkened. "We will hunt him down and kill him."

"I don't think so." He had faith that Draigo would carry out his mission; Gilbertus had gambled everything on that hope.

Anari waited in heavy silence for a long moment, but didn't argue with him. "Leader Torondo knows who and what you are. He will never rescind your sentence."

"I wouldn't expect him to. He is a man of clear-cut convictions. He follows a path that allows no room for learning or growth, to his detriment."

"He follows a holy path. I came to tell you to prepare yourself."

Gilbertus was relaxed, calm. He had meditated for hours and visited his Memory Vault that held all the bright spots of his life. "You're the one who is about to kill a man. Shouldn't *you* prepare yourself?"

"I am merely meting out justice. My sword is sharp. What more do I need to prepare?"

Gilbertus found it amusing. "And my mind is sharp. What more do I need to prepare?"

Flustered, Anari shook her head. "You were raised among the demon machines. They made you strange."

She left the prisoner tent, and Gilbertus returned to his meditation. Curiously, he found that he was able to focus better than he ever had in his life, and he understood why. He needed to cram all of his important thoughts into very little time.

AFTER TRYING TO rescue Headmaster Albans, Draigo spent most of the darkness eluding the Butlerian hunters. They chased after noises in the swamps—but he hardly made any sound at all. The hunting parties shouted back and forth, so that he knew exactly where they were. Overanxious for revenge, they blundered along, and the Mentat easily eluded them.

Still, he felt an emptiness in his chest. This wasn't sport. The Headmaster's life was on the line . . . and he had refused to be saved! If what Gilbertus said was true—that the Erasmus memory core still existed, and Anna Corrino needed to be rescued along with it—Directeur Venport would be very interested in both. Draigo had come to Lampadas in the hope of finding powerful allies against the barbarians. Even more important, he had *promised* his friend and mentor, Headmaster Albans, that he would keep Anna Corrino and the Erasmus core safe.

It was nearly dawn by the time he circled back toward the besieged school complex. He made his way through the sangrove swamps, threading the safe path through the hazards.

He was astonished when, out of the underbrush, Anna Corrino approached him, as if she expected to find him there. "You are Draigo Roget." She seemed to be reciting a file. "You trained for five years at the Mentat School, and scored higher than any other Mentat candidate. You graduated and were released. You are allied with Venport Holdings. No one at the school knew the identity of your benefactor until you were later encountered at the Thonaris shipyards."

After listening to the young woman rattle off the résumé of his life, Draigo said, "I came here to rescue the Headmaster, but he refused to accompany me. Instead, he made me promise to find you and . . . a thinking machine."

Anna laughed. "Erasmus and Headmaster Albans discussed letting you in on the secret some time ago." She paused as if listening to a voice only she could hear, then nodded to herself. "Erasmus says he wishes they had done it sooner. You would have been a great help to us."

"My ship can take you far from Lampadas, where you will be safe."

"Erasmus, too?" She self-consciously touched a bulge in her blouse. "Don't take us to Salusa Secundus, though. Salvador will destroy Erasmus because he does whatever the Butlerians tell him to."

"I have no intention of letting that robot memory core come to harm, and I won't let you become a hostage to the Butlerians either," Draigo said. "You should no longer be a pawn, Anna Corrino. First you went to the Sisterhood, then to the Mentat School, and now the Butlerians want you. But Directeur Venport has an isolated place to keep you where you'll be completely safe."

"No one can know," Anna said. "Not about me, or about Erasmus."

"No one will know. I promised Headmaster Albans."

As dawn brightened the sky, Draigo led her and her precious package out of the swamps, away from the Mentat School, to his hidden ship.

THE SUNSHINE FELT bright and warm on Gilbertus's face as the guards led him out of the prisoner tent. Lampadas had a yellow-white sun, and even though he had lived here for decades, the daylight still felt wrong to him. He'd been born under the bloated crimson sun of Corrin, a red giant whose light was so harsh that Erasmus had made him wear eye protection. Other slaves who worked outdoors went blind before they grew old . . . but in Erasmus's pens few human captives ever grew old.

Manford Torondo did Gilbertus a kindness by not binding his hands, and Anari Idaho did not manhandle him as he emerged into the central camp. Gilbertus showed no fear. He knew his students would be watching from the observation platforms, and he only hoped that the spectacle of his execution would provide enough of a distraction that Draigo could get Anna Corrino and Erasmus safely away.

He had no idea what sort of plan Draigo might develop. That was out of his hands. Erasmus would also understand the danger they faced. But Anna Corrino . . . she was a wild card. Even so, Gilbertus had faith in all three of them.

Deacon Harian and Sister Woodra stood at the edge of a cleared area in full view of the walled school complex. Gilbertus looked up, although the sun dazzled his eyes. He saw figures up on the school walls and observation decks.

The Butlerians had brought out a special chair from the headquarters tent, and Manford Torondo sat upon it, looking like a king on a little throne.

Gilbertus halted before the Butlerian leader, who had been propped up so that their eyes were at the same level. Manford said, "Even though I am saddened by your behavior and I feel betrayed by you, Gilbertus Albans, I still see the Headmaster of this school and the Mentat who helped me accomplish good things for the Butlerian cause."

Gilbertus raised his chin. "And I deeply regret having done any of them. I erred in trying to protect myself rather than standing up for my principles. I should have openly defied you long ago. You are wrong."

Hearing this, the Butlerians went into a barely suppressed fury. Gilbertus had promised himself he would make a statement, but he also had to be careful, because this mob could cause inconceivable damage to the school, not just to him. "You'll have me as your spectacle, but I remind you of your oath. You *will* save my school."

"I will save your school," Manford said. "I'll save the Mentats from themselves. They will continue their training, but they'll be reeducated. Mentats need to understand that their entire purpose is to supersede computers, not emulate them."

Gilbertus remained stony, realizing that was the best promise he would get. He knew Manford would alter the terms however he wished, and would make whatever justifications he needed.

He was not afraid of Manford's attempts at indoctrination, since he had trained his students how to *think*, rather than to blindly follow any doctrine. Gilbertus had given his cherished students the method, and their minds were tools that the Butlerians could not take away, short of killing them. The next Mentats would have to be careful and find ways to continue the great school, or perhaps Draigo might set up another Mentat learning academy someplace safe.

Gilbertus felt confident that Mentats would continue in some form or another, no matter what happened to him. And if the Mentats survived, then this was a worthwhile bargain.

Anari stood there, her sword gleaming in the bright dawn. Deacon Harian glared at him with loathing, blaming Gilbertus for the machines using human shields at the Bridge of Hrethgir, and for the generations of suffering before that. The accusations were ludicrous, and Gilbertus didn't bother to look at him.

Manford said, "You committed horrific crimes against your own race, Gilbertus Albans. If you recant and beg for forgiveness with all your heart and soul, God may forgive you. But I can make no promises, and you *will* die today."

"I wouldn't want you making me promises on God's behalf. He may not feel obliged to honor them."

Harian looked even more offended than before, but Manford merely nodded. "That is your choice, Headmaster. God will do with you as He wishes."

Gilbertus gave a last smile. "I look forward to debating him."

Without being asked, he turned to face Anari Idaho and sank to his knees. He heard distant cries of dismay from the observation platforms and growls of outrage from the Butlerians, but it all retreated to a buzz in his mind.

"I know you're a good Swordmaster and your blade is sharp," he said.

Anari's voice cut crisply through the air. "I will do my job."

He bowed his head, closed his eyes, and withdrew into his Memory Vault, where he had many decades of life to revisit. He knew he had very little time, and memories moved at their own speed.

Gilbertus had spent the first portion of his life on Corrin, with all the care and teaching Erasmus had given him, yet now in memory he returned to his happy times on Lectaire, the seven years when he'd been a normal human being leading a quiet life, in good company. He'd made his first human friends there, including Jewelia, the first person he'd ever loved, an experience he held within him as a long-term treasure, even though it had not turned out as he hoped. Gilbertus also relived the pain of his broken heart, when she had chosen someone else, instead of him.

He remembered Jewelia's sweet, caring face, her carefree laugh, the good times they spent together. By now she would be old and quite possibly dead, but in his Memory Vault she remained as young and vibrant as the last time he saw her.

He spent that bright moment with her now, and didn't feel the pain when the sharp sword made its deadly arc.

*Sand flows through my veins, dust fills my lungs, and the taste of spice lingers in my mouth. The desert is inside me and cannot be washed away.*

—desert hymn

H e discarded everything from offworld before returning to the desert. He felt like a prodigal son with no family to receive him. Taref had no place to go, not on Arrakis, not anywhere.

Thanks to the largesse of Directeur Venport, he could have bought himself the finest home in Arrakis City and a tanker of water to fill his household cistern. He could have traveled to Caladan, as he'd once fantasized . . . but that dream had crumbled into ashes, and he wondered why it had ever seemed important.

In his galactic journeys he had felt rain and sleet on his skin, and although those were wondrous experiences, Taref could not measure them against watching a yellow sunrise spill across the dunes, or the smell of raw melange from a fresh spice blow so pungent that it made him want to pull out his nose-plugs and inhale the desert's bounty deep into his lungs.

Taref didn't want to return to his sietch, though, at least not in defeat. He had ideas but didn't know what to do with them. The desert would help him find himself.

He considered his modified distilling suit, the one VenHold had given him with sophisticated "improvements." It was comfortable and functioned efficiently, but it smelled wrong, felt wrong. He stripped off the suit, intending to dispose of it, but realized he had only offworlder clothes with him, which would not let him survive in the desert. Instead, he sold the suit to a blue-eyed vendor, who immediately saw its value. Taref accepted the man's first offer, caring only that he had enough money to trade for an old but serviceable distilling suit. He should have thought of that before throwing away the money that Venport gave him, scattering coins in the street and watching scavengers rush in to retrieve them.

He carefully looked over the offered distilling suit before accepting it from the vendor. No true Freeman would ever surrender a good stillsuit, so this one must have come from the body of a dead man. Taref studied the fittings and seams and discovered where a knife puncture to the kidney area had been cleaned and repaired. Such things happened all the time. No desert dweller would let a suit go to waste, but would fix and reuse it. Taref donned the garment, fitted it to his body, and pronounced it acceptable. Then he left the vendor's shop and discarded his offworld clothes. They were worthless to him.

Though Directeur Venport had covered up the assassination of Emperor Salvador Corrino, Taref felt the stain of his own actions on his conscience. The Imperial Barge had escaped—but it would likely be lost, since he had sabotaged its navigation systems. He remembered, though, that he had not taken the time to finish his work, upset by Manford's ghost. Still, what he *had* done should be more than enough to make certain the barge was never seen again.

He learned that Directeur Venport had purged the records of the Arrakis City spaceport and the orbital tracking systems. Everyone back on Salusa Secundus would be mystified when the opulent Imperial Barge vanished en route— another tragic loss, like so many other ships that had been lost recently, due to the dangers of galactic travel. . . .

Taref also wanted to vanish. The desert would enfold and caress him, in spite of its dangers, which were at least familiar to him. Maybe he would die, and maybe he would be saved, but he needed to find out one way or the other.

He left the city behind, along with its ways that were nearly as alien to him as those of Venport Holdings. Taref had his stillsuit, a literjon of water, spice, and food. A man of the desert required nothing more.

As a dreamer, he'd once led a difficult life in the sietch, estranged from his father and brothers and from many of the other Freemen. They only wanted to keep doing things as they'd done them for centuries, never daring to extend their experiences beyond a parochial comfort zone.

Yes, Taref had seen things far away from that life, and learned from his experiences. He had dreamed, but had come to realize he'd been dreaming of the wrong things. Now it was time for a change. Again.

Alone, he wandered into the furnace-hot, shimmering wasteland.

*When I gaze up into the night sky, I see as many opportunities as there are stars.*

—DIRECTEUR JOSEF VENPORT, excerpt from
a speech to business associates

Making his way across the small Caladan spaceport, Vorian Atreides hardly noticed anyone around him, did not hear the noise of conversation or the engines outside as the occasional shuttle arrived and departed. It was early evening, and he was alone after a long day of last-minute preparations.

Tragedy seemed to follow him like a shadow. He had to leave beautiful Caladan, again.

Vor felt scarred inside, as if he had been broken and improperly healed. A dark fear lingered in his heart—not for himself, but for everyone in his extended family. Any member of his bloodline was in danger, because the Harkonnens blamed him for the fall of Abulurd decades ago, and Griffin's death on Arrakis only last year. They would seek vengeance on any Atreides they could find.

Tula Harkonnen had vanished, but records showed that a small cruiser had been stolen from the Caladan spaceport right after Orry's murder, and after she had attacked Vor in his room at the inn. He didn't know where the murderous Harkonnen girl was going, but Tula had slipped away, leaving a trail of blood that someday he might be able to follow.

She'd left a bloody message of vendetta, and Vor had sent an urgent warning to anyone who claimed Atreides lineage on Caladan. Yet he could not stay there and risk them further, so he made it known that he was leaving. He would go back to Kepler, despite the Emperor's proscription—a promise that had been forced on Vor out of Salvador's pique. But Vor would risk Imperial ire to protect his dispersed family. Maybe they were in danger, too.

He didn't know how many of his descendants he could locate. Back during the early years of the Jihad, when he was a young officer traveling from star system to star system, he'd had lovers on many different planets. Vor sent an urgent message to the banking representative on Kolhar who had helped him arrange discreet financial transactions over the years, including the recent infusion of wealth to Lankiveil. The bank had contacts across the Imperium, and Vor ordered a detailed research report on all possible Atreides descendants.

*We will never forget,* Tula Harkonnen had written. And then she had disappeared from Caladan.

Did all of House Harkonnen seek the vendetta? How far had the poison spread? Griffin had come after Vor, too. While working with Vergyl Harkonnen on Lankiveil, Vor had been invited into his home, shared his food. But even though he had secretly rescued the family from financial ruin, they would not embrace him if they ever learned who he was. Believing that Vorian Atreides had harmed innocents in their family, they would take revenge on innocents in his extended family.

Xavier Harkonnen had been Vor's sworn enemy before Serena Butler's Jihad, then became his closest friend after Vor switched sides. Decades later, Xavier's grandson Abulurd had been like a son to Vorian, his military protégé, until the young man's cowardly disgrace. Even though Vor had saved Abulurd from execution, sending him into exile instead, the Harkonnens did not consider that a favor.

Generations later, Griffin Harkonnen hunted Vor down, intending to kill him. Now his sister Tula expanded the bloodshed, murdering Atreides descendants who had never even met Vor until recently. With Shander and Orry dead, Willem was the next likely target—and now Willem had sworn vengeance against the Harkonnen murderers. Vorian foresaw a spiraling cycle of bloodshed and retaliation. When would it ever end?

In the spaceport building, he watched through a large viewing window as his designated shuttle set down in a pool of light and prepared to release its passengers. He had spent hours with a distraught Willem, confessing the chain of events that had led to the murders. What had seemed like distant and esoteric family history was now painfully relevant.

When Vor offered to remain on Caladan, to help stand guard over Willem and other Atreides cousins, the young man resented the suggestion. "If Harkonnens come to Caladan, I will kill them myself . . . but if you leave here, maybe they'll hunt you instead. So go far away, and I'll keep myself safe."

It felt like a crushing weight on Vorian's shoulders. Willem, too, blamed him.

And so Vor had booked passage on the next outbound spacefolder, wherever it was headed. At the first opportunity he would transfer to another route and make his way to Kepler, warn his family there. After that . . . he didn't know where he would go, but it couldn't be anywhere that would expose his family to additional attention.

Now, in the reflection of the spaceport's plaz window, he saw a tall, thin figure approach from behind. Vor didn't need to turn in order to recognize him; he felt his pulse speed up as he wondered what Willem was doing here. "You shouldn't have come here." Vor looked sidelong at him. "I told you it isn't safe to be seen with me."

Willem looked ready to argue. "I've decided to go with you. I'm strong, I can fly ships, I can fight. I can help you find the Harkonnens." He held up a ticket for Vor to see.

"I'm not hunting Harkonnens. I'm going to warn the rest of my family, who are your distant cousins. I don't need my"—stress blocked Vor's mind for a moment, and finally he finished the calculations—"great-great-great-grandson with me, looking for vengeance. There are things I need to do, quickly and efficiently."

Crossing his arms over his chest, Willem said, "For years I served in the Air Patrol, so I know how to handle myself in a crisis. I can be cool, and I am not out for blood. But with Orry dead, and Uncle Shander . . . and my parents, there's not much left for me on Caladan. I can stay behind, alone, and be reminded every day. Or I can go with you."

Vor met the young man's urgent gaze, saw a hint of Leronica there, from across the generations. And he saw a bit of himself, too. Something in Willem's demeanor reminded him of his own cocky determination when he'd been a young officer, the confidence and certainty in his own abilities.

Vorian Atreides had come to Caladan to regain a grounding in his life, to find his family and reestablish a long-lost connection. That connection was not about a *place*, but about the bonds of blood. "I'll let you convince me, then," he said with a small smile. "But I won't have a loose cannon at my side seeking revenge."

Willem's eyes shone with gratitude. The shuttle up to the spacefolder was ready to be boarded. "I'm levelheaded. But if a Harkonnen tries to kill me or you, I'll kill them first."

Vor said, "I can accept that." Together, they boarded the shuttle.

*How do we measure the loss of Salvador Corrino? Is it a blow to the Imperium, or do the people actually benefit from his demise? The answer rests in large part on the shoulders of his brother, our newly seated Emperor.*

—"anonymous" pundit (name ~~known,~~ but withheld)

The Imperial Barge had vanished somewhere in the vast emptiness, and the ache left a hole in Roderick's chest. As the weeks passed and no word came, he could not escape the grim conclusion. Salvador was gone!

After being pressed for answers, Directeur Josef Venport said that the Emperor and his entourage had inspected the spice-harvesting operations and then departed as scheduled. An Imperial investigation team descended upon the Arrakis spaceport, but found only a notation in the log that the barge had departed on its slow, safe journey with old-fashioned FTL engines.

The mechanics and engineers who had checked the opulent barge before its departure from Salusa faced intense scrutiny, but their records were impeccable. The spacecraft had passed all routine safety tests. Under interrogation by a Truthsayer, the Arrakis City maintenance crew revealed nothing other than a routine servicing.

Roderick dispatched another team, including two Scalpel practitioners, to interrogate the members of House Péle who had last worked on the vessel before Salvador confiscated it as punishment for their fraudulent schemes. Even the most skeptical questioner found no evidence that House Péle had planned some subtle sabotage in retaliation for their immense political and financial losses.

Salvador was gone. Navigation accidents occurred, and too frequently. Emperor Salvador Corrino had vanished, along with his ship and crew. An ignominious, but not unexpected, accident.

In a recorded message to Roderick, to express his concerns and condolences, Josef Venport shook his head sadly. "Space travel involves risks, and far too many ships disappear. Look at the appalling record of EsconTran. Even though the Imperial Barge avoided using foldspace technology, the design of the FTL engines was centuries old. If only all vessels would use my Navigators, then we could ensure their safety. Let us hope that Emperor Salvador has only been delayed, and will arrive safely soon."

But the Emperor had been missing for weeks past his expected arrival.

Now, Roderick Corrino faced his own challenge. He stood alone in the Audience Chamber, staring at the unoccupied green-crystal throne, listening to the silence, seeing the *emptiness* where his brother had held court so many times. A deep sadness washed through him, but this had to be done. The business of the Imperium must continue. The Emperor had been absent for too long.

Just as heartbreaking, their sister, Anna, was still missing on Lampadas, with no sign of her at the overrun Mentat School. Roderick felt another twinge of anger. Yet another violent riot caused by Butlerian mobs, and Headmaster Albans had been executed after an unbelievable accusation. Roderick felt sorry for the Headmaster, who had seemed like a reasonable man. Had the whole Imperium gone insane?

Perhaps the mad Butlerian movement was at last imploding. He could only hope.

Roderick felt the burn of anger and dismay deep inside him. A Butlerian riot had killed sweet Nantha, another killed Headmaster Albans, and now Anna had also disappeared in the upheaval. Maybe Manford was actually holding her as a hostage for future leverage. But why would he keep her hidden? Maybe she had escaped—or worse, dear Anna might be dead.

He decided to send an army to Lampadas to interrogate the Butlerians, to search for his missing sister and learn what had really happened. Manford would not like it, but Roderick didn't care. The mad dog of a Butlerian leader had to be put in his place. And now Roderick was in a position to do what had to be done.

First, though, he would deal with the matter of the empty throne. Each day Haditha had been counseling him, supporting him, and listening to him. "You must take the throne—provisionally. The Imperium requires more than just the hope of a leader. Where there is doubt, there is weakness. If your brother returns, you can step aside." She came close, held him. "But you must become the Corrino Emperor."

Knowing he could no longer delay, he called an urgent meeting with the highest-ranking members of the Landsraad and his most valued advisers. While waiting for them to arrive, Roderick stepped onto the raised dais and peered into the translucent facets of the great throne, where the reflections created a glittering green universe. It was the throne that Faykan Butler—crowned Emperor Faykan

Corrino—first used when he forged the Imperium out of the rubble of the Jihad. The throne had held Emperor Jules Corrino and then Emperor Salvador Corrino . . . the *Corrinos*. Roderick had not dared to dream that he would be the Emperor one day. Nor had he wanted it.

He had spent so much time at his brother's side that he had few close friends among the nobles and courtiers. Salvador and Anna had demanded most of his attention in their own ways, so that he had little left for Haditha and his own children. Even Nantha.

Now, however, he would have to concentrate on his own political alliances, if he hoped to succeed as the acting Emperor.

Of those he trusted in the palace, the Truthsayer Dorotea was well respected, but she had not yet returned from her mysterious mission to Wallach IX, and he didn't have as much trust and faith in the other Sisters. For the most part, he would be alone with his own decisions.

Hearing a murmur of voices, Roderick watched the highest-ranking members of the Landsraad file into the chamber. He stood beside the throne and waved them forward. They had appointed Naza Ibilin as their spokesperson. She was a small woman, normally quiet and subdued—at least publicly—but she wielded a great deal of influence behind the scenes. She stepped to the dais, gave a brief, formal bow.

"What happened was a terrible thing, Prince Roderick. Whether Emperor Salvador is dead, or unable to return here, the result is the same. The Imperium must have an Emperor. No one questions the succession. The noble houses of the Landsraad beg you to accept the crown so that the peoples of all planets can be reassured."

A number of leading nobles stepped forward to join Naza Ibilin. "Times are troubled enough, Prince Roderick," said Chamberlain Bakim, a man of about Roderick's age. "At this time of tragedy, you are our salvation, and can assure stability. We look to you to lead us."

Roderick knew the parliamentary rules regarding succession—he had, in fact, reviewed the document recently, although it made his heart heavy—and this was certainly a quorum. He realized that the crowd was composed almost entirely of moderates, none of Directeur Venport's most vehement supporters, and none of the most vocal adherents to the Butlerian pledge. Good.

"You want me to become Emperor." He placed his palm on the cool surface of the throne, and the nobles fell immediately silent. "With my brother gone, the Imperium needs a strong leader. Our planets are being torn apart by this feud between Venport Holdings and the Butlerians, a feud that seems to disregard the Imperial throne. That must change. We survived the thinking machines—are we so determined to destroy ourselves?"

Naza Ibilin interjected, "That is why we must schedule your coronation quickly, Sire."

Glancing at the ornate trappings of the chamber, he was reminded of the glorious history this great room represented, including the end of the League of Nobles and the formation of the Imperium. Roderick felt responsible for much more than the Corrino name.

"I accept it," he said, "though if my brother should return, I will declare that he is the rightful Emperor and will step down from the throne."

The nobles muttered, some with obvious dissatisfaction, some in approval. It was possible that they believed his words were merely a pro forma statement. A few, he supposed, might even assume that Roderick had secretly assassinated his own brother.

A chill ran down his back.

Haditha entered through the chamber doors and made her way up the steps of the dais. She had aged since Nantha's death, but he still found her as beautiful as ever. Haditha stood proudly at his side, next to the throne. And in a quiet voice, as if they were the only ones having a conversation, she said, "You must do this, my gallant husband. No one else can draw the Imperium together."

He looked at her long and hard, feeling emotions well up inside him as he thought of the good things she represented in his personal life—his anchor, his beloved wife, the mother of his children. In some ways Haditha was stronger and wiser than he was. He saw all he needed to know in her eyes.

OVER THE NEXT several days, Prince Roderick, soon to be *Emperor* Roderick, received messages from Directeur Josef Venport and Leader Manford Torondo, oddly similar communications in which each man offered both condolences and congratulations. Manford's message sounded terse and false, and made no mention of the missing Anna. Venport's message dwelled upon the "complex and difficult" situation surrounding the proposed Imperial control of spice harvesting and distribution operations. He said he hoped that Roderick would be amenable to "extensive consultation on the best way to move forward on this important commercial and strategic matter."

Salvador had never been confident enough to stand up to Manford Torondo, but Roderick intended to be a stronger leader. He was not intimidated by the fanatical demagogue. And now that his sister had vanished, he had a great many questions for the Butlerian leader. But he would not protect VenHold's position as the dominant power in the Imperium either. It was time for the Corrinos to become the power they were destined to be.

Roderick had the two message cylinders on the desk in his private study, adjoining the palace apartments he shared with his family. Haditha had been with him when he opened the messages, and they had read the letters together.

Glowering at the signatures, he swept the cylinders onto the floor and rose to his feet. "Those two men are tearing the Imperium apart, and I will not have either of them at my coronation. I will show them that I am not weak, nor am I afraid of either of them. This throne will no longer be irrelevant."

He had ordered General Odmo Saxby to put the Imperial military forces on high alert, but years of Salvador's rule had left them unprepared and in disarray. Their warships were customarily transported in VenHold spacefolders, and they were at the mercy of wherever the pilots took them. Roderick vowed to eliminate corrupt officers and whip the Imperial Armed Forces into shape, but that would take time and considerable effort. Some of the noble houses would not be happy to see those officers relieved of duty, because of the flow of political and financial favors that had led to them receiving their positions.

Roderick intended to begin with Saxby, a man who had very little backbone, despite his high rank. Obviously, he was being propped up by influential noblemen, but the new Emperor was prepared to battle them. If the Landsraad League fell, those nobles would lose everything.

Haditha agreed, but understood the battle to come. "Shall I take our children someplace safer? Or *send* them someplace safer, while I remain here at your side? If there is unrest, you will not want to be alone—"

Thinking of Nantha, they exchanged mournful gazes. Finally, he said, "Our living children must be kept safe. Javicco will be Emperor someday. And as much as I want you protected so that I can rest easy, I'd like you to remain here with me. I'll need your advice."

Haditha kissed him and headed for the door. "I'll make all the arrangements . . . and I'm glad you're not trying to send me away. I don't think even Imperial guards could have made me leave."

*For too long, the Imperium has been ruled by greedy noblemen whose
faith is weak. They hardly give any thought to the common man.*
  —SWORDMASTER ANARI IDAHO, comment to Manford Torondo

Mother Superior Valya Harkonnen arrived in time to witness the unexpected coronation of Emperor Roderick Corrino I. Her timing was accidental, but impeccable.

In transit from Wallach IX, she was accompanied by Sister Olivia and six others, including four of the orthodox Sisters who had come with Dorotea. In her new role as Mother Superior, Valya wore a robe more ornamented than her previous garments, but her most important trapping was her confidence; her personality was both armor and sword. She was the leader of the unified Sisterhood and not yet twenty-five years old—although she carried thousands of years of experience from the Other Memories inside her head.

When the eight Sisters tried to make their way to the Imperial Palace, though, the celebratory throng made passage impossible. All around the city, Imperial soldiers wore formal cloaks and armor, protected by body shields.

The Mother Superior drank in details, asked questions, and quickly discovered that Roderick was about to assume the throne. Emperor Salvador had vanished in a space-travel mishap and was presumed dead—coincidentally close to the time when Raquella and Dorotea died.

Sister Olivia had parallel thoughts. "It seems to be a time for new leaders, Mother Superior."

Valya responded with a thin smile and noticed the orthodox Sisters nodding. Keeping her voice pitched low, she projected her words so that only her companions could hear. "Emperor Salvador was no friend to the Sisterhood. Let us not forget what he ordered on Rossak—even Dorotea was burdened with guilt for her part in that. Let us hope that Roderick will be a different sort of Emperor."

In the crowded streets, Valya sent two of the orthodox Sisters ahead to find other members of Dorotea's faction, to inform them that the Mother Superior had arrived. When she and her companions finally drew in sight of the plaza that fronted the palace, Valya heard someone shout to them.

Among the gathered celebrants, she recognized a stocky woman who had once served beside her as an assistant proctor on Rossak, Sister Ninke. She was one of the women who had adamantly opposed the use of computers and had gone with Dorotea to the Imperial Court. Nevertheless, Ninke had seemed like a sensible person, not prone to hysteria.

As their Mother Superior, Valya would have to stop thinking of these other Sisters as traitors. She needed their talents, especially the Truthsayers, to add to the Sisters on Wallach IX. Trust, though, would be a long time coming, and loyalty could only be earned over time, through actions.

Ninke had more gray hair than before, though only a year had passed since they'd seen each other. Despite her size, she moved deftly through the crowds. She gestured. "This way!"

She led Valya, Olivia, and their companions around one side to a more open space. They flowed through clusters of people who were pushing their way forward for a better view of the coronation ceremony. When Valya's path became blocked, she raised her voice and said in an authoritative tone, "Move aside! Imperial business!"

It wasn't the forceful, commanding Voice she had used as a weapon against Master Placido or Sister Dorotea, but the people responded nevertheless. Spectators scurried out of the way, blundering into others as they did so. With surprised or angry glares, they looked at the troupe of women as they marched through.

Ninke said, "We received the transmission when your ship arrived, and the Sisters are prepared for your arrival." Her gaze locked on Valya. "Crown Prince Roderick was expecting Dorotea."

"Roderick needn't worry," Valya said. "He will have his replacement Truthsayer, and your own Sisters will explain the agreement that Dorotea and Mother Superior Raquella reached. The Sisterhood must be strong and unified again."

Still unsure, Ninke continued to lead them forward. "We have a private box from which to observe the coronation ceremony. Zimia was not prepared for the influx of travelers from across the Imperium. Security is extremely tight, to prevent another backlash and frenzy. Leader Torondo was not invited, and neither was Directeur Venport. Prince Roderick was afraid their presence might cause unnecessary agitation."

*And indeed they might,* Valya thought.

When the Sisters reached the central square, a new path opened for them. Ninke spoke to one of the uniformed soldiers waiting at a stairway to the observation pavilions, and an Imperial guard escorted the women to a private box. From that vantage they could see the coronation stage and the green-crystal throne that had been placed there. A large group of Dorotea's followers awaited their arrival. Valya knew most of them.

Sister Esther-Cano and other Sisters rose to their feet and gave curt bows when Valya approached; then all resumed their seats. Valya sensed hesitation and uneasiness, questions and buried challenges. She hoped that with four orthodox Sisters vouching for her claims, Dorotea's followers would honor the agreement with Mother Superior. If not, Valya was prepared to fight them in personal combat and kill any dissenters.

Nearby boxes were crowded with gaudily uniformed functionaries, including the Court Chamberlain, the Imperial Protocol Minister, and a variety of invited guests. In front of the stage sat rows of elegantly dressed delegates from various Landsraad houses and leading commercial conglomerates. Valya did not see any VenHold business representatives.

Roderick Corrino emerged on one side of the flag-draped ceremonial stage, wearing a scarlet-and-gold uniform decked with silver epaulets, and gleaming medals and bright ribbons on the chest; a galaxy of small gold stars ran down the arms and encircled the wrists. A golden-lion pin sparkled at his collar. He waited while an additional security perimeter was set up in front of the coronation stage, a cordon of honor guards brandishing projectile rifles.

The orthodox Sisters pressed closer to Valya and her companions from Wallach IX. Esther-Cano leaned forward. "We have many questions for you, Sister Valya."

Remembering this woman's personality, her moods and weaknesses, Valya put an edge on the tone of her response, driving it deep. "Mother Superior Valya."

Esther-Cano recoiled as if she'd been lashed, then struggled to recover. "Yes. That is one of our questions."

"You have been informed that I am the new Mother Superior, per the wishes of Mother Superior Raquella, cemented by the suicide of Reverend Mother Dorotea."

"A convenient suicide . . ." Esther-Cano's voice dripped with suspicion.

"You are a Truthsayer—so hear the truth. In her last days of life, Mother Superior Raquella forced Dorotea and me to make peace, for the good of the Sisterhood. We both agreed. Your Sisters witnessed it."

She saw the Salusan Sisters listening, knew she had to select her words carefully. "After Mother Superior Raquella passed away, Dorotea plunged a knife into her own throat. The ashes of both women are now scattered across the grounds of the new school on Wallach IX." She narrowed her gaze, hardened her voice. "I am your new Mother Superior."

Olivia said, wide-eyed, "She speaks the truth."

Ninke, Esther-Cano, and several of their companions looked troubled, glanced at one another. Ninke finally said, "She speaks the truth, whether we like it or not."

Valya used her most compelling, throaty Voice to reinforce her words. "We are no longer foes or rivals. You and the others here *will* accept me as your Mother Superior. Today, we have a new Emperor, and a new Sisterhood. Help me make us all stronger."

Ninke was the first to bow in acquiescence. Then the other Salusan Sisters did the same, some with greater reluctance than others.

The crowd noises diminished when a green-robed High Priest marched out on the stage carrying the priceless Imperial crown on a golden pillow. Another priest walked beside him holding an overlarge tome, a special volume of the *Orange Catholic Bible*. Salvador had been the first Emperor to use the new publication in his coronation, and Roderick intended to maintain the tradition.

A tall man with a deeply cleft chin, the High Priest stood behind Roderick and raised the jeweled crown high as his assistant priest read a long passage from the illuminated pages of the *Orange Catholic Bible*. Valya was impressed that the holy man could hold the heavy crown so high for so long. Amplifiers transmitted the words out over the crowd and across Salusa; the ceremony was also being recorded for immediate distribution around the Imperium.

When the crowd began to show signs of restlessness, the assistant priest finally concluded, "The Imperium is the very soul of the human race, and the Emperor is its heart. Do you, Crown Prince Roderick Corrino, swear fidelity to your people, to your honor, and to the Imperium?"

"For as long as I live." Roderick formally bowed, as he had rehearsed.

The High Priest set the crown on Roderick's head. "Long live Emperor Roderick Corrino the First. May your reign shine as long as the stars!"

The plaza erupted in boisterous applause and cheers, with so much excitement and giddy relief that Valya worried the mobs might work themselves into a frenzy. But Imperial soldiers had been stationed at strategic points, some with stun darts or canisters of soporific gas. All those seated rose to their feet, while the assistant priest stood at the front of the stage, sprinkling a container of iron-red holy dust onto the audience.

As the newly crowned Emperor gazed out at the crowd, he was joined by his wife, Haditha, and their surviving children, all dressed in regal finery. Haditha's long scarlet-and-gold gown glittered with a thousand jewels. The boy Javicco wore a princely outfit, and the two daughters were dressed in matching gowns.

Valya watched the fledgling Emperor with the intense focus she had developed through Sisterhood training and noticed that Roderick looked neither happy nor eager to begin his new role. Apparently he would not be an Emperor who reveled in trappings or power, but a man who accepted and *endured* his responsibility. His smile was strained. According to reports Valya had read, Roderick had genuinely loved his brother, even though Salvador was never much beloved by his people, nor known for great deeds.

After years of uninspired rule, the Imperium was in a fragile, turbulent state. Emperor Salvador had committed a grave error, she thought, when he decided to seize all melange operations on Arrakis, just before his mysterious (and convenient?) disappearance. An accident? An assassination? She couldn't believe Josef Venport would be so bold.

Venport Holdings had, however, reiterated its embargo against any world that signed the Butlerian pledge, and there were persistent rumors that Directeur Venport was increasing the number of armed ships in his force. To what purpose?

Meanwhile, antitechnology fanaticism still ran rampant, and she'd learned that Manford's followers had overrun the Mentat School on Lampadas. And that Anna Corrino was missing. Valya knew the vapid girl was not capable of surviving difficult circumstances, although she would make a good hostage. Valya felt a twinge of sympathy; she had not disliked the Corrino girl while pretending to be her friend . . . but Valya had moved on to greater things.

This was an uncertain time. Valya knew that the Sisters—including those loyal to Dorotea—had excellent sources of information, and she decided she would take time to learn the details, analyzing Roderick's motivations and the alliances hidden in the politics. As Mother Superior, she had to understand the entire tapestry if her Sisters were to pull the right strings. Once she had all the new information, she would see that loyal Sisters were assigned to important houses in the Landsraad, where they would advise nobles, while knowing the overall plan that Mother Superior Valya would develop. . . .

After the coronation, an endless reception line formed. The procession had been organized in advance, yet it still seemed chaotic. Standing formally, and patiently, the new Emperor greeted hundreds of dignitaries, including the Sisters, who flowed forward like a flock of black birds.

Valya stood at the front, as a Mother Superior should. With a formal bow, she introduced herself, not sure that Roderick Corrino would know who she was, even though she had previously visited the court. And he might not know that she had taken his sister under her wing at the Rossak School.

"I am Mother Superior Valya, ranking member of the Sisterhood after the death of Mother Superior Raquella. My Sisters are here to serve you, Sire. I will travel regularly between Wallach IX and Salusa Secundus to coordinate matters."

He seemed puzzled. "Where is my Truthsayer Dorotea?"

Valya bowed, avoiding his gaze. "I am sorry to report that she died on Wallach IX of a self-inflicted wound. We will provide the Truthsayer you need, more than one if you require. We will strive to make your reign as strong as possible. In our unified Sisterhood, you have an even greater ally than you did before."

Roderick hung on to his silence for a moment, then said, "As my investigations continue into my brother's disappearance, I may have need of many Truthsayers."

Valya nodded and moved along as the rest of the Sisters gave their congratulations. She felt strong, satisfied, and confident that she would be remembered by future generations—not only by the Sisterhood but by House Harkonnen.

Using her rapidly increasing influence, she would open doors in the Landsraad for the Harkonnens to pass through. Perhaps the Emperor could find a position for her brother Danvis.

And one day, she thought, there may even be a Harkonnen Emperor.

*Murder is murder, no matter the justification.*

—NORMA CENVA

K illing an Emperor was no small thing.

During the flight from Kolhar to Salusa Secundus—a respectful time after the coronation, as commanded—Josef Venport explained his actions to Norma Cenva.

She had helped him eliminate the Imperial Barge at Arrakis, because he told her it was necessary, but he wasn't confident that she fully comprehended his rationale for doing so. Her thoughts and concerns were vastly distant from the realities Josef had to deal with. Now, however, he needed her to focus on the crisis and grasp the importance of the political course he had mapped out for the Imperium.

With Roderick as the new Emperor, a rational man who was already predisposed to despise the Half-Manford and his barbarians, they no longer needed to fear the looming dark ages.

On the Navigator deck in front of the broad observation windows that offered a view of the entire universe, he spoke with his great-grandmother even as she folded space and moved the ship from Kolhar. She floated inside her tank full of swirling orange gas, but he couldn't tell whether she was listening.

After the aurora-light display around the ship ceased and they settled back into normal space in the Salusan star system, he repeated his last few sentences, until Norma cut him off. "I heard and absorbed all data." Her voice sounded tinny across the tank's speaker system. "I am ancient, but aware."

She could help him save the Imperium now. The dangerously incompetent

Salvador and his entourage had vanished down the gullet of a sandworm; no trace remained of the spice operation, and the Imperial Barge was lost in the vastness of space, due to Taref's sabotage. Now that Roderick Corrino had been crowned, human civilization had a chance to survive the dark forces of ignorance, so long as he worked with Josef. The grim future Norma had foreseen no longer needed to come to pass.

"It only stands to reason—" he began again, then caught himself with a dark chuckle. "*Reason!* The Imperium needs more of that. We can now assure a renaissance instead of cultural darkness." He smiled with relief and optimism.

Through the swirling orange gas he saw her tiny mouth form into a barely perceptible smile. "That would be preferable . . . but not assured."

He paced in front of her large tank. "*I* will assure it, Grandmother. Roderick Corrino understands the interconnected ties of commerce, the business of governing vast populations, the need for trade instead of superstition. He and I need to meet in private to find a mutually viable path out of the mess Salvador created."

"The Emperor might consider you part of that mess. He did not invite you to the coronation."

Josef frowned. It disturbed him that he had not been on the guest list for the grand coronation, but Manford Torondo had also been kept away. Perhaps the new Emperor wanted to appear neutral until he consolidated his power. Josef realized he might have pushed too hard and too quickly. He assumed Roderick would be anxious to disband the fanatical Butlerians, just as Salvador had broken up the Rossak Sisterhood.

On this trip, accompanied by Norma Cenva, he would seek to heal wounds and begin the important work of moving the Imperium forward.

She drifted in her tank as the spacefolder entered orbit and slid in among the space traffic. "The immediate future is elusive," she said, "but I foresee great turbulence."

His tone was dismissive. "Roderick Corrino is a man who makes well-considered decisions, and we have the same goals. Together, we will control the barbarians and defeat the Half-Manford."

Norma's detachable tank moved on suspensors, and she accompanied him to the VenHold shuttle. As the craft descended, Josef gazed at the lush greenery, lakes, and snow-kissed mountains below. Salusa Secundus was one of the loveliest worlds in the Imperium. Even so, he preferred industrial Kolhar, which made him think of a bright and efficient future.

Since he was the Directeur of Venport Holdings, Josef secured a prime landing spot. The moment he stepped from the craft, with Norma's large tank floating behind him, he heard a roar of crowd noises and amplified music coming from the city. The postcoronation celebrations continued, even several days afterward.

The manicured grounds of the Imperial Palace and the associated Landsraad Hall, along with the various bureaucratic ministries and office buildings, took up more area than the rest of the capital city. Approaching the palace proper, he and Norma stopped at a security gate, where they were subjected to scanners that confirmed their identities. Moments later they were escorted into the palace by a contingent of guards, who remained with them. They were told to wait in an anteroom outside the Imperial Audience Chamber.

Following the coronation, Emperor Roderick had filled his schedule with meetings as Landsraad representatives, planetary interests, and businesses all tried to earn his favor. Josef's appointment had been swept into that chaos, but he had enough clout, and spread enough bribes ahead of time, to secure a prominent slot in Roderick's calendar. Yet even Directeur Venport had to wait.

When his time finally arrived, an hour overdue, Josef passed through the large central doors, his shoulders squared and chin held high. Norma accompanied him in her suspensor-borne tank, drawing wide-eyed stares and murmurs of awe. A dozen Imperial guards followed close behind them.

Josef looked up at Roderick Corrino on the green-crystal throne, with his thick blond hair and patrician features. If only that man had been born before his brother, the history of the Imperium would have taken a vastly different turn. Finally, after thirteen years of a false course and destructive distractions under Salvador's rule, human civilization could achieve the greatness it deserved. Back on track. Populations could be free from the tyranny of extremes—both the tyranny of thinking machines and the tyranny of the Butlerians' irrational fear. Feeling great hope now, he couldn't keep from smiling as he stepped up to the dais.

"Emperor Roderick Corrino, I come to congratulate you and swear my allegiance. I look forward to many great goals that the Imperial throne and Venport Holdings can achieve together." Perhaps he smiled too much.

Roderick looked awkward on the throne. His expression showed no warmth. "Salvador may yet return, Directeur. My brother's fate is still a mystery, and our investigation continues. I have Truthsayers to assist me in finding answers."

Josef felt the chill in the air. Did Roderick suspect him of something? Cioba had told him about the skills of the Sisterhood's Truthsayers. He had been so careful to leave no evidence, but if a Truthsayer were to interrogate him about Salvador's disappearance, he doubted even Norma could help him.

He responded with carefully chosen words. "We all want the truth about our beloved Emperor, Sire." He drew a breath. "But the Imperium is far larger than any one man, and your responsibilities now extend across hundreds of worlds, and countless trillions of people who are your loyal subjects—including myself. I am here to assist you in any way you deem fit."

From her tank, Norma's voice resonated, startling the audience in the chamber. "The spice is essential. Operations on Arrakis must continue unhindered. Our Navigators require melange."

Josef was glad for the distraction. "Sire, we should discuss certain spice operations on Arrakis, Imperial interactions with Combined Mercantiles. Your brother asserted a claim to the entire industry, but the implementation of such an idea is complex and, frankly, impractical. It would needlessly disrupt spice commerce across the Imperium to the many who depend on it for health and vitality. We should proceed with caution so as not to cause any unnecessary turmoil." He bowed his head slightly in deference. "Of course, in this and in all matters, I seek your Imperial wisdom."

Months ago, Draigo Roget had estimated the number of people addicted to melange to be in the billions, and Josef had not waited quietly while Salvador made his clumsy claims. He had already armed most of his VenHold ships, and was ready to put battleships in place around Arrakis, should it come to a direct showdown against the Imperial Armed Forces. Roderick Corrino would have his spies, but VenHold had numerous hidden resources of its own. Josef would have more than enough force to defend both Arrakis and Kolhar, but that was not the outcome he desired. He hoped the new Emperor would become his partner, rather than a hindrance.

Roderick remained silent as he pondered, then finally spoke. "Directeur Venport, the Imperium needs to prosper, but there is much more we need to accomplish. My father and grandfather helped form this Imperium after the Battle of Corrin, and now I want to ensure that we lay a stable moral and commercial foundation for future generations." His expression softened and he already looked weary of all the problems. "With the resources and cooperation of Venport Holdings, it is possible for us to achieve that prosperity together. I believe we have a mutual vision."

"I concur, Sire. We should focus on *building* rather than destroying. We must choose hope over fear. To that end, I beg you to consider strenuous efforts to control Manford Toronto and his dangerous Butlerian fanatics. On Baridge, they destroyed one of my ships, its cargo, crew, and a priceless Navigator. Here in Zimia, they killed your poor daughter and countless others, burned parts of the city. Emperor Salvador may have let them run unchecked, but you—"

The sounds of turmoil among the audience—mutters of agreement and disagreement—grew loud.

Roderick looked gray and angry. He leaned forward. "I am well aware of that, Directeur Venport. I agree that something must be done."

To hide his elation, Josef bowed his head and pretended to be meek. "If there is any way that Venport Holdings can help, Sire, we—"

A courier burst into the Audience Chamber, rushing toward the throne. Imperial guards braced themselves to stop the intruder, then touched earadios, listened to urgent announcements, and let him pass.

Josef looked around, wondering what was happening. Norma Cenva drifted in her tank, and her face came closer to the transparent walls. Her words emerged from the speakerpatch, addressing Josef, although others nearby could hear. "The Imperial Barge just returned, battered, but intact. They were lost in foldspace, but the pilot was talented and desperate. He managed to bring the barge back home, and the surviving crew just broadcast an urgent message."

The courier bounded up the steps to the throne, gasping, and spoke to Emperor Roderick.

Josef felt as if an executioner's blade were swinging down toward him. The barge was intact? Then the witnesses were alive! Taref had failed to properly sabotage the emergency Holtzman engines.

The Imperial crew knew that Josef had betrayed and murdered Salvador, and the barge itself had barely escaped from the attacking VenHold ships around Arrakis. If they had somehow survived and returned, they would tell the new Emperor that Josef Venport had caused it all.

He turned to Norma in her tank, whispering, "We are ruined!"

Even before the courier finished his breathless message, Roderick Corrino rose from the throne, his face filled with sickened fury. "You, Directeur Venport! You *assassinated* my brother!"

He shouted for the guards, who raced forward, drawing their weapons. Josef was surrounded by them and by hundreds of audience members. They would tear him apart. He saw no way to escape.

"This is not a scenario I foresaw," Norma Cenva said. "Once again, I must rescue you."

Josef felt a tingle, and the Audience Chamber around him blurred and crackled. With a pop of displaced air, Norma folded space around them and whisked her own tank and Josef Venport away.

*When studying history, spectacular failures can provide great inspiration to improve.*

—ERASMUS, *Latter-Day Laboratory Journals*

When the spacefolder carrying Draigo Roget's ship arrived at Denali, Erasmus finally let himself believe they were safe. Their circumstances had dramatically improved, and he was intrigued by all the new experiences that awaited him and Anna Corrino.

But that was small consolation for the loss of Gilbertus, and very probably the end of the Mentat School; the teachings would either be banned or drastically altered by the foolish Butlerians. He still experienced great confusion, a turmoil in his thought processes that was completely unfamiliar to him. For centuries he had strived to understand emotions, but now that he had a better grasp, the independent robot found that he didn't like them at all.

Erasmus felt deeply disturbed. He thought back to the day before, when Draigo's scout ship had raced to the covert spacefolder in orbit over Lampadas. Even from there, the robot had continued to observe through his linked network of spy-eyes, but without his usual analytical detachment. He'd felt unsettled curiosity as he watched his dedicated ward kneel down amidst the jeering barbarians, in full view of the Mentat school. This sense of loss was not strictly quantifiable.

Erasmus had rescued the young man from slave pens on Corrin, mentoring Gilbertus and treating him exceptionally well. He had changed the slave boy's life, and his own. Both had grown from the experience.

And it had all culminated in the horrific scene on Lampadas. Surrounded by rabid Butlerians, Gilbertus had bowed his head and closed his eyes. Interestingly, his expression had been filled with remarkable contentment, enviable peace. A smile had even curled his lips at the last moment. Erasmus did not understand.

Then the Swordmaster had lopped off his head, extinguishing a fine and efficient mind.

Upon seeing the death of his student, his protector, and his friend, a jolt had gone through the robot's gelcircuitry—a blinding flash that made him unable to process for a moment. In what seemed like an eternity, everything changed for Erasmus, as if the fundamental laws of reality had become different. He had not expected this at all.

Erasmus had seen countless humans die in the centuries of his life, many of them at his own hands, but he had never previously felt anything similar to this. Gilbertus was gone! The companion who had been such an interesting debater, such an avid learner, such a . . . such a caring, protective friend. Gone. Dead. *Murdered!* This could not be repaired. Gilbertus could not be replaced. Erasmus had never before experienced such a sharp, painful *loss.*

Something shifted in his malleable programming. Erasmus could not be cool and objective; rather, he felt dismay, disgust, and anger. And then with a cascade of realizations, data linking to data, he had another epiphany, a completely unexpected insight, another breathless revelation. He had an answer that he had been trying to find for more than two centuries.

Was *this* what had driven Serena Butler into such an irrational, hateful rage when he threw her noisy, crying child off a balcony? Incandescent, helpless rage and loss? Now he thought he grasped what had produced her immediate blind reaction. It all made sense in a way that it never had before. He understood the spark that had ignited the Jihad, with all of its tremendous consequences.

Gilbertus was gone. The Butlerians had killed him. His mind surged with countless reactions, all of them dark, violent, vengeful.

And now he brought those feelings with him to Denali.

Although Erasmus kept track of the different factions of humanity, especially the machine sympathizers and antitechnology fanatics, he now experienced actual loathing and *hatred* toward the people who had harmed the human who had become the equivalent of a son to him.

Yes. From all of his studies, that must be the sensation he was experiencing. *Hatred.* Along with unquantifiable sadness at watching the blood spill out and Gilbertus's headless body collapse to the ground.

Erasmus *despised* Manford Torondo. Erasmus grieved for Gilbertus, who had given his life to preserve his beloved school. Those violent savages had destroyed it all. Erasmus felt strong resentment at the unfairness of the situation. *Unfairness.* These new thoughts and emotions were fascinating to him, and quite unpleasant. They threatened to overwhelm his circuitry.

Gilbertus was *dead!* And the robot decided he would have to do something about that. . . .

Draigo Roget and Anna Corrino were tense and frightened as they descended to cloud-swirled Denali. Sitting on the edge of a passenger bench, Anna removed her package with the robot's core, unfolded the wrappings, and showed the gelsphere to Draigo. After measuring the Mentat's expression, Erasmus could tell that Draigo was awed and intrigued.

The Mentat said, "Anna, I'm taking you and the robot to a safe haven, away from politics and fanatics. Directeur Venport established this place as a refuge where the greatest minds could create the best defenses to save civilization. These researchers will find the robot's memory core infinitely fascinating."

Erasmus spoke into the transceiver hidden in Anna's ear, and she repeated his words aloud. "Erasmus is confident that we will find the Denali research center just as fascinating as they find him."

"This is not a pleasant world," Draigo cautioned, "quite unlike the Imperial capital on Salusa. And dangerous, with a poisonous atmosphere—you can't go outside the domes without special protective gear."

"I'll be fine," she said, "as long as I can stay with Erasmus."

During their journey, the robot had reviewed his stored memories of Gilbertus Albans, and had made projections of his growing friendship with Anna Corrino. Yes, he cared for her, as well. He would be greatly angered and saddened if she were to die, too.

He also analyzed his undeniable fury toward the Butlerians, a genuine sense of raw outrage. It was fascinating to channel his thoughts in new and untried pathways, *human* pathways. He had urged Gilbertus to leave Lampadas well before the Butlerian menace grew out of hand. Now he could only think of going back there to destroy the fanatics in their nest.

That would require some planning. . . .

Draigo piloted the craft down toward a complex of domed buildings. Although the equipment inside this vessel was primitive by thinking-machine standards, the robot could still use it, so he accessed the ship's sensors, and scanned the poisonous vapors until he discerned the laboratory complex and habitation modules. Down there, the domes were filled with rational objective scientists who hated the barbarians as much as Erasmus did—and he would find them useful.

There were many new possibilities. Maybe the Denali scientists could even create a new body for him. Surely they had the resources. He would convince Anna Corrino to speak on his behalf, and then his situation would improve a great deal. Yes, many things could soon change.

When the ship settled onto the landing zone outside the reconstructed hangar dome, Erasmus was overjoyed to see the welcoming party that emerged to meet them. Anna Corrino pressed close to a side windowport, peering at the movement through the murky air.

Four cymek walkers strode toward the shuttle, armored warrior forms like giant mechanical crabs, with pistons pumping and strong legs driving them forward. They were powerful, ominous, threatening—absolutely wonderful!

Erasmus hadn't seen cymeks for a long time, and these appeared to be new and efficient.

The most fearsome one spoke. "I am Ptolemy, head of the new Titan project. Welcome to Denali." Half a dozen more cymek forms emerged from the swirling, poisonous mists. "We are preparing an army."

Erasmus scanned the giant mechanical forms and realized he looked forward to what this place had to offer. If he, the cymeks, and sympathetic humans worked together, they could accomplish great things.